CITY OF
JASMINE

Center Point
Large Print

Also by Deanna Raybourn and available from
Center Point Large Print:

A Spear of Summer Grass

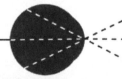

**This Large Print Book carries the
Seal of Approval of N.A.V.H.**

CITY OF JASMINE

Deanna Raybourn

CENTER POINT LARGE PRINT
THORNDIKE, MAINE

This Center Point Large Print edition
is published in the year 2014 by arrangement with
Harlequin Books S.A.

The text of this Large Print edition is unabridged.
In other aspects, this book may vary
from the original edition.
Printed in the United States of America
on permanent paper.
Set in 16-point Times New Roman type.

ISBN: 978-1-62899-153-6

Library of Congress Cataloging-in-Publication Data

Raybourn, Deanna.
City of Jasmine / Deanna Raybourn.
pages cm
Summary: "Five years after her husband's death, aviatrix Evangeline Stark receives a mysterious photo causing her to believe her husband did not die when the Lusitania sank. Seeking answers, she goes to Damascus and finds nothing is as it seems"—Provided by publisher.
ISBN 978-1-62899-153-6 (library binding : alk. paper)
1. Women air pilots—Fiction. 2. Missing persons—Fiction.
3. Damascus (Syria)—Fiction. 4. Love stories. 5. Suspense fiction.
6. Large type books. I. Title.
PS3618.A983C58 2014
813'.6—dc23
                                                    2014016076

For Tara Parsons on this first grand adventure.

Two small figures were beating against the rock; the girl had fainted and lay on the boy's arm. With a last effort Peter pulled her up the rock and then lay down beside her. Even as he also fainted he saw that the water was rising. He knew that they would soon be drowned, but he could do no more . . .

"We are on the rock, Wendy," he said, "but it is growing smaller. Soon the water will be over it."

She did not understand even now.

"We must go," she said, almost brightly.

"Yes," he answered faintly.

"Shall we swim or fly, Peter?"

—*Peter and Wendy*, J.M. Barrie

ONE

The desert is a lonely place to begin with. And there's nothing lonelier than being with someone you loved who stopped loving you first. It ended in the desert, the fabled rocky reaches of the Badiyat ash-Sham, with a man I had already buried once. But it began in Rome, as all adventures should, and it started with a scolding.

"Aunt Dove, dearest, I know you do like to make an entrance, but driving the ambassador's car through his wife's rose garden was a bit much, don't you think?"

Aunt Dove grabbed the parcel of letters and cuttings forwarded by the British ambassador's office and began to riffle through them. "Oh, look at the piece the New York newspaper published on our stop in Bulgaria. Wasn't Tsar Boris a lamb to let us land there?"

She bent over my shoulder, causing her turban to slip a little. She poked it back into place with a stiff finger as she handed me the cutting. "Although I must say, I didn't like the way that tsar was leering at you," she said, peering at the photograph. "But I suppose he could have been worse. He has rather a nice moustache, and personally, I would rather take my chances as a Bulgarian tsaritsa than spend another night with those villains in London."

"Aunt, the Ritz is not run by villains."

"They made a terrible to-do about Arthur," she said with a brisk nod to the little green parrot drinking from her teacup. "He didn't mean to make such a mess, but he was startled by an omnibus." She clucked at him and he put out his little brush of a tongue to drink his tea.

Aunt Dove crumbled a tea biscuit for him while I fixed her with a severe look. "And don't change the subject. The ambassador's wife is particularly put out about her roses. She says they're utterly destroyed and the cost to replace them will be seventy pounds."

"Don't fuss, darling. I've already spoken to the ambassador. He's willing to overlook the little matter of the roses if I have dinner with his friend, some American tycoon with money to burn. Apparently the fellow is thinking of sponsoring us. He has a company, something to do with powder—washing powder? Face powder? I forget. In any event, a little charm and a flash of bare ankle ought to do the trick."

I pursed my lips. "Cynicism is an unattractive quality in a woman, Aunt Dove."

"So is starvation," she reminded me mildly.

I sighed and reached for the pile of letters and cuttings. My plan to fly my pretty little Sopwith biplane over seven seas was keeping the wolf from the door, but barely. Reporters adored the story since the headlines practically wrote themselves—

Society Aviatrix to Pilot Across the Seven Seas—but newspaper stories didn't pay the bills. Our tiny collection of sponsors had to be constantly reassured—a job I left most often to Aunt Dove. I could smile and simper with the best of them when I had to, but it always left a sour taste in my mouth to do it.

At that moment the door opened and Wally, my mechanic and dearest friend, entered—all five foot eleven inches of perfectly formed English gentleman. He flopped into the nearest chair with a sigh and Aunt Dove poured him a cup of tea.

"I deserve stronger," he told her with a fond smile.

"Wally, how is my baby?" My beloved plane had suffered a few nasty injuries during our landing in Rome, but if anyone could sort her out, it was Wally. He was officially known to London society as the Honourable Vyvyan Walters, eldest son and heir to the Viscount Walters, but he was never happier than when he'd shed his Savile Row suits for a pair of coveralls and a set of spanners.

"The *Jolly Roger* is in grave condition," he told me, his expression severe. I wasn't entirely surprised.

"But you can save her?" It wasn't just the trip I was thinking of. I might have bought her second-hand as a means of making a living but through the journey she'd become something more—rather like an exotic pet that required frequent

11

repairs and devastatingly expensive upkeep.

"I can, but I don't really see why I should bother if you're going to be so cavalier with her. I've told you before, she's *delicate.*"

I blew him a kiss. "I'm a brute and you are an absolute prince, Wally." I threw him a parcel of letters. "The post was waiting for us. If I'm not mistaken, there's something from your father."

He groaned. "Doubtless the usual refrain." He pitched his voice low in a perfect imitation of his father's plummy public-school tones. " 'Why don't you settle down? Get on with it already, boy. The title needs an heir. I'd even approve you marrying that Starke woman if it got me a grandson.' "

Aunt Dove shook her head, setting her turban to wobbling. "The older generation can be so unforgiving of the young." Wally and I exchanged amused glances. Aunt Dove was at least twenty years senior to Wally's father.

We spent a pleasant half an hour reading letters and passing around cuttings from assorted newspapers. I perused the last with familiar irritation. "My God, they don't even try to be original. It's always precisely the same thing—'Explorer and aviatrix Evangeline Merryweather Starke is engaged in an heroic attempt to fly her biplane, the Sopwith 1 1/2 Strutter called the *Jolly Roger*, across the seven seas of antiquity. Mrs. Starke travels with her aunt, the legendary Victorian traveller Lady Lavinia Finch-Pomeroy, last

12

surviving daughter of the 7th Earl of Sheridan, her mechanic, the Honourable Vyvyan Walters, and Lady Lavinia's pet parrot, Arthur Wellesley. Mrs. Starke's late husband was Gabriel Starke, explorer, mountaineer and archaeologist of note, tragically lost in the *Lusitania* disaster.'" To my disgust, beside the photograph of Aunt Dove and me in our slim leather aviatrix suits was a picture of Gabriel taken just before our marriage. I tossed the clipping to Aunt Dove for her inspection.

"Hmph," she grunted, looking at Gabriel's photograph. "I always said he was far too handsome for his own good. It isn't helpful to a man's character to have a face like that."

She wasn't wrong. If he'd been a sculpture, Gabriel Starke would have been a masterpiece, created by a genius in a leisurely and generous mood. Each of his features had been beautifully moulded with an extra stroke of grace from a master's hand. From the most startling blue eyes I had ever seen to a chin marked by a decisive cleft, he was unspeakably gorgeous. It was irritating beyond measure.

Aunt Dove sighed. "I always thought he looked like a seraphim, you know, one of those noble warrior angels, all fire and muscle and unearthly beauty."

I pulled a face. "If Gabriel Starke was an angel, I assure you he was a fallen one."

She peered closely at the article and looked up,

blinking. "Ought they to call you a widow, dear? After all, when Gabriel died you were in the process of divorcing him." She passed the clipping back and I looked down at the image of the man I had married in haste. The photographer must have annoyed him. He was wearing an expression I knew quite well. The sleepy drop of the eyelids meant he was immensely bored, but the upward quirk of the well-shaped lips meant he intended to make his own fun, most likely at someone else's expense.

"He died before it could be finalised," I reminded her, a trifle waspishly.

Aunt Dove went on. "Shame they never gave him a nice little honour after he died. A tidy KBE on his gravestone and you might have been Lady Starke."

I ignored her as I crumpled the clipping into my fist. "I ought to have gone back to my maiden name. If I travelled under 'Merryweather' all of this Starke business would be forgotten."

Wally snorted and crumbled up another biscuit for Arthur.

"Oh, don't, Wally," Aunt Dove ordered. "He's getting fat as a tick as it is."

Wally moved to take the plate away, but Arthur dropped his beak smartly and nipped him just hard enough to draw blood.

"Feathery bastard," Wally muttered, sucking his finger.

"Damn the kaiser," Arthur said, bobbing his head in satisfaction. He applied himself to his biscuit and Aunt Dove threw up her hands.

"Very well, but don't complain to me if you get indigestion," she warned him. She shook her head. "It never does to argue with parrots. They might speak, but they simply never *listen*."

She glanced at the clock and rose, gathering up her letters.

"Lord, look at the time and I'm dining with a Savoyard prince tonight. I think I might have been engaged to him once."

"You *think?*" Wally asked, his eyes popping.

Aunt Dove smiled sweetly. "Eighteen seventy-eight is a bit of a blur, dear boy. That's the year I discovered absinthe. Now, you children have a lovely evening and don't wait up. Come along, Arthur." He flapped to her shoulder and then up to the top of her turban, narrowly avoiding the enormous paste emerald brooch she had used to pin the thing in place.

They left in a cloud of feathers and musk perfume, and Wally turned to me. "Is it very wrong that I want to grow up to be your Aunt Dove?"

"In that case, growing up has nothing to do with it," I said, flipping through my letters. "She still thinks she's twenty, exploring the world as a Victorian adventuress. It's never occurred to her that time has marched on. Heavens, here's something from the fuel company."

"What do they want?"

"I daren't open it. The last bill was just too ghastly. I'll look at it tomorrow and maybe I'll be lucky enough to lose it before then." I tossed aside the bills and read out the most salacious snippets of news from home to Wally.

He stretched out his long legs and laced his hands behind his head, offering an occasional comment on the gossip. "I cannot believe Delilah Drummond has remarried so soon after throwing over poor old Quentin. The sheets weren't even cold before she said 'I do' to that Russian princeling—" He broke off. "Evie? What is it?"

I stared at the photograph that had just fallen from the pile of cuttings. My hand felt cold, colder than any living hand ought to feel.

"Evie? You look as if you've seen a ghost," Wally said.

"That depends," I said in a small, hollow voice. "Do ghosts photograph?"

I did not faint, but I must have been green enough to frighten Wally into shoving my head between my knees until I was breathing normally again. He held me there for at least a quarter of an hour, his hand firm on the back of my neck.

"I'm fine," I said to my knees, my voice sounding marginally stronger. I tried again. "I am fine, really."

"I don't believe you," he said, narrowing his

16

eyes at me. "How many fingers am I holding up?"

"I will hold up a very particular one if you don't let me sit up," I warned him. He sprang back and I eased myself to a sitting position. "You must be worried," I told him. "You didn't even scold me for saying something unladylike."

"I don't think I've ever seen a face go that colour," he replied. "You were positively green."

"What colour am I now?"

He screwed up his eyes. "A sort of yellowish parchment-white. Not very becoming, if I'm honest. Now, what's this about ghosts?"

I handed over the snapshot. Wally stared at it, his mouth agape, and after a long moment passed it back. "Where did it come from?"

I shrugged. "There was no envelope. It was simply stuck in with a bunch of letters and cuttings."

"It means nothing," he said firmly. "It must have been taken on one of his expeditions before the war. You said Gabriel was always haring off to parts unknown before you married him."

"Turn it over," I instructed.

He furrowed his brow as he read the inscription on the back aloud. " 'Damascus, 1920.' Why the devil would Gabriel be in Damascus?"

I swallowed hard. "I think the better question is why would Gabriel be in Damascus five years after he died?"

17

Wally rose and went to the drinks tray. A moment later he handed me a whisky and poured another for himself. "Forget the tea. Strong drink is the only solution."

I obeyed and took a deep swallow, grateful for the burn of it.

"What would he be doing in Damascus?" Wally repeated. "Did he have any connection with that part of the world?"

I nodded. "He was born there. His father was rather high up in the army, posted to the consulate in Damascus when Gabriel was born. And then Gabriel went back to do a brief season of digging there when he was at school studying archaeology." I paused. "I'm not wrong. It *is* Gabriel." It was a statement, but he understood what I was asking.

"It certainly looks like the photographs I've seen of him. Perhaps someone put on that inscription for a bit of a joke—a cruel one," he added. "But people can be spiteful and Gabriel did make rather a lot of enemies in his time. A man cannot be that handsome and successful and still be universally liked. Mark my words, it's a vicious prank and nothing more."

I peered at the photograph more closely. "I don't think so. Look at the corners of the eyes very closely. There are lines there he didn't have. And there's something about his jaw even under that disgusting beard. It's firmer, it's—" I scrutinised the jaw through a thicket of untidy hair. "It's resolute . . ." I said, hesitating. "I've always wondered, you know."

"Wondered?"

"Whether he was actually on the *Lusitania*. I know it sounds mad to even suggest it. He was on the passenger list. People saw him on the ship once they'd put to sea. And they never recovered a body, so of course, I believed it when they said he'd been lost. At least I think I believed it."

"But, darling, why wouldn't he have been on the ship?"

"I don't know. I just keep thinking of him the last time I saw him, when he left me on that steamer in Shanghai. The whole expedition to China had been such a disaster, I kept telling myself it had to get better but it never did." I faltered. Wally knew the whole story. He'd been treated to it once during a maudlin night with too much gin and too little sleep. I told him everything—how Gabriel and I had met at a New Year's Eve party thrown by my friend Delilah, how we had eloped that very night. I described the romantic dash up to Scotland and the hasty wedding. It was our very own fairy tale.

But Gabriel and I hadn't found our happily ever after. Almost immediately after the wedding he had begun to change. There were mysterious telephone calls and cryptic looks, and we began to quarrel even before we left for his expedition to China. I had thought the trip would be a sort of belated honeymoon, a chance to smooth out the little bumps in Matrimony Road. But China is where it all fell apart. The dashing, impetuous man I'd married had become a stranger almost overnight. He retreated behind a façade of cool detachment, holding himself aloof from me. He avoided my bed and my company, and he broke my heart a thousand different ways but the most painful was with cordial indifference. The man who'd swept me off my feet was nothing like the distant stranger I had left China with, a man who had picked a howling quarrel with me, then quite civilly agreed to let me divorce him. We had left Shanghai on separate ships.

"It was like I never even knew him at all," I told Wally as I stared at the photograph. "He just escorted me to the ship as politely as if I were an acquaintance and lifted his hat in farewell." I broke off, swallowing hard. "It's absurd, but I always hated to think it was the last memory I would ever have of him."

"You were divorcing him," Wally pointed out.

"Yes, but it was so unlike him, at least it was unlike the man I thought I married. That moment when I stood on that deck watching him leave was the very worst of it. It was like saying goodbye to a stranger."

"I don't suppose most divorces are terribly amicable," he said reasonably. "After all, no one likes to get chucked away like last night's dinner."

20

"I suppose."

"And weren't you the one who asked for a divorce?"

"Yes, but—oh, never mind! I've wasted too many years thinking about him already. Let's just forget this and get on with the trip. Hand me the map book, will you? I want to plot the course across the Caspian."

I rose hastily and threw the photograph into the fire in a savage gesture then snatched it back almost as quickly. The burned edge of it singed my finger and I sucked at the tender skin, cursing under my breath. I couldn't bring myself to completely destroy the photograph, and I didn't want to think too hard about what that might mean. I walked to the wastepaper basket and dropped the photograph inside. "Damn him."

Wally rose calmly and retrieved it. He put it into my hand, folding my fingers gently around it.

"What did you do that for?" I demanded.

"Because it's time you stopped running, Evie. For you, Gabriel Starke is past and present, and somewhere, I don't know how, perhaps your future, as well. You'll never be free of him if you don't go and find out."

"Go?"

He sighed. "Woman, you try my patience. To Damascus. You must go to Damascus and find him if he's there."

I blinked up at him. "But why? For what possible purpose?"

"That's up to you, my dear. Strike him, swear at him, kiss him or kill him, I don't much care. But you will never bury your dead so long as there is a chance he is still alive in this world."

I looked at the photograph. The edge was charred, but the image was clear. Gabriel's expression was as inscrutable as I remembered. "No," I said finally. "Oh, it's tempting, I'll grant you that. But we still have the tour to finish."

I waited for Wally to contradict me, but he didn't. A change of subject was in order.

I nodded towards his own letters. "What did your father have to say?" I asked.

He slumped further into his chair, crossing his long legs at the ankle and staring up at the ceiling. "Much as I expected. I must marry. I must have sons."

"Same song, second verse," I said lightly.

He lowered his head and smiled. "Oh, a new tune, though. He's threatening to cut off my allowance."

He passed me the letter and I skimmed it quickly. Certain damning phrases jumped out at me . . . *wasting your life . . . feckless . . . dishonour to the name . . . not much time . . . doctor not optimistic.* I gave it back to him.

"I'm so sorry, Wally. What will you do?"

He shrugged. "What can I do? I must go home to Mistledown. I can hold him off for the last leg of

22

the trip, but no more adventures after that, I'm afraid. Egypt will be the end of the road for me, love."

I slipped to the floor and put my head on his knee. He ran an absent hand through my short curls. "I ought to take him at his word and marry you," he said after a while.

"That's the whisky talking." I turned my head to look at him. "Have you ever considered telling him the truth?"

His smile was sad and distant as a martyred saint's. "Telling the Right Honourable Viscount Walters that his only son and heir is a poof? Have a heart, dear girl. He's already got one foot tickling the grave. That would finish him off."

"I imagine you're right."

He sipped thoughtfully at his drink. "I suppose we could get married, though. I would get respectability and you'd have a lovely title to lord over all those nasty people who have nothing better to do than gossip about you."

I slipped my hand into his. "Putting one over on the society cats is hardly reason enough to get married."

"With you I could provide the estate with an heir," he mused.

"But would you want to?"

He reached down and kissed my cheek. "No. Not even with you, and I adore you. I'll simply have to go back to Mistledown and make the best of things. I shall be a proper lord of the manor, and when the time comes, it will all pass to a feeble-minded cousin in Ireland."

"Is he really feeble-minded?"

"Well, he's Irish, so it's difficult to tell," he said with a twinkle. I slapped at his leg.

"Don't be catty." I picked up the photograph. "I can tell you think I'm an awful fool for not going to Damascus."

"Yes, I do."

"But why?"

Wally leaned down and put his cheek against mine. "Because somewhere in your very large, very tender heart, you are hoping it was all a terrible mistake and that he is alive."

I reared back as if he'd struck me. "Hoping! What an extraordinary thing to say."

"But a truthful one. Evie, everyone else sees the brave face. Everyone else sees the big smile and the plucky girl who flies her little plane and waves for the cameras and flogs boots and face cream. But I see everything else. I see the shadows under your eyes when you've sat up half the night thinking about him. I see the hunted expression you get anytime his name is mentioned. And I see that somewhere beneath the sophisticated, glamorous façade of the barnstormer who crosses the globe with nothing but her dancing slippers and her best lipstick is the heartbroken girl whose husband called her bluff and left her sitting on a ship when she thought he would come crawling back."

I blinked back unshed tears, my throat tight and hot. "Damn you."

"People are always damning me," he said with a sigh. "And it's always because I'm right."

I looked at the photograph again. "Do you really think he's there?"

He shrugged. "I haven't the faintest idea. The point is it doesn't really matter, dear girl. What counts is that you find some answers once and for all. You've spent the last five years running away from everything, dashing off on another trip just so you wouldn't have to think about how you were going to pay the butcher or the baker."

"You forgot the candlestick maker. And you're quite wrong, you know. Those trips were *how* I paid the bills."

"Nonsense. You could have learned to type and taken a nice job in an office somewhere. You could have married again. You could have accepted the annuity Gabriel left you. There were a hundred other ways to keep a roof over your head, my love, and you managed to choose the only way that kept you running. Well, it's time to stop. Face down your ghosts. Exorcise them once and for all. Forgive them, forgive yourself and get on with the business of living."

I thought a long moment. "And what if Gabriel isn't a ghost? What if he really is alive?"

"Then you must find him and demand answers. You deserve them."

"I suppose so," I said slowly. "I imagine I could get one of the newspapers to underwrite a detour before the Caspian flight. Aunt Dove's most successful book was her memoir of travels in the Levant in the '80s. I could tell them we're retracing her steps, meeting up with old friends, that sort of thing. I could promise some camel caravans and desert nomads for local colour. They'd lap that up. And I know she would love to see her old friends. I could tell her I want a little rest before the rigors of the Caspian trip."

"See? You're two steps ahead as usual, winkling out the difficulties. You're halfway to Damascus already."

I smiled. "You're right, of course. I do deserve an end to it. If Gabriel's gone, I ought to be able to put him behind me once and for all. And if he's alive . . ." I hesitated then gave him a broad smile. "If he's alive, I'll let you hold him down while I thrash him."

"Excellent notion. I'd love nothing better than to get a few licks in myself. I've always hated him."

"Why should you hate him, Wally? You never even met him."

He shrugged. "He had everything I ever wanted in life and left it on a ship out of Shanghai. I could kill him on that score alone."

I jumped up and kissed him on the cheek. "You don't really want me," I reminded him. "I am not at all your type."

"Oh, but how I wish you were."

TWO

The next day the editor of a newspaper in Los Angeles came through with tickets for the Orient Express, and Aunt Dove began to pack. She insisted on bringing Arthur along—"Roman air is insalubrious to parrots, dear"—and I left her to go in search of Wally. He was still tinkering with the *Jolly Roger*, whistling a bit of jazz as he worked.

"How's my darling?" I called, patting her wing. It had been my idea to paint her to resemble a pirate flag. The black highlights lent her a certain gravitas while the dazzling white skull and cross-bones on her tail said I meant business.

Wally looked up from the engine. "Your aeroplane is fine and so am I, thanks for asking."

"Can I fly her to Venice?"

"Depends. Do you feel like landing her in the lagoon? Venice is water, pet."

I pulled a face. "Not the Veneto. There's a darling little airfield where we can get some smashing pictures before Aunt Dove and I catch the train to Constantinople."

He considered then nodded. "She'll be fine for

that, but no further. I'll take the train up to Venice and finish working on her there. As soon as she's able, I'll hopscotch her down to Damascus. There's a small airfield just outside the city and the ambassador has already contacted the authorities for you, although I'm surprised he knew who to ask. Are we still in charge over there or is it the French now?"

I rolled my eyes. "Wally, do you ever actually read the newspapers we get? It used to be a vilayet of the Turks. We liberated it and there's an interim Arab government now. The French are hanging around to act as advisors and we're out."

He shrugged. "Makes no difference to me and they change their minds every week. I think it's a conspiracy on the part of mapmakers to sell their wares."

"More like another souvenir of the war," I reminded him.

At the end of the war, the Ottoman Empire, once stretched tautly from North Africa east to the Silk Road and north to the Balkans, had been shattered into a thousand pieces. Britain and France had swept up the choicest bits for themselves, leaving the crumbs for others. Unfortunately it had meant breaking a slew of promises to the native Arabs that they could have a country of their own after the war in exchange for their help in throwing off the Turks, the largest and most powerful of the German allies. These accords had left the whole of the region seething with rebellion and resentment with British and French overlords attempting to maintain an uneasy peace, while Arabs rightfully demanded autonomy. The trouble was the French had been meddling in the Holy Land ever since the Crusades and the British authorities weren't about to be left out of the oil fields in southern Mesopotamia—particularly not since Churchill had set his heart on building an air force.

"Will you have trouble getting through Constantinople?" he asked.

"Shouldn't do, although Aunt Dove is insisting on giving me a six-shooter to carry. She says Turks can't be trusted."

His expressive brows inched upwards. "A six-shooter?"

"Goodness, I don't know what it is. Something that makes a bang and persuades people to stop doing things you don't want them to do. It looks like a child's toy actually, small enough to fit in my palm and inlaid with mother-of-pearl. I feel quite like a gangster's moll."

"Did she mind the change in plans?"

"Not at all. In fact, she's rather happy to get Arthur Wellesley out of Rome. She said he's picking up Popish habits. She heard him reciting the Paternoster in Latin this morning. In any event, it might not be a bad idea for you to keep the ambassador's details handy. We might need a little

29

diplomatic assistance if Aunt Dove decides to misbehave."

He rolled his eyes to heaven. "Saints preserve us."

I patted the *Jolly Roger* lightly. "Mind you tighten everything up. I have a little surprise."

The surprise was a series of barrel rolls I pulled off over the Piazza San Marco. As I heard it later, the Italian authorities were not amused and the pigeons in the square flapped about irritably, but Aunt Dove thought it was all great fun and the reporters lapped it up like kittens with cream. The only one who protested seriously was Arthur, who kicked up a tremendous racket and then played dead for the better part of an hour while Aunt Dove fussed over him with warm brandy. He feebly opened his beak when she spooned the brandy into it, and when she cracked some pistachios for him and drizzled them with honey he hopped around, fluffing out his feathers and making a queer chortling noise that meant he was very happy indeed.

We rested in Venice a day before boarding the Orient Express, and I blessed the instinct that had caused our friend in Los Angeles to book two compartments. Aunt Dove was delightful company, but she snored like a fiend, and Arthur tried my patience at the best of times. I spent most of the journey reading up on the political situation in the region—as pretty and fickle as a spring

30

thunderstorm—and the rest of the time staring out the window at the passing Balkans. It was hard to imagine that this peaceful, beautiful countryside had been the start of such a bloodbath, I mused as I watched hill town and pasture roll past. There were stunning mountain gorges and pastoral and village scenes like something the Brothers Grimm might have conjured out of a storybook. And with every passing mile, I found something new that I would have liked to have shown Gabriel.

Damn. There he was again, hovering at the edge of my life like a ghost that just won't quit. When he'd first been reported missing and presumed dead at the sinking of the *Lusitania*, I had spent months catching glimpses of him out of the tail of my eye. Psychosomatic, Aunt Dove had pronounced firmly. She'd prescribed demanding war work and long country walks to clear my head. She'd even found me a job working at a convalescent hospital run by Wally's mother at their estate at Mistledown. Because his mother was a viscountess and an unrepentant snob, she insisted on taking only pilots as her patients and she wanted a very select group of nurses to attend them. She gave us splendid uniforms of crushed strawberry-pink with clever little caps designed to show off our hair. Most of the girls worked there only to catch a husband, but I had other ideas. I made friends with the lads, and within a few months, I understood the rudiments of flying. And that was what saved me when I thought I would drown in regret after Gabriel. For the first time since he'd been lost, I slept whole nights through, and I didn't see him around corners and in shadows. I learned to say goodbye, to get on with the business of living.

But now, the nearer I got to Damascus, the closer he felt. I slept badly and dreamed of him when I did. And when I had time alone, I found myself remembering.

I was staring out the window of the Orient Express, a book open on my lap, thinking of the last time I'd seen him, when the door to my compartment opened and Aunt Dove slipped in, a dozen necklaces of polished glass beads clacking as she moved.

"That's Baroness Orczy's newest effort, isn't it?" she asked with a nod to the book in my lap. "I heard it's quite amusing. Pity you're not enjoying it."

I perked up. "What makes you say that?"

"You've been stuck on the first page for the last two days. You're brooding. And from the way you're toying with your wedding ring on that chain, I'd say it has to do with Gabriel."

I dropped the chain as if I'd been burned. Since I had been waiting to divorce Gabriel when he was lost, I didn't have the right to call myself his widow, I reasoned, no matter what society and the law said. But I hadn't the heart to chuck the ring away, either. I had worn it on a chain since the day of his funeral, tucking it securely into my décolletage even though it brought back the most painful memories of all. I hadn't expected a wedding ring. We had eloped, and it had seemed like a particularly romantic bit of conjuring that he had managed to get me a ring. He pulled it off my finger on our wedding night to show me the inscription.

"When did you have time?" I had demanded.

He smiled. "It's mine." He held up his hand and I saw that the slender gold band he'd worn on his smallest finger, tucked under his Starke signet ring, was missing. "I found a jeweller to inscribe it this afternoon while you were looking for a frock to wear to the wedding. Have a look inside."

I peered into the ring, puzzling out the script in the dim light. "*Hora e sempre*," I read aloud.

He gave me a mock-serious look. "It's Latin."

"Yes, I may not have gone to university, but I'm not entirely uneducated," I said, giving him a little push. "Now and forever."

He dropped the ring back onto my finger. "I mean it, you know," he said, his tone light, but his eyes desperately serious. "I suspect I'll be a rotten husband, really frightful, in fact. I'm not very good at living up to anyone's expectations but my own, and I'm abominably selfish."

I looped my arms about his neck. "Yes, you're a monster. I still married you."

In spite of my teasing tone, he didn't smile. Some melancholy had come over him and he put his hands to my wrists, pinning them gently.

"Damned if I know why. What I'm trying to say, Evie, is that my best is a bloody poor thing. But I'll give you that best of mine, now and forever. Just don't expect too much, will you?"

I had thrown my arms completely around him then, as much because I couldn't bear the look of hunted sadness in his eyes as from passion. Some hours later, when he slept heavily, one leg thrown over mine, his face buried in my hair, I closed my hand tightly so I could feel the ring bite into my hand. *Now and forever.* We had lasted four months. . . .

I let my gaze slide back to the passing Balkan countryside. "Those are particularly nice cows."

Aunt Dove gave a sigh and took a seat, her beads still clacking. "If that's meant as an encouragement to me to mind my own business, it's feeble. Try again."

"Mind your own business," I said, smiling.

She shook her head. "It isn't good for a woman to brood, you know. I think you need a man."

"Of one thing I am certain, I do *not* need a man."

Her expression was sympathetic. "Darling, I know you love Wally dearly, but I think there's something you ought to know."

I rolled my eyes. "Oh, heavens, Dove! I know that already."

She gave a sigh of relief. "Thank God for that. I thought I was going to have to explain to you about boys who go with other boys. Did you figure it out for yourself or did he tell you?"

"A little of both," I admitted. "One night we had rather too much gin and not enough to eat. I told him the whole story of Gabriel and sobbed a bit in his arms, and then he was holding me. Everything went sort of soft and blurry, and we fell into a kiss. I realised after about two minutes that neither of us had moved. It was what I imagine it would be like to kiss a brother. Or Arthur Wellesley. Just nothing there at all."

"Really? Curious. One of the best kissers I ever knew was a poof—but he was royal. Perhaps it makes a difference," she said consolingly. "But that doesn't change anything, child. You need a proper seeing-to."

"A 'seeing-to'? What on earth—" I held up a hand. "Never mind. I don't want to know."

She pursed her lips. "Sex, dear. I'm talking about sex. You need some. And badly, I should think."

"Aunt Dove, we are not having this conversation. Not now, not ever."

She pretended not to hear me. "It isn't your fault, my dear. I imagine after a man like Gabriel Starke, I'd be a bit choosy about my male companions, as well. But just because you won't find someone to . . . er, fill his rather large shoes, so to speak, doesn't mean you can't have a perfectly pleasant time of it."

"How do you know he had large shoes to fill?" I demanded. The fact that she was entirely correct was beside the point.

She smiled. "Because for the duration of your brief marriage you looked like the cat that ate the canary. Now, you fought like tigers and he was a crashing failure as a husband. That leaves the bedroom. Clearly, things were satisfactory there. *More* than satisfactory, if I'm any judge of these things, and I think I am. But just because you are still pining for Gabriel, that's no reason not to have an interesting time of it. In fact, I think you should. A woman's insides need lubrication, you know. They'll go all dry and stick together otherwise."

I ignored her vague grasp of biology and seized on something else. "I'm not pining for Gabriel. I can't imagine why you'd think so."

She rose and kissed the top of my head. "Child, you're transparent as glass." She went to the door. "I seem to remember the last thing Gabriel Starke ever gave you was a copy of *Peter and Wendy*. Interesting that you named your aeroplane the *Jolly Roger*."

She closed the door before my shoe hit it, neatly marking the glossy wood.

The brooding over my failed marriage had taken its toll by the time we reached Constantinople. I was snappish and tired, with dark circles under my eyes, but the photographers were waiting. I powdered my face and painted my lips with the brightest crimson lipstick in my box and posed for photographs with a smiling Aunt Dove and a moulting Arthur. He shed bright green feathers all down the train platform, but by the time we had settled in for the last leg of the journey to Damascus he had perked up. Aunt Dove flirted her way through Customs outrageously and as a result, our bags weren't so much as opened, much less searched. She plied me with pistachios— which I was darkly afraid had once been intended for Arthur—and in due course we arrived in Damascus. The approach to the city was not the finest. For that we ought to have come from Baghdad, crossing the desert to find Damascus shimmering in its oasis with the snowy bulk of Mount Hermon looming up behind. But rolling through the orchards of olive and lemon, pomegranate and orange, we saw Damascus standing on the plain, a gleaming, jewelled city of white in a lush green setting. It smelled, as all ancient cities do, of stone and smoke and donkey and spices, but over it all hung the perfume of the flowers that spilled from private courtyards and public gardens. Sewage ran in the streets, yet to me it would always be the city of jasmine, the air thick with the fragrance of crushed blossoms.

We collected a taxi at the station and after a harrowing ride through narrow streets, the driver deposited us neatly on the walk in front of the Hotel Zenobia, a new establishment in a very old structure. Once a pasha's palace, it had been only recently converted to a private hotel. It was decorated in the traditional Eastern style with courts fitting together like so many puzzle boxes, each with its own staircases and tinkling fountains where gilded fins darted through the pale blue petals of the lilies. Outside, the manager—a tall, elegant Belgian—was waiting. He bowed and kissed Aunt Dove's hand, murmuring something into her ear. She dropped her eyes and gave him a doelike look from under her lashes, and before I knew what was happening, he snapped his fingers for porters and in a very short time we were ensconced in the largest suite in the hotel. It was a delicious mixture of Damascene luxury and European sensibility with a wide veranda and comfortable sitting room linking our bedrooms. The bedrooms had modern furniture, but the sitting room was fitted with traditional Eastern divans, long and low and thick with tasselled silk cushions.

The maids bustled, unpacking and hissing at one another in French and Arabic, occasionally breaking into giggles when they discovered something unexpected like my leather aviatrix suit or Aunt Dove's French underwear. But I merely stood and surveyed the surroundings while Aunt Dove flipped through the post that had been waiting for us.

I gave her a suspicious look. "Do you know the manager? From before I mean?"

Her expression was determinedly innocent. "Who? Étienne? Oh, our paths have crossed from time to time." Before I could ask more, she took me in hand. "We're travel-fatigued," Aunt Dove pronounced. "It happens when one passes too quickly from one culture into another. I've always said trains were uncivilized. One ought only ever to travel by steamship or camel."

"So sayeth the woman who has learned to fly my aeroplane," I remarked. A large bowl of orchids had been placed upon a low table between the cushion-strewn divans and I bent to sniff it.

Aunt Dove waved off my remark. "That is entirely different. Aeroplanes are novelties, not real travel. No one would ever want to use them for anything other than publicity. Now, I want a beefsteak and a cigarette and a stiff whisky, not necessarily in that order. Go and wash for dinner, child. It's time to see Damascus."

Thanks to a broken strap, I was ten minutes later than Aunt Dove in getting ready and found her in the crowded lobby. She was wearing a gold turban with her great paste emerald brooch and an armful of enamelled bangles that clattered and clinked as she gestured. The lobby was one of the many courtyards of the hotel, this one furnished with the usual divans and endless pots of flowering plants and palms. Soft-footed servants trotted back and forth with trays of cocktails and little dishes of nuts while a discreet orchestra played in the corner. The place was thronged with international visitors, most of whom were craning to get a look at Aunt Dove. She was chatting animatedly with the handsomest man in the room. There was nothing unusual about either of those things. She often dressed with originality, and one of her greatest skills was finding the most attractive and charming men to do her bidding. She caught sight of me just as I descended the stairs and waved an elegant hand.

"Evie, darling, come and meet Mr. Halliday. He's a British diplomat posted here to keep an eye on those wily French."

I extended my hand and he took it, staring at me intently with a pair of delightfully intelligent grey eyes. "How do you do, Mr. Halliday? Evangeline Starke."

"Miss Starke," he said, shaking my hand slowly and holding it for an instant longer than he ought.

"Mrs.," I corrected gently. "I am a widow."

A fleeting expression of sympathy touched his features. "Of course. The war took a lot of good men."

I didn't bother to correct him. Gabriel had died during the war—just not doing anything useful like actually fighting.

He glanced to Aunt Dove. "Lady Lavinia was

just telling me about your Seven Seas Tour, but she needn't have. I've been following your exploits in the newspapers. It's dashed thrilling. Will you be doing any flying here?"

"Not just yet. My plane is still in Italy. Aunt Dove and I are here for pleasure. We mean to relax and revive before we move on to the Caspian for the next leg of our tour."

"Damascus is the place for that," he assured me. "Lots of picturesque sights and loads of delicious gossip, but it's just the spot for shopping or lounging in a bathhouse or lying by a fountain and letting the world pass you by."

Those pursuits would interest me for about a day, but I smiled. "I'm very interested in how the interim government is faring, as well. I know the French are determined to meddle, and I'm curious how their efforts compare to the British presence in Palestine."

Mr. Halliday's brows lifted in delighted astonishment. "I say, beauty and brains. What a refreshing combination! Most women only want to talk tea and scandal, but if you really want to know the truth of the political situation, I am more than happy to give you the lay of the land, so to speak."

Aunt Dove smelled the opportunity to make a new conquest and leaped on it. "How very kind of you, Mr. Halliday. My niece and I were just about to go to dinner. Won't you join us as our guest?"

He accepted quickly, extending his arm to

Aunt Dove. I followed, watching him as he deftly negotiated the crowds to secure a taxi and handed her in. He turned to me and I put my hand in his.

"Mrs. Starke," he murmured.

"Evie, please," I told him.

To my amusement, he blushed a little. To cover it, he gave swift and fluent instructions to the driver and turned to us with a beaming face. "I think it's going to be a devilishly good night."

In fact, it was an extraordinary night. The restaurant where we dined was very new and very French with exquisite food and wine. Aunt Dove was at great pains to be charming to Mr. Halliday, who himself was a delightful companion. A tiny European orchestra was tucked behind the palms, playing popular music, and as the evening progressed, bejewelled couples rose and began to dance. I was tired from the journey—or perhaps it was too much champagne—but the whole of the evening took on an otherworldly quality. It seemed impossible that I had come so far in search of a ghost, and as I sat sipping at my bubbling wine, I began to wonder if I were making a tremendous fool of myself. The war was over. And on that glittering night, it became quite apparent that the world had moved on. Why couldn't I?

Mr. Halliday was charming company. He was an expert storyteller, and his anecdotes about the expats and officials in Damascus ranged from the highly amusing to the mildly salacious. But he'd chosen his audience well. Aunt Dove loved nothing better than a good gossip, and much of our meal was spent chatting about her travels in the South Pacific, an area Mr. Halliday longed to see.

"Oh, you must go!" Aunt Dove instructed. "If nothing else, it's a lovely place to die."

Mr. Halliday burst out laughing then sobered as he looked from Aunt Dove to me. "She is serious?"

"Entirely," I admitted. "Auntie won't travel anywhere she thinks would be unpleasant to die."

"That's why I don't go to Scandinavia," she said darkly. "It's far too cold and bodies linger too long. I'd much rather die in a nice warm climate where things decompose quickly. No point in hanging around when I am well and gone."

Mr. Halliday looked at me again and I shrugged. "Ask her about her shroud."

"Shroud?" His handsome brow furrowed.

Aunt Dove smiled broadly. "Yes, a lovely *tivaevae* I picked up last time I was in the South Pacific."

"*Tivaevae*?"

"A quilt from the Cook Islands," I explained. "Auntie travels with it in case she dies unexpectedly. She wanted something nice for her cremation."

"You ought to come up and see it," she told him, leering only a little. "It's quite the loveliest example of South Pacific needlework—all reds and aquas and a green so bright it matches Arthur perfectly."

"Arthur?" Mr. Halliday looked well and truly lost.

"My parrot, Arthur Wellesley," she replied.

She beckoned the waiter over for another bottle of champagne, and Mr. Halliday threw me a rather desperate look. "I wonder if I might prevail upon you for a dance, Mrs. Starke? Lady Lavinia, if you will excuse us, of course."

Aunt Dove waved us off and I rose and moved into his arms for a waltz. He was a graceful dancer, but not perfect, and it was those little missteps that made me like him even more. He apologised the second time he trod on my feet, pulling a rueful face.

"I am sorry. I don't seem to be able to con-centrate very well this evening." But his eyes were warm and did not leave my face.

"All is forgiven, Mr. Halliday," I said.

"John," he said automatically. "Your aunt is an entirely original lady," he said. "Like something out of mythology."

"She can be," I agreed. "By the way, if you haven't any interest in sleeping with her, you ought to know what she means when she asks you to come up and look at her shroud."

He tripped then, and it took him a full measure of the waltz to recover.

"Mrs. Starke—Evie. Really, I would never presume to believe that I would behave in so ungentlemanly—"

I cut him off. "Mr. Halliday, it's none of my business what you get up to. I just wanted to offer a word of warning in case her intentions came as a surprise. They often do."

"Often?" His voice was strangled.

"She is affectionate by nature," I explained. "Demonstrably so. And while many gentlemen are receptive, it can be a trifle unnerving when some poor soul goes to her rooms actually expecting to see her shroud or examine her stamp collection."

He smiled, almost against his will, it seemed. "Does she have a very fine stamp collection?"

"She doesn't have one at all."

"Oh," he said faintly.

"Sometimes gentlemen misunderstand her intentions," I explained. "It occasionally results in unfortunate events. I shouldn't like to see a repeat of the Aegean."

"The Aegean?"

"There was a young man who thought she was actually kidnapping him. It was all a tempest in a teapot, I assure you, but he happened to be the son of the local magistrate, and things got rather out of hand. That was when I took up drinking as a hobby."

He smiled deeply, and I saw he had the suggestion of dimples. It wasn't fair, really, to compare them to Gabriel's. His had been so deep a girl could drown in them when he smiled. In repose, Gabriel's face had been decidedly handsome, but when his mouth curved into a cheerful grin and his dimples flashed, the effect had been purely devastating.

Something of Halliday reminded me of him, a trick of the light, the curve of a high cheekbone, perhaps. But Halliday's eyes were a mild grey where Gabriel's had been such a startling blue I had sometimes looked into them and completely lost my train of thought. There was something similar to Gabriel's lazy grace in Halliday's gestures, his economy of movement, but the effect was of a serviceable copy instead of the glamour of the real thing.

Of course, that wasn't Halliday's fault at all, so I smiled back and he tightened his hold. We danced on until the end of the song. When it finished I started to step back, but he did not let me go. "One more?"

I went willingly into his arms. It was a delicious feeling after so many years without Gabriel, and I found myself thinking an unmaidenly thought or two as we moved. The song came to an end, but he made no move to stop dancing and neither did I.

Just as the conductor raised his baton for the next number, the maître d' thrust his head behind the palms to speak to him. The conductor shrugged and something changed hands—money, no doubt—for the conductor leaned forward and murmured something to his musicians.

They fumbled with their sheet music, casting aside the next song on their list, and launched into a pretty little prelude. Mr. Halliday and I began to dance again, and just as he swung me into a graceful turn, I felt a shiver run down my spine.

"Evie?" His eyes were full of concern, his arm tight about my waist.

" 'Salut d'Amour,' " I said.

"Beg pardon? Oh, yes, I think it is. Pretty little piece, isn't it? Shame I've such a wretched memory for music. Never can remember who wrote it."

"Elgar," I said stiffly. "It's Elgar."

His expression brightened. "Of course it is. Now, Evie—Mrs. Starke? You've gone quite pale? Are you feeling all right?"

I forced a smile. "Quite, but suddenly the room seems beastly hot. Forgive me. I must excuse myself for just a moment."

He held onto my hand, patting it solicitously. "Anything you like. May I take you back to the table?"

"The ladies' cloakroom, I think."

He walked me as far as the door and I turned to put my hand to his sleeve. "Would you mind going to check on Aunt Dove? I oughtn't have left her quite so long. I'm feeling frightfully guilty."

He hesitated. "If you're certain you're all right."

"Perfectly. Just a little warm. I will bathe my

47

wrists and be right as rain in a few minutes. Please don't trouble yourself. Go order some more champagne and I will be back to the table by the time it arrives."

He trotted off and as soon as he was out of sight, I ducked behind one of the palms. I waited until the maître d' strode by and jumped out to pluck at his sleeve.

The poor man nearly jumped out of his skin. "Madame! You have startled me."

"I apologise, but I must speak with you."

He preened a little, stroking his moustache. No doubt he was accustomed to intrigues in his establishment, but I had other fish to fry. I leaned closer.

"It is a matter of some delicacy, monsieur."

"*Naturellement.*" He put on a conspiratorial smile and laid a finger to the side of his nose. "This way, madame."

He led me to a quiet little alcove sheltered from the rest of the club by a carved screen. "What may I do for you, madame?"

"The song the orchestra is playing now, 'Salut d'Amour—' why are they playing that piece?"

He shrugged. "It is a pretty and popular piece, madame."

"I think it is more than that. I believe you paid the conductor to play it. Why?"

His dark eyes gleamed. He was enjoying himself. "Madame is observant."

"Madame is a little impatient, as well. Why did you pay him? Did someone pay you?"

He shrugged again. "It is customary to pay extra for special services," he said blandly.

The hint did not go amiss. I fished in my tiny beaded bag and withdrew a paper note. His eyes lit with avarice and he plucked the note from my fingers, whisking it into his pocket before I could object.

"To answer your question, madame, yes. I was asked to make this request of the conductor."

"By whom?"

He rolled his eyes heavenward and I took out another note. He made to take it, but this time I held it just out of reach.

He sighed. "Ah, madame grows cynical. *Quelle dommage.* Very well. I was given money to request the song, but monsieur was most insistent that it be played immediately."

"Describe monsieur for me, please."

He thought. "My own height, perhaps a little less slender. Dark hair and dark eyes with tiny moustaches. An Arab," he added. "And a very young one. Not yet twenty."

My racing heart slowed. It could not be Gabriel. The maître d' was less than five foot eight and inclined to slight embonpoint around his middle. Gabriel had been six feet even and well-built. Even more damning, although he had dark hair, his gentian blue eyes would have given him away even if he could have passed for someone almost two decades his junior, which I distinctly doubted.

The maître d' winkled the note out of my fingers. "Does madame have any more questions?"

"Yes," I said suddenly. "How much did he pay you?"

"Two hundred francs."

"And how did he pay?"

"In two 100-franc banknotes, madame."

"You gave one to the conductor?"

He gave an indulgent laugh. "Madame underestimates me. I gave him fifty francs."

I pulled out the largest banknote I had in my bag. "Give me the notes he gave you."

He took the note from me and held it up to the light.

"Oh, for heaven's sake, I'm no counterfeiter!"

He threw up his hands with a gusty sigh. "Madame must forgive my cynicism, but it is the burden of the Frenchman. When a lovely woman wishes to pay him far more for his money than it is worth—" He trailed off, leaving me to draw my own conclusions.

"You're quite right to be cautious. But I think there may be something for me on one of the notes."

He lifted his brows, a delighted smile playing about under his moustache. "La! An intrigue! Why did madame not say so before?"

He drew out the two hundred-franc notes and

handed them over, happily pocketing the larger note I had given him in exchange. He leaned over while I examined the notes.

"What do they say, madame? Anything?"

I scrutinised the notes in the dim light. "Nothing," I said, but even as the word was out of my mouth, I saw it. In faint pencil, on the very edge of the note. REAPERS HOME.

"But what does this mean, madame?"

I forced a bright smile and brought out another banknote to press into his hand. "It is an assignation. I must trust in your discretion, monsieur."

He pocketed the banknote swiftly as he bowed. "But of course, madame! I am the very soul of discretion. It is more than my life is worth not to be," he added with a wistful smile. No doubt he had seen his share of intrigues and thought himself a sort of Cupid, helping them along. Or he simply enjoyed the extra money he extorted for his silence.

I slipped the notes into my décolletage and slid out of the alcove, fluffing my hair as I made my way back to the table.

Halliday rose and handed me a fresh glass of champagne.

"Feeling better?" Aunt Dove asked.

"Much. It was wretchedly hot on that dance floor," I said, turning from one to the other with a smile. I lifted my glass in a toast. "To Damascus. To old friends and new."

We drank together and Halliday and Aunt Dove fell into conversation about what we ought to see and do in Damascus. I tried to keep up my end, but my thoughts kept turning to the banknotes rustling in my cleavage, and when Halliday at last dropped us at our hotel I was grateful to bid Aunt Dove good-night and go directly to my room. To Aunt Dove's disappointment, Halliday hurried away, and I felt a trifle guilty I had warned him off. He was a big boy. I had no doubt he could take care of himself and would be gentleman enough to be gracious to Aunt Dove when he rebuffed her advances. Still, it was sometimes better to head off trouble at the pass, I had found, and I would have hated to lose Mr. Halliday as a connection. I had a feeling he could prove useful to us, and with so little to go on, I wanted every possible advantage in tracking down the facts behind the photograph.

I pulled out the banknotes and studied them again. There was nothing remarkable about them, no other pencilled messages, no distinctive scent. Just those two words and the song the orchestra had played. "Salut d'Amour." It was a beautiful melody with just a touch of nostalgia to save it from sentimentality. There was something haunting and old-fashioned about it, and although Gabriel and I had quarrelled good-naturedly about music, it was the one song we had agreed upon. I could never convince him that jazz was going to be the next big thing any more than he could make me love Palestrina. But "Salut d'Amour" had been ours. We had danced to it the first night we met and every night after. No matter how badly we fought or how cold our silences had become, every evening after dinner Gabriel had started up his gramophone and played it, taking me in his arms and leading me into a sweeping turn that left me dizzy.

I tucked the banknotes into my cleavage and wound up the tiny gramophone I carried with me on my travels. It took me a few minutes to find the right recording, but at last I did. I went to the window, opening the pierced shutters to look out over the sleeping city. The moon was waxing and hung half-full like some exotic silver jewel just over the horizon. From the courtyard below rose the scent of jasmine on the cool night air. A slender vine had wound its way up to the balcony, and I reached out, pinching off a single creamy white blossom. I lifted it to my nose, drinking in the thick sweetness of it as it filled my head, sending my senses reeling. There was something narcotic about that jasmine, something carnal and ethereal at the same time. I crushed the petals between my fingers, taking the scent onto my skin. It was not a fragrance to wear alone. It was too rich, too heady, too full of sensuality and promise. It was a fragrance for silken cushions and damp naked flesh and moonlit beds. I rubbed at my fingers, but the scent clung tightly, keeping me company as I sat in the window, listening to a song I had almost forgot and thinking of Gabriel Starke and the five years that stretched barrenly between us.

THREE

The next morning I popped in to see Aunt Dove just as she finished her breakfast in bed.

"Oh, this apricot jam is absolutely exquisite. Did you have some, dear?" she asked, feeding the last bits to Arthur Wellesley on a piece of bread.

"I did, and it was sublime. What shall we do today?" I asked. I was already washed and dressed and only the tiniest bit put out that she hadn't even risen yet.

She gave me a wan smile. "Do you mind terribly going on without me? I'm afraid I've caught the indolence of the East and I'm feeling lazy as a harem girl today."

It wasn't the East so much as the relentless travel of the past few months, I thought. Her complexion was a little paler than I liked, and in spite of her delight in the jam, most of her breakfast had gone untouched.

"You're off your feed," I said, helping myself to a fig. "Shall I call the doctor?"

She flapped a hand, startling Arthur, who retreated to the bedstead, squawking irritably.

"Heavens no! You know what English doctors are like—all purgatives and little pills. No, I just need rest, child, and I'll be right as rain tomorrow. You'll see."

"If you're sure," I said a trifle uncertainly.

"Quite," she assured me, clipping off the syllable sharply. "Now, I don't like the notion of you bumbling around Damascus on your own. You're far too pretty for that. You will want a dragoman."

"Aunt Dove, really! I hardly think they go in abducting women off the streets. I'm sure I shall be perfectly safe."

She wagged a finger at me. "I mean it, Evie. I know this part of the world. Arabs could teach the English a thing or two about courtesy, but there are more than Arabs in Damascus. Some of those wretched Turks—"

I held up a hand before she had a chance to warm to her theme. "I'm sure there are perfectly courteous Turks to be found, as well. But if it makes you happy I'll engage a dragoman and see the city in style. Is that better?"

"Much." She began thumbing through the letters on her tray, clearly finished with me now that I had promised to be a good girl.

I left her then, dropping a kiss to her cheek and nearly getting pecked by Arthur for my troubles. I opened my phrasebook and began to sound out a few key words. I was so immersed that I completely missed the last step of the stairs, stumbling neatly into a young Arab man.

He caught me, setting me gently on my feet, then dropped his hands at once, bowing gracefully.

"Oh, forgive me, *sitt*! It is not proper to put hands upon a lady. I have offered the gravest offence."

"Don't be silly. You saved me from a nasty fall," I said, smiling to reassure him I was not offended.

I didn't bother to ask how he knew to address me in English. The hotel catered to an international crowd, and English or French was any Damascene's best bet if he wanted to make himself understood.

I thought my smile and pleasant tone would convince him I was not bothered, but he looked up at me, his expression stricken.

"But you must permit me to make amends."

I bit back a smile. He was very young, no more than fifteen, I guessed, and so earnest, I hadn't the heart to let him think I found him amusing when he was taking the whole thing so seriously.

I inclined my head with as much gravity as I could manage. "That isn't necessary," I assured him. "There is no offence, and I thank you for your quick thinking."

I moved to go past him, but he darted in front of me, his dark brown eyes snapping brightly.

"Then the *sitt* will consider hiring Rashid as dragoman," he said suavely.

That time I did smile. He was slender as a girl and far younger than the dragomen who clustered about the court waiting for clients. But he had a true entrepreneur's spirit, and he had seized the advantage in speaking to me.

Still, I thought a fellow with experience might be best, so I shook my head.

"Thank you, but no."

I stepped forward and he dodged in front of me again, his striped robe billowing.

"Then the *sitt* speaks untruly, for she has not forgiven me," he said, his face mournful as he turned those expressive dark eyes heavenward.

"Oh, really, that's not fair," I said, laughing. "You can't think I would actually hold a grudge over something so trivial. I promise, I haven't. It's just that I want a dragoman with experience."

He rose to his full height, which was very nearly my own, and lifted his chin as his hands sketched a graceful gesture. "I have experience, *sitt*. I am a gentleman of this city."

The words were spoken with a solemnity beyond his years, and I suppressed another smile.

"And I suppose you have twelve cousins who all own shops and want you to bring business there, is that it?"

He scowled a little. "I have no kinsmen in *trade*," he said, nearly spitting the word. "I am a son of the desert." He finished with a little flourish and a phrase that sounded something like *ibn al-Sahra.*

"You are a Bedouin then?" I asked, fascinated in spite of myself. To the casual traveller, all

Arabs were alike. But I had learned enough from Gabriel to understand that the Bedouin were special. Nomadic and proud, they were held to be the very embodiment of Arab virtues. They were more than a little fascinating, and I found myself giving way almost before I knew it.

"I haven't much money to pay you," I warned him. I had finally opened the fuel bill for the *Jolly Roger* and it had been so horrifying I had thrust it at once into the toe of an old boot.

He made another graceful gesture and named a price. It was so low, no other dragoman would have taken as much to get out of bed in the morning, but I was in no position to question him. I agreed and he grinned—a beautiful, engaging smile. He was a remarkably handsome young man, and he must have set a dozen hearts fluttering back home.

But he was all business as we ventured into the city. He might have charged me a pittance, but he was determined to be the best dragoman in Damascus. He hailed taxis, nipping neatly into traffic to snatch them up before anyone else could. He kept a sunshade firmly over my head, scolding me for coming out with only a small-brimmed hat as we made our way through the old city.

Rashid was as good as his word. He was knowledgeable and courteous, and when it was time to lunch, he guided me to a small restaurant where a Western woman eating alone would not attract too much unwanted attention. There was no menu—only Rashid, speaking firmly to the staff about what he wanted. They brought out dish after dish of delicious things, from stewed chicken with pistachios to a pomegranate custard that melted on my tongue. I finally pushed away from the table, groaning a little as I did so.

"I ought never to have doubted you, Rashid," I told him. "That meal alone was worth engaging your services."

He made another of his courtly bows. "Now, the *sitt* must see the city as only a Damascene can show it."

"I thought you were a son of the desert, *ibn al-Sahra*," I replied mischievously, mangling the phrase as I tried to repeat what he had said earlier.

"Only a son of the desert can truly appreciate the city of princes," he replied smoothly.

He guided me through the temples and mosques and *souks*, making our way from one end of the old city to the other. Together we strolled the stony streets and Rashid, much to my surprise, kept his word about keeping the merchants away. He waved off the fruit sellers and spice merchants alike, turning down offers of excellent prices on rugs and perfumes and brassware. It was only when a fabric merchant flung himself in front of us and unrolled his wares that I paused.

"You know, that stuff isn't half-bad. I think I'd like to have a look," I told him.

He rolled his eyes. "It is not good enough for the *sitt*, but he will have better inside the shop."

"Will he?"

He shrugged. "Of course, *sitt*. He will not keep his best wares in public view. The most special things are guarded for the very best customers."

I followed him into the shop where the merchant stood bowing and expressing his delight at having an exalted English lady in his place of business. He ordered his wife to bring tea and while we waited he showed me his stock.

Rashid frowned at him and the merchant held up his hands, darting a quick apologetic glance at me. "But I think you would not be interested in such trifles. For you I will bring out the very best of my fabrics."

His wife entered with the tea then, and we paused to observe the customary civilities. I had already learned that negotiations with an Arab were not a thing to be undertaken quickly. Like most Easterners, they were immensely hospitable and expected any interaction between people, even strangers doing business, would be punctuated with refreshment and pleasant conversation. In this case, the tea tray was laden with glass cups full of black tea heavily sweetened and spiced with a little crushed cardamom. His wife had brought biscuits, as well, dry things that tasted a little soapy, but I soon discovered they were edible if I dunked them quickly in the tea.

"Ah, how clever madame is!" the shopkeeper proclaimed, and he dunked his, as well. He leaned closer and gave me a knowing look. "My wife is very beautiful and she bears me sons, but her cooking . . ." He rolled his eyes heavenward, and threw up his hands.

We drank several small, heavily sweetened glasses of tea while the merchant talked about his shop. He had taken the business over from his father, who had sold beautiful fabrics, as well, and *he* had learned the trade from *his* father, and so the conversation went, pleasant and innocuous, but heightening my anticipation besides. It was masterfully done, and by the time he unrolled the fabrics, I was already persuaded I would buy from him no matter the cost.

He needn't have bothered with the theatrics. The fabrics would have sold themselves. In the end, I chose for Aunt Dove an inky blue damask, heavy and expensive. "It will make a splendid dressing gown for her," I mused aloud. "Perhaps with a nice hanging sleeve. Something deliciously medieval. She can play at being Eleanor of Aquitaine."

The merchant bowed, but Rashid gave me a disapproving look. "The *sitt* does not buy for herself? This will not do." He went to the shelves and rummaged through the treasures until he unearthed a deep green silk shot with gold. "This, *sitt*. A gown of this to match the green of your eyes."

"I don't have green eyes. They're brown," I corrected.

He shook his head. "They are the same colour as the spring grass on the breast of Mount Hermon," he said flatly. "Green and brown mingled together. This is a welcome colour to the Bedouin, *sitt*. I do not make a mistake."

"Fine, they're hazel," I responded, compromising. "And I suppose this green will light them up."

"In this colour, the *sitt* will be irresistible to all men."

I raised a brow at him, but he wasn't wrong. Green did bring out the best in my eyes, coaxing the hazel to something altogether more brilliant. Gabriel had loved me in green for that very reason. I hadn't worn it since his death, but in that crowded little treasure trove of a shop, I did not let that stop me. I signalled to the merchant that I would take a length of it, and I threw in a length of white patterned on white, as well. Rashid nodded his satisfaction at the price and told the fellow to send them along to the hotel when they were parceled up.

When we emerged into the sunlight, I felt a little dazed after so much time in the dim shop and so many glasses of sweet tea. We walked slowly so that I could enjoy the shop fronts, and I sighed over one piled high with gorgeous confectionery.

"All things shall be as the *sitt* wishes," he said. He darted into the shop, my stalwart cavalier in a striped robe. I moved on to the next window wondering if Rashid were going to present a problem. He had been sweetly authoritative, but the last thing I needed was a boy following me about like a hound puppy. A wiser woman might have paid off Rashid and let him go at the end of the day, but it occurred to me he was a stellar dragoman and seemed to know everyone and everything about the city. It was just possible he might be able to help me stumble onto some clue to Gabriel's whereabouts.

Rashid returned quickly, wearing a satisfied expression. He reached into his robe and pulled out a paper parcel, opening it to reveal a slab of pistachio toffee layered with crushed, sweetened rose petals. "For you, *sitt*. That you may know fully the sweetness of Damascus."

"How lovely. Thank you, Rashid." I broke a piece free and nibbled a little off one corner. "Oh, that is sublime!"

He made a grave bow. "Now I think we shall go to the Great Mosque."

He led the way while I walked slowly, eating my rose-scented toffee. The Great Mosque was the centrepiece of Damascus, the most recognisable landmark in the whole city, and while we made our way there, Rashid gave me a brief history lesson.

"The Umayyad mosque is the Great Mosque of Damascus, *sitt*, and one of the largest and oldest in the whole world. There has been a holy place in this spot for more than three thousand years. First, the pagan gods of which your Bible speaks. Then the Romans built a temple, and after that the Christians made a church here. But after this came the Umayyads, the great caliphs of this land. They were architects and poets. They settled the nomadic tribes here and built the city as it stands today—magnificent!" At this he threw his arms wide to encompass the whole of the dome that shimmered in front of us. "And it is the fourth-holiest place to the followers of the Prophet, peace be unto him."

As it happened, showing the proper respect meant draping myself with the shapeless black robe and head covering that Rashid rented for me at the door. The garments were tolerable, although I suspected they'd be suffocating to wear on a hot day. I could not imagine how the Arab women tolerated the beastly things, but as I looked around at the dozens of women similarly attired, I suddenly understood their compliance. The veil had been ordered by men to protect female chastity—a sensible precaution since their honour was dependent upon their womenfolk not getting up to mischief—but women had found certain advantages to the arrangement. To begin with, once veiled, a woman was virtually impossible to distinguish from any other. Oh, certainly, one could judge the colour and shape of the eyes, and perhaps learn something from the hands, but it would take a keen eye to pick out a familiar shape under the enveloping yards of black fabric. There was something almost anonymous about wearing the veil.

But it still seemed a small consolation for walking around in a shroud, I grumbled to Rashid. He said something about eunuchs then, but I could scarcely hear for the veil covering my ears, and by then we had reached the shrine of John the Baptist. It was a small chapel, really, with intricately carved stone and gold filigreed windows set with green glass that glowed in the afternoon light. Above it all hovered a green dome that looked like something Hawksmoor would have designed. The whole effect was quite grand and rather pretty in an overdone way, and not what one would expect for a fellow who went around living rough in the desert and eating locusts.

When I had seen my fill, Rashid guided me out to a little garden attached to the north wall and into a small stone structure with curiously striped marble walls. Inside was a tomb hung with emerald-green satin, heavily embroidered and tasselled in gold.

"The tomb of Salah al-Dln, known to your people as Saladin!" he proclaimed with a flourish. He proceeded to talk at length about his accomplishments, but he needn't have bothered. Saladin had been one of Gabriel's heroes. More than once we had passed the time, waiting for a train or sitting on the windswept deck of a ship, by telling stories. I loved fairy tales and the stories of childhood and folklore, but Gabriel preferred poetry or real history—usually the Crusades and often Saladin. He'd had a particular fondness for the great Islamic general who had defeated Richard the Lionheart so soundly.

One night in particular, sailing through the midnight waters of the Pacific en route to China, he'd even worked out the Battle of Hattin for me using coins and bits of paper. His eyes had gleamed in the dim light as he detailed the battle and its significance in history. Reality had fallen away and I had seen it all so clearly—the medieval armies clashing on the parched plain, the silken tents fluttering in the breeze, the thirst-raddled men falling under the curved blades of the Arab defenders who had risen under Saladin's standard to defend their homeland. And after all was finished, Saladin had taken up the most sacred relic in Christendom, the Holy Cross itself, carried into battle by the Bishop of Acre and left in the dust. Saladin had carried the last remnants of the Crucifixion into Damascus in triumph and had been known as a wise and just ruler before his untimely death.

And here I stood, at the foot of the great man's tomb. The German kaiser had stood in the very spot some years before, laying a golden wreath onto Saladin's effigy as a gesture of respect to his Ottoman brothers. But when the advancing Allies had entered Damascus, T. E. Lawrence—the flamboyant Lawrence of Arabia—had wrenched it off and sent it to the museum in London with the coolly dismissive note—"Have liberated this from Saladin as he no longer requires it." It had been a grand gesture, and if any part of Gabriel endured, I knew he would have appreciated it.

The tomb itself was oddly moving, a perfect combination of excess and austerity, and I lingered for a while before Rashid guided me into the sunlight. I blinked hard, dazzled, as I heard a voice hailing me.

"Mrs. Starke! Evie, what a delight!"

I blinked again to find Halliday bearing down on me with a wide smile.

I returned the smile, then realised he couldn't begin to see it through my veil. "Mr. Halliday, how nice to see you. But how could you possibly recognise me through all of this?" I asked, plucking at my heavy robes.

He pulled a rueful face. "One gets accustomed to seeing past veils and things. For instance, in your case, I knew you by how you moved."

"How I moved?"

"Like a dancer," he said, then covered it quickly with a cough and a tinge of a blush. He glanced to Rashid, who was glowering in my shadow. "Who is this fellow, then?"

"This is Rashid, my dragoman."

Halliday's gaze was dubious. "A bit young for the job, don't you think? You must let me arrange for a proper guide."

Rashid's slender nostrils flared and his hand twitched as if he would have loved nothing better than to return the insult. But he was wise beyond his years. Instead, he smiled and inclined his head. "I am the best dragoman in the city. Perhaps the gentleman is new to Damascus and this is why he does not know me."

To his credit, Halliday smiled. "Well, that's put me in my place, hasn't it? Steady on, old boy. If the lady is happy with your services, it's not for me to complain. Now, have you seen the tomb of John the Baptist?"

He guided me around the rest of the mosque and gardens, giving me a thorough grounding on the architecture and history of the place, with Rashid following behind. I might have expected a glare or a sulk, but Rashid's expression was one of carefully schooled indifference, and it began to worry me. It meant he was far more sophisticated than I had understood. He realised that showing his feelings would only get him booted from his job, and he concealed them with masterful nonchalance. It was a remarkable piece of dissembling, and it was only when he neatly guided me to the ladies' corner of the mosque that I realised he was deliberately paying back Halliday for monopolising me.

"I am desolate," he said, quickly stepping into Halliday's path, "but this is the section reserved for the ladies. The *sitt* must go alone," he added, his face impassive.

Halliday gave him a long look then smiled at me. "So you must. Have a look 'round and I'll be here when you finish."

Rashid took me into the courtyard to the fountain where I had to wash to purify myself, then guided me back to the prayer halls. He went no further, but stood at the edge of the ladies' corner, keeping watch. I wandered off, admiring the decoration of the mosque on my own until I came to a little bench and realised my feet were unaccountably sore from all the stone streets. I sat and fanned myself, enjoying the peace and quiet of the spot. In the distance, I could see Rashid standing as still as marble while Halliday roamed restlessly. After a moment, a tall, tweedy sort of woman sat next to me. She wore no-nonsense brogues under her borrowed black robes and her hair was obviously cut short—wisps of it stuck out from under her veil at odd angles. Her hands were large and there was an air of masculine competence about her. She nodded towards my companions.

"Your man friend seems a nice enough chap, but I've known donkeys who know more about ancient architecture. Must be a diplomat."

I smiled in spite of myself. Poor Mr. Halliday.

"Yes, he is attached to the British consulate here."

She snorted. "Useless breed, diplomats. Spend all their time at drinks parties and thinking up ways to interfere where they oughtn't."

I lifted my brows a little. "Oh, dear. That sounds personal."

She smiled, the edge of her eyes crinkling with good humour. "I confess it is. I've had more trouble with diplomats than any other sort since I've been here, always mucking about at the site and interfering. They've no concept of good scholarship."

My heart began to drum against my ribs. "The site?"

She gave a nod. "Excavation site in the desert. Don't know if you speak the lingo, but it is called the Badiyat ash-Sham. We've uncovered a caravansary next to one of the old Crusader castles, and I know that won't impress you, but it ought to. Everyone wants tombs and palaces, but you can learn a damn sight more from a simple thing like a village wall or a caravansary."

"And you're excavating now?" The inscription on Gabriel's photograph had said Damascus, but the background was clearly somewhere in the desert, the vast open reaches of the Badiyat ash-Sham.

"Trying to," she said with some disgust. "If it weren't for the bloody French, we'd have had the whole thing unearthed by now. As it is, we're months behind. Every fortnight they're out there, taking pictures and poking their noses in and demanding new permits and new reports."

Taking pictures. Without planning it, I thrust out my hand. It wasn't proper for me to introduce myself, but since she had spoken first, I doubted she would be the sort to stand on ceremony. "I'm Evangeline Starke."

She took my hand in hers, a wide, capable hand with a surprisingly gentle grip. "Anna Green, although everyone calls me Gethsemane," she said, almost bashfully.

"Gethsemane? How extraordinary."

"I did my first excavation work outside Jerusalem and had a rather significant find—hang on, did you say Starke? You're that aviatrix, aren't you? A relation of some sort to Gabriel?"

"His widow, actually."

"Oh, it is a small world," she said gruffly. "I met the lad once, years ago. He was digging out here. So young I think he must have still been at school. I heard he went down with the *Lusitania*." She paused as if collecting her thoughts and when she spoke again, her tone was brisk. "Well, lots of fine lads lost. Least said about that the better." We fell into an interesting chat then. She was a lively conversationalist, as happy to discuss the state of the political situation in Damascus as she was the complications of digging in the desert, and we passed quite a pleasant half hour before she

71

looked up. "Ah, your friends look restless," she said, nodding to where Halliday was studying his watch.

Her expression was one of avid curiosity, and I seized on the hint she had offered earlier.

"Would you like to meet Mr. Halliday, Miss Green? Surely the more friends you have in the diplomatic world, the easier it will be for you to secure the permits you need?"

I didn't have to ask twice. She bounded up and accompanied me out of the ladies' corner to where Rashid and Halliday were waiting. I introduced Miss Green and Halliday and we made arrangements to meet for dinner the following evening. Halliday would have seen us to our hotel, but Rashid stepped smartly in front of him and hailed a taxi, bundling me inside and slamming the door before springing up front to sit next to the driver.

Halliday leaned in the open window and gave me a knowing smile. "I won't press the matter, then. But tomorrow night you are entirely mine," he said, blushing furiously at his own forwardness. I waved goodbye, but Rashid kept his profile strictly averted. He offered to show me more sights, but I was tired after the long day of trudging the streets of Damascus, and wanted to look in on Aunt Dove.

"Thank you for a lovely day, Rashid," I told him. "It was the perfect introduction to Damascus."

"Truly, *sitt*?" he asked, his eyes wide with pleasure.

"Truly." I pressed the coins into his hands, adding more than I should have. To my astonishment, he did not even count them. Perhaps he was less astute a businessman than I had thought.

"I will come tomorrow," he promised, and before I could tell him I wasn't sure I even needed him for the day, he vanished into the crowd, his slim figure slipping into the shadows as easily as a ghost.

I hurried upstairs to Aunt Dove, not entirely surprised to discover her propped up on the divan, a fashion magazine in one hand and cigarette in the other. She had wound up my gramophone and was playing the newest jazz records while Arthur Wellesley bobbed his head furiously.

"I quite like this new music of yours," she said, "although I think Arthur disapproves."

"Then you ought to turn it up," I said waspishly.

She laughed and waved me to the cocktail pitcher. "Have a drink, child. You must be exhausted."

"I shall be grateful for an evening in," I confessed. "I've spent the whole day walking, but it's been brilliant." I spent the next hour describing the sights and sounds and telling her about Rashid and meeting Miss Green. I finished by explaining we would be dining with Miss Green and Halliday the following evening.

"A party!" she exclaimed, her turban wobbling

happily. "And that Rashid fellow sounds a first-rate dragoman, although I'm surprised at him charging so little."

I had wondered the same, but I felt vaguely insulted that Aunt Dove made a point of it. "I can take care of myself, you know, darling. If he attempts to abduct me into the desert, I promise I will fend him off."

She puffed out a sigh of cigarette smoke. "Bedouins don't carry off their brides as if they were Sabine women, Evangeline, although I will admit they are rather *deliciously* masculine. I think it must be the diet. They eat few vegetables, you know. I always think a man who eats vegetables loses something of his vigour." I thought of young Rashid and said nothing. In spite of his tender years, he was decidedly authoritarian. It didn't bear thinking about what he might be like when he matured. Aunt Dove was still talking. "Very well, child. Enjoy yourself with your little dragoman. Now, speaking of sex, what do you think of that tasty Mr. Halliday?"

FOUR

The next day Aunt Dove decided to stay in the hotel and hold court—something she occasionally did when we arrived in a city. She simply arranged herself in the most public spot, sat expectantly and within minutes she invariably gathered a crowd of people about her. Some were old friends, many were new, and some were merely thrill seekers eager to gape at the famed traveller Lady Lavinia Finch-Pomeroy, a Victorian legend in the flesh. They would ask her for photographs and stories, and she was always delighted to oblige, staying so long as she had an audience, and I was more than happy to let her. Very occasionally her little soirées managed to land us a sponsor or two, and from time to time with a discreet hint she managed to get a little something knocked off the price of the hotel altogether or a free luncheon for her troubles. Hotel managers were usually delighted to oblige as her devotees were quite happy to order quantities of food and drink, but it was the admiration she longed for most of all, I realised. She had been so famous in her youth, and her middle years had been dull ones, tarnishing the bright gleam of her fame. Being out and about again, surrounded by people who would thrill to her adventure stories, was like a tonic to her, and I encouraged her to indulge.

Of course, in this case, she might just as easily have been intending to get me out of the way to engage in a tender afternoon with the charming Étienne, the hotel manager, I realised, and I hurried out of the suite to find Rashid. To my astonishment, he was nowhere to be found, and in his place Halliday waited, hat in hand, and a broad smile lighting his face.

"Surprised? I took the day, told the office to go hang because I was going to show a lady the city," he said, offering me his arm. I wondered what had become of Rashid, but I had often been told the Easterner had a more flexible sense of time and I made up my mind to adopt the habit myself as long as I was in Damascus. I took Halliday's arm, and together we wandered the *souks*, each devoted to a different trade—silversmith, bookseller, tailor, mercer, tobacconist. There were coppersmiths and birdsellers, dealers in antique furniture and Persian rugs all calling their wares and bantering, and over it all hung the scent from the perfumers and spice merchants whose fragrant wares brought buyers from across the East. Halliday showed me the souk el-Jamal, the odiferous camel market, and afterwards we braved the din of the souk el-Arwam, where armourers and weapon-makers cried their wares next to the sellers of shawls and water pipes. Through it all wove the beggars pleading for alms, and the public scribes selling their skills for a few coppers. Vendors offered roasted peas and sweet pastries while others carried steaming urns of tea to provide refreshment on the street.

It was a glorious riot of colour and noise and scent and Halliday kept up a commentary straight out of Murray's guide book. I felt a little wistful for Rashid's much more colourful delivery. The boy had shown me the great bazaar that stretched all the way to the walls of the Umayyad mosque and explained how the roof had been torn off when the Turks left, opening the arcaded shops up to the sunlight for the first time in half a millennium. He had described the scene the day the city fell to the conquerors, Arab and Westerner marching together to drive out the Turks, how the women of the city showered them with flower petals and sprinkled them with attar of roses until the cloud of perfume wafted over the desert sands all the way to Baghdad. Rashid could paint a picture with just his words, and although Halliday tried, he didn't have the knack for it. We stopped at a quiet coffee house just outside the *souk*, and he ordered a pot of coffee and some pastries.

When the refreshments came, the coffee was nearly thick enough to stand a spoon in and terribly gritty. I pulled a face and he laughed.

"You must strain the grounds between your teeth. Like this." He demonstrated, and after a few attempts, I got the hang of it. The pastries were crispy and stuffed with nuts and bathed in warm honey. Those were much more to my taste and I stuck a finger in my mouth, licking off the succulent stickiness.

"I know. I've appalling manners. Pay no attention," I instructed him.

He smiled, his slight dimples in evidence. "I think you're everything that is charming and unfettered. You're like a breath of fresh air, so different to the girls I knew back in England, Mrs. Starke."

"You were supposed to call me Evie."

He shook his head slowly. "I want to. It just seems like such a dashed impertinence. I mean, you're Evangeline Starke. You're becoming something of a legend in certain circles." He hesitated. "And I have looked into your husband. A man of many talents. That sort of thing could put a man off of wooing," he added lightly.

"Some men," I corrected. "I ought to feel sorry for them."

"Do you feel sorry for me?"

I tipped my head, taking him in from firm jaw to broad, innocent brow under a silken fall of dark blond hair. It was a good face, a decidedly English face. I shook my head. "No. I think you like me for me."

"I do. More than I ought," he said, a certain bleakness coming into his eyes.

"Oh, dear," I said. I smiled, but didn't dare laugh. "Is it as bad as all that?"

"It is," he returned, matching my light tone. "Appearances to the contrary, I'm rather desperately poor. Haven't a bean of my own to offer a woman."

"If it's any consolation, you make a good showing for a fellow who's up against it."

He shrugged. "Splendid genes and nothing to show for them. My grandfather is the Duke of Winchester."

I gave him my best po-faced expression, and he

burst out laughing. "Bless you for that. I should have known tossing out his title wouldn't impress you. I've seen the cuttings from places like Monte Carlo and Biarritz. I know you've met your share of Russian grand dukes and American millionaires. A plain English duke must seem like rather small change in comparison."

"The Russian grand dukes are all poor as church mice and just looking to get their names into the newspapers so they can make a few quid themselves. And the Americans are after publicity for whatever they're selling—rubber tyres or bath soap or cough medicine. They'll be gone as soon as my headlines are. At least being the Duke of Winchester is something to hang your hat on. It still means something in England."

"Not for me," he said. His expression didn't turn pitying and I liked him better for it. "My cousin will inherit. I'm the second son of the third son. No title of my own, and twelve relations between me and the strawberry-leaf coronet. I'm left to make my way in the world with a good name and a few decent suits."

"And some good connections," I pointed out. "Surely your grandfather knows people in the diplomatic corps who might help you along."

He smiled. "You don't know Grandfather. He has been locked in his study writing a treatise on the subject of Tudor tax laws since 1893. Oh, he creeps out for Christmas, but the rest of the time he's content to stay in his study. I think the housemaid occasionally dusts him and turns him to face the sunlight like an aspidistra."

I laughed and he carried on, still lightly, although I suspected it was an effort.

"So, that's me. Educated and tailored beyond my means, but with great hopes. What of you, Evie? See, there, I managed it. Next time I promise it will sound almost natural."

"I'm like you, making my own way as best I can."

"But there is a double-barrelled surname in your family tree, as well," he prompted.

"Ah, the Finch-Pomeroys. My grandfather wasn't as grand as yours—only an earl and on my mother's side, so it doesn't much count. When Grandfather died the whole caboodle went to a cousin who kicked it in '07 and then onto his nephew. Everything has passed so far away that the current earl is a perfect stranger. I've never even seen the estate myself, although Aunt Dove grew up there with my mother."

"And where is your mother now?"

"Dead," I replied succinctly. "She married badly."

"A footman?" he asked with a bit of a twinkle in his eye.

"Worse. A writer, and a dead broke one at that. But they were very much in love. There was a good deal of laughter in that house, although neither of them had the sense God gave a goose. If Papa sold a story, he'd spend every penny in a day. I remember when he sold a book of poetry and he went straight from the bank to the furrier. He bought Mama a silver fox stole she had to pawn a week later to pay the butcher's bill. It was always furs for Mama or pearls. And for me, it was books, beautiful books with silk ribbons to hold my place. It was always Christmas when Papa sold something—the trouble was he didn't sell much."

"He sounds a remarkable man," Halliday said softly.

"He was. As good as they come and guileless as a lamb. He always thought the next great adventure was just around the corner. When I was eight, he sold his first novel. He was so happy, he glowed with it. There were new frocks for me and for Mama, and that night he took us to the theatre. *Peter Pan* had just opened, and he was determined to get the very best seats. He took us to Simpson's first for roast beef and I ate more than I have ever eaten in my life. And when the play was over he took us for ice creams and told us he had bought a share in a business in New Orleans. He was leaving the following week for America to investigate his new investment." I paused. I didn't tell the story often, and the words were rusty and stuck in my throat. "Mama insisted upon going. I think he knew she would. He was desperately pleased she didn't want to be parted from him. So they dropped me in the midst of a pack of aunts and sailed for America."

Something in my tone must have warned him. His eyes were soft and his voice was gentle. "What was it?"

"Yellow fever. Turns out there was a beastly epidemic raging. They died within a week of one another. That's the only mercy in the whole story."

"Good God," he said faintly.

I shrugged and affected a casual air I did not feel. "It all happened so long ago, it's almost like talking about strangers."

"Still, I imagine that sort of thing leaves a mark," he said quietly.

"It does, rather. I try to be responsible. I try to take care of the things that matter like keeping food on the table and shoes on our feet. But sometimes . . . well, sometimes I do very thoughtless things. Like running away with Gabriel Starke the night I met him."

His expression was delightfully scandalised. "You didn't!"

"I did. We eloped to Scotland after we met at a New Year's Eve party. A mutual friend invited us both because she intended to match us up with other people. But we danced together and that was it. A *coup de foudre*. We both felt it—at least I thought we did. In any event, he had a fast car and somehow I found myself on the road to Scotland, ready to marry a man I hadn't even known six hours before."

To his credit, Halliday looked more amused than shocked. "It sounds terribly romantic."

"That's very kind of you. I think it sounds mad."

Something shrewd stirred in his eyes. "The song you danced to the night you met Gabriel Starke. Wasn't 'Salut d'Amour' by any chance?"

He gave me a kindly smile and I returned it. "Got it in one."

"Ah. Pity, that. And here I thought I was sweeping you off your feet," he told me with a rueful lift of his silky brows.

I laughed. "Don't give up so easily. Just because I've learned to keep my feet on the ground doesn't mean I can't be wooed."

"But you don't really keep your feet on the ground, do you?" he countered smoothly. "You're always dashing off in that aeroplane of yours. I must say, I've done a bit of flying myself, and it's a devilish thing for a lady to try. You astonish me, Evie."

"But there's nothing astonishing about it," I protested. "It was the most logical thing in the world. I worked at a convalescent hospital during the war. I brought them tea and read their letters from home and played cards with them. They were pilots, most of them American and terribly young and so sweet it broke your heart just to see them all swathed in bandages and aching for a chance to get back into the action before it all went away. I adored them, but I could only read so many letters and play so many games of cards before I wanted to scream. So I made them teach me about flying instead. It gave them no end of a thrill to talk about it, you know, and they were terrifically good teachers."

Halliday smiled. "You liked them."

"Immensely. They were just boys, really. Like brothers to me."

He shook his head. "Surely not all of them. I imagine more than a few found themselves smitten with you."

I shrugged.

"You surprise me. I would have thought the dash and romance of a pilot would have turned any girl's head."

I grinned. "Well, there was the odd kiss or two, but nothing more. There was only one I almost lost my head over, but it would never have worked."

He leaned forward, resting his elbows on the table. "Aha! Intrigue at last. Was he a pilot?"

"Yes. He was the one who took me up the first time."

"One of those daring Yanks, no doubt," he said, pulling a face. I laughed.

"Almost. He was Canadian by birth but brought up in Africa."

"Good God. Colonials," he said with a shudder.

"And Ryder was more rustic than most," I told

him. "He helped form the flying corps in British East Africa. He was shadowing the highest ranking ace in our flying corps when the fellow was shot down. Ryder came with him to Mistledown while he recuperated, but he was bored out of his mind. He amused himself by borrowing a pal's Sopwith and getting me in the air."

"A direct and dashing way to a lady's heart."

"True. I might have been smitten by any man who taught me to fly. But Ryder was something special."

Halliday's voice was soft. "You were in love with him."

"No. Not even halfway. But I was grateful to him. He was the one who got me airborne, convinced me I could do it. He flew like a buccaneer and he taught me everything he could before he was sent back to Africa."

"Did you keep in touch with him?" Something like jealousy tinged Halliday's voice, and I enjoyed that.

"The occasional postcard. It's all very polite and respectable," I said with a prim mouth.

Halliday leaned closer still. "It's no business of mine, but I wonder if I should believe that."

"It's the truth," I assured him. "Ryder never laid a finger on me. Of course," I said, slanting him a wicked smile, "I put considerably more than a finger on him, but that's a different matter."

Halliday's eyes widened and his mouth

85

dropped open, but his expression was not entirely disapproving. "You seduced him?"

"I tried, but bless him, he wasn't having any of it. He understood why I did it and he turned me down so sweetly I couldn't even be angry with him."

"Oh, dear."

"I wanted him for all the wrong reasons." I shrugged. "He reminded me of Gabriel. I don't know why—entirely different men. But there was something fine about Ryder, something deeply good, and that was what I thought I had seen in Gabriel once. It brought up feelings I thought I had buried."

"No man wants to be a woman's second choice," he said, his voice low. His gaze was intent, his eyes searching, and after a moment, perhaps not seeing what he wanted in my face, he sat back and adopted a lighter tone.

"And how did you go from student pilot to world-famous aviatrix?"

"I started barnstorming. I thought I could make a living at it, but Aunt Dove's money dried up and suddenly I had her to take care of. And so many girls had taken up barnstorming it wasn't enough just to be a woman pilot anymore. I had to do something to set myself apart. It got so competitive the manager of one aerial circus wouldn't even give me a try-out, so I stole an aeroplane and pulled a barrel roll over his head. He screeched like a monkey, he was so furious. He threw me off his airfield and swore he would make certain I never got another job flying anywhere. He was as good as his word. Every other outfit refused to see me after he told them what I'd done. It wasn't long before I didn't even have enough money for a cup of coffee at a corner house. I was feeling desperate, horribly so, and suddenly the walls of our little rented room just seemed to close in on me and I had to get out. I went to the park—Kensington Gardens. I wandered for hours, not even paying attention to where I was, until finally my legs gave out and I just sat. And do you know where I was?"

His expression was rapt. "Where?"

"At the foot of Peter Pan himself. I was sitting at the base of the statue. And I looked up at him and thought of that last night with my parents at the theatre and I thought of Gabriel always dashing around after adventure and never really growing up and I began to weep. Not a pretty, dainty little cry but an absolute storm of sobs. It was appalling—I make the most awful noises when I cry, and my eyes go very small and my nose runs like a tap. But I couldn't seem to stop. I just sat there, bawling my eyes out until I couldn't cry anymore. It was a relief actually. I had never cried properly over Gabriel. But I cried that day, and when I was done, I looked up at the statue again, and everything suddenly made sense."

He cocked his head. "How so?"

"The last gift Gabriel ever gave me was a copy of *Peter and Wendy*. The frontispiece has an illustration of all the most important characters—Peter, the Darlings, Tiger Lily—and looming from the left is Captain Hook. Well, an aeroplane is rather like a sailing ship, isn't it? I decided if Hook could have a *Jolly Roger*, so could I. I could remake myself as a sort of modern-day pirate and adventurer. I looked up Wally, a friend from the war who happened to be an ace mechanic. He gave me the money to buy the Strutter and we christened her. I painted a skull and crossbones on her tail and let it be known I would fly anything for a price. I hauled important papers and the occasional passenger, although it's entirely illegal. I even ferried a pig once. And I flew a case of champagne from Paris to London for a French breeder to celebrate winning Ascot. My name was in the newspapers enough that I began to attract sponsors. When I had enough, I arranged the Seven Seas Tour."

"Crossing the seven seas of antiquity in a modern ship," he said admiringly.

"Just so. Like a pirate of old."

"Only rather prettier," he said, his cheeks blooming pink.

I went on as if he had not spoken. "And I invited Aunt Dove to come along to sweeten the deal for the sponsors. She is meat for the newspapers. They can't seem to get enough of her—no doubt because they never know what she's going to say."

He gave a short cough and patted his mouth. "She is an original," he said gallantly.

"And so we started off, and here we are. Heading for the Caspian next and lands as yet unseen."

"Here you are," he said softly. His eyes were warm, and for an instant, his hand hovered over mine. But he dropped it to the table and when he spoke, his tone was bright but forced.

"Have you finished your coffee? Then let's be off. There's something I want to show you." He fished coins out of his pocket while I tactfully turned away. Through the window I caught a flash of striped robe, but as soon as I blinked it had gone. It meant nothing, of course. There were thousands of such robes in Damascus, and doubtless hundreds on that street alone. Still, when we emerged from the coffee house, I looked about for a glimpse of a familiar profile or that slender, darting figure.

"Everything all right?" Halliday asked.

I slipped my arm into his and gave him a smile. "Perfectly."

He led the way, winding through a few small backstreets until we came to the Gate of the Sun, the Bab Sharqi, the most ancient way into the city, and from there down into the street called Straight.

As we walked he told me the history of the road, how it had been built by the Greeks and improved by the Romans with arches and colonnades.

"On this road, you will find synagogue, church and mosque, sitting cheek by jowl and getting along rather nicely together," he explained.

"It's good to think such things are possible somewhere in the world."

He paused, propping his hand against a bit of Roman stonework. "This has been here since the time of St. Paul, when he stayed at a house in this very street. The man is long gone, and yet this bit of stone endures. Astonishing, isn't it? How many temples and tombs outlast us all? They were put there by the hands of men, at the orders of kings and priests, and yet they stand on long after the men of power have dried to dust."

" 'All human things are subject to decay, and when fate summons, monarchs must obey,' " I murmured, hearing Gabriel's voice ringing on the words as he had once spoke them.

"What's that?" he asked.

I shuddered as if a goose walked over my grave. "Just a bit of poetry."

"It sounds familiar. What's it from?"

I shook myself free of the past and smiled up at him. "I can't remember."

He returned the smile and extended his arm. I slipped mine through his and we walked on in the warm sunshine, the smell of jasmine faint on the air as somewhere behind us trailed a ghost who whispered poetry in my ear and teased a breeze to touch my cheek.

That evening we dined with Miss Green, and our companions met us in the hotel court. Aunt Dove was wearing another of her turbans, this one an Indonesian batik pinned with a great lump of turquoise while her favourite green brooch winked from her considerable décolletage. She looked like a particularly winsome peacock, and Miss Green, subdued in a stern and rusty black gown, complimented her. Halliday looked every inch the proper English gentleman in his beautifully tailored evening clothes while I had shimmied into a darling little black dress dripping with silver bugle beads. Halliday's brows raised and stayed there when he saw me.

"I say," he breathed as he took my hand.

I dimpled at him. "I shall take that as approval."

"Rather," he agreed. He turned to Aunt Dove. "Lady Lavinia, resplendent as usual."

She gave him a fond look and fluttered her lashes a little while Miss Green organised us. She insisted upon taking us to a proper Levantine restaurant not far from the main bazaar. "Authentic fare," she promised as our taxi alighted outside a nondescript stone building. "The real Damascus."

Mr. Halliday manfully hid his reluctance, and we

made our way to a thoroughly nondescript-looking place with no sign and a beggar reading in the doorway. He held out a cup towards us, never taking his eyes off of what looked like a copy of *Les Misérables*.

"Pay no attention to Selim," Miss Green instructed. "Just step over his stump. That's right." She ushered us through the stout wooden door and into a courtyard with a fountain. Across the courtyard, a pair of elaborately carved wooden doors had been thrown open and delectable smells were wafting from inside.

Miss Green grinned. "Trust me, Mrs. Starke."

She led us into one of the most beautiful rooms I had ever seen. The walls and floor were tiled in extravagant patterns and the ceiling soared overhead to a graceful gilded dome. Another fountain stood in the center, this one festooned with lush water lilies and the darting flash of goldfish. Lanterns with coloured glass panes hung about the room, interspersed with golden cages full of songbirds. The brass tables were low and surrounded by piles of silken cushions. The proprietor, a plump, jolly sort of fellow, greeted the archaeologist with great affection and bowed repeatedly as he showed us to a table directly underneath the golden dome. We seated ourselves as best we could—Miss Green with a surprising sinuous grace and Aunt Dove with a decided plop. Halliday waited until I was settled with my feet tucked aside before taking the cushion next to me, arranging himself into a languorous posture.

"When in Rome," he murmured.

Just then, a rather shabby character appeared, an Englishman, and from twenty paces I could tell he was another archaeologist from the telltale stoop. His hair was dirty with streaks of dull grey and his teeth, protruding unpleasantly from an unkempt beard, were of the prominent and horsey sort. His eyes—which might have been a pleasant dark brown once—were rheumy, and his features were set in a scowl.

"All right, Green. I'm here to make nice. Introduce me before I change my mind."

Miss Green jumped up with alacrity. "Rowan, I'm so glad you could join us. Lady Lavinia Finch-Pomeroy, Mrs. Starke, Mr. Halliday, may I present the co-leader of our expedition, Mr. Oliver Rowan. Rowan, you might have met Mr. Halliday before. He's attached to the British diplomatic delegation This is Lady Lavinia Finch-Pomeroy and her niece, Evangeline Starke, the aviatrix."

Mr. Rowan seated himself next to Miss Green. She graciously served as hostess, ordering local specialties for us and instructing us how to eat politely—with the right hand only. Almost as soon as we sat, waiters began to appear. The first came carrying brass bowls of hot, perfumed water with petals floating lazily on the surface. We dipped our fingers and dried them on soft linen then turned our attention to the food. Platter after platter was set before us, rich dishes of stewed meats and vegetables and tiny, delectable meatballs, and heaps of couscous jewelled with pomegranate seeds. There were smaller dishes of spicy sauces and savoury pastries as well as nuts and olives and dried fruits, all of it accompanied by discreet but potent glasses of *arak*, the anise-flavoured liqueur of the region.

When we had eaten our fill of the savoury courses, the desserts came—more pastries but these filled with nuts and citrus custards and drizzled with honey. There was a sorbet of pistachios and another of rosewater, and we ate ourselves into a stupor. The conversation, which had ranged from books to travel, turned more serious when Miss Green addressed Mr. Halliday.

"I think you might be a useful fellow to know. Those Frenchies think because they've sponsored part of the expedition they can send their government advisors out from Damascus to harass us on a routine basis. Could do with a bit of British support in getting them to let us be," she told him firmly.

"Hear! Hear!" Mr. Rowan grunted through a mouthful of couscous. A few bits of it were stuck in his beard and I turned away with a grimace.

Halliday put up his hands. "Dear lady, I am the most minor sort of functionary, I assure you. My days consist of reading and composing the lowliest of memoranda, which I am given to understand are sent to very unimportant people and where they are quickly filed away never again to see the light of day. My influence would be less than nil."

Mr. Rowan made a noise that sounded like "hmph." Aunt Dove leaned over to put a hand on Mr. Halliday's sleeve.

"Now I don't believe that for a minute," she drawled flirtatiously. He ducked his head with a worried expression and I smiled behind my glass. I *had* warned him she would try. Her seduction techniques varied from the painfully direct to the engagingly subtle, but her single most effective strategy was persistence. In this case, it afforded me a chance to hint to Miss Green that an invitation to her dig would be most welcome. I turned to address her, but she was busy giving instructions to the waiter. I held my tongue, watching Mr. Rowan. He was contentedly munching his way through a pile of flatbreads, washing them down with quantities of *arak*.

The waiter bowed and left and Miss Green turned to me, her cheeks flushed and her hair standing on end. "I say, this is a jolly meal," she said happily. I wondered if she had sampled too much of the *arak*; if so, I had chosen my moment well.

"What do you think of Damascus, Mrs. Starke?" Mr. Rowan asked suddenly.

"It's enchanting," I told him honestly. "My husband and I meant to come together, but we never had the chance."

Miss Green looked a little uncomfortable at the mention of my late husband, and Mr. Rowan seemed supremely bored as he picked at his teeth. I tried a different tack.

"How is the excavation going? A caravansary, I believe you said?"

At this Miss Green warmed immediately, going into painfully detailed descriptions of the site. But I had not been an archaeologist's wife for nothing. I was able to ask intelligent questions, and when I queried her on the significance of the proximity of the site to an old Crusader castle, she fairly glowed.

"But civilians never understand that sort of thing! Yes, indeed, it is significant." After spending another quarter of an hour describing exactly *why* it was significant, she trailed off. "I say, it is nice to have someone really appreciate what we are doing out here." Mr. Rowan gave a decided belch and covered his mouth with his napkin.

I smiled my most winsome smile at the pair of them, but neither of them seemed inclined to take the thing further. "I would think a dig site would be immensely interesting to visit." There, if that didn't coax an invitation, nothing would, I thought grimly.

Miss Green opened her mouth, but Mr. Rowan

chose that moment to burp again, this time a little less discreetly, and he lifted his glass of *arak* in my direction. "To desert endeavours," he proposed. We all clinked glasses and drank deeply. And somewhere overhead in one of the gilded cages a little bird began to sing.

At the sound of the glasses, Halliday turned his head. "I say, what sort of toast is this? Are we celebrating?"

"We are toasting Mrs. Starke's appreciation of ancient history," Mr. Rowan proclaimed, his vowels only slightly slurred.

"She does indeed," Halliday agreed. "What was that bit of poetry you quoted at me? Something mournful about all human things and decay and monarchs?"

He wrestled with the words for a moment before I cut in and repeated the quotation.

" 'All human things are subject to decay, And when fate summons, monarchs must obey.' "

Mr. Rowan nodded into his *arak*. "Donne, isn't it?"

"Dryden," I corrected, baring my teeth in a smile. He smiled back and I saw his own teeth were almost aggressively yellow.

Miss Green flapped a hand. "All those metaphysical poets—they all run together in one's head after a while."

"Dryden wasn't metaphysical," I told her quickly. "He was Restoration."

"Was he?" Her tone was polite, but she was clearly bored talking of poetry.

Mr. Rowan perked up. "I know a bit of poetry." He cleared his throat. "'There once was a man from Nantucket—'"

Miss Green cut him off before he could finish, but Aunt Dove leaned over, her expression consoling. "Don't worry, Mr. Rowan. I like a good dirty limerick myself. Have you heard this one?" She launched into a verse I didn't dare let her finish, but before I could stop her, Halliday cut in smoothly with a little laugh, changing the subject slightly.

"I'm not surprised at Mr. Rowan knowing only limericks. Archaeologists are scientists, Mrs. Starke. You'll seldom find stonier ground to sow the seed of poetry than that."

Mr. Rowan gave him a thin smile. "I don't know. I should think a bureaucrat would be even more lacking in imagination."

Halliday smiled in return. "I daresay you're right, Mr. Rowan. After all, an archaeologist must look at a handful of clay bricks or crushed pots and be able to recreate the past. I suppose that requires a prodigious imagination."

Aunt Dove raised a glass. "In my experience, all souls are receptive to poetry provided they are sufficiently lubricated. To *arak* and the Restoration poets," she pronounced.

We toasted them and the conversation turned to

war reparations and the moment to invite myself to the dig passed fruitlessly. I shredded a pastry in my fingers as I listened to the others talk. And, upon my most recent revelation, drank several glasses of *arak* in quick succession. After a long while, Mr. Rowan's chin slid to his chest as he gave an audible snore.

Miss Green gave a low chuckle. "Time to see this one to his lodgings, I think. It's never a party until someone's drunk too much *arak*." She waved off our efforts to pay our share of the dinner, insisting it was an honour, and we were bowed out of the restaurant by the sleepy staff.

We delivered the archaeologists to their modest lodgings—academic expeditions were not well enough funded to permit them to stay anywhere more exclusive—then Halliday saw us safely to our hotel, although he made a hasty exit when Aunt Dove mentioned her stamp collection. He gave me a meaningful look as he took his leave, and I smiled warmly at the lingering feeling of his hand on my shoulder.

Aunt Dove and I said good-night and went to our rooms. I washed and put on my nightdress and opened the pierced shutters to the spill of silvery moonlight. From the high ivory minaret of a nearby mosque, I could hear the muezzin's call to prayer, the *Salat al-Isha*, the evening invocations that remembered God's presence and dwelt upon the quality of Allah's mercy.

I turned down the lamp until it was the merest suggestion of light, a pinprick of something that was not quite darkness, and slid into bed. The call faded away, and after a while I heard the bells of a Christian church chiming in the night. A chill breeze passed over my face, ruffling my hair. Suddenly, some sense of otherness roused me, a shadow that detached itself from the wall and moved close to my bed.

I had kept my hand under the pillow, and as the figure moved, I curled my fingers around the grip of the tiny mother-of-pearl pistol Aunt Dove had given me in Italy. With one smooth gesture, I leaped up to a sitting position, opening the lantern and levelling the pistol at Mr. Rowan. And when I spoke, my voice was perfectly calm.

"Hello, Gabriel."

FIVE

To his credit, Gabriel didn't look surprised. "You expected me."

"Of course I did. I even did you the courtesy of leaving the shutters open."

He flicked a glance to the window. "Damn. And I went to all the trouble of picking the locks, too."

He turned back to me. "You may as well put the gun down, you know. You won't shoot me."

"You seem very sure of that."

"Well, it isn't so much that you won't shoot me as that you can't." He opened his hand and a palmful of bullets fell onto my coverlet.

"Damn you." I put the gun down and crossed my arms over my chest. "Very well. I suppose we can be civilised about this. Make yourself comfortable. That disguise must be painful."

"You've no idea." He straightened, rolling his shoulders back and shedding the archaeologist's stoop for the beautiful posture I remembered so well. The shadow he threw on the wall behind him grew as he eased himself up to his full height. He loosened the mouthpiece, with its terrible yellow teeth, and shoved it into his pocket before taking out a small tin and his handkerchief.

"You might not want to watch this part."

"I'm not squeamish," I told him, which we both knew was a lie. But I was curious, and I watched the process with fascinated horror.

Slowly, carefully, he reached up to his eyes and levered out a pair of almond-shaped lenses that covered the whole eyeball. I put out my hand and he gave me one to inspect. I held it to the light, marveling at the thinness of the glass and the delicacy of the painted brown iris. "Clever," I told him as I handed it back. "It's the one thing I couldn't figure out about the disguise."

"They're hideously uncomfortable and most of the time I wear coloured spectacles, but in close company I take the precaution of covering up my own," he said blandly, batting his lashes. He was entirely correct about that. They were remarkable eyes, and no one, having once seen them, would forget them.

"The beard is appalling," I pointed out.

"Quite disgusting. I'm always getting bits of food stuck in it, but it's entirely my own, I assure you," he said, tugging at the hairs on his chin.

I got out of bed and went to him, standing so close I could see the first tiny lines just beginning to etch themselves at the corners of his eyes, lines he had not had the last time I had seen him. Slowly, deliberately, I drew back my hand and slapped him as hard as I could across the face.

He rocked back on his heels, turning his head back slowly. He was smiling.

"I entirely deserved that."

"I just wanted to make sure you weren't a figment of my imagination."

"Satisfied now? I am flesh and blood, as you can see," he added, daubing the blood away from his lip.

I went to the bed and sat with my back against the pillows.

"When did you figure it all out?" he asked in a conversational tone.

"I knew you'd sent the photograph yourself when I found the banknotes. *REAPERS HOME.* It's an anagram of the inscription on my wedding ring—*hora e sempre.* Really, Gabriel, a child could have cracked that. I hope you haven't been spending your time composing codes for an international spy ring. You'd be something worse than useless."

He gave me a ghost of a smile, the same buccaneer smile that had gotten him into and out of more trouble than most men see in a lifetime. "Have a heart, love. I was in a hurry. Besides, I thought you'd enjoy a little cloak-and-dagger stuff."

He swayed a little on his feet. "Are you still intoxicated?" I asked pleasantly.

"Not much. I vomited most of it as soon as I could get to my bottle of *ipecacuanha*. Nasty stuff, but it does the trick. Got rid of what was left in my stomach, but there was a fair bit of it already in my blood. God, I loathe *arak*."

"You did a tremendous job convincing me otherwise."

"I wasn't trying to convince you. But it seemed a good idea to persuade your associates that I was precisely what I claimed to be."

He swayed again, and I drew up my feet. "Oh, for God's sake, sit down before you fall over and hurt yourself."

"You always were thoughtful," he said, giving me that small smile again as he settled himself at the foot of the bed. His shadow still loomed on the wall behind him, larger than life and inky black.

"It's not kindness. I just don't fancy mopping

up your blood. Now, where should we begin?"

Gabriel hesitated. "I know I owe you the whole story. But now isn't exactly a good time."

"I think I deserve more than evasions, Gabriel."

His jaw tightened. "As I said, I am aware of what I owe you, Evie. Believe me when I tell you I am not in a position to explain, at least not yet."

"Believe you? Veracity isn't precisely your strong suit. You faked your own death," I reminded him.

"I had no choice."

"So you say." My voice was pleasantly neutral and a good deal calmer than I felt. "I should so like the chance to make up my own mind about that."

He sighed. "I can't discuss it just yet. I'm still making sense of it all myself. The less I involve you the better."

I rolled my eyes heavenward. "Then what am I doing in Damascus, Gabriel? Sending me that photograph to lure me here was your doing. The banknotes and the song at the restaurant were arranged to show me I was on the right track. And now you won't explain why?"

"I can't," he said simply. "I know it's too much to ask you to take my word for it, but I can't explain any of it yet."

"Then why am I here? And perhaps more to the point, why are you here?"

He had the grace to look uncomfortable. "I want to make amends."

"Amends? Gabriel, you make amends when

you play the wrong suit in a game of bridge. You cannot possibly make amends for faking your own death."

"Fine," he growled. "Call it atonement, then. Penance. I did a terrible thing to you and it's in my power to make it right, or—" he hurried on as I opened my mouth "—as right as I can. Look here, I'm not asking for forgiveness. What I did is so far beyond that it would be laughable to suggest you could ever find it in your heart, and God knows, I don't deserve it. But I want the chance to do something for you."

"There is nothing on earth you could *possibly*—"

He held up a hand. "Yes, there is. I've acquired something . . . valuable. But you'll have to take my word for it."

"Take your word for it? Not bloody likely! Besides, if you have something for me, why not bring it here—" I broke off. "Oh, my God. You can't bring it because you're involved in something illegal. And that's why you faked your own death five years ago, isn't it? You're a *criminal*."

He winced. "*Criminal* is such an ugly word. And a subjective one."

I opened my mouth to blast him, but he held up a hand. "Let's not quarrel, pet. I haven't the stamina for it just now." He gave me an appraising look. "I must say, you're taking this all much better than I expected," he said, his tone mildly amused.

"What did you expect? Hysterics? Violence?"

"I don't know what I expected," he said quietly. "But you were a flighty girl when I saw you last, not this cool, composed woman who travels with a loaded pistol and plans for midnight visitors."

I set my chin mulishly. "I've grown up, Gabriel. I had to."

"Another sin to drop at my door," he said lightly. But his eyes were bleak and he looked away. When he spoke again, his tone was brisk. "I can't stay long. Matters are . . . complicated. I have to get back to the dig site and sort a few things out."

He reached into the breast pocket of his filthy khaki shirt. He drew out a small tin tobacco box and opened it, rifling through an assortment of oddities until he unearthed a grubby bit of paper. He handed it over, but I hardly liked to touch the thing it was so disgusting. "That's the man you'll need to see in London after I've brought you what it is I have to give. He will give you the money—and it will be a substantial amount," he added.

I placed the dirty paper carefully on the bedside table and gave him a level look. "Why me?"

It might have been easier for him if he'd looked away, but that sharp blue gaze never wavered. "Because I hurt you. As I said, this will make amends."

"And you can scrape me off your conscience, is that it?"

He went on, still never taking his eyes from my face. "I've no one I can trust. Except you."

I shook my head. "You've no one in the whole world you can trust except the wife you abandoned five years ago? Gabriel, that might well be the saddest thing I have ever heard."

He flashed me his buccaneer smile. "You have no idea. Now, will you help me?"

"What do you need me to do?"

"Just sit tight in Damascus. I've stashed my little find for safekeeping. When I am able to retrieve it, I'll bring it here. The rest is up to you."

"How long will it take you? I can only stay in Damascus a fortnight. I have obligations," I told him, thinking of the tour I had quite possibly wrecked for the sake of what might be nothing more than a chase of the wildest, goosiest variety.

"I'll leave first thing in the morning for the dig. A day out, a day to get my hands on the item and two days back into the city. I will deliver it to you by the end of the week, *inshallah*," he added.

"*Inshallah*? My God, you have changed. You were an agnostic the last time I saw you."

His smile was grim. "I've learned to hedge my bets. If I don't show up by the start of next week, forget I ever contacted you. Just go on about your business and get out of Damascus. I'll find another way to get the thing to you. If that's the case, I want you to go on, sooner rather than later." He

107

rose to his feet in languid motion, his shadow stretching as he died.

"How did you know where to find me?" I asked. "Where to send the photograph?"

"Everyone knows the name Evangeline Starke. You're famous." He reached into his pocket for the horrid lenses and slipped them into his eyes. Next came the mouthpiece and then the stooped posture. "By the end of the week," he promised. He slid into the darkness and left, so quietly I might have imagined he had been there at all.

There was not even a crease where he had sat on the coverlet. Only the handful of bullets he had slipped from my pistol betrayed that anyone had been there at all. He might as well have been a ghost, I thought, as I blew out the lantern. Except I had made him bleed. It was a very small consolation.

The next few days were torturous. Aunt Dove and I visited more of the tourist sites, posing for photographs in all of the *souks* and palaces and outside of mosques. We met Syrian gentlemen from the interim government and their veiled wives; we dined with French advisors and lunched with British expatriates. It ought to have been a whale of a time, but I kept one eye on the calendar, watching each day creep past in a blur of stone streets and perfumed courtyards. Halliday was often in attendance, always attentive to Aunt

Dove, but clearly seeking us out for my company. From time to time his hand brushed mine or he let his gaze linger a moment too long for comfort. The air was thick with possibility and things unsaid. But for the moment I was content not to say them. Gabriel occupied far too many of my thoughts to spare any good ones for another man. Not yet. Not until I had laid his ghost once and for all.

My greatest consolation was the reappearance of Rashid the morning after the dinner party. Aunt Dove and I descended to the main court to find him there, waiting patiently as a dog at the foot of the stairs. He offered no excuses for his absence, but his praise for Aunt Dove was so fulsome, she was eating out of his hand in a matter of minutes. He put himself in charge of Arthur Wellesley, letting the little parrot ride on his shoulder through the streets and feeding him titbits of fruit and teaching him Arabic phrases. He somehow made himself a part of our ragtag household, and he spent just as much time making himself useful in our rooms or running errands as he did acting as our tour guide.

As the days passed, my mood sank lower and lower, and Aunt Dove took me aside to give me a boots-up-the-bum speech while Rashid cleaned out Arthur's old cage. He had just brought the parrot a ghastly new cage from the *souk*, a filigreed affair so heavily gilded it looked like something out of an Arabian Nights fantasia. I thought it was horrid, but Aunt Dove merely cooed at him and tipped him lavishly for his thoughtfulness. He set about clearing out the old one and laying out seed and water in Arthur's new quarters while the bird had a snack on Aunt Dove's turban.

She pulled me down next to her on the divan, plucking Wally's latest letter out of my fingers as she pitched her voice low. "Now, dear, you're a handsome girl. Everyone says so. It is time to close the deal," she advised me.

"I beg your pardon?"

She waved her hands, scaring Arthur from his dish of seed onto her head. "Damn the kaiser," he muttered irritably from the top of her turban.

"My darling," Aunt Dove continued, "Halliday is a patient man. *Too* patient. He's let you call the tune and he's danced it. Now, I've warmed him up for you, but I can't keep stringing him along. It's time for you to give up the goods, Evangeline."

I choked down my surprise. "What did you have in mind?"

She shrugged. "Heavens, child, you've been married. I should think you know how to get things started. Show him you're *open*. Men are the dearest creatures, but none of them is very bright. If you want one, you've got to show him. Be direct!" She paused, her eyes brightening. "Do you have a nice collection you could invite him up to see? Coins? Cigarette cards?"

"I'm sure I could think of something," I said faintly.

She patted my hand. "That's my girl. Now we've cleared the air, I think you ought to have a treat. With Rashid's help, I've arranged something quite special, quite special indeed."

I narrowed my eyes. Aunt Dove had a unique notion of what constituted a treat. It might be anything from a mule ride to the rim of a volcano to a baby crocodile in the bathroom.

"We are going to have a bath," she announced.

To my relief, the bath was a proper Turkish *hammum*, a holdover from the days of Ottoman occupation. Rashid led us to the bathhouse in the old quarter of the city, another of those sprawling but nondescript buildings from the outside. He bowed low, indicating we should enter while he waited outside, but some secret amusement danced in his eyes. Doubtless the notion of a houseful of nude, fragrant women, I decided with a sigh of impatience. I hurried in, stopping just inside the anteroom with a gasp. It was a virtual palace, gilded and tiled and filled with fragrant steam. The scent of ancient perfumes—cinnamon and frankincense and cedar—hung heavy in the air, mingling with the more delicate notes of the flowers whose crushed petals floated in the various pools.

But the pools, I soon learned, were not the point

of the place. It began with a disrobing that left us each a slender towel to cover our modesty. We were hurried into a low-ceilinged chamber where attendants ladled water onto coals so that great clouds of steam hung thickly in the air, leaving us feeling oddly light when we moved into the next room. There, a mixture of beet sugar and lemon juice was cooked up, stirred constantly until it bubbled at which point it was whisked off the fire and pasted onto us. Before I knew what they intended, strips of muslin were applied and then torn away, taking the candied mixture and everything else with it. Aunt Dove then explained about Mohammedans and their views on body hair. A few *extremely* personal services followed, and then we were hurried off to be stretched and massaged and scrubbed and wrapped in wet sheets and gently flogged with small branches of herbs. Our hair was washed and our nails cleaned, and finally we were sent into the main bath to relax.

Women of every age and description frolicked about, as naked as the day they were born, entirely free of embarrassment, and once I gave myself up to the heavenly sensations of the steaming water I thoroughly enjoyed it. After a long soak, we were wrapped in warm, dry sheets and seated on divans with sweetmeats and glasses of mint tea to refresh ourselves. Aunt Dove promptly fell asleep. I felt as light as thistledown, all of my cares evaporated in the steam. I was dozing gently when I heard my name.

"Mrs. Starke! Fancy meeting you here!"

It was Miss Green, wrapped in a sheet, as well, her complexion flushed deeply red and her hair once more standing at attention. Her flesh was mottled and wobbling, but she looked as happy as any bacchante.

"Hello, Miss Green. My aunt was determined to show me the full Damascene experience," I told her. I glanced to where Aunt Dove was snoring gently on her own divan and motioned to Miss Green to share mine. She seated herself and we took glasses of sweet sherbet from the attendant.

"It's quite relaxing, isn't it?" she asked, her voice conspiratorial. "Makes one feel almost indecent to be so free of cares."

"Have you lots of cares?"

She rolled her eyes heavenward. "My dear Mrs. Starke, you've no idea. The Arab interim government simply have their hands full with trying to run the country. They've left the archaeological business to their French advisors, and the French have been extremely difficult, threatening to revoke our permit because they have decided to object to the presence of a German on our staff. It's the rankest prejudice because no one who ever met Herr Doktor Schickfuss could ever think him anything but a gentleman and a scholar."

"So the French authorities are holding a grudge against him because of the war?"

Her lips tightened. "The rankest prejudice," she repeated. "They would only have to look at the fellow." She pitched her voice low. "He looks exactly like Father Christmas." She giggled, and I began to wonder if there might have been something illicit in the herbed smoke. But Miss Green, like most scholars, simply spent so much time in her own head that any true relaxation made her giddy as a child. She went on. "He is quite short, you see, not exactly an *elf,* but very short indeed. And he is plump and his whiskers are white as snow. He is a gentleman and a gifted linguist. He is quite invaluable to our team, does all the odd jobs no one else can be bothered to do."

She carried on with her litany of Herr Doktor Schickfuss' virtues, but I fell to thinking. Miss Green was co-leader at Gabriel's dig site in the Badiyat ash-Sham. He had told me to stay put in Damascus, but he was three days overdue. My instructions had been to leave Damascus if he didn't show. I had no intention of helping him carry out any sort of criminal enterprise, that much was certain. But there was no way of knowing what Gabriel was really up to, and the curiosity was eating me alive. I thought back to what he had said early in the conversation, and more important what he hadn't. Gabriel's manner had always been indolent. His expression of perpetual lazy

114

amusement at the world had slipped when we talked. Naturally his experiences would have changed him, but there was some scent, some whiff of danger, I had caught in his conversation. I hadn't pressed him, but he was clearly involved in a dangerous business. What precisely was he risking in getting his find to me? And more important, had he already fallen into danger?

A shudder ran down my spine, and Miss Green stopped short. "I say, Mrs. Starke. Are you quite all right?"

"Entirely," I told her, summoning a smile. "I came over all goosefleshy just then. Too much time in the heated rooms, I think."

"Yes, English constitutions aren't always suited for Turkish bathing."

I ought to have paused then. I should have considered my options carefully, weighing them and judging the consequences. But of course, I didn't.

Instead, I leaned forward, smiling my most winsome smile and determined not to take no for an answer. "Miss Green, I would like to be very forward indeed. How would you like to take me back with you into the Badiyat ash-Sham? I have a yearning to see the desert."

The arrangements were swiftly made. Miss Green accepted my forcing myself on her with good humour and within two days we were on our way.

Aunt Dove had been remarkably agreeable to my going, and even Rashid seemed resigned, although secretly I had expected him to sulk a little. He was in our suite, teaching Arthur a few new phrases as the bird watched from Rashid's shoulder, cocking his head and regarding me with his menacing little eyes.

"*Asalaam aleikum*," he said, thrusting out his feathery neck.

"*Aleikum asalaam*," I returned, feeling perfectly idiotic.

"Long live the Saqr al-Sahra," he murmured—or something that sounded very like it.

I turned to Rashid. "I'm afraid I don't know what that phrase means."

He grinned. "It is not a phrase, *sitt*. It is a name. Like Lawrence of Arabia."

I blinked. "You know Colonel Lawrence?"

He shrugged. "Not I. My uncle, the sheikh of our tribe, met him. He says Colonel Lawrence is nothing compared to the Saqr al-Sahra."

"Who is the . . ." I hesitated then attempted the phrase, mangling it so badly Rashid went off in fits of laughter.

He wiped his eyes and said the phrase again, slowly, until I could repeat it perfectly.

"Why do you keep saying *sahra*," I demanded. "We're a thousand miles from the Sahara. It isn't even on this continent."

Rashid sighed. "It is merely the Arabic word for

desert. And the phrase I have taught you, it means falcon of the desert, *sitt*. The Saqr is a legend, a warrior who unites his people to fight against the Turk. This is why he is better than Lawrence. The Saqr is one of us, a true Bedouin. Perhaps you will meet the Bedu when you are in the Badiyat ash-Sham and they will tell you of his deeds. Perhaps you will even meet with my Bedu, and I will introduce you to the sheikh, my uncle."

"Meet your Bedu? You mean you are leaving Damascus?"

He shrugged. "It is time for me to go into the desert again, *sitt*."

I gave an impatient sigh. "Rashid, I had hoped you would keep an eye on my aunt while I was gone," I said softly.

He shrugged again, taking refuge in silence. I sighed again and he turned back to the bird to teach him another choice word or two. I went to Aunt Dove.

"I've had a wire from Wally. He ought to turn up with the *Jolly Roger* in a day or so. You can show him around Damascus, and by the time he's properly settled, I will be back. That ought to be fun for you. You will be all right in the meantime?" I asked her.

"Oh, don't fret about me, child. I daresay I'll come up with some way to amuse myself, although Halliday will be downcast, I've no doubt," she said, giving me a disapproving look. "Perhaps I'll see about entertaining him while you're gone," she said brightly. "I could put in a few good words for you."

I thought of warning him, but there seemed little point. I packed a single small holdall for the trip, kissed Aunt Dove, blew a raspberry at Arthur on my way out the door and skipped down the stairs to find Miss Green just entering the court.

"Morning, Mrs. Starke! Ready to go, I see. And you've packed lightly," she said, eyeing my single small bag. "Good girl. Wouldn't do to bring too much. We'll be lucky if Mother Mary gets us to the site, never mind our luggage."

"Mother Mary?"

"That's our nickname for the motorcar. Come and see."

Outside idling in the street was one of the most curious vehicles I have ever seen. It was an old Ford van but scarcely recognisable. It had been painted in violent shades of yellow and blue with an enormous image of the Virgin Mary emblazoned on the bonnet. Through the cracked glass of the windscreen I could see a statue of the lady perched on the dash. Various bits and pieces of the vehicle were lashed together with baling wire and from within came the most astonishing smell of unwashed human and chicken droppings.

"We've little money for things like automobiles," she said with the barest trace of apology. She leaned into the car and roused the driver, who was sleeping peacefully. "Daoud, get up at once. Shove the chickens into the backseat. You will ride with them and Mrs. Starke will sit up front with me."

The driver, a native fellow wearing a filthy striped robe and a vacant grin, did as he was told, touching his forehead as he bowed to me. "Greetings, *sitt*."

"Hello."

Miss Green did not bother to lower her voice. "That's Daoud. He's an imbecile, poor fellow, but a useful enough worker so long as you tell him precisely what to do. I told him to collect the chickens I'm taking to the dig site. Only trouble was, I neglected to tell him to bring the coop," she said, scowling at Daoud. He was lazily flapping his robe at the chickens that paid no attention to him whatsoever. "Oh, give it up, Daoud!" Miss Green instructed. With characteristic efficiency she hoisted each squawking chicken up by the feet and tossed it neatly into the back. She brushed a quick hand over the front seat, scattering feathers and other unspeakable things.

"Climb in, Mrs. Starke. Nothing in here that will hurt you."

I did as she told me and she gunned the engine. "Here we go!" she declared, and we sailed majestically into traffic. "We are on our way."

SIX

The drive was nothing like I imagined. I had pictured a long journey over rough terrain, with dust and grit filling my mouth and eyes and the sun beating hot overhead as my throat slowly parched and my skin tightened. It was a thousand times worse. Unlike the tall sandy dunes of popular imagination, this desert was simply an endless stretch of rocky nothingness. The road did not even deserve the dignity of the name; it was a track in the long scrubby wastes of desert, dotted here and there with low bushes and the occasional outcropping of rock. From time to time Miss Green would point out the crumbling tower of a ruined Crusader castle or a particularly note-worthy bit of rock wall surrounding a well from antiquity, long since run dry. The landmarks were few and difficult to see, and the further we travelled, the more I began to wonder what on earth I had got myself into. The track branched off in several places, and in some spots disappeared altogether. But Miss Green seemed to know precisely where she was headed, and she did not hesitate, plunging forward at each turning with confidence and as much speed as she dared. As she drove, she described the staff I would meet at the dig site.

"There are the labourers, locals, of course, and then there are the Hungarians, the Thurzós, to whom I am cordial but secretly despise. They despise me, as well, but are even more cordial than I am, so you needn't fear we will draw knives over the dinner table," she said with a little chuckle. "The Thurzós are brother and sister, and we have a little joke about them being spies although they claim to be linguists, and I must admit, they do know their stuff."

"Spies!"

She shrugged. "Of course. The area is thick with them. That's what we get for digging out here where half of Europe is involved in making nations." She gave me a narrow look. "You do understand what the situation is, don't you?"

I hesitated. I had spent the entire journey on the Orient Express refreshing my memory and Halliday had added a few choice details, most notably about the Arab Bureau in Cairo directing British regional interests as far as Baghdad. By the time Miss Green and I set off, I probably knew as much as any minor government functionary and possibly more. But it occurred to me there was nothing like the horse's mouth. Listening to Miss Green's take on things wouldn't tell me any more than I already knew about Syria but it could tell me a hell of a lot about her.

I smiled girlishly and fluttered my lashes a little while I shrugged. It was revolting, but I had pegged Miss Green as the tweedy, academic type, and that sort always thought girls like me with our fluffy curls and red lipstick were about as intelligent as the average sofa cushion. With such women it is always best to let them explain things to you. They liked to feel superior and it freed up a lot of time to think about shoes or choosing the best route across the Caspian Sea.

Right on cue, Miss Green puffed out a long-suffering sigh. "You ought to know, Mrs. Starke. It's important," she said firmly. "The Turks were masters here for centuries, and they were complete bastards about it, to be perfectly blunt. I presume you know they sided with Germany in the war?" She slid me a glance and I bristled. Maybe I had overdone it a little if she were going to go quite so far back in her explanations.

"I did know that!" I assured her a trifle acidly.

She shrugged. "That's more than Daoud knows and it's his country. In any event, the Turks sided with the Germans, two empires walking out cosily together. In the meantime, England and France got together and realised this was a strategic area, a *very* strategic area. If the Turks could be kept busy here, they couldn't aid the Germans on the Continent. And as a starting strategy it worked rather well. We agitated the locals and got them to kick up a fuss against Turkey."

"If memory serves," I said carefully, "we incited them to rebellion by promising to support them in establishing a homeland—a promise we have since broken. This interim government has no real power, does it?"

She flapped a hand. "It's all very complicated," she said vaguely. I was not surprised. Broken British promises made for awkward conversation in the Levant. Lip service to Arab independence had been paid by allowing Prince Faisal, son of the Sharif of Mecca, to call himself king, but by never giving him the merest scrap of power, the Europeans had made it clear precisely who was in charge. Gabriel had always been stern on the subject of Arab independence and I had agreed with him. Imperialism was an outdated philosophy and one that had no place in the twentieth century. But clearly Miss Green was a horse of a different colour, and I had no intention of insulting my hostess before we'd even arrived at the dig.

I prodded her to go on. "I do know that after the war we English kept charge of things here, but I understand we have now retreated to Palestine and Mesopotamia, leaving the French with their hands all over the interim government."

"Just so. And it's played hell with our excavations, I can tell you. The bloody French advisors are making all the same mistakes here they made in Egypt before we got there!" she said, throwing up her hands. The car veered sharply but she jerked the wheel and got it back on track. The chickens protested bitterly. Daoud took the loudest onto his lap and began to pet it.

"In any event," she went on, "the French advisors have let us dig, but they keep an eye on us. And I have heard we have our own spies trotting about in the desert keeping an eye on *them*."

"To what end?"

She shrugged. "Whoever knows? It's all down to little grey men at Whitehall who know nothing and who don't ever walk further than Downing Street. But it plays havoc with my dig because they keep the French agitated and that means the French keep coming round demanding to see paperwork. Rather handy to have the Thurzós on staff. Hungarians have a sort of glamour about them, I always think, even if they did side with Germany in the war. This pair speak a dozen languages and manage to smooth things over, especially Erzsébet. She's got a way about her."

Before I could ask about Erzsébet's way, she carried on, ticking off members of the expedition. "Then there's Herr Doktor Schickfuss. I told you about him already. The very best of chaps, but the French will kick up a fuss about us having a German around. Took me the better part of this week to persuade the French not to chuck him out." She glanced back and spoke sharply. "Do not make a pet out of that creature, Daoud. It will be in the cookpot tomorrow morning."

Daoud clutched at the chicken, which clucked in

alarm. Miss Green turned back around. "Fool," she said, but there was no heat to her words and I suspected she was fond of the fellow. "Where was I? Oh, excavation. We've a local foreman who is quite well-trained and an obliging chap. He puts up with all of Rowan's bloody-mindedness."

I studied my nails and adopted a casual tone. "Mr. Rowan is difficult to work with?"

"All geniuses are, and Rowan is more of a genius than most. He doesn't usually do field work— terribly reclusive and made a name for himself writing scathing critiques of other people's dig reports. Apparently he had a rough time of it in the war and doesn't like to talk about his past, so don't go upsetting him with questions," she warned. "Quite a coup to get him here, but his pet subject is Crusader castles. Our caravansary formed part of the construction of one of the castles. The place is in ruins now, scarcely two stones stacked on top of each other, but he's quite in heaven, prowling about the place at all hours. He's the worst sort of archaeologist, completely driven. I don't think the man sleeps three hours a night. But he is a stern taskmaster and expects as much out of the rest of the crew and somehow gets it. One doesn't mind so much when one realises he drives himself just as hard."

"Still, if he's such a tyrant, I wonder why you don't all look for a more accommodating staff member."

"We are co-leaders," she said proudly. "We were dashed lucky to get him." Her manner was a little stiff then, and I wondered wickedly if she had formed a *tendresse* for him. She was an extremely pragmatic woman, not the sort one would expect to harbour romantic fantasies. But in my experience, those were the women who always fell the hardest—and often for entirely indifferent men like dance instructors and hairdressers.

"You must be tired," she said. "Why don't you try to sleep? It will be hours yet and the view won't change at all, I promise you."

I folded my coat into a sort of pillow and closed my eyes, as much to give myself a chance to think as time to rest. As I shut my eyes, I saw Miss Green look back at Daoud, and this time her expression was warm and when she smiled at him, she coloured a little. I closed my eyes firmly then, but I spent many miles thinking about Miss Green and her peculiar little companion and exactly what their relationship might be.

We arrived just as night began to fall, having stopped only twice for food and water and to stretch our legs, and twice more to dig out the car when it bogged in a soft spot. The workers were filing away from the site, a long line of weary men in striped and plain robes, barefoot or sandalled and singing lowly as they walked. The others were preparing the evening meal and closing down the site for the day, although they all left what they were doing when Mother Mary chugged into view. I looked around to get my bearings, surprised to find the site was so large. Miss Green had exaggerated the decrepitude of the castle only slightly. Most of it had fallen into great heaps of stone, but a few courses of the keep still stood atop one another enclosing shadowy rooms, and somehow, silhouetted against the setting sun, it seemed grim and forbidding with its thick tower and heavy crenellations. The caravansary had been laid out at its foot, a series of warehouses and storerooms and lodgings opening off one another. A little distance away, a sort of camp had been established, with a long low building to serve as the storehouse for artefacts. Another small building, scarcely more than a shack, had been set aside for a common room where they ate and sat together in the evenings. A small room opened off the back for Mr. Rowan's lodgings, and the rest were scattered about in tents. "You'll have to share my tent, I'm afraid," Miss Green told me. "It's quite comfortable, as tents go, and I'm a sound sleeper."

She flapped her hands to get the chickens out of the car and scolded Daoud into finding a cage to put them in. Just then a man and woman approached, the woman as smartly turned out as if she'd stepped out of a Parisian bandbox. Her desert costume was beautifully tailored, and I did not need Miss Green to tell me this was the

Hungarian aristocrat. She introduced herself as Countess Thurzó and pointed to her companion. "My brother, Count András Thurzó."

He bowed low, and I was astonished at the resemblance between them. They were two peas from a very handsome pod, slender and short, and both of them blessed with enormous black eyes and chocolate-box complexions.

"Mrs. Starke is on a world tour. She's a famous aviatrix, you know," Miss Green told them. "She's a keen interest in archaeology. Her late husband used to dig."

"My condolences, madame," Count Thurzó murmured as he bent over my hand.

"Good God, Green, did you let Daoud drive? I've been waiting two days on the post." I turned to see Gabriel approaching in his disguise as Mr. Rowan. He looked like Zeus on a bad day, all thunderous expression and angry scowl behind his wretched beard. He wore coloured spectacles that darkly shadowed his eyes and turned the colour to mud. He blinked nearsightedly at me as he came close.

"Mr. Rowan, how nice to see you again," I said lightly. I put out my hand. "It is so kind of you to welcome me to your site."

He took my hand, but with a show of reluctance, and dropped it instantly, as if he'd been scorched. "It's nothing to me, although I don't much care to have amateurs about. Too much of a bloody nuisance, frankly. But I daresay if you can remember to shake out your shoes to free the scorpions and check your cot for snakes before you bed down, you'll manage," he said, his tone decidedly bland. He played the benign curmudgeon with a mildness that would have been entirely convincing to anyone who didn't know him as well as I did. A tiny muscle at the corner of his eye twitched and I knew he was enraged with me and doing his level best to hide it.

"I won't get in the way," I added with my most winsome smile. "And I promise I won't inconvenience you."

He scowled then gave me a dismissive shrug. "I shan't even notice you're here, I assure you, Mrs. Spark."

"Starke," I corrected coldly.

He shrugged again and turned to Miss Green to issue a series of orders. Countess Thurzó put her arm through mine. "Do not pay him attention," she advised softly as she drew me away. "He is always cranky. I think he is dyspeptic," she said with a faint smile. "Now come this way and I will show you to Miss Green's tent. You will want to make yourself tidy for dinner."

I had a quick wash and changed into clean clothes just in time for the evening meal. At dinner I was introduced to Herr Doktor Schickfuss, a kindly, ruddy-cheeked fellow who was vastly more welcoming than Mr. Rowan had been and inclined to flirt in that harmlessly charming way elderly men have.

"How wonderful to have a fresh face," he said to me as we settled in at the table. "It is very nice." His accent was distinctive, with a pronounced sibilance to his esses and a softness about some of the consonants as his *v*'s and *w*'s slurred into one another.

In fact, I decided in short order that he was a darling—full of hilarious stories about various mishaps at other digs—and sweetly courteous, making quite certain my plate was full and my glass topped up throughout the evening. The Thurzós were the merest bit aloof, not pointedly so, but in that very correct way that most well-bred Continentals have with new acquaintances. Miss Green was tired after the long drive and said little apart from a brief argument she and Mr. Rowan had over the location of their efforts.

"Three weeks and not a damned thing more interesting than a potsherd in the current spot," he said bitterly. "I've a mind to shift the fellows down a bit, towards the south end of the site."

"To the storerooms?" Herr Doktor Schickfuss asked, his plump cheeks wobbling with excitement. He leaned to me. "There are lodgings behind that I believe may have belonged to someone of importance, perhaps even a local official who might have left some record of his time here."

"Anything written must first pass through our hands," Countess Thurzó said sharply. "You know that, Herr Doktor."

His expression was a little wounded. "Of course, dear lady. It has never been said that I am not fully cooperative with my colleagues."

"Naturally," Count Thurzó soothed. "Erzsébet did not mean to suggest otherwise, did you, sister?"

She gave the German a thin smile. "Certainly not. But there was the little matter of the seal last month—"

Herr Doktor flushed deeply and before he could open his mouth to remonstrate with her, Mr. Rowan held up a hand. "Enough, all of you. I won't have bickering at dinner. Carry on outside if you must, but leave it there."

There were murmurs around the table, but the matter was dropped instantly, and if anyone thought it odd that Rowan, rather than Miss Green, had cracked the whip, they didn't betray it. As she pushed her fork tiredly around her plate, Miss Green said, "You know, Rowan, I rather think it might be interesting to have a go at the castle itself. I realise it's a ruin, but there might be some important things to be learned from it. For example, I don't know if you've studied the engravings in the chapel—"

"Banal in the extreme," Mr. Rowan returned coldly. His smoked spectacles gave him an inscrutable look, and he turned to the Thurzós, who were both taking an avid interest in the conversation. "Besides, Miss Green, I don't think I need remind you that we only have permission to excavate the caravansary. I doubt the authorities would look favourably on us pushing the limits of our permits."

"But surely—" she began.

Suddenly, Rowan, stood, throwing his napkin down. "I am turning in. We will begin at the southern end of the site tomorrow."

He stalked out, as much as he could with his stooped posture, and it was as if someone had let the wind out of the room.

Miss Green dropped her fork and pushed her plate away. She gave me an apologetic smile. "Don't mind too much about Rowan. It's quite normal for archaeologists to get like this in the middle of a season, particularly if things haven't gone as well as we would have liked."

"Is it a poor season?" I asked.

The Thurzós laughed and Count András explained. "For linguistics, no. There is ample carving on the lodgings and storerooms at the site. But as to significant artefacts, very little has been unearthed. Nothing but pots and beads, pots and beads, piles and piles of pots and beads."

"Those pots and beads tell us a very great deal about the day-to-day life of the people who once lived here," Miss Green said wearily. "Now, if all you want is gold, you'd best take yourself off to Egypt."

"Egypt!" Herr Doktor scoffed. "There is nothing new to be found in Egypt. It has all been looted in antiquity. To think something wonderful might yet be found there is silliness."

Miss Green rubbed her face, and I wondered if she were dangerously close to weeping. There was something brittle about her mood, and the conversation had been thorny. I rose then.

"I'm afraid I'm rather tired, Miss Green. Would you mind if I went to our tent?"

She shook her head. "Of course not. I'll walk with you." We bade the others good-night and she lit a pair of lanterns, handing one to me as we left the small building. In the distance, we could see the hunched form of Mr. Rowan as he made his rounds over the site.

We readied ourselves for bed and doused the lanterns, and after a while I heard her heavy snores. I must have dozed, for I awoke some time later, after the moon had set and the darkness pressed against me.

I could not say what had awakened me, but then I heard it, a faint noise, so slight I could almost imagine it. Gooseflesh raised on my arms and I realised what it was. Pan-pipes. Gabriel had loved all forms of music, but for a connoisseur he had had appallingly lowbrow tastes at times. He refused to appreciate my jazz, but he adored pan-pipes he'd played as a boy, and he often used them to relax.

And now it crept into the tent, coaxing, luring. I fumbled with the fastenings, and it took several minutes before I freed them and emerged into the clear, cold desert air. The melody was faint and seemed to come from everywhere and nowhere at once, no doubt a trick of the desert air. I peered into the flat darkness, thinking of the *jinn*, the malevolent spirits of desert folklore. They were particularly fond of travellers, I recalled with a shudder. And then I pinched myself hard, realising this was no doubt Gabriel's attempt to signal to me. He might have chosen something less melo-dramatic, I fumed as I moved out from the cover of the tent, but then again he'd always had a flair for the dramatic, I thought bitterly.

I saw a figure, white and shadowy, moving slowly towards the castle ruin. I set off after it, but I had not gone three feet before I tripped heavily over a rock and fell, cursing into the darkness.

"Frau Starke, is that you?" Herr Doktor groped his way towards me, swinging a lantern high as he came near.

"Yes, I'm so sorry to have disturbed you."

He helped me to my feet. I looked towards the castle but the ghostly figure was gone, vanished into the night.

"Disturb me? I am an old man, I do not sleep well and I am often restless," he told me. "I too often rise in the night to attend to the demands of nature. But you must not wander about in the dark, my dear. It is dangerous in the desert." As if on cue, a jackal chose that precise moment to howl, and I shuddered, the hair on my neck raising as the creature carried on its mournful cry. Herr Doktor patted my hand and walked me back to my tent, and I said nothing, grateful for his assumption I'd been answering a call of nature. It was as good an explanation as I could have thought of on my own.

I thanked him and he waited until I was safely inside. I heard Miss Green's healthy snores as I eased into bed. I lay in silence several minutes before I heard Herr Doktor walk slowly away. I strained my ears, but the melody did not come again, and after a long time, I slept.

I woke to a chilly, brilliant morning. The sun touched everything with its warm light, gilding the wrecked stones and huddled tents into a scene of actual beauty. Miss Green's bed was empty and I hurried to wash and dress and present myself for breakfast. She was just coming to collect me with a clutch of boiled eggs and flatbread and a steaming mug of tea.

"I'm afraid you've missed the proper cooked breakfast, but I didn't like to wake you, you were sleeping so soundly," she said by way of apology.

"No matter," I told her. "I had a restless night."

She nodded towards the tea. "That will soon sort

you. The Hungarians complain to no end, but it's bracing stuff."

She was not wrong. The cook had stewed it until it was thick with tea leaves and so heavily sweetened it made my teeth ache. But I was wide awake after drinking it, and she took me on a tour after I had eaten.

We made our way down to the southern end of the site, away from the castle, and just as Gabriel—in his guise as Mr. Rowan—had instructed, the men were busy excavating the storerooms. There were a series of structures, some completely razed with nothing but a stone outline to show where they had once stood. Others were in better repair, with low walls and some even with lintels over the doorways. There were very clearly courtyards and even a few staircases.

"For the rooftops," Miss Green told me. "Very common in this part of the world. In hot weather, one might take meals or even sleep up there to take advantage of the cooling breezes."

She strode on, pointing out the most interesting bits and pieces until Daoud ran up to her, gesticulating wildly. She listened then turned to me, rolling her eyes.

"Problem with the men and, wouldn't you know, Rowan is too busy drawing the map to take them in hand. I'll sort it out and be back in a tick."

She walked away with Daoud, leaving me on my own to explore the site, but I hadn't gone a few steps before András Thurzó appeared.

"Good morning, Mrs. Starke," he said, inclining his head in a courtly gesture.

I smiled. "Your Continental manners put the fellows I know to shame, Count."

"I am delighted you find it so. How do you like our little dig, madame?"

"Very interesting, at least the bit I've seen."

He held out his arm. "Then it must be my privilege to escort you to what you have not seen."

I hesitated. "I was waiting for Miss Green."

"Then we must hurry if we are going to miss her," he said with a conspiratorial smile. I laughed and took his arm.

"Count, I think you might be a scoundrel," I said as he led me into the depths of the caravansary. I glanced back to see Erzsébet Thurzó watching us closely as we went. I smiled, but she merely turned her head and went back to her work.

We walked for some time and the count explained the site thoroughly, but always with a few interesting details thrown in to keep my attention. Between the courtly gestures and his insistence on being alone, I had expected him to try something and steeled myself to give him a good shove if he needed it. But as the morning wore on and we covered more ground, he showed no signs of playing the lover. Occasionally his hand lingered a moment too long on my back as he guided me, but otherwise his manner was perfectly correct—slightly nervous even, and he seemed distracted, checking his watch every quarter hour or so. He was serious as the grave, and although he did toss in a few complimentary phrases now and then, each time he did, I had the oddest feeling he was merely conversing by rote, saying things he felt he *ought* to say rather than things he actually meant.

I wondered exactly what he was up to, but listening to him drone on about substrata wasn't going to tell me anything. So I batted my lashes and kept touching his arm, and when I put a finger into the cleft in his chin and he shied like a pony, I knew. He was keeping me busy for some purpose of his own. It obviously wasn't seduction and I couldn't imagine what it might be, but I was getting a little tired of wandering around in the sun. The shadows had shortened considerably, and it was drawing close to time for luncheon. I sat on one of the low walls and patted my face with a handkerchief.

"Are you too warm, Mrs. Starke? Please, allow me to offer you some water," he said quickly, obviously glad of something to do. He knelt in front of me to open the flask and pour out a little water, and as he did so, I happened to glance at a scribble chalked onto the wall beside me. It was faint, almost illegible, but I could make out two words: *REAPERS HOME*. Next to them was a series of letters. *XIIA*.

I stared at them a long moment, then jerked my head back as the count handed me the cup, but his eyes had drifted to the chalked markings. I smiled and took a long sip. I held it out for more and when he had refilled it, I jostled my own hand, spilling water on the chalk.

"Oh, how clumsy of me!" I said, righting the cup. But the job was done. The words were obliterated instantly. I smiled at him. "I do hope I haven't been very stupid and damaged something of value," I told him.

He returned the smile, but thinly, and when he spoke, it was with scarcely veiled irritation. "On the contrary, Mrs. Starke. These stone walls have stood for many centuries. A little water cannot possibly harm them."

"I am glad to know it." I batted my lashes some more, and he dove for his watch. Whatever he had been waiting for, it was apparently finished. His expression relaxed instantly and he rose, replacing the cap on his flask.

"It's very nearly time for luncheon. We must go."

I followed obediently to where the rest of the party were finishing up the morning's work. Apparently there had been a find of some value and the atmosphere was buzzing. Miss Green waved me over to show me the goods. It was a cache of modest jewellery, wrapped in a rotting piece of fabric. There were bracelets and clasps and a particularly nice necklace in a Roman style. The workmen were round-eyed with excitement, clapping the fellow who had found it on the back as he accepted the congratulations of the staff.

Miss Green turned to me. "He's right to be happy. He'll get a reward exactly commensurate with the value of the find. Standard practise to encourage the men not to steal from the site," she explained.

"They will have half a day's holiday tomorrow, as well," Count Thurzó stated. "Although that is a touch generous for such a modest find."

Miss Green turned on him. "What did you expect, Count? The crown jewels? It is a perfectly exciting find. Why, look here—" She went off on a highly technical explanation of why the necklace was significant. I thought I was the only one not following, but the count held up his hands with a smile.

"You ladies and your jewellery!" He clearly intended the mockery to be in good fun, but Miss Green took offence.

"Now see here, Thurzó—" She was clearly building up a head of steam, so I slipped to the edge of the crowd and thought of the message on the wall. Gabriel wanted me to meet him at twelve—midnight to be precise since he had chalked an *A* after the numerals. Where, he hadn't indicated, and it occurred to me the best I could do was stay awake and wait for his signal.

Gabriel appeared then to inspect the find, and

140

amid much celebrating and shouting, made the proper noises and paid out the finder's fee. The men were to be given an early luncheon, and as the crowd moved away, he flicked a glance at me, his brows lifted. He didn't need to speak for me to understand the question. *Did you get the message?* I gave him a single nod in reply and he blinked once before turning away. The entire exchange could not have lasted more than a few seconds, and anyone who had not been looking for it would not have noticed.

But as Gabriel walked away, I looked up to find Herr Doktor watching us both, a small smile playing about his lips.

The celebratory luncheon was a lengthy affair with several courses of rustic food and much telling of stories, although the mood varied wildly depending upon where one ate. The workmen sat in the shade of the castle keep, eating apart from the staff and sharing what sounded like ribald jokes. The staff were much quieter, and an odd atmosphere seemed to have settled upon them. As Mr. Rowan, Gabriel said almost nothing, ate swiftly and was off again minutes after he joined us, but the rest showed an inclination to linger.

We began by talking of the state of archaeology after the war and this rather naturally led to a discussion of what it had been like during those tumultuous years.

"Awful," Miss Green said mournfully. "It was the purest form of agony not being able to get here to dig and having no idea what was happening to our sites."

"Had you been digging here before the war?" I asked, idly toying with a bit of flatbread.

"We had all been here at various sites," Countess Thurzó put in. I noticed that Herr Doktor had fallen silent and seemed a little morose. No doubt talk of the war was a difficult thing for a man who had been on the wrong side of it. I asked him what he thought of the location and he nodded slowly.

"Yes, there is no better spot on earth than the Badiyat ash-Sham for excavation," he said.

"Really? You surprise me, Herr Doktor. I would have thought Egypt—" Before I could finish, he waved his hands.

"Not at all, Frau Starke! Oh, the Egyptians have their ancient kings, but this is all. If you peel away the Greco-Roman influence, what is there? Uninteresting people doing uninteresting things in rock tombs. But here!" He opened his arms expansively. "Here the whole world was at a crossroads. This is the Silk Road, madame, and it is here that merchants came from as far away as China and Persia, winding down the Tian Shan mountains, crossing vast expanses of steppes to bring silks and spices. They came from India, from Nepal, out of the Hindu Kush they came, carrying with them all the secrets of the east in their camel caravans from Baghdad to Palmyra to Damascus. And from Europe we went out to meet them, bringing our God and our gold. We traded philosophies, and music and dance, and when our Crusader knights came to these lands, they collected these things and took them back to Europe."

His bright blue eyes were shining as he talked, painting a vivid picture of life as it had once been.

"Imagine it, dear lady, when the camel caravans walked these stony hills, laden with their perfumes and silks, the fat merchants and the wily thieves who preyed upon them. For they were vulnerable, these rich men who came bearing goods from the mountains across the plains. The desert tribes learned to attack them and carry off their treasures on swift horses. But still they came, for the trading was too good, and in this way everyone profited."

"You make it all sound quite romantic, Herr Doktor," I told him.

Countess Thurzó gave a short laugh. "Not entirely. They brought bubonic plague with their pretty silks. But Herr Doktor likes to see only the lovely, isn't that right?"

He gave her a sad smile. "It is true, it makes life more pleasant this way. The youth today, you do not always see that it is better to look for the beauty in life. But, alas, Countess Thurzó is not wrong. The Silk Road lasted until gunpowder and disease took their tolls. But before this, ah, madame, what a time to be alive!" He pointed out the window. "Can you not see them if you try? The Persian conquerors who once swept over this land like a plague? Or the plump merchants with their laden camels? Or the Crusader knights who believed this land was once promised to them by God?"

"That's right," I said, "this was once part of the kingdom of the Outremer, was it not?"

"The kingdom over the sea," Miss Green said a little dreamily. It amused me that she was not immune to the romanticism of the German Doktor.

"When all the great kings of Christendom united to fight the infidel and claim this land where Jesus once trod in His own name," he added.

"I don't know," Count Thurzó said, his expression thoughtful. "My sympathies have always been with Salah al-Dln."

"Mine, too," I told him with a grin.

"Yes, well, enough of metaphorically raking up dead bones," said Miss Green briskly. "We ought to go outside and get to the real thing."

We dispersed then, but Countess Thurzó gave me a long look as she walked away, and I suddenly felt quite alone out in the desert with a group of strangers. I smiled at Miss Green. "I think I'll lie down for just a bit."

She nodded. "The heat. It takes newcomers sometimes. Just be very glad you're here in late winter. Summer doesn't even bear thinking about."

She bustled away to get back to work and I made my way back to the tent we shared. It took me approximately three seconds to realize my things had been searched. It had been done in haste, and things had been put back almost but not quite the way I left them. Doubtless whoever did it figured I wouldn't notice, but then they weren't flyers. I was, and I had been trained by the best. Ryder might have been a daredevil with half a death wish, but he'd been raised in the African bush, where a moment's inattention can kill you. He took his flying seriously and the one thing he had beaten into my brain was method. Day in and day out we drilled the same things, and he had told me stories that curled my hair about how little slackness it took to kill a flyer who wasn't careful. Order, method and attention to detail—those were the things that kept a pilot safe, and I'd left his tutelage as well-trained as any aviator could be. I had thought he was training me to be a pilot, but the truth was he'd trained me to be an adult. I'd learned to follow through with things, to plan ahead and most important to check my gear. I knew where every item in my possession was and I knew how I'd left it.

And as I tidied away the few items I had brought with me, I noted that nothing was missing, only disarranged. My papers in particular had been thoroughly gone over, but there was nothing in them to indicate anything unusual. There were a

145

few maps, some identification papers and a few unanswered letters from friends back home— perfectly appropriate and expected for a traveller abroad. Gabriel's photograph and the two bank-notes were buttoned securely into my pocket along with the little pearl-handled pistol Aunt Dove had given me. I hadn't brought anything of real value with me except my wedding ring and that was still on a chain around my neck, tucked inside my clothes. Whoever tossed my things must have been mightily disappointed, I thought with a smile. No doubt some poor worker, driven to exhaustion for low wages, had seized the opportunity for a little petty theft. It was just his bad luck that I hadn't anything more valuable than my hairbrush on hand.

SEVEN

The rest of the day passed quietly. The workers dug, the staff supervised and the sun beat down mercilessly overhead. We all washed and met for another somewhat stilted meal. The odd atmosphere at the luncheon table stayed, no doubt made worse by Gabriel's foul temper in the guise of Dr. Rowan. One of the men had unearthed a sizeable potsherd only to break it through clumsy handling, and Rowan's reaction could be heard all over the dig site. He swore loudly in English and fluent

Arabic, sometimes lapsing into sputtering as he tore at his hair and gestured wildly. He fretted over the loss of the potsherd at dinner, and resisted all attempts by Miss Green to jolly him out of it.

To my surprise, he did not retire early, but sat, nursing a glass of whisky and sucking at his false teeth in irritation as he perused the latest issue of the *Revue Archéologique*. After a while the others began to talk more naturally, and everyone seemed in better spirits as we turned in for the night. Miss Green fell asleep almost immediately, but I lay awake again, staring into the darkness. The moon had waned and the night was much darker with only starlight to illuminate the long plain of the rocky desert. I turned onto my side, and just then I heard the sound again, the faint coaxing of the pan-pipes, rising on the night air.

I listened for any movement, but Miss Green was snoring heavily. Slowly, carefully, I eased out of the cot and slipped into my clothes. I shook out my boots and slid my feet into them, lacing them as best I could by feel. I had fallen into the habit of keeping the pistol on me, so I slipped it into my pocket. The music was fainter now and I fumbled with the fastenings of the flap. At last I was out in the chill of the desert night, pausing only a moment to let my eyes grow accustomed to the starlight and the pale shimmer of the rising moon. I could barely make out the traces of the stones at my feet and I picked my way carefully towards the music. It seemed to be coming from the ruin of the castle keep, and I cursed myself for not bringing a torch. It felt like hours before I reached the stones, but I kept going, lured on by the faint sound of the music. As I crept closer, I could just make out the faint glow of a lantern.

I moved slowly over the stones, falling twice and nearly breaking my neck once. And with every stumble I cursed Gabriel and his sense of the theatrical. By the time I found him in the remains of the chapel in the crumbling castle, I was ready to give him a piece of my mind. He held up his hand and put a finger to his lips as soon as I opened my mouth. He beckoned and I followed him behind the altar and down a narrow, twisting stone stair. It led into a tiny crypt where a pair of Crusader knights had been laid to rest. Their stone effigies were crumbling to dust, but I could just make out the proud features of their faces. One had been sculpted lying in the traditional pose but the other was sitting upright, his blind stone eyes staring out at the world. It was an arresting piece and any other time I would have paused to admire it, but at the moment I was too enraged to take it all in. Gabriel popped back up to the chapel to make sure we weren't followed, and by the time he returned, I'd built up a full head of steam.

"Gabriel Starke, this is not what I signed on for. Those pan-pipes are the most absurd—"

"And effective," he said, spitting his mouthpiece

into his palm. "Anyone hearing them might assume it was one of the local lads having a bit of fun. No one would associate the thing with me except you." He pocketed the pipes and took off his dark spectacles, rubbing his eyes with his thumbs. "Christ, that feels better."

"Don't swear," I told him. "You're in a church."

"If you didn't like that, you really won't appreciate this. Why the f—" I held up a hand and he moderated himself. "What the devil are you doing here? I told you in the plainest terms that you were to wait for me in Damascus. Now, kindly explain to me how you heard that to mean, 'Please come out and find me in the middle of the desert'?"

I studied the effigies and waited for him to finish. Gabriel could rant with the best of them, and I had learned during our brief marriage it was best for him to get it out of his system before attempting to reply. He cleared his throat impatiently.

I turned back to him. "Oh, is it my turn? I wanted to make sure you'd done all your fussing first. It was always so distracting when you kept on and *on* about something."

"I never—" he began, but snapped his mouth shut hard. His jaws were grinding against one another, and I shook my head.

"Don't do that. It's very bad for your teeth."

"Evangeline Rosemary Merryweather Starke,

there is absolutely nothing to prevent me from shooting you and leaving your body here for the jackals. Don't try my patience."

I snorted. "Don't be stupid. Jackals would never manage those stairs," I said with more bravado than I felt. For all I knew, jackals were ace stair climbers. "Now, as to why I've come, I should think that would be obvious. I thought you needed help."

He stared at me, his lips parted in astonishment. "You're not that daft," he said in a dazed voice. "You cannot be."

"Well, apparently I am because I'm here," I returned cheerfully.

"I don't know whether to kiss you or kill you," he murmured, sitting heavily on the stone lap of a sitting knight.

"Neither, if you please. I'm not sure which would be more disturbing. Now, I am right, aren't I? You are in some sort of trouble?"

His annoyance seemed to drop away, and when he spoke it was with an air of resignation. "You could say that. I ran into difficulties getting the item. I decided it was better to stay here and keep my head down. I'm sorry for that. I really wanted to get the find to you."

I blinked at him. "My God. Being dead agrees with you. Do you realise that's the first time you've ever apologised to me?"

"Is it? How curious."

"Isn't it? Now, what sort of trouble and what can I do to help?"

"Why the devil should you want to?" he demanded. "Evie, I lied to you. I committed the grossest, rankest betrayal. I pretended I was *dead*. You ought to be furious with me."

"Who says I'm not?"

"Well, you're doing a damned fine job of behaving otherwise."

I sighed. "Gabriel, what you did was unforgivable. But I have learned a lot since you left me in Shanghai, and one of the things I've learned is how to put things in a cupboard and shut the door when it isn't time to deal with them."

His brow furrowed. "Come again?"

"It's basic pilot training. You cannot fly if you're emotional. In fact, it's one of the main objections to teaching women to fly at all. In order to get my licence, I had to prove I could be as dispassionate as any man. I had to take whatever I was feeling at any given moment— rage, fatigue, euphoria, *anything*—and put it aside to focus entirely on the job at hand. I had to learn to separate myself from any situation and assess it coolly and without prejudice."

"Something I know a little about," he said with a wry twist of his lips.

"I imagine so. Now, don't think for a minute I have forgotten or forgiven. I haven't. You behaved unspeakably. But this is my chance to get rid of you forever, with a perfectly clear conscience, and I intend to take it."

His eyes brightened with something like malice. "Does that mean your conscience wasn't already clear where I was concerned?"

"I may have made some mistakes in our marriage," I conceded.

"Mistakes?" He laughed aloud. "You *dared* me to divorce you."

I folded my arms over my chest and gave him a cool glance. "Do you really want to hash all of that out now? Or shall we get to the matter at hand? What sort of criminal game are you playing and how can I help you get out of it?"

He was silent a moment, clearly weighing how much to tell me. "Fine," he said at last. "I haven't been able to retrieve the item I wanted to give you. Things are at sixes and sevens just now in the Badiyat ash-Sham, and there are any number of villains about. It makes things awkward."

I rolled my eyes. "I'm terribly sorry for your inconvenience. Now, suppose you tell me what this find is and we can proceed from there."

He smiled, his eyes sparkling with some unholy delight. "It's quite remarkable." He paused, waiting for me to start guessing, but I refused to play. I studied my nails instead. "I mean, it's extraordinary, Evie. The find of a lifetime—of a century."

I buffed my nails on my shirt and swore. "I'm

sure all archaeologists think that about their pet finds," I said sweetly. I yawned. "You always did love melodrama, Gabriel. What is it? A gold seal? A glazed pot? A mummy?"

He fixed me with a cold look. "A Levantine mummy would hardly generate any interest whatsoever in archaeological circles as you well know, so stop pretending to be stupid and think of where you are."

"We are outside Damascus, the most ancient inhabited city in the world, the site of Crusader sieges—"

His face had taken on an alert look, and I caught the smell of something tantalising. "It's a Crusader relic."

"Not a Crusader relic," he corrected. "*The* Crusader relic."

"Oh, for God's sake, you will have to narrow it down! Crusader knights were as prolific a set of liars as modern politicians. They claimed to have bodies of saints, the Holy Grail, the True Cross —" I broke off again as he smiled a slow, triumphant smile.

"You aren't serious. You cannot have found it."

"But I did."

"The True Cross," I whispered. It wasn't possible. St. Helena, mother of Constantine the Great and inveterate magpie of religious relics, had travelled to the Holy Land to collect the True Cross, not scrupling about a bit of torture to get her way. When she'd found it, she had cut it up and had the largest bit set in a gold-and-silver cross studded with precious gems. The result had been dazzling to look at and so sacred it had been carried into battle at the head of armies. It was rumoured the thing could cure the dying and even change the direction of the wind.

I stared at him in disbelief. "Gabriel Starke, that cross was lost at the Battle of Hattin. Saladin himself took it from the Bishop of Acre, and afterwards he carried it into Damascus in triumph. It was never seen again. It was lost to history."

"Until now."

His smile was exultant, but I shook my head. "You cannot have found it," I repeated.

"I am not a man to be underestimated," he reminded me.

"You always do this," I murmured. "Just when I think you can't surprise me, you pull another rabbit from the hat. Just how many tricks do you have up those filthy sleeves?"

His smile was undiminished. "As many as I need."

I cudgelled my brain, dredging up every last fact he had ever told me about the Cross. "Little wonder you've had trouble getting it out of the desert," I remarked. "If the Bishop of Acre carried it at the head of an army, it must be massive."

"It was. Once," he corrected. "Western chronicles didn't record it, but the Cross was badly damaged

154

in the Battle of Hattin. Much of it was burned, and what Saladin took to Damascus was a fragment. The portion he salvaged was embedded in the floor of the Great Mosque and it stayed there until Tamerlane sacked the city in 1400. He burned the mosque, and the cross was taken up again and carried off to Samarkand. It was forgot for many years, but eventually it made its way back here, to the Badiyat ash-Sham, to a group of Christian monks who had the thing reset in gold and crystal. But shortly after it was finished, one of the habitual tribal wars broke out, and the monks were scattered. One of them managed to hide the Cross for safekeeping and left a notation of its whereabouts in a manuscript. I came across the manuscript a while back and followed the trail to the Cross."

"It won't do, Gabriel," I told him rather more gently than he deserved. "The Cross belongs to the dig site. You have to turn it over to Miss Green."

"I won't." His expression was indignant. "I found it myself well before Green launched her dig. I was unaffiliated with any expedition and on entirely other business when I discovered it."

I furrowed my brow. "What other business could you possibly have in the desert besides archaeology?"

He gave me a bland look. "An ethnographical study on the variations in the Bedouin tribes of the Badiyat ash-Sham."

"Liar. You loathe ethnography. You always said it was work fit only for academics, not real archaeologists. I repeat, why are you here?"

"I like camels."

"All right, then. Don't tell me. I'm sure whatever it was would make me an accessory after the fact. But surely you understand the government won't possibly let it out of the country."

"The French control the interim government at the moment," he corrected, "and they would never let the locals keep it. It's a valuable piece of Crusader history, and the French know it. They would do exactly as I'm doing. They'd get it right out of the desert and into a museum."

I narrowed my eyes. "Gabriel, the man's name you gave me on that wretched piece of paper— who is he?"

He muttered something unintelligible.

"Gabriel?"

"Oh, very well. He's the curator for mediaeval antiquities at the British Museum."

"You intend to have me *sell* the Cross to the British Museum?"

"They can afford it," he said, waving an airy hand. "Two birds with one stone, pet. I get the Cross where it belongs, and I would be free and clear of my obligations to you."

"There were no obligations," I reminded him. "I thought you were dead."

He rose, standing so near to me I could smell the

familiar scent of his skin through the rank, filthy clothes and appalling beard. Memories rushed at me from all sides, and I fisted my hands at my sides as he smiled down at me.

"Did you really?"

"Yes," I lied. His nearness was confusing, and I stepped away as if to inspect the knight who lay flat on his back. I peered at the inscription on his tomb while I collected myself.

"I can't quite make it out," I said. Gabriel did not move closer.

"It says '*Nec Aspera Terrant.*'"

"'No fear on earth,'" I murmured. "The same as your signet ring."

He touched the little tin box tucked in his breast pocket. "It's a common old motto but a good one. I haven't carried much with me from one life to the other, but the ring at least made it."

"The ring but not the wife," I said softly.

His hands tightened and his nostrils went white. But his voice was low and even. "Fair enough. I won't fight you, Evie. I haven't the stomach for it. Sharpen your claws on me as much as you like."

"That takes all the sport out of it," I said, baring my teeth in a smile. "Now, what you haven't told me is why you didn't just pack the bloody Cross up and bring it to me yourself instead of dragging me out to the desert."

He shrugged. "Things have got quite dangerous out here with the French attempting to exercise an

157

authority that isn't entirely official. The Bedu don't entirely appreciate being told what to do. Besides which, there are bands of renegades left over from the war to contend with, brigands, thieves and opportunists. A person can't go two steps without falling over someone nefarious out here. It complicates retrieving the Cross, you know. It isn't the sort of thing one wants to go around parading in front of thieves and brigands. A fellow could get killed that way."

"You're afraid," I accused.

He opened his mouth then closed it on a smile that did not reach his eyes. "Yes, Evie, if that makes you happy. I'm afraid. I meant to have you in and out of Damascus with the artefact. Now, I don't like the notion of you being here any longer than necessary. I want you to go back to Damascus. If I don't contact you in two days, get right out. Get out and don't look back."

I thought it over. "Is it dangerous for you to retrieve the Cross?"

He rolled his eyes. "It's *complicated*. The French aren't actually supposed to have an official presence out here, but that isn't stopping them. They're sending patrols from Damascus with an eye to taking over some of the old Turkish garrisons. Clashes are growing more frequent and more violent and not just among the people you expect to find out here. When I went to get the Cross, I found a detachment of armed and rather testy French Foreign Legion deserters were camped out where I stashed the bloody thing. It would have been suicide to retrieve it."

"Are they still there now?"

"No, they moved off yesterday in the direction of Palmyra."

"Then why don't we go and get the Cross now?"

He gave a short laugh. "You think it's that simple? It isn't the corner shop, you know. It's a desert oasis half a day's journey from here over extremely rough country. Not to mention, I have to take extreme care not to be followed." He hesitated. "I suspect someone from the dig site might have an inkling that I've found something. I don't know who to trust anymore."

He passed a hand over his face, raking his fingers through the knotted beard. It must have aggravated him to no end. Gabriel had always been fastidious, even on expedition, groomed to perfection under the most trying of circumstances. But Mr. Rowan's character was more slapdash and unkempt. It was not a bad strategy, I reflected. Few people would ever have connected the stooped and cranky Mr. Rowan with the larger-than-life glamour of Gabriel Starke. But it must have been a lonely life, hiding himself from everyone, even his closest companions, I thought. . . .

I started with a sudden realisation. "You don't trust Miss Green. That's why you planned to fetch the Cross when she was in Damascus. But the deserters scuppered your chance and now she's back and you can't go because you won't take the chance she's the villain."

"I might have made a slight miscalculation in taking a post with Green's expedition. We met once, years ago, and I thought she'd never be able to connect the schoolboy named Gabriel Starke with the cantankerous old devil called Rowan. But she might be sharper than I gave her credit for. I think she may have searched my things once. I can't prove it, but she is the likeliest suspect. The rest of the staff were down at the dig."

"I wonder if she was the one who searched mine," I mused.

His gaze sharpened. "What did you say?"

"I wonder if she searched my things, too. Someone went through them today, but nothing was taken. Oh, drat. It can't have been her—she was busy overseeing the excavation of that little find of jewellery."

"Someone is looking for information," he said grimly. "They are looking to tie us together."

"But that isn't possible," I pointed out. "Your identity is perfectly established as Mr. Rowan, and the only time Rowan and I met in public was when Miss Green introduced us. She would have already known that."

"But there is our past history."

"We—Mr. Rowan and I—do not have a past

history," I pointed out. "There was nothing for her or anyone else to find to tie us together."

He said nothing, but his colour had faded to something sickly white.

"Gabriel?"

"The cuttings," he managed. "If anyone found the cuttings, they'd know there was a connection between us."

"What cuttings?"

"Your exploits around the world," he said, his tone cold. "Newspaper photographs of you with your various conquests—the newspaper magnate whose chin you were tickling, you draping yourself over the Bulgarian tsar, that English mechanic that you keep as some sort of pet."

"Wally is not a pet," I returned hotly. "And as for Boris, he was simply my host and the Bulgarians are a surprisingly demonstrative people—" I broke off. "And why on earth would you have cuttings of my travels?"

"I had to keep track of your whereabouts to know where to send the photograph," he said, biting the syllables off sharply. "But it might be enough to prove a connection between us." He swore fluently for several minutes. I waited for the tantrum to pass and hoped it wouldn't take long. The stone floor was decidedly uncomfortable.

Finally, he fixed me with a piercing gaze. "You have to go back to Damascus. Tonight. I'll drive you. I'll make up some story about you taking ill.

No one will believe it, of course, but it will at least get you out of harm's way."

"And you're coming back here?"

"I do have a job, you know," he reminded me. "The character of Oliver Rowan was a damned nuisance to establish. I'd rather not leave him behind."

"If you're going into the desert, anyway—" I began.

He held up a hand in refusal. "Absolutely not. I'm not taking you. It's simply too risky." His manner turned brisk. "If I can manage to get my hands on the Cross after I run you back to Damascus, I will, but that is the most I can promise, and if I were you, I shouldn't count on it. Now, don't look so glum, child. I will give you instructions on precisely how to find the hiding place. Perhaps someday, when all of this is over, you can come for it."

He rose, flicking dust from his trousers, and I stared at him, openmouthed. "That's it? That's all you have to say? You're going to drive me back to the city as if we just had tea at the vicarage and call it a day?"

For a moment something sharp and hot flared in his eyes but he smothered it, giving me a cool look. "I've already explained the dangers, my dear. To both of us. Do you really thirst so much for my blood?" he asked lightly.

I thought of the Cross and all it represented. It

was the holiest relic in Christendom. Men had died gruesome deaths for it, and although it carried a bloodstained legacy, it deserved to be in a museum. I was determined to see it there, even if that meant crawling halfway across the Badiyat ash-Sham and risking my neck to get it.

At least that was what I told myself as I stepped to stand toe-to-toe with him. The real reason to stay with Gabriel in the desert—the only reason—was one I didn't even dare to think about.

"If you didn't want me involved, you shouldn't have sent me the photograph. I am not letting you stay entangled in this life of crime. You must break free of it and grow up, Gabriel. Do the right thing for once in your life." I should have known an appeal to his better nature would get me nowhere. He merely gave me a long, cool, level look and said nothing. I squared my shoulders and adopted a brisker tone. "I don't like to use such tactics, but you're forcing my hand. Either you guide me into the desert to retrieve the Cross, or when you take me back to Damascus, I will wire every major newspaper in the known world *immediately* with the entire story."

"You wouldn't dare." His hands went to my shoulders, gripping hard, and I felt a rush of sheer inexplicable joy. This was the man I had married. The Gabriel Starke I had known was brilliant and mercurial and up for anything. But I hadn't understood how quickly he could change, settling a mask of indifference so swiftly over his features it seemed to be all there was to him. I had learned that lesson the hard way, bitterly and with many tears, and for an instant I was savagely happy to have goaded a reaction from him. I smiled up into his face as his fingers dug into my flesh.

"Careful, darling. Remember, I bruise easily."

Instantly he recovered himself. He removed his hands, thrusting them into his pockets. He was in command of himself, but not fully. His hands were still fisted, but his tone was bored and I realised I had not truly reached him. He was as distant as a star and twice as cold. "My dear child, this seems to be a game to you."

I stood my ground, matching his tone. "Yes, and for extremely high stakes. But you haven't figured out yet that we are on the same side. So let go of my arms and get the keys to Mother Mary. We're going after the Cross whether you like it or not."

EIGHT

Gabriel argued the point for another half an hour. He stopped just short of threatening me outright, and when he saw I wouldn't budge, he tried appealing to my sense of reason by explaining exactly what dangers we might face. In the end, he gave in with extremely bad grace and a great deal of swearing, and I smiled to myself to see his sangfroid slipping so badly. He was finding it more and more difficult to keep up his pose of cool detachment, and every bitten-off curse seemed like a victory.

We agreed that he would go and fetch some water and food from the storeroom while I made my way to Mother Mary. We would drive a little way down the track that led to Damascus, and when the ground was suitably rough to hide the traces, we would turn eastward into the desert.

"You understand we will have to leave it almost immediately?" he warned. "There isn't a vehicle built that can withstand the rigours of the Badiyat ash-Sham proper. We can manage a mile or two before we shall have to leave it and walk into the desert. It will be rough and I can promise you won't enjoy it."

"It is dear of you to be concerned, but I am sure I will manage just fine," I assured him sweetly. He cursed again and stomped off as loudly as he dared to secure the food and water. He returned a little while later looking slightly less grim.

"The night watchman is snoring behind the tents, thank God," he told me. "I'm not at all certain whether I should dock his wages or give him a bonus." We held our breath as we opened the driver's door to Mother Mary. I slid in and he came immediately after, so close behind he nearly crushed me. He gave me an irritable shove and I took the goatskins of water and packets of food from him as he let out the brake. We dared not start the engine, but it had been parked on an incline, and it coasted smoothly away from the camp. As we put distance between ourselves and the site, I looked back. A shadow, small and plump, detached itself from one of the tents and stepped onto the dirt track. It was impossible to be certain, but it looked very like Herr Doktor Schickfuss. I told Gabriel and he shrugged.

"Bugger all I can do about it now," was all he said. He told me he'd left behind the note we discussed, explaining I'd been taken ill and he had decided to drive me to Damascus and would return as soon as possible. "That story wouldn't deceive even a fool like Daoud, but it might buy us a little time before anyone actually comes looking for us. Now, keep a sharp eye out behind while I try to find a place to turn off."

I turned around and sat, watchful and alert, until he turned off the track. We went further than I expected, bumping along rougher and rougher terrain until at last he swung the vehicle behind a boulder and stopped. "This is as far as she goes," he told me. He collected half the food and one of the goatskins, handing me the rest. He rummaged in the glovebox for a moment, emerging with two items—a small medical kit and a torch. "It won't last forever, but we'll be glad of it tonight." He pocketed the items as he got out of the car and beckoned me to follow.

"Hang on a tick," I told him. I lifted the bonnet of the car and reached into the hot engine carefully. I tinkered with the wires a moment, yanking them this way and that.

"What on earth are you doing?" he demanded.

"Disabling Mother Mary. That way, if anyone finds her, they won't be able to use her to follow us," I told him.

He shook his head. "Do you always make things complicated?" He picked up a rock and brought it down with a decisive blow to the fuel tank. Petrol spilled out into the sand as he dusted off his hands. "Let's go."

I trotted after him.

We walked for miles, moving from patchy, scrubby dirt dotted with rocks and shrubs through long barren sandy swathes and back again. There were hills to scramble over, some of them rocky and others deceptively soft, tripping up inattentive feet—and it was cold, far colder than I'd ever realised a desert could be. I thanked heaven for the fact that I'd put on my boots and picked up my warmest jacket before leaving the tent. I'd left behind my toilet articles but nothing of importance. My papers and my pistol were tucked into my pockets, and as we clambered over the hills and through the bushes, I felt a surge of something like excitement. This was a proper adventure, far away from advertisers and formal dinners and bill collectors. It was glorious, and I moved as swiftly as I could over the desert, fairly flying as I followed. Gabriel never once looked back but carried on, relentlessly, ever forward, until at last he paused, lifted his face to the dimming stars and pointed.

"That little outcropping has an overhang that will shield us. We'll rest awhile and then push on."

"If you're stopping on my account, don't. I can keep going," I assured him.

He gave me a cool look. "I wouldn't dream of stopping for you, my dear. There is a track nearby that is heavily travelled by the Bedouin. I want to observe it for a little while in daylight to see if there's anyone about and whether they might be friend or foe. Until I know it's safe to venture out in the open, we'll stay sheltered."

He moved on and I followed into the little outcropping. "Mind the stones," he warned in a casual tone. "Might be snakes bedded down there."

"I know you're still put out that I'm making you do this, but there's no call to be childish. You can't frighten me with talk of snakes. It's the desert, Gabriel. One expects snakes."

"Oh, you're right not to be frightened," he told me in the same breezy manner. "After all, cobra around here hunt at night. They're probably all heading in to rest now. Looking for some lovely sheltered rocks and maybe a nice warm human to cuddle up to."

"Never mind the snakes. I suspect the most poisonous creature around here is you."

"Me? I'm cut you would think so, cut to the bone," he said in mock horror.

"Jest all you want, but I know this mood, Gabriel. You've been forced into something you didn't want and you're sulking. Petulance was never a good colour on you and the years have done nothing to improve you."

He took a long pull off his goatskin of water and said nothing. I did the same and looked to the pale pearl-grey streaks of dawn just rising at the eastern edge of the desert.

It seemed as good a time as any to try to get some answers. "I don't suppose you'd like to tell me what you were really doing out here when you found the Cross? Or why you faked your death?"

"I need my beauty sleep," he said. And he folded his arms over his chest and closed his eyes.

"Fine. But this conversation is far from over, Gabriel. Sometime you're going to have to tell me what you've been up to. I deserve more than the Cross, you know. I deserve the truth, too."

He said nothing. He gave a gentle snore, and since he might well have been faking, I gave him several minutes to fall properly asleep. When his face had relaxed and his arms dropped to his sides, I eased my bootlace free and slipped it through the loop of his trousers. It took deftness and patience, but I worked slowly and at last had it hitched through. I tied the other end around my wrist and made myself as comfortable as possible. Pearly light was spreading across the desert sky, casting long shadows and warming the sand. Somewhere in the distance I heard the cry of a hawk as it rose on the sharp edge of the cold morning breeze to hunt. And I slept.

I woke with a jerk when Gabriel tried to get up.

"What the f—"

"Language, Gabriel," I said absently.

He plucked at the bootlace. "What is this?"

"Insurance," I said, yawning and stretching. "I didn't absolutely trust you not to leave while I slept."

"Don't give me ideas," he returned coolly. We both drank from our goatskins and Gabriel produced a handful of dried apricots. "Eat."

I chewed one and pulled a face at the pliant, supple warmth of it.

"What's the matter with it?" he demanded.

"I don't much care for flaccid food."

He laughed, a proper belly laugh, and while he was regarding me with delight he nearly choked on his own apricot. "Christ, I have missed you."

Before I could respond, he hauled me to my feet and yanked the bootlace free. "Let's go have a look at that track," he said, stuffing another apricot into my mouth with his filthy fingers. I followed him slowly, picking my way along until I reached his side.

He was crouched along the edge of the track, and as I knelt he pointed to a set of blurry prints in the sandy soil. "These were made by a small raiding party of Bedu."

"How can you tell?"

"A caravan would be larger and have camels in train. These are all on horseback and riding fast. Luckily they're southbound. We can follow the track north a little while and make better time than if we kept scrambling over the rough bits. Come on then."

He set off at a quick jog and I fell into step behind him. As with our travels of the previous night, he never looked back. But I caught him stealing sidelong glances and realised he was checking the position of my shadow as we moved. We stopped occasionally for water and a handful of nuts and for Gabriel to gauge our position with nothing more than the angle of the sun to help him.

"Time to cut east again," he told me, and we struck off the track for the wasteland somewhere between Damascus and Palmyra. We might have been anywhere in those hundreds of miles, and suddenly I felt quite small. I don't know if I stiffened or made a noise, but Gabriel stopped abruptly. "What's wrong?"

"It just occurred to me how vast it all is. It's like flying. Just you—a tiny speck in an infinitely larger emptiness."

He paused a moment. "And both can be deadly.

Mind you keep up." He set off again, this time at a punishing pace. We trotted, for hours it seemed, and much later, when my bones had begun to ache and my muscles were shrieking in protest, we came to an oasis, a very small one, with a well and a small fringe of palm trees. To my horror, Gabriel strode right past it.

"We aren't stopping?"

"No. It's a *bir*, the village well. Too busy."

"Gabriel, there isn't a soul around."

"Now there isn't. In another hour, there could be two dozen women there taking on water."

"And we can't stop, not even for a minute?"

He whirled on me, his expression wholly indifferent. "This was your idea. Either keep up or stay behind. But if you stay, I suggest shooting yourself with that absurd little toy you carry. It's nicer than dying of thirst or snakebite or brigands."

He turned sharply and walked on. I followed meekly. He was right, of course. He had warned me the trip would be hard, but I had insisted and I had only myself to blame. He moved quickly, but I kept up, grateful that flying demanded the highest level of fitness. I had worked hard to develop the stamina I needed to control the *Jolly Roger*, and as we trekked through the desert, I called on every bit of it. The day was hot and the sun was almost as merciless as Gabriel. We stopped more often for water, and I ate the dried fruit he handed me without complaint although it was unpleasantly warm and fleshy, with pulpy bits that stuck to my teeth as I chewed.

At last the sun began to sink below the horizon, leaving long bloodred streaks behind as if the sky itself had been lashed with a whip. A freshening breeze sprang up and with it came a low, mournful sound echoing over the desert.

"Jackals," he told me, and I nodded, too tired to speak. The desert itself began to sing then, a long, low sound so mournful it made my heart rise in my throat. It creaked and sighed like the sea, empty but not silent, and as we walked, it seemed that the desert itself watched us.

Soon after, he stopped us to rest again. We were both too tired to talk, and after we had drunk our fill and each eaten a handful of nuts, he motioned for me to try to sleep. I hesitated, and he cursed, unbuckling his belt and lashing the end of it to my wrist. He tugged at the buckle to show me that it would not pass through the loops.

"I can't get free without cutting the loops with a knife, and you'd be awake long before I could manage it. Happy? Now go to sleep. I'm not leaving you," he said, his voice cold and distant. But I felt oddly comforted, and before I could reply, I slept.

Some time later he shook me awake, his hand bruising on my shoulder. He made me drink again then pushed me to my feet. We walked on, and I saw the stars were out, glittering overhead with a cold and distant light. He navigated swiftly by them, quickening the pace as we drew near. At last we reached an oasis—or at least the remains of one. The pool of water that must have once nourished the earth had dried, and without it, the palms had withered and died. The bricks at the edge of the abandoned well were crumbling to dust. The cover had long since blown away, and from the depths of the well I could smell the rotting stink of some animal that had wandered too close and fallen in.

I could not imagine where in this nasty little wasteland Gabriel could have found to hide the Cross, but before I could ask, he dropped his goatskin and began to strip off his shirt and boots.

"What are you doing?" I demanded.

"Preparing to climb into the well, child, what does it look like?"

I glanced around. "Where is your rope?"

"I do not require a rope," he said with a scornful glance. Off came his socks then, and he was bare save for his trousers, which he rolled to the knee. Even though it had been five years, I was interested to see he was fit as ever, sleek muscles stretching from his wide shoulders to a pair of hips as narrow as a girl's. But when I looked closer I could see a few fresh scars acquired on his travels.

He drew a sizeable knife from his pocket and clamped it between his teeth, looking for all the world like a pirate prince. He swung himself onto the crumbling course of bricks on the top of the well. Several wobbled and fell as he touched them and I swallowed hard. He motioned for me to shine the torch down into the well and I took it, grateful for something to do. The shadows around the oasis moved and shifted in the darkness, and more than once I fancied I heard sounds like the rustling of old ghosts. I had heard of the *jinns* that were supposed to haunt such places, demons and malevolent spirits that stalked the unwary traveller. Such tales were easy to laugh away in the city, but there, as the darkness pressed against us from every direction, it was not difficult to believe.

I shivered a little as I held the torch high for Gabriel.

He took the knife out of his teeth long enough to bark at me, "Don't shine that bloody thing in my eyes, woman," then put it back in and began to clamber down into the well. He wedged his fingers and toes into the cracks between the bricks, the mortar long since worn away. It was dangerous, bloody work, and more than once he slipped when a brick crumbled under him and he had to catch himself one-handed. He grumbled and complained all the while, sending up a steady stream of irritation muffled by the knife in his mouth, but all directed at me, I had no doubt.

At last, when he was halfway down the well, he

stopped. Hanging by one arm, his legs braced far apart by thigh muscles that had gone rigid with the effort, he plunged the knife into the remaining mortar and began to scrape. In a few minutes it was over. He was climbing back up with a bundle hanging over his back. He reached the top in a lather of sweat and bloody hands and feet and took the goatskin I handed him. He tipped his head back and swallowed for whole minutes, taking in the last of his water. When he'd finished, he used his knife to slice open the empty goatskin then put it aside. He took the bundle off his back carefully, reverently even, and unwrapped all but the last layer of cloth. It had been tied into lengths of soft leather, now covered in mould and dirt, but he left these behind, keeping only a single wrapping of decaying velvet as he pushed it into the goatskin that had held his water. He fished in his pockets for the little medical kit he'd retrieved from Mother Mary, and by the light of the torch stitched it closed with a large needle and a length of catgut. When he'd finished, it looked like any other goatskin carried by a desert traveller.

"I can't believe you didn't let me see it," I told him as he packed up his medical supplies. It was typical of him that he attended to the Cross with such care and entirely neglected his own scrapes and bruises.

"You'll have the rest of your life to stare at it."

He pulled his shirt and boots back on and hefted the goatskin with the cross. "Now, we're going to find someplace to rest, and hopefully get clean because I am forty days beyond filthy and I can't bear the stench of myself, and then we're getting you back to Damascus, *inshallah*."

Suddenly, the shadows at the edge of the oasis shifted again, materialising into a group of people. They flicked on their torches, shining them directly into our eyes.

"Mr. and Mrs. Starke, you will please oblige us by turning over what you have just retrieved from that well," said a cultured voice.

Gabriel sighed loudly. "You made good time, Thurzó. Better than I would have expected."

Squinting, I swung my own torch around and was just able to make out the Thurzós and a small band of native fellows draped in the usual striped robes and headdresses. Countess Thurzó looked a trifle less tidy than usual and her brother's hair was wildly askew, but it was the pistol in his hand that caught my attention.

He smiled at Gabriel. "We were lucky enough to find a cordial group of desert gentlemen willing to rent us their horses," he said, and I could just hear the jingle of harnesses from some distance off. They'd been lucky. We had been walking upwind of them, which had kept the sound and smell of the horses at bay.

He gestured to the pouch with his pistol. "I

must repeat my request, Mr. Starke. I will have the Cross, please."

"The Cross!" I whipped my head around to Gabriel. "I thought you hadn't told anyone."

"I hadn't," he said with an unpleasant smile. "But I would lay a fiver I know who did."

At that moment one of the native fellows moved into the light a little and I saw it was Daoud, Miss Green's simple manservant.

I looked at Gabriel and he shrugged. "I suspected I was followed one day, but I never caught sight of who it was." He flicked a cold glance at Daoud. "I gather you followed me and decided to see what was in the well after I left?"

Daoud merely gave a blank grin and shrugged, but Countess Thurzó stepped forward. "He is not so stupid as you think. He saw a good business opportunity when it presented itself."

Gabriel rolled his eyes. "Why the devil didn't he just take it then and save us all a great deal of bother?"

She shrugged. "It takes time to arrange for a buyer for such an object, as you yourself no doubt discovered."

He gave another bored sigh. "All right, then. You've bested us. Nothing to do but take our medicine and swallow it." He hefted the goatskin bag carefully and tossed it with a light underhanded throw to Count Thurzó. The fellow caught it neatly and felt the shape of the Cross through the bag. He gave a nod to his sister and she turned back to us, peering at Gabriel with her torch trained closely on his face as she scrutinised the differences in his face without his lenses and various pads and mouthpieces.

"Your disguise was most effective, Mr. Starke. It was only when I searched Mrs. Starke's things and yours that I began to suspect who you really were. It seems obvious now that you concealed your identity all the while in order to keep this find for yourself."

Gabriel shrugged indifferently. "A fellow has to earn a living, you know. And digging in these bloody rocks gets old after a few decades. Thought I'd make a few bob when I found that, but you've found me out. Nothing for it but to take my punishment and let you haul us back to Damascus to the authorities."

Countess Thurzó started to speak but her brother stepped forward and murmured something in Hungarian. They quarrelled briefly, and Countess Thurzó gestured emphatically. But whatever the trouble, her brother clearly carried the day. The countess turned on her heel without another word and strode into the darkness in the direction of their horses.

Count Thurzó sighed and turned to us. Gabriel's expression did not falter. He was playing the hail-fellow-well-met, but the count was having none of it. "It is very nice that you are gracious in defeat, Mr. Starke, but that does not alter the fact that you cannot be allowed to live."

My heart lurched against my ribs and I heard an odd ringing in my ears from far away. Gabriel's perfect imitation of the outraged, overly civilised Englishman never slipped.

"I say, that's unsporting. Just unsporting is what I call it. And to think we didn't bother to shoot you when we could have—" He broke off with a sudden startled glance towards me, his expression panicked, but Count Thurzó seized upon what he had almost said and smiled. He came to me and patted my pockets, giving a little sound of satisfaction when he emerged with my tiny pistol.

Gabriel spoke up, his voice rising almost hysterically. "You can't force her to use that on me. You *mustn't*." Count Thurzó looked at Gabriel's pleading face, then to me, his eyes strangely bright as he held out the pistol. His expression was apologetic but his gaze was implacable.

I stared at the pistol glittering on his palm. "I don't—"

"Take it, madame. And shoot him. Or I will." His voice shook with excitement, and I realised then he was new to violence. If he and his sister had been hardened criminals they would have plotted this out in advance, but they hadn't—the argument bore testimony to that. And now that Gabriel had blurted out his idiotic fear that they would make me shoot him, the count had seized upon this as an extremely elegant solution to the problem of what to do with him. If they shot Gabriel, they might be held for murder. But if I did it, their hands were clean. If the authorities ever became involved, it would be their word against mine, and they could always devise a plausible motive for me to have shot Gabriel. They could claim he had abducted and insulted me, that we had been conspirators to take the Cross and had quarrelled, that I had simply gone mad. The possibilities were legion.

The count's eyes were searching as he looked at me. I glanced at Gabriel and he said nothing. His only gesture was an almost imperceptible flicker of one eyelid. If I hadn't been looking for it, I would have missed it altogether. I looked up to see the count was looking grimly determined and behind him his henchmen stood, immovable as the hills themselves, while Daoud smiled his meaningless smile.

I reached out and took the pistol.

"You are a resourceful man, Count Thurzó," I told him.

"One learns survival of necessity when one has lost a war," he reminded me as he relieved me of my torch. "Now, please get on with it." He stepped back sharply and kept his pistol raised, protecting himself in case I should change my mind.

"I have a fully loaded weapon and I am an

excellent shot," he told me. "You might wound me, if you are very lucky, but you will not kill me, and I promise you my revenge would not be pleasant."

I shuddered and turned back to Gabriel. I lifted the pistol and looked into his eyes. He dropped his eyes, and I was grateful. It would be easier without him staring at me. I lowered my gaze to the pocket of his shirt, a small square of khaki directly over his heart. I stared at it until everything else swam out of focus and there was nothing but that patch of fabric and nothing else in the world.

And then I pulled the trigger.

NINE

Gabriel collapsed facedown onto the ground. He gave a single shudder and lay still, so perfectly, impossibly still that the count's relief was palpable. "Congratulations, Mrs. Starke," he said. "You have the nerve of a Hungarian. It takes real courage to shoot a man when you can see his face."

"Go to hell," I told him.

He clucked his tongue at me. "That is not nice. Now, I would offer to bring you with us, but I see no need to burden myself with witnesses. You can make your way out of the desert as best as you can. Without water and horses, I think you will not get far. In fact, I would put your chances at no better than one in a thousand. But you might surprise me. You already have."

He started to go then turned back. "I leave you your torch and the pistol in case you find it necessary to take matters into your own hands when the thirst gets to be too much to bear. My friends are heavily armed, so I would not suggest you try to delay us on our departure. Goodbye, Mrs. Starke."

He turned on his heel and left with his companions.

I waited until I heard the jingle of their horses' harnesses fade into the distance before I turned to where Gabriel lay in the dirt. I knelt beside him and rolled him over, not an easy task as he was entirely dead weight. His eyes were rolled back into his head, and for the second time in a week I pulled back my arm and slapped him hard.

He came to, coughing as if he would bring up a lung, and when he could speak, he pointed a shaking finger at me and called me a vile name.

"Yes, well I just bloody well saved your life, so I think you might be more inclined to thank me than insult me."

He wheezed and coughed for several minutes more while I hunted through his pockets. In the past he had always carried a flask of whisky and I was relieved to see old habits died hard with him.

I waved it under his nose and he sat up, cursing, to take a long pull. When he finished, he looked marginally better.

He reached into his pocket, the very pocket where I had shot him, and pulled out the small tobacco tin. Embedded in the lid was the flattened slug from the pistol.

"Well, at least you understood the signal I gave you when I looked down at my shirt. Thank Christ you don't own a proper gun or I would have been dead for sure."

"You silly ass. You took a terrible chance letting me do that," I told him. My hands were shaking as I took the flask from him and drank deeply.

He held up a hand, his tone gentle. "Don't scold, Evie. It was our best hope." He got to his feet, wincing a little.

"Does it hurt?" I asked him.

"Like hellfire and I'm going to have a bruise akin to a mule kick."

"Then you ought to rest," I told him, pushing him back.

He swayed but kept his feet. "We have to get out of here. I don't trust them not to come back."

I rolled my eyes, but there was no arguing with him in that mood. I picked up the goatskins of water and the packets of food and started off in the direction the Thurzós had taken.

Gabriel's sharp voice stopped me. "You can't go that way."

"Why ever not? It's the way to Damascus, isn't it?"

"Yes," he said, his tone exaggeratedly patient. "And that's where the Thurzós are most likely headed. I'd rather not be headed the same direction, if it's all the same to you."

"Don't you want to get the Cross back?"

"Evie, what I want now is a hot meal and a hotter bath. The Cross is gone, and that's unfortunate, but there's nothing we can do about it now."

"Nothing we can do about it?" My voice rose, incredulous. "We can go after it. There are only half a dozen of them and from what I saw, the Thurzós don't much care to get their hands dirty."

His jaw went slack as he listened. "You're mad, do you know that? I thought people who flew aeroplanes understood about calculated risks."

I flapped a hand. "If we only took calculated risks no one would ever have had the nerve to get into one of the damned things in the first place. When you took that Cross from its hiding place, you took responsibility for it. And now that it's fallen into nefarious hands, it's your obligation to retrieve it. What's the matter, Gabriel?" I taunted. "Lost your nerve?"

He stepped close to me, so close I could see the dirt ground into his face, the brilliance of the blue irises in whites that were heavily shot with red. He was exhausted and battered and I had just shot him. It occurred to me I might have been a little more sympathetic, but I refused to back down. I stood toe-to-toe with him, lifting my chin and giving him a long, cool stare.

After a moment, he eased away, giving a wheezy laugh. "Oh, you nearly had me. Not a bad strategy to bait me into doing what you want. A few years ago, I'd have fallen for that. But not anymore. I don't give a sweet bloody damn about your approval, Evie. You can think I'm a coward or that I've lost my nerve—embroider it on a cushion to sleep with at night. But I'm not going after the Cross. I am getting you safely out of here and washing my hands of the whole affair. And you can argue all you like, but you're doing things my way or, so help me God, I will truss you like a turkey and carry you over my shoulder all the way to Palmyra."

I blinked. "Palmyra?"

The very mention of the broken-pillared ruin of Queen Zenobia's desert city was enough to set the pulses racing. Nestled in the heart of the desert, the tumbled stones of the once-fabled city lay amid the sands, sad relics of what had once been the most vibrant and elegant city between Mesopotamia and the sea. It had controlled the silk route from India from its colonnaded streets, and over it all stood the great temple of Ba'al, where the stars were charted and now only the whispers of the *jinn* broke the silence of the sands.

"Stop it," Gabriel ordered.

"Stop what?"

"Romanticising the place. It's a load of bloody great rocks in the middle of the desert. The only reason I'm heading there is because it's precisely the opposite direction from Damascus."

I rolled my eyes. "And I suppose archaeology is all about broken pots and desiccated mummies for you? I've seen you light up like a little boy at Christmas when you see a particularly nice temple, Gabriel. There are a dozen other places that would serve just as well. You're choosing Palmyra because you're as smitten with it as you are with Saladin and Petra and the Dome of the Rock and everything else in this part of the world," I finished, spreading my arms to encompass the barren landscape before us.

"Don't take this amiss, duck, but I'm hungry and thirsty and you just shot me. Quarrelling seems a bit of a waste of effort. Now, I'm going that way," he said, nodding towards the north and east. "You're welcome to join me. If not, have a nice life and mind the scorpions."

He strode off with a jaunty stride, and I muttered one of his favourite swear words under my breath as I followed.

When I reached his side, he paused and gave me a penetrating look. "How much did you enjoy pulling that trigger at me?"

I thought a moment. "Less than I expected but more than I should have."

He nodded. "That sounds about right."

Shortly after we left the oasis, Gabriel turned and made for a line of low hills perhaps a quarter of a mile distant. We had gone half the way when he whirled around. Behind us, a lone figure sat on horseback on a ridge, silhouetted by starlight. Horse and rider were motionless, but the rider seemed to be watching us. A low cloud obscured the figure a little, and it was impossible to see more.

"Gabriel?"

"I don't know who it is, but I don't like it. A friendly Bedouin would have made his presence known. He wouldn't just sit there watching. Keep making for the hills," he said, giving my bottom a shove. I didn't even bother to slap him for it. I doubled my pace, and we pressed on. Gabriel turned every hundred steps or so to look behind, squinting into the shadows thrown by the starlight. Finally, when we had almost gained the hills, the night breeze gusted a little, blowing the cloud from the ridge. As the cloud lifted, the lopsided moon rose, silvering the desert landscape and illuminating the figure on horseback.

I sucked in my breath and Gabriel reached for my pistol. He fired once into the air. The horse was well-trained. It did not move, but the figure on its back did. It raised a hand in a gesture of goodwill and bowed from the waist. We hurried forward into the hills, but still he sat, sinister and silent.

And as we scrambled over rocks and thornbushes, I wondered how on earth Herr Doktor Schickfuss had found us.

After twisting our way through the hills for what seemed like hours, Gabriel eventually settled on a quiet little cave tucked so far into the earth even a fox would have had trouble finding it. He shoved me far into its depths, and we collapsed onto the dirt floor.

"How did he find us?"

"Bugger me if I know," he said, wiping the sweat from his brow. "But at least he knows we're armed and he won't dare these canyons on horseback in the dark. We'll be safe until morning."

"Why don't you have your own gun? It seems that someone in your business ought to carry some sort of protection."

"A gun is simply an invitation for another fellow to shoot you," he said sleepily. "Besides, you don't know what my business is. Who says it's dangerous?"

"Gabriel—" I began.

He held up a hand that was covered in dirt and blood and deep scratches. "I can't, Evie. Just let me rest now. You're welcome to abuse me later."

He held up the end of his belt with a cynical smile and I grasped it, too tired to buckle it properly.

I was too restless to sleep, and I kept reliving the moment when I had pulled the trigger. It might so easily have gone wrong. I might have missed or the tin box might not have been strong enough to stop the bullet. I could so easily have killed him but that didn't seem to trouble him at all, and I began to worry if he had something of a death wish.

"Gabriel?"

He was slow to answer, but I knew he had not been asleep. "Hmm?"

"Do you want to die?"

"Perhaps," he said with a mocking light in his eyes. "After all, 'to die would be an awfully big adventure.'"

"Stop quoting *Peter Pan* and answer the question," I told him irritably.

He gave a low laugh. "I won't. It's absurd."

"It isn't, not really. You did let me shoot you," I reminded him.

"To avoid being shot by András Thurzó," he returned. "I saw his gun and yours and chose the better odds. Nothing more."

"And you talked in Damascus about making amends. Atonement, I think you said. Those are words men use when they're thinking they won't be around much longer."

"Planning my next funeral, love?" His tone was amused. "Might be easier for you this time with an actual body to bury."

I turned away from him, coldly furious. "How very like you to make a joke about one of the most wretched days of my entire life."

He said nothing, and the silence fell heavily between us.

"I shouldn't have said it was like you to make a joke," I told him. "I've come to understand that I don't know what's like you and what isn't. I thought I did once—when I married you. At least before you changed. Or perhaps you didn't change. Perhaps that cold stranger I found myself married to in China was the real Gabriel Starke all along."

"Perhaps the façade is what you married," he said quietly.

"I think it must have been. But he was a hell of a façade. He was everything a girl dreams of, but I daresay you know that if you created him. You didn't miss a trick, did you? You thought of every detail—the beautiful clothes and the elegant manners, the fast car and the penchant for poetry."

"Ah, yes," he said in the same soft tone. "Which one did I use on you that first evening we met? Now I remember. Donne, wasn't it? 'License my roving hands, and let them go . . . before, behind, between, above, below.' I must say, I never expected you to take me so literally. Your enthusiasm was most gratifying."

Something in my face stopped him. He didn't say another word on the subject but swore viciously under his breath as I turned away from him and curled up, miserable as I hadn't been for a very long time. I slept, and when I slept, I dreamed he had left with the Cross and I was left alone with a grinning pile of bones in the corner of the cave. The bones rose up and came together to form Herr Doktor Schickfuss and he smiled as he came near me, holding out the long bones of his fingers to touch me.

"Evie, for God's sake, wake up." Gabriel shoved me hard and I woke to find him looming over me, buckling his belt back into place.

I scrambled to my feet. "Bad dream," I told him, a trifle unnecessarily. "What do you think Herr Doktor is after? Could he know about the Cross?"

He shrugged. "Hell if I know. There's no telling how many people Daoud took into his confidence. But we must try to slip out of here without him seeing us. I know a track out of these hills that's as obscure as you can get, and with any luck we'll run across some friendly Bedu who can help get us to Palmyra."

"With any luck? Gabriel, has that been your plan all along? I thought you were some sort of criminal mastermind and that leaving the car in the desert was part of some grand strategy, but it appears you've been making it all up as you go along."

He rolled his eyes heavenward and dropped his hands. "There isn't a manual for this sort of thing, you know. You assess the situation and follow your gut and do your best. And sometimes luck plays a bloody great hand in it all. So, yes, I am very much making it up as I go along, and right now, we are going to eat something and get the hell out of these hills in case Herr Doktor or the Thurzós are lying in wait outside preparing to put a bullet in my brain."

He snapped his mouth shut, but not before I realised what he had said. "The Thurzós? Why should they come back? They have what they want." His gaze drifted, so I leaned into his line of vision. "Gabriel? They have what they want, don't they?"

"Not entirely."

I felt a chill whisper in my blood. "What did you do?"

He hesitated then leaned over to the dirt floor of the cave, sketching quickly with a finger. "This is the basic structure of the Cross after it was reset by the monks. It's gold, set with some precious stones—cabochon, of course. It was fashioned before jewellers learned to cut proper facets."

He pointed out the location of the main jewels with his fingertip and I groaned.

"You've taken the jewels."

"Not the jewels," he said quickly.

"What then? The Cross is only valuable because of the jewels and the—" I gave a little shriek of horror. "You didn't! Oh, Gabriel, how could you?"

"The crystal heart holding the wood from the Holy Cross is the most valuable part of the thing," he protested. "When I found the Cross I couldn't very well leave it where it was, but I couldn't come into the camp with a stinking great bit of gold, either. You've seen the camp—it's as busy as Victoria Station and there are few secrets. The best I could do was separate the two parts and stash the gold in the well at the dry oasis."

"What did you do with the crystal?"

"Put it in a safe place," he assured me. "It is still a tremendous find."

"But not nearly as significant as it would be with the gold of the original Cross of Acre surrounding it."

His eyes narrowed. "I know what you're thinking. The answer is no."

"Gabriel, I realise the crystal centrepiece is a find, possibly a significant one, but in order to be truly meaningful, it must be reunited with the Cross. They are two halves of the same coin."

"Evie—"

I knew he wanted me to let him off the hook, to say I understood it was too dangerous, to give it all up and go back to Damascus and leave the adventure when it had only just begun. And something within me rebelled at the thought of surrendering, of letting go of what we had started. But even more than that, I knew if I let him go now, he would never buckle down and see anything through in his life. It was time, once and for all, for him to seize the chance to do the right thing and give up his adolescent ideas.

I fixed him with a scathing look. "We cannot give up on it, particularly now that the Thurzós have it. They'll sell it to a private collector and it will disappear. No one will dare exhibit it outright, and that piece of history will be lost. It belongs in a museum and honestly, I don't see why you're making such a fuss about going after it."

He spluttered in disbelief. "A fuss? Have you forgot they made you shoot me?"

I flapped a hand. "It all turned out fine. You weren't actually hurt, after all."

He gave me a wounded look. "It is bruising spectacularly, I'll have you know. And they won't be half so cordial the next time, I promise you."

"Ah, but the next time will be on our terms," I assured him. "Just wait and see."

Once more we argued at length, and once more Gabriel gave in with bad grace and a good deal of very fluent profanity. He shoved some food and water at me, and we ate and drank a sparse meal before we gathered up our things. He had roughed a map of the desert onto the cave floor and we discussed the best route for intercepting the Thurzós. We had assumed they would head straight for Damascus, but I raised the point they might just as easily be making for Baghdad to the east.

"But Baghdad means crossing into British Mesopotamia, and I'm not sure they'd want their presence noted at the border," he mused. "If they were smart, they would indeed head straight for Damascus as we'd anticipated and then out again as quickly as possible."

"Wouldn't they want to stay in Damascus to find a buyer?" I questioned.

"Not with you still on the loose." He smiled thinly. "They would have to hedge their bets that you might just possibly survive to make your own way to Damascus. Far safer for them to head to Beirut and then Europe and get rid of the Cross there, most likely to an unscrupulous private buyer."

"Would they know how to find one?"

He shrugged. "Probably. The countess mentioned the complexities of securing a buyer, but it's rather easy for an archaeologist to find a collector who is avaricious without being terribly concerned with provenance. They won't get as much for it, of course, as if they'd been able to put it up at auction and let the great museums fight it out at the bidding, but it would still be enough to make it worth their while—if they get out of the desert alive."

I blinked at him. "What are you talking about?"

"I didn't much like the look of their friends. Daoud's nothing to write home about, but the others with them were from the south, renegade Bedouins who have been cast out of their own tribes for any variety of offences. They've got damned little to lose, and the Thurzós aren't exactly hardened criminals. A bit of mutiny in the ranks wouldn't surprise me at all."

"Do you think this is the first time they've turned their hand to serious crime?"

"I should say so. Oh, I've no doubt they did a few unsavoury things in the war—most of us did. But they made several crucial mistakes for real criminals."

"You ought to know," I muttered. He carried on as if I hadn't spoken.

"They didn't inspect the Cross when they took it. They didn't make sure you'd killed me. They didn't even take your water away from you to ensure you'd die of thirst. Mark my words, this won't end well for them unless they have bloody good beginners' luck. They're soft, and softness is a liability in this sort of game. If one intends to have any success as a criminal, one must harden oneself up. I don't approve of bloodshed, but those two will have to learn to like it if they mean to make anything of themselves as villains."

He left me to meditate on that while he packed up our meagre gear. I slung my goatskin on my back and followed him out the mouth of the cave.

The first shot at us went wide, chipping stone off the edge of the rock. Before the echoes had even died away, I was flung to the ground with Gabriel on top of me. A sharp pain throbbed in my back, and Gabriel's dead weight did nothing to improve it.

I shoved hard at his shoulder. "Gabriel, are you hit?"

He lifted his head, shaking it slowly. "No. Now lie still." He lifted himself onto his forearms, his face inches from mine, his blue eyes bright even in the dim light of the cave. He turned his head sharply and tossed a rock out the cave. Immediately a pair of shots answered, and he turned back to me.

"Bloody buggering bollocking hell," he muttered. He levered himself up and put out his hand. I reached for it and fell back, wincing. "Evie? What's wrong?" He did not wait for a reply. He reached down and flipped me onto my stomach, yanking my shirt free from my trousers to bare my back.

"Thank Christ," he said. "It's just a bruise. You landed on a rock." He released me and I stuffed my shirttail back into my trousers.

"How you manage to make that sound like my fault when you're the one who threw me onto the ground—" I began.

"For God's sake, not *now*," he ordered. "Get out your pistol and get to the back of the cave. You might like the option of using one of those last bullets on yourself if things go awry."

"Oh, don't be so grim, Gabriel. There has to be something we can do."

"In case you missed the point, we have a villain out there ready and willing to make us very permanently dead. We have one small pistol of extremely dubious use."

"It's maddening when you insist upon seeing the worst in a situation."

"What exactly do you suggest we do?"

I shrugged. "You're the criminal genius. I leave it to you to think of something. In the meantime, I'm going to finish the dried apricots. I rather like them, after all."

I sat on the floor of the cave and took the remaining apricots out of my pocket, lining them up on my leg. I ate them slowly, savouring each one. He finally threw up his hands and settled in next to me.

"I presume you have formulated a plan?" I asked pleasantly.

He sighed and reached for an apricot. "It isn't much. But I think I ought to give myself up. If you keep very quiet and hide here, they might not realise we're still together. I can try to engage them."

"Oh, you are an ass. That's a daft plan. First, of course they know we're together. If it is Herr Doktor, he saw us come into these hills together. You might persuade him I've done a runner for about two minutes but that won't do either of us much good. And they'll simply shoot you and take me, so I don't know what you think that will accomplish. And if it's the Thurzós, they don't yet know you're still alive."

"It would be a nasty surprise," he said mildly. "But I prefer the tactic of evasion."

"How, exactly?"

"I will keep an eye on the front, you go inspect those webby, dark corners of the cave and see if you can find a back way out."

"That plan does not much appeal to me," I assured him. "I don't like spiders and I'm even less enthusiastic about bats."

He gave a bored shrug. "You may change your mind when the water's run out. You realise they don't have to come up here. They only have to wait us out."

"Then we wait," I said grimly. "Something will happen, I'm sure of it."

And so we waited. It was hours, but nothing happened apart from a few stray shots being fired at the mouth of the cave. I didn't know if they did it to frighten us or to annoy us, but Gabriel retaliated by singing a selection of truly filthy songs in a variety of languages at the top of his voice.

"For a man with such a keen appreciation of music, you are truly tone-deaf to your own talents," I told him.

He shrugged. "It's not meant to be pretty. It's meant to show them I'm not cowed." He grinned again, and I stared at him.

"I can't make you out at all," I told him finally. "I thought I understood you when I married you, but I was wrong. And now I find I know you even less."

He gave a light laugh. "Good God, Evie, you didn't even know my middle name when we married. I don't think two people have ever rushed into matrimony so swiftly or on such a flimsy basis as we did."

"I think we had reason enough, at least I did then," I said in a still, small voice.

"I suppose an appreciation of Elgar and some rather heated kissing is enough," he answered with a shrug. "Certainly enough for marriage these days with everyone and their little dog getting hitched and unhitched in the blink of an eye."

"It wasn't like that," I told him. "We married each other because we were in love, *desperately* in love."

His eyes were cool and a tiny smile played about his lips.

"Were we?"

"Yes, we were, damn you! I loved you, and you loved me, too, or at least I thought you did. You made me believe it and even when we went to China and you changed and turned so cold and distant and pushed me away, I loved you then, too."

He rose slowly, and his expression was carefully neutral, giving nothing away.

"I know I hurt you terribly, Evie. It was never my intention."

"Of course it wasn't your intention," I thundered at him as I rose to stand toe-to-toe. "If it had been your intention it would have made you a monster. But it doesn't alter the fact that you *did* hurt me. I've pretended for years that it didn't matter, that because I was the first one to say the word *divorce* I could keep my pride and tell myself I left you. But we know the truth, don't we, Gabriel? We both know if you'd given me the slightest indication that you still loved me—a word, a glance, *anything*—I'd have come crawling back to you, on my knees, over broken glass if you asked it. But you never did. And I may like to believe I'm a bigger person, that I could forgive you, but I'm not sure I ever did, not because you left me but because you took him away, too."

"Him?"

"The man I fell in love with. I didn't much care when *you* left," I raged. "You were so strange and cold by then it was a relief to be done with you. But you wrecked my memories of that dashing, impossibly wonderful boy I fell in love with when you went. You might have at least left me that."

He swallowed hard, and when he spoke, his voice was flat and calm. "I had no idea."

"Yes, well, why should you?" I demanded. "It isn't the sort of thing a man would think about, but that's how a woman feels. I wondered for the longest time if I were half-mad, did you know that? I wondered if somehow I had made him up,

202

the Gabriel Starke I married. But I didn't. I married a *sterling* man and somehow I woke up a month later with a stranger I didn't recognise. I don't know why or how you changed, and it doesn't matter anymore. It cannot matter. But you were wrong to take him from me, and I wanted you to know that."

He handed me a handkerchief and I wiped my eyes and blew my nose.

I moved to hand the handkerchief back and he waved me off with a single elegant gesture. He had drawn himself up, his chin high, his expression inscrutable.

"There are too many sins on my account to number," he said softly, "but I think that must be the most terrible."

I said nothing and he cleared his throat, adopting his post of cool detachment again. "Now we know where we stand with one another, I am confident it won't trouble you too much if something should go amiss with me. It's almost dark and the shifting light will make it quite difficult for a marksman to hit us. I will go and have a squint outside and see how things stand. You really ought to have a look 'round the back for an exit. If we can creep out that way it will simplify matters immensely."

I nodded mutely, all the fight suddenly extinguished. I felt lighter, suddenly, as if a burden I'd been carrying for years had been plucked off my shoulders. It had been awful to tell him those things; jaggy, prickly, thorny things I had said in the hopes of hurting him. But it was heavenly to speak my mind. No matter what happened now, I had held him to account for what he had done, and the exchange left us both a little shaken. He was quiet when he gave me a few matches from his little tin box and turned away. I did not look at him as he made his way to the front of the cave. I struck one of the matches and groped my way to the back, feeling each crevice and niche for something more.

Gabriel's hunch had been right; there was more to the cave than met the eye and there *were* bats. I stepped carefully to avoid disturbing them, holding the match low and moving cautiously. It took ages to make my way around the twists and turns, but just when I was about to give up, the flame of the last match flickered and went out.

"Blast," I muttered, but as my eyes grew accustomed to the dark, I realised there was a thin line of light just ahead. I pushed on, guided by the light, and found a slender opening. I was just about to push my way through it when a hand clamped onto my shoulder.

I screamed and jumped backwards. A bat stirred overhead, and Gabriel put a finger to his lips. "Don't wake them," he warned. "I've a horror of the bloody things."

He held a match up, dazzling my eyes, but I

could see he looked worse than when he'd set off.

"Goodness, Gabriel, what happened to you? You look as if you'd fallen down a hill."

His clothes were dirtier than ever and a long bloody scratch marred one cheek, running from just below his eye and down into his beard. He put a hand to it.

"I did," he said quickly. "Fell right down. Made a bloody awful racket. I'm surprised you didn't hear it."

"I couldn't hear a thing. I was too busy finding this," I told him in triumph, showing him the exit.

"Well done," he murmured.

"And what about you? Were you shot at?"

He shook his head, his manner distracted. "Not closely. The light was against the count and he missed his shot."

"The count! So it was the Thurzós after us?"

"Just the count, as near as I could make out," he said smoothly. He hesitated then hurried on, his lips very white in the dark mat of his beard. "I hate to be the bearer of news, but I should probably tell you—the count won't be troubling us again."

The match went out just then, singeing his fingers. He swore and struck another, and by the time he had, his colour was normal again.

"What do you mean he won't be troubling us?"

"I'm afraid the fellow is quite dead. He had a fall, bless him. It was a stupid thing, so ridiculous

I wouldn't have believed it if I hadn't seen it with my own eyes, but he slipped and landed quite the wrong way."

"The wrong way?" He put a finger to his neck and I felt my stomach turn to water. "He broke his neck?"

"It's rocky out there," Gabriel said lamely. "These things happen in the desert."

I swallowed hard. "I'm sorry for the countess, but not for us. God only knows what he might have done. And I'm sorry you had to see it," I said kindly. "I'm sure it wasn't pleasant."

His eyes were oddly flat. "No, it wasn't."

"Still," I said briskly, "it's an ill wind that blows no good for someone. We'll make the best of it and get away while we can, shall we?"

He blew out the match and followed me through the little opening, cursing when his shoulders stuck fast. It was only with a great deal of effort and a bit of lost skin that he wriggled free, but eventually we both emerged into the waning sunlight. The desert had never looked more beautiful. The fading light washed the rocks in colour—honey and primrose and velvety purple.

I turned to Gabriel. "I'm sorry about what I said earlier. I was upset, you see. And I oughtn't blame you for what went wrong between us. I daresay I was a fool for ever thinking you were someone you are not."

"I daresay you were," he returned. But he smiled

as he said it, and for just a moment, it was not painful to be with him.

He turned his face to the north. "Come on, duck. We've a lot of walking to do."

TEN

We walked the whole of that night, plodding on until all I knew was the ache of my own body and the chill wind that wrapped around us. Gabriel found another well, this one a mere trickle, and he forced me to drink the foul water, taking as much himself as he could stand. He unearthed a handful of palm dates from a sad, thin tree and handed them to me, bullying me into eating them even as I gagged on the sourness. He pushed me on, into the sands, telling me the whole time how bloody lucky I was that I hadn't come in summer. He showed not a jot of sympathy; his entire mood was grim and relentless, pricking my temper to frequent outbursts and leaving me in such a state of annoyance that I charged ahead of him just to get away. I walked some twenty yards ahead, correcting my course when Gabriel shouted epithets about my sense of direction. At last the sun began to rise, the morning shadows stretching long over the cruel beauty of the desert, and the breeze began to die.

I paused, letting the warm sunlight play over my

face. Gabriel stood at my side, and after a moment he lifted his nose, sniffing.

"What is it?" I asked sharply.

"You don't smell that? You always did have a monkey's sense of smell. It's horse sweat."

"You're making that up," I began, but no sooner had I started than a group of horsemen topped the small rise ahead of us. They were garbed in black robes and riding smart Arabian horses with elaborate bridles and small heads. "Bedouin!" I breathed.

I moved forward, but Gabriel grabbed my arm. "Not so fast. Bedu come in two varieties and these . . ."

He didn't bother to finish the thought. The rifles pointed directly at us told the story clearly enough. We put our hands into the air as they rode at us. They began firing a hundred feet away and circled us, shooting at the ground and grinning and shouting things in Arabic.

"What are they saying?" I asked Gabriel. "I'm afraid my Arabic only goes so far as ordering in restaurants and shops."

"Allah is good, Allah is great, and we are their prisoners," he said calmly.

"Well, I suppose it could be worse," I replied. "At least they might feed us."

Just then one of the Bedouin detached from the group. He wore one of the native headdresses, a sort of veil down his back with a small bit of it draped to conceal his face from the sand and wind. As he came near, he dropped the veil to reveal a wide smile. And a familiar one. "Daoud!" I said, starting forward. A shot at my feet stopped me in my tracks.

Daoud bowed from the saddle and grinned from me to Gabriel. The blank expression he had worn the entire time I had been at the dig was nowhere in evidence. In its place was a look of sharp intelligence, and I realised the guise of simpleton had served him well. No doubt he had picked up quite a bit of information pretending to be a dullard.

"Greetings." He peered at Gabriel with narrowed eyes. "I think you have been concealing things."

"It's a long story and we're hungry," Gabriel said pointedly.

"Of course. You will come with us to be our honoured guests," Daoud proclaimed.

"That's very kind of you," I told him. "But if we're guests why exactly were you shooting at us?"

"Because you will be our guests whether you wish it or not. So long as you give us what we want, we will take very good care of you and there will be no problem."

"And what precisely do you want?" Gabriel asked.

Daoud's smile deepened. "We want the Cross that belongs to us, the spoils of war taken by the great and honoured Salah al-Dln—all of it."

Gabriel's expression was pained. "I'm afraid we haven't got it, old boy."

Daoud's smile did not waver. He leaned out of the saddle to come quite close to us.

"Then we have a problem." He gave a series of instructions in Arabic and before we could object, Gabriel and I were both swiftly bound and helped onto horses to ride pillion—me behind Daoud and Gabriel behind one of his compatriots.

"Was this part of your plan?" I asked Gabriel sweetly.

He swore viciously and I realised he hadn't even heard me. He was struggling with certain anatomical difficulties for a man presented by riding pillion. I turned my attention to Daoud.

"He was telling the truth, you know. You remember—you were there. The Thurzós stole it from us."

Daoud waved a hand. "Madame Starke, one does not talk business before the demands of hospitality have been met." Without warning he kicked his mare sharply in the side and she sprang forward. I grabbed Daoud's robe and held on for dear life.

The journey took us well into the day, and it was afternoon by the time we reached their small encampment. A few of Daoud's men had stayed behind, but our appearance roused them, and with much shouting and waving of guns we were brought into the camp. We were given water to drink and for washing our hands, and at Daoud's instruction, we were untied and taken into a low black tent and made to sit side by side upon a cheap Turkish rug.

"If he feeds us, I will willingly be his harem girl," I whispered to Gabriel as my stomach gave a terrific growl.

"My dear child, if he feeds us, *I* will be his harem girl," Gabriel retorted.

I furrowed my brow. "Do Bedouin have harems? I feel I ought to be prepared just in case."

Gabriel rolled his eyes heavenward. "Now who's the ass? The *harim* is a Turkish institution. Only city folk have them."

"But the Bedu do take more than one wife?"

"As Mohammedans, it is their right, yes. But I hardly think you need worry yourself. The last European woman to find trouble in one of the eastern deserts was Alexine Tinne, a Dutchwoman, and that was fifty years ago."

"What happened to her?"

"Impaled with a Bedouin spear after having her arm cut off. Or was it a Berber spear? Now that I think of it, I seem to recall she was in one of the African deserts."

"Good God! But still, if that was fifty years ago and it was the last . . . it *was* the last?"

"Of course not. People come to grief in the desert all the time. I was trying to distract you."

"From what?" I demanded.

But the flap of the tent was flung back and Daoud entered with a cohort of his men. Behind came a pair of others carrying platters with flatbreads, a pungent sort of sour goat's cheese and a hot, greasy rice dish studded with bits of stewed vegetables. Daoud signalled that we were to help ourselves, and remembering the strictures about eating only with the right hand, we dove into the platters.

Daoud joined us in a gesture that I suspected was intended to allay our discomfort. He was a genial host, telling stories and asking interested questions about my travels prior to coming into the Badiyat ash-Sham. He was particularly taken with the notion that I flew an aeroplane, and I expanded on that until we had eaten and drunk as much as we could. At last the platters were taken away and Daoud summoned a tall contraption I recognised from the shops in Damascus. It was a water pipe, a *nargileh*, and it had been prepared for him so that all he need do was apply a glowing coal and take several long puffs. When it was going, he offered it to Gabriel, who took a long appreciative drag, then passed it to me.

I pulled hard at the mouthpiece, filling my mouth with the sweetly fruited smoke and holding it there before I blew it out in a slow, steady stream.

Daoud laughed and said something in Arabic.

212

"He is impressed. Most women don't handle a pipe that well."

I smiled. "I learned to smoke from the soldiers I helped nurse at a convalescent home during the war."

"The Great War?"

I blinked. "Was there another?"

Daoud bared his teeth in a smile that was almost as winsome as it was sinister. "Madame Starke, out here there is always war."

So we smoked and Daoud listened as I talked of my travels. He was particularly interested in the Seven Seas Tour. We went outside so I could sketch out for him the seas I planned to cross.

"They're not the modern seven seas, you understand," I explained as I roughed in the positions. "I chose the seven seas of antiquity. They're much nearer together, you see, and much smaller."

He mused over the wide swathes of water I had drawn between the bits of land. "It is too much water. I do not like it."

"But your own people know the importance of the sea," I protested. "They took the port of Aqaba from the Turks with the help of Colonel Lawrence."

He smiled the smile that was nothing like his idiot's grin. "But the sea is not ours, Madame Starke. We are masters of the desert," he said, throwing his arms wide.

I turned to look from horizon to horizon, and endless blackness outside the small circle of warm lamplight. It was pierced here and there by the brightness of stars that barely pricked the inky nothingness. "But the desert is a sea," I told him. "It is vast and relentless and it can take a man's life with ease. Only the clever and the brave survive."

No flattery seemed too thick for Daoud. He preened every time I larded a little into the conversation, and by the time we returned to the tent, we were chattering away like old mates. Gabriel sat quietly, his expression alternately bland or sour depending on the topic. Daoud and I ignored him and continued to talk as another *nargileh* was filled and bowls of dates were carried in.

We nibbled and smoked and the talk turned back to my experiences as a pilot.

"I have seen aeroplanes, of course," Daoud offered. "They flew over the Badiyat ash-Sham rather more often than one would like." His expression was pained, and I thought of how terrifying it must have been for people whose lives had carried on largely unaltered through the centuries to have come face-to-face with the horrors of mechanised warfare.

I said as much, and he nodded. He talked then of his village, the settlement far to the south where the women and children lived while the men were out raiding. The village moved, of course, herding their flocks between grazing lands, but the faces and the quarrels and the friendships were unchanged. He told me of a brother lost to the Turks and another lost to an overzealous bit of British artillery.

"But worse than this, Madame Starke, is the war that rages among the Bedu. We cannot agree on what should become of us."

I nodded. "You know, the nomadic peoples in the United States were much the same as yourselves. They followed herds of animals called buffalo—like enormous cows, really—across great grassy plains and fought among themselves. They couldn't unite to fight their common enemy, either."

"And who was their enemy?"

"Well, the white settlers who kept moving westwards. They wanted more land and the native peoples were pushed and squeezed. And then the white people hunted all the buffalo until there were none left to feed the natives."

"And what became of these natives who were like the Bedu?"

I did not flinch from his clear gaze. "They died. Or were pushed onto foul little bits of land that are no good for farming or grazing. Everything they knew was destroyed."

He pounded the earth with his fist. "This! This is what I fear if the Bedu do not come together in agreement. The English and the French will break us into pieces because they want the cities or they want the oil fields of Mesopotamia. But what of the people?"

"And what are you doing about it?" I demanded coolly.

He gave me a blank look. "I?"

"Yes, you're busy trotting around the desert abducting people and planning to steal priceless artefacts. That *is* why you went to the dig in the first place, isn't it? You thought if you pretended to be a halfwit and kept your ears and eyes open you'd find something of tremendous value and make off with it. One trinket from a good archaeological find is worth years of desert raiding. It could keep your people comfortably, I quite understand," I said, holding up a hand as he opened his mouth to protest. "But what good does that do after this year? You cannot repeat the trick. Your description would be circulated among the digs. You'd never be hired again. And then what? You've fed your people for another season but no further. And by then the French mandate may have been formalised. They may have established outposts in the desert, rounding up the stragglers and rebels, putting Bedouins to the sword and protecting their own interests. And what will you have done to stop it? Nothing. In fact, you will have given them a perfect excuse with your lawlessness to come out here and interfere. Is that what you want, Daoud? To bring the ire of the French authorities to bear upon your people?"

His mouth hung slack and he darted a look at Gabriel, who was sitting quite still in the shadows. Gabriel said nothing and his expression was carefully neutral.

"Let us go," I went on. "Set us free, Daoud. We have no quarrel with the Bedu. We want only prosperity and peace for the great warriors of the desert." I paused to see if I had laid it on too thickly, but Daoud was more susceptible than I thought. "You are the sons of lions," I said, my voice ringing with conviction. "You are the children of the wind, masters and first-born sons of the Badiyat ash-Sham. You are the true nobility and the greatest part of nobility is mercy. I cast myself upon your goodness, o' son of the lion, and I ask for your gracious mercy and compassion as a child of Allah, the merciful and compassionate."

I bowed my head and waited for his gesture of mercy. Instead, there was a hoarse, grating laugh, and Daoud doubled over in mirth. Tears rolled down his cheeks, and when he wiped them away, he said, "Oh, Madame Starke, that was most impressive. And we Arabs are the most senti-mental folk in the world. But I am afraid you're not dealing with an Arab."

I blinked at him as Gabriel muttered an oath under his breath. "Not an Arab?"

Daoud gave me a thin smile. "Not a full-blooded

one at any rate. My father was Bedu, but my mother was French and brought me up to know the ways of her people, as well. So, while I might be a— What did you call it? A 'son of the lion'? I am gifted with a great deal of very sound Gallic common sense. Mine is a Cartesian brain, Madame."

I sat back on my heels. "Drat."

The smile deepened. "Indeed. In fact, it was my experience with the perfidious ways of Europeans which enabled me to understand what the Thurzós were planning. Naturally, they did not think to guard themselves against immoderate speech when they were in the presence of a native with a reputation for idiocy. You're quite right—it was a most useful pose. Now, I must thank you for the enormously entertaining interlude, Madame Starke, but I think it is time for me to leave you. I would like a little sleep before we set off tomorrow."

He motioned for two of his men to tie us up— back to back, which was just as well. Gabriel was smirking and I would have struck him if I'd had my hands free. They left us, taking the lamp with them, and when the tent flap dropped, we were in darkness.

"Don't say it," I told him, my teeth gritted.

Behind me, I felt his body shaking with silent laughter. I dug my elbow into his ribs, but that didn't stop him.

"What's the matter, Evie? I'm sure we'll get out of this just fine. Why don't you call on Allah the merciful and compassionate to give us a hand?"

"At least I tried," I returned hotly. "Some criminal genius you are! You just sat there like a bloody great lump saying nothing and letting me prattle on—" I carried on abusing him for a full minute before I realised he was busy fumbling with our bound hands. "What are you doing?"

"Cutting the ropes," he replied in a cheerful tone.

"Gabriel! You have a knife? How absolutely *brilliant.*"

"A moment ago I was a bloody great lump."

"I don't remember saying anything of the kind. Oh, do be careful with that thing! You nearly nicked an artery."

He sighed. "You don't have arteries there, my daft little duck. Now shut up and let me concentrate. It's bad enough I can't see."

I fell silent as he worked on the ropes, sawing carefully. At last I felt a pop and one of them loosened. But we were still tightly bound, and I realised it was going to take a very long time for Gabriel to free us. I felt my arms begin to shake a little from the strain and the long night without rest. I occupied myself by reciting poetry in my head. *"This is the forest primeval,"* I thought.

"Are you thinking of 'Evangeline'?" Gabriel asked suddenly.

"How on earth did you know that?"

I felt him shrug in the darkness. "You always do it when you're anxious."

"I forgot I ever told you that. Yes, I was. 'Ye who believe in affection that hopes, and endures, and is patient, Ye who believe in the beauty and strength of woman's devotion, List to the mournful tradition still sung by the pines of the forest; List to a Tale of Love in Acadie, home of the happy.'"

Gabriel groaned. "Not aloud, I beg you."

"It's a perfectly splendid poem, I'll have you know."

"You only think that because your father named you after it, for which I believe he ought to have been horsewhipped. No one should be named after a Longfellow poem."

"Longfellow was a brilliant poet."

He snorted. "Brilliant? He was bloody useless, as bad as Wordsworth and his daffodils with all that talk of primeval forests and happy trees. If you want proper poetry, you want Marvell."

"Marvell? You call that proper poetry? It's *rubbish*." I cudgelled up a few lines from memory. "'Ye living lamps, by whose dear light the nightingale does sit so late.' It's a poem about *glowworms,* for heaven's sake. As I said, rubbish."

"Rubbish, and yet you can recite it," he countered smugly.

"Because you used to prattle on about them until I wanted to scream blue murder," I told him.

220

"And I never understood how someone with such a keen appreciation of baroque music could find pleasure in the foulness of Donne. He wrote a poem romanticising a flea."

"It was a metaphor."

I opened my mouth to argue, but suddenly he gave a heave and the ropes snapped free.

"Done," he said with a darkly satisfied note.

"Now what?"

"Now we wait."

If I could have seen him clearly, I would have punched him. "What do you mean we wait? We're free!"

"Not so loud unless you'd like Daoud and his chums to come back and take care of that," he hissed. "I've got us free, but they've only just turned in. We need to give them a chance to nod off properly before we try to get out of here. Stretch your legs a bit, but don't make any noise. I'm going to see if I can loosen a tent peg on the backside for us to slip out."

I did as he instructed, moving my legs and arms to get the blood moving freely again. I felt surprisingly exhilarated in spite of my exhaustion. A good sparring match with Gabriel had always had that effect, I reminded myself. Although why he should pick a fight over something as stupid as poetry at just that moment . . .

After a long while he slid back to my side. "I've loosened enough we should be able to slip under.

There's a guard, but he doesn't seem much interested in actually guarding anything. He keeps wandering off."

"How long do you intend to wait?"

"I'll let you know," he said shortly. I huffed a sigh and began to recite *Evangeline* again in my head. I had reached a particularly poignant line—"So came the autumn, and passed, and the winter—yet Gabriel came not"—when I had had about as much as I could stand. I got up and went to where Gabriel had loosened the tent pegs. Without so much as a "by-your-leave" I lifted the tent fabric a few inches, peered into the starry darkness and rolled myself out into the cold air of freedom. Gabriel was right behind me, not swearing because neither of us dared to speak, but I could feel the rage vibrating in him as we scurried through the sand and over the little rise behind the tents. We gained it without incident, and then the next, and finally, when we were some distance away and well out of sight, he turned on me.

"That was the bloody stupidest thing—" he began. He was raging quietly, for sound carried easily in the desert at night, but I knew he was building up a good head of steam and I flapped a hand at him.

"Gabriel, *hush*. It's done and fussing at me isn't going to change that. And if you thought it was such a poor idea, you didn't have to follow me, you know."

"What was I going to do? Let you stumble around the desert on your own and get killed for your pains? Or worse, let them take their fury at you out on me?" How he managed to sound injured when I had just effected an escape eluded me.

"I *think* I just got us out of a rather sticky situation, so let's not get too high and mighty about my helplessness, shall we?"

"Then would you like me to keep quiet about the fact that you're heading the wrong way?" His tone was icily polite, which, frankly speaking, wasn't much of an improvement on his raging, but I'd take what I could get.

I followed meekly as he turned us northeast and began to trot. We covered some ground before he stopped with a groan. "This is damned pointless. We ought to just go back to Daoud."

I shook my head as if to clear it. "I'm afraid the desert air seems to have damaged my hearing. I thought I heard you suggest going back to Daoud."

He sighed, and for the first time in our little adventure, he looked defeated. The posing and posturing was gone, and the expression in his eyes was solemn. "Evie, we're a good forty miles from Palmyra and we've no water. We're in a part of the desert I'm not particularly familiar with. We've got Countess Thurzó running off with the Cross, we've got Herr Doktor skulking around for God only knows what reason, we've got Daoud, who will, I hope you realise, be after our heads once he finds us missing."

"All the more reason to move quickly," I said.

He opened his mouth then snapped it shut again. He lowered his head a moment, and when he lifted it, his mask of insouciance was firmly back in place. He drew himself up as if steeling himself for an ordeal.

"Come on, then," he said briskly. "First one to water gets the cleanest drink."

As we walked, we speculated on the whereabouts of Countess Thurzó and the Cross. "She ought to be in Damascus by now enjoying a hot bath and a nice meal," I said, feeling my stomach rumble at the thought of a nice savoury steak.

"Perhaps," he said, drawing out the word slowly.

I stared at him. "What are you thinking? Why on earth would she hang around the desert when she has the Cross?"

He shrugged, his expression evasive. "I don't know. She could have a buyer here in the Badiyat ash-Sham."

I considered this. It was vaguely possible, I supposed. There was money in some of the desert tribes. Some of them, like Daoud's people, were poor as church mice. Others were rumoured to be quite prosperous—usually through charging enormous fees to safely escort trading caravans and travellers through the desert.

"But who?" I asked.

He stroked his thick grimy beard. "I can think of a few Bedouin who would be absolutely delighted to hang one of Saladin's trophies on the walls of a city house and who have the funds to pay through the nose for it."

"City house?"

"The richest Bedu have houses in Damascus. Some of them split their time between the city and the desert. Best of both worlds, really."

"Like Jane Digby," I mused. The lady's romantic amours had scandalised Europe for the better part of the nineteenth century. A daughter of one of England's oldest families, she had taken to the Continent when she fell pregnant with her lover's child, and a series of *mésalliances* had followed. She'd had a string of noteworthy lovers, from rebel lords to crowned heads, but the most notorious had been her Bedouin prince, her last husband and by all accounts the love of her life. She'd happily spent almost thirty years dividing her time between their Damascene mansion and his desert tribe. In the city life was not terribly dissimilar to the one she'd known back in England with social calls and entertaining and shopping taking up much of her time, but the rest was wild desert raids and modest warfare, where she was often to be found riding her Arabian mount and handling a rifle as competently as any man. I was just imagining myself astride a horse, leading a charge with rifle blazing, when Gabriel's voice cut into my reverie.

"You'd hate it."

"I beg your pardon?" I blinked rapidly. "Hate what?"

"Life as a Bedouin woman. Even if you did marry a prince. You're far too uppity to take to life under a veil."

"How on earth—" I bit off the question. "I was thinking no such thing."

"Oh, for God's sake, don't lie. I can read you as clearly as the morning newspaper. You were thinking how dashing it would be to live that life, swanning about Damascus half the time and leading desert raids the rest."

"It does sound tempting," I admitted.

"And you would hate it," he repeated. "It seems like adventure but it's an endless cycle of sun and barren land and camels—as repetitive as life in an English village if you think about it. Only rather more tribal skirmishes and fewer village fêtes. Now, if you're quite through wool-gathering, we were in the middle of a discussion. I'd very much like some food and water, and you look so exhausted, I'm beginning to wonder if it mightn't be a very great kindness just to shoot you here." I stared at him, aghast, and instantly his expression softened. "Never mind. It's all right, Evie. We'll manage."

"Not if you keep underestimating me, you great

ass," I said, giving him a hard shove. I reached into my pocket and pulled out the packets of bread and dates I had managed to secure. From inside my shirt I took the small goatskin full of water and waved it at him. "Now, we have food. We have water. And we have a plan—we are moving on towards Palmyra. There are people there and at least a dozen oases between here and there. If we're lucky we'll stumble on one. If not, the desert is crawling with Bedouin and some of them are bound to be friendlier than Daoud, particularly if we offer to pay them. When we get to Palmyra, we're going to eat until we can't hold another bite and we're going to drink our own body weight in water. Then we're going to bathe because, my *God,* you smell like something three days past death, and then we are going to organise an expedition to get that Cross back. What we are not going to do is go back, not for one single minute."

His jaw went slack and he opened his mouth to speak, but I stepped forward, poking him hard in the chest. "I mean it, Gabriel. I spent the whole of our blessedly short marriage doing what you wanted. I said 'Yes, Gabriel' and 'No, Gabriel' and you despised me for it, and well you should have. I wasn't myself with you. I was so desperately afraid of losing you that I acted like some sort of jellyfish. Do you know what sort of wife I was, Gabriel? I was *invertebrate.* I had no backbone with you. And you needed my backbone and so did I. You needed someone to bring you down to earth and make you act like a responsible grown-up for once. It was the worst mistake I ever made, rolling over and letting you walk all over me with your great filthy boots. I let you have your way about everything and where did it get me? Standing on the deck of a steamer in Shanghai watching you walk away without a care in the world while I broke my heart over you. Well, I'm not that girl. I never was, I was just too in love with you and too frightened of losing you to show you who I really was. Here I am, Gabriel—the girl you should have married but didn't. I smoke cigars and I barnstorm and I wear red lipstick and I do as I damned well please. And when this is all over and I have that Cross, I am going to divorce *you* and we won't ever have to see each other again. But at least you'll know what you were missing. Now, point me in the direction of Palmyra because that is where we're going."

Without a word, he reached out and pulled me into his arms, and before I could take a breath his mouth was on mine. It wasn't gentle and it wasn't sweet, and if he'd ever kissed me like that before, just once, we wouldn't have been headed for divorce court. When he set me on my feet again I pulled back my arm and slapped him for the third time in a week.

He rubbed his hairy chin. "We really must give

some thought to breaking you of the habit of physical violence."

"Why on earth did you do that?" I demanded.

His expression was dazed, but not from the slap. He shook his head slowly. "The same reason you slapped me. I simply didn't have a choice. Palmyra, you said? This way."

He turned and began to walk. And somehow, for all my fine speech and taking the bull by the horns, I had an unwelcome suspicion that Gabriel had somehow found the upper hand again.

ELEVEN

We had only walked an hour or so before the sun began to rise, and for a moment, as that long yellow light gilded the entire world, it felt like a promise that everything was going to be all right. I lifted my wind-roughened face to the golden warmth. Soon it would be hot, searing everything below including us, but for the moment, I could worship it. I closed my eyes and sniffed deeply, smelling the few scrubby plants that managed to survive. There was something that smelled like sage, and for a moment, I thought of all my favourite dishes—crisp potatoes and new bread and roast goose with sage stuffing.

"Good God, if your stomach roars any louder

they'll be able to track us by the sound of it," Gabriel said irritably.

I stuffed a date into my mouth and didn't answer. It was just like him to ruin a perfectly lovely moment.

I ate another date and sulked while Gabriel drank and rested. He looked awful—pale under the ruddy sunburn he had acquired and his cheeks were so obscured by overgrown beard even a pirate crew would have thought him disreputable.

He opened one eye and looked at me quizzically. "Admiring the view?"

"Actually I was thinking how frightful you look."

"Clearly you haven't got a mirror."

I opened my mouth to let him have it, but nothing came out. He cocked his head. "No response to that? Come on, Evie. I miss scrapping with you."

I didn't bother to answer. I merely sat, my eyes fixed upon the horizon. Gabriel noticed the direction of my gaze and swiveled his head. In the distance, a cloud of dust and sand was coming and just before the cloud was a party of darkly robed horsemen brandishing rifles. Bedouin.

"Not again," he muttered.

I sighed and stood, brushing off my hands. Gabriel stood at my side and together we waited. There was no point in running simply because there was nowhere to run *to* in that vast nothingness.

"I'm really beginning to despise this desert," I told him.

He didn't respond. Instead, he narrowed his eyes at our approaching company and then turned to me with an equally casual tone. "There's a good chance this isn't going to end well, my dear. If it doesn't, don't bother burying me. Just take the tin box out of my pocket and send a postcard to my mother, will you?"

"Your mother already thinks you're dead," I reminded him.

"Yes, well I never liked her much. Maybe this shock will kill her."

"Gabriel Wilberforce Starke," I began, but there was no time for more. The horsemen were upon us, and I stared openmouthed at the first of them to reach us.

"Good day, Frau Starke! Herr Rowan," cried Herr Doktor Schickfuss. "How pleased I am to have found you."

He was followed by Daoud and his compatriots and I rolled my eyes at the sight of them. "Honestly. Over 200,000 square miles of desert and it's him again," I muttered to Gabriel.

Daoud was smiling broadly, as was Herr Doktor, and it seemed silly to make a fuss just because we'd been caught a second time. I moved forward with a sigh and put up my wrists to be tied.

Gabriel had other plans. Or perhaps his reluctance was just an excuse. He lashed out with his fists and two of Daoud's men were prone on the desert floor before they knew what happened. It occurred to me once again that Gabriel might not be terribly skilled as a criminal genius. He entirely missed Daoud leading his horse around behind and turned a fraction of a second too late. One swift kick to the jaw from Daoud's boot and a second to his cheekbone and Gabriel went down, his eyes rolling back in his head as he hit the ground hard enough to shake it. Herr Doktor's eyes rounded and he made some guttural exclamation as he smiled. He seemed to be enjoying himself thoroughly.

"It is like the earthquake when he falls! Boom!" he said with a nod towards Gabriel's prostrate form.

I shrugged and held up my wrists as Daoud bound them, a little less gently than the time before, and hauled me up onto his horse behind him. Gabriel was trussed like a Christmas goose and draped over the back of another horse, his head lolling as we moved out.

Daoud turned his head and flicked Gabriel a malicious glance. "I like him better that way."

"So do I," I replied. "But you're wasting your time. We already told you we don't have the Cross. Countess Thurzó does and she's well gone, probably already in Damascus by now." Of course, she could be absolutely anywhere in Syria at that point, but short of torture, I wasn't going to give Daoud a single piece of helpful information.

Daoud shrugged. "I know precisely where to find the countess—and the Cross, when I want them. Unfortunately, the Cross, as you must know, is incomplete, and I believe you know the whereabouts of the heart of the relic."

"But I don't!" I told him. "I promise. I'll swear on anything you like."

He merely smiled. "Come. We have much to talk of, Madame Starke." But apparently not just yet. He touched his horse's flanks and we were off again, racing across the desert and into the lowering curtain of purple twilight.

Gabriel bounced around like a sack of turnips, but the journey didn't seem to do him much harm. He came to when they cut him off his horse and he rubbed his jaw, cursing at Daoud and giving me hateful looks into the bargain.

"That bruise is turning a spectacular shade of violet." I nodded towards his cheekbone. "I have a dancing frock just that colour."

He said something obscene that I didn't quite catch but went peacefully enough as they herded us into the same low black goat's-hair tent we'd escaped from two hours before. "Home sweet home," I murmured.

"I swear to God, Evie, one more word, and I will tell Daoud to use your bones for a toothpick," Gabriel vowed.

I would have responded, but Daoud turned to us after giving instructions. "We will rest here today," he said with a courteous little bow. "First, we will eat together, for the custom of desert hospitality must not be forgotten."

Within moments we were seated on the same cheap Turkish rug, eating precisely the same food as the previous meal. In fact, I suspected it was exactly the same dinner, warmed over and served again.

I scooped up a greasy handful of vegetable stew with a bit of flatbread and crammed it into my mouth like a farmhand. It wasn't very good, but it was hot and filling and I was making up for lost time.

While I ate, I took stock of the gentlemen. Gabriel, with his unkempt hair and assortment of bruises, looked a mess, but Daoud had a sort of careless elegance in his robes, and the little German was almost as tidy as a Thurzó. His complexion had pinked up under the desert sun and wind, but his eyes were bright and his white beard was neatly clipped with a tremendous pair of moustaches waxed to little curls at the end.

"I admire your moustaches, Doktor," I told him.

Gabriel made a faint gagging noise, but Herr Doktor smiled and simpered. "You should have seen them before the war," he told me. "Nine inches on either side!"

"Well, they're much nicer than the kaiser's," I

told him. He bowed at me, and I decided it was time to take the bull by the horns. "So what's your interest in all this, Doktor?"

His great white bushy brows rose. "My interest? The Cross, of course! Since the greatest of Holy Roman Emperors, Frederick Barbarossa, led the Third Crusade, it has been the holy quest of the Teuton to protect the most precious relics of Christendom."

"Didn't he die in a Turkish river?" Gabriel asked pleasantly. "Drowned in his own armour, if I recall. He never even made it to the Holy Land, much less led the Third Crusade."

The old gentleman flushed a dark red and lifted his finger to wag it at Gabriel. Before he could get going, I poured a little oil on the troubled waters.

"But the Third Crusade would never have happened if the great Barbarossa hadn't pushed Richard the Lionheart to go," I said quickly. "Everyone knows that."

Gabriel snorted but said nothing more. His jaw must have been screaming in order for him to give up so easily, but the little German settled back, mollified.

"Excellent," I murmured. "No point in fighting the Third Crusade all over again."

"Particularly as we all know Salah al-Dln won," Daoud added smoothly.

Herr Doktor threw him a pained look, but Daoud went on munching contently. "Tell me, Daoud," I said, keeping my voice pleasant, "how did you and Herr Doktor come to work together?"

Daoud shrugged. "There are two groups of people who seek treasure, madame—brigands and archaeologists, and both will pay dearly for what they want. When the Thurzós moved so quickly to accept my proposal, naturally I wondered which other archaeologists might be willing to do the same, and for an even greater sum of money."

"That's rather brilliant," I told him in perfect honesty.

He quirked a smile at me. "As I said, a Cartesian brain."

"And you, Herr Doktor," I said, turning to his partner. "You have the funds to secure such a find?"

"I will." He and Daoud exchanged the complacent glances of a pair of intriguers who both think they've gotten the better of a bargain.

Suddenly, I was struck with an idea. "Daoud, did you approach any of the other archaeologists first?"

He shrugged. "Only Miss Green, but she does not have money."

Gabriel growled. "Gethsemane knows, then?"

"Not what the relic is," Daoud corrected. "Only that I have the means of acquiring something very special and very expensive. But she does not have the money, so I do not talk to her. I turn instead to Herr Doktor."

Schickfuss was beaming happily, his cheeks glistening with grease. "My muscum will pay much for this. It will go far towards improving the spirits of my saddened homeland," he said, a faint shadow in his eyes.

"Your homeland bloody well can't afford it," Gabriel said with a merry laugh. "How do you intend to pay Daoud? With cobblestones pried up from the Unter den Linden?"

Daoud looked at Schickfuss curiously, but the little German was staring at Gabriel, his eyes popping. "How dare you speak so slightingly of my homeland?" He rose, clapping his hand to his belt, where I noticed for the first time a small knife marked with the Teutonic cross of the old empire. He ranted on, but Gabriel merely chewed his food, and I hurried to settle the old fellow.

"Herr Doktor, please, I'm sure he didn't realise what he was saying. The pain from his jaw, and he hasn't eaten properly in days, and hasn't slept much, and of course, he's still terribly upset from when I shot him—"

Schickfuss stopped midrant and stared at mc. "You shot him?" He peered at Gabriel then nodded. "This I can understand. But what was it that tempted you to shoot him?"

"Well, it's rather a long story and I'm afraid I'd rather not go into it just now. Why don't we all sit down and have a nice dinner? You can tell me more about your plans for the Cross and the museum, and he will keep his mouth shut. If he doesn't, perhaps we'll shoot him again."

At length, Herr Doktor permitted me to coax him into sitting down and finishing his meal.

Daoud, who had continued to eat without the least concern, nodded at the German. "I told you Madame Starke would try her charms on you. She talks too much, but you will get used to it."

"No, you won't," Gabriel interjected.

Daoud laughed, and by the time we were finished eating, the atmosphere had grown positively chummy. I learned that Daoud had a wife and two sons, and that Herr Doktor hailed from Silesia.

"Such beautiful country, Frau Starke!" he told me. "Have you never been? Ach, you must go and fly over it in your aeroplane. Such beauty must be seen best from above, I think. So lovely a land as God accounted himself pleased when he made it. Of course, what will become of it now . . . ?" He trailed off unhappily. "Always the rest of Europe fights over us. We have been Polish and Prussian and Bohemian. But really, we are Germans." His face was woebegone, and I felt a pang of sympathy for him, but Daoud made an unpleasant noise.

"How do you think we feel? At least it's your own kind fighting over you. Our land doesn't even belong to us, so I think we will speak no more about who is to be pitied."

Of course, there was no reply to make. Daoud

was entirely correct. It was tiresome enough that Europeans quarrelled among themselves for bits of their own continent; it seemed pure bad manners they insisted on doing it elsewhere.

Herr Doktor looked uncomfortable, and Daoud did not attempt to soothe the moment. He rose, beckoning his fellows to come and clear away the food and bind me up again.

Gabriel quirked a brow inquiringly. "Not me? Let me guess, I'm the after-dinner entertainment."

Schickfuss chuckled while Daoud gave a grin that didn't quite reach his eyes. "As a matter of fact," he said, reaching a hand under Gabriel's arm and hauling him to his feet, "you are."

I started to rise, as well, but one of the guards shoved me back onto my heels and motioned for me to stay. The men moved out of the tent then, and only Daoud had a backwards glance for me. "Do not fear, Madame Starke. I will leave him in one piece. Mostly."

He dropped the flap of the tent and I was left alone, although I had little doubt guards were posted outside, and probably far more diligent than the first lot. I had seen only one of them since we'd been returned to the camp and he had been sporting a blackened eye and a sour expression, doubtless the result of Daoud's disappointment at the fellow letting us escape.

The next few hours were not pleasant ones. I couldn't tell if they'd taken Gabriel into another tent or left him outside, but I could hear raised male voices from time to time and other sounds I didn't like to think about. At one point I heard Gabriel's quick, taunting laugh, and what followed turned my stomach to water. I crawled far away from the tent flap and curled up as best I could with my hands bound behind me. I must have slept, for the sky was just beginning to grey when the flap was lifted and Gabriel was chucked inside. He landed limply on the Turkish rug and did not move.

Daoud came in behind him followed by Herr Doktor. Daoud looked oddly satisfied as he regarded his handiwork, and I noticed his hands were marked with blood. He came to me and took a knife from his belt. One quick slash and I was free, chafing my wrists as he stepped back.

"I will not bother to bind him. He'll be no trouble to me now."

He gave me a broad smile and turned on his heel and left. Herr Doktor lingered a moment, his eyes inscrutable. "I will send water and food."

I dared not look at Gabriel. "Is he—"

"No." He hesitated as if he wanted to say more, but instead he left me quickly and without another glance at Gabriel.

I rolled my wrists and flexed my fingers. I stretched my sore back and when I couldn't find any other reason to delay the inevitable, I went to Gabriel. It wasn't as bad as I feared, although I had no doubt if he were conscious he would have informed me otherwise with a few choice words.

He was sporting a few fresh bruises on his face and on his arms there were odd little cuts that had bled freely. I opened his shirt and the bruise he'd gotten from being shot was blooming magnificently, but there seemed little else wrong with him. His legs were not bleeding at all from the looks of his trousers, and I poked at his ribs to see if anything else ailed him except the minor contusions on his face.

"You enormous faker," I said. "They didn't do a thing except poke you once or twice in the face and make a few nicks on your arms. I've done worse in crash landings." He stirred as I spoke, reaching out a hand to me. As he stretched his arm, he gave a deep groan and dropped it again, his face contorted in pain.

"Gabriel," I said, a trifle uncertainly. He didn't respond, and I felt a horrible suspicion dawning. I tugged as gently as I could at his shirt and he gave another deep groan, this one of protest as well as pain, but I didn't stop until I had rolled him onto his stomach. His shirt was soaked in blood, great stripes of it, some freshly red, some dark and clotted. I crawled to the corner and heaved quietly for a moment. When I was done, I wiped my mouth and went back to him. I gritted my back teeth together and seized the edge of his shirt, curling my fingers so tightly I thought the bones would break.

"Not all at once, Madame Starke," said Daoud from the flap of the tent. He was followed by one of his men with a basin of hot water and a few other oddments. "I have brought useful things," he told me.

He watched as his man set down the water and an old robe along with a battered tin of some dried-up salve with Turkish writing on the label.

"How did you do this?" I asked evenly.

He gave me a thin smile. "I am skilled with a riding crop."

"Bastard."

Daoud shrugged. "He was stubborn."

"Yes, well, that I can believe. I hope you got what you want."

The smile deepened. "Indeed, madame. I am leaving you now. Herr Doktor will remain behind with a few of my men to guard you." He nodded towards Gabriel. "The information he gave me may not be entirely accurate. I might have a few more questions for him."

He strode out and left me with Gabriel. He hadn't given me a knife, so I had to use my teeth to tear the robe into strips. I soaked one of them in the water and used it to saturate the remains of his shirt. It took a long time to coax it free, but eventually I managed and only a little fresh blood flowed when I pulled it off. I washed him as best I could and saw that the wounds were long but very thin and rather shallower than I had expected.

Daoud had used a small whip with a slender lash. I pried open the tin, breaking a few fingernails in the process. The salve inside smelled evil, but it was better than nothing. I softened it with some of the hot water and larded the rank stuff into his wounds. He stirred and protested, but I told him to shut up and finished the job. I bound up the worst of his wounds, and wished we'd saved a little of the whisky, as much for me as him.

As if I'd spoken aloud, Herr Doktor entered with a small flask. "How is he? A little schnapps would not go amiss, I think," he said. He opened the flask and handed it to me. "But first for the lady. I think this is not an easy thing for you."

"Oh, I don't know. I like my men bloody and unconscious," I said brightly.

But my hand trembled as I took the flask and the shrewd old eyes missed nothing. The schnapps burned straight to my belly and I gasped, choking a little as I handed the flask back.

"An old family recipe." He eased an arm under Gabriel's chest, and with surprising economy of movement, shifted him onto his side. Gabriel stirred and Herr Doktor gave him a sip of schnapps. Gabriel swallowed it down, followed quickly by two more gulps, then dropped his head. Schickfuss arranged him comfortably then gave me another long pull on the flask. He nodded approvingly as I didn't choke that time.

"You like the schnapps, Frau Starke," he said

with a smile of delight. "It is good to take what is fine about the old country, no? Some things we must not forget—including how to take care of our friends."

His gaze sharpened suddenly and I stared at him. He smiled as he realised I was beginning to understand. "Now, dear lady. Let us put our heads together and devise a way to escape with our companion."

I gaped at him and he handed back the flask without a word. I took another hefty swallow and only stopped when the tent began to swim around me. I shook my head to clear it.

"You're not a friend. You're in league with Daoud."

He spread his hands. "Sometimes one must do a little ill to effect a greater good."

I shook my head again, trying to fit the pieces together. "You mean you're here to keep Daoud from doing him more harm?"

His mouth turned down, his moustaches vibrating with disapproval. "Violence is distasteful, madame, particularly the violence of a brutal man. There are fine men in the desert, fine men of noble character. Regrettably, Daoud is not one of these. He is a little rough in his enthusiasms. He needed some persuading to consider the idea that our Mr. Starke might have some more useful information and it would be best to keep him alive."

"Mr. Starke? I suppose Daoud told you who he is?"

He shrugged and said nothing.

"So he has you to thank for his life at least. I'll make sure he writes you a nice thank-you note," I told him. He looked a trifle hurt, and I rolled my eyes. "What did you expect? A parade? You helped Daoud find us and bring us back here in the first place."

"Daoud was already well on his way to finding you when I joined him," he said, his manner stiff. "I did all that I could to protect you. *Both* of you," he said with a meaningful lift of the brows.

I sighed. "I suppose I owe you a bit of thanks for that. But unless you happen to have a vehicle outside and a quantity of morphine, I don't see how we're going to move him more than twelve feet. He's a dead weight, and between you and me, rather a considerable one."

"I am not fat," Gabriel muttered from the rug. "It's muscle."

With a guttural groan, he shoved himself up onto one arm. The arm shook but it held him as he opened one bloodshot eye to look at Herr Doktor. "Give me more of that rubbish you call liquor and I can walk anywhere. I'm not sticking around for Daoud to take another go at me, if it's all the same to you," he added with a quick glance at me.

Herr Doktor obediently passed over the flask.

Gabriel downed a significant amount, and the more he drank the sadder Schickfuss looked. "It came all the way from Breslau," he said as Gabriel drained the last drops.

"It went to a good cause," Gabriel told him. He took a great breath, wincing as he did, then forced himself to his knees.

"If you're going to puke, don't get it on my shoes," I told him.

He gave a single roar like a bull and forced himself upright onto his feet. He swayed but didn't falter. "I need a shirt," he said, his voice hoarse. I picked up the bloody rag he'd been wearing with my two fingers.

"This will have to do. We're fresh out of clean shirts."

He struggled into it with a great deal of swearing, but only a few of the wounds opened, and he was looking a little steadier. He turned to Herr Doktor. "How many are out there?"

Herr Doktor counted on his fingers. "Three, I think. I have a plan."

Gabriel didn't wait to hear it. He fisted his hands together and pushed past us, thrusting open the tent flap. As soon as he strode into the sunlight, two of Daoud's men jumped up from the campfire in front of the tent, reaching for their weapons.

Heaven only knows what Gabriel would have done then, but before either of them could cock their guns, two quick, muffled pops sounded and they slumped to the ground. The third and final guard emerged from an adjacent tent, but as he opened his mouth, a third pop sounded. He slid onto his stomach and lay perfectly still, bleeding urgently into the sand beneath him.

Gabriel and I stared at Herr Doktor, who was looking regretfully at the elegant pistol in his hand. It had been fitted with a neat little silencer, and the pops made by the weapon were no louder than the slipping of a cork from a bottle of champagne. "I told you I had a plan."

He guided us around one of the tents and threw his arms open wide with a showman's flourish.

"But that's—"

"Mother Mary," Gabriel said through gritted teeth. It was crouched there like a great hulking beast.

"But I tore out a handful of her wiring!" I protested.

Herr Doktor clucked his tongue at me. "Frau Starke, there are ways to manage such difficulties. Even in the Badiyat ash-Sham."

I threw open the bonnet and peered in. The tangled nest of wires had been put back into perfect order and the fuel tank Gabriel had smashed open had been neatly patched.

Herr Doktor gave me a sheepish smile. "I like to tinker with engines. I was not a linguist during the war, you know."

"What exactly did you do?"

He preened himself a little. "I am a man of many talents."

Herr Doktor opened the doors and waved us in. I took the front passenger seat and didn't bother to look back at Gabriel. He would manage under his own power—no doubt with a great deal of swearing and gritted teeth—and he wouldn't thank me for interfering.

The old gentleman reached down and sparked two wires together. Mother Mary shuddered to life and we started off. "I must be cautious here. We do not wish to be bogged in the sand," he explained. "I think none of us would like to be apprehended by Daoud after he has seen my little mess."

He negotiated the terrain expertly and pointed us east, not towards Palmyra, but not Damascus, either. I glanced back to see Gabriel had crawled into the vehicle on his belly and was lying face-down on the rear seat.

Herr Doktor fell silent then, and his features sagged a little. The exhilaration of effecting our escape had run its course, and he seemed tired. "This is a young man's game," he told me.

"I think you must be a mind reader, Herr Doktor," I replied.

"Pah. I have lived a long time, and always I like the pretty girls. It is not difficult to know what they think. You study something the whole of your life, it's no strange thing to become something of an expert."

I laughed aloud and he gave me one of his twinkling smiles. "I don't suppose you are going to tell us why you came to our rescue? Or what you hope to gain from this?"

He nodded. "All in good time, dear lady. Now, if the snores coming from behind us are any indication, the good gentleman has fallen asleep. I think you should rest, as well. We have a long drive, and I know the way. You are safe, *liebchen*."

After the war, I wouldn't have thought a German endearment would move me at all, but something about his tone warmed me.

I did as Herr Doktor told me, and almost as soon as I curled up, I fell dead asleep. When I woke, the long afternoon shadows were falling across the desert and looming ahead of us were the crumbling remains of a tall stone tower.

"Heavens, what is that?" I asked him.

"That, dear lady, is the Crusader castle, Castel La Soie. It was built by a Provençal knight who came to fight with Count Raymond of Toulouse during the First Crusade. Raymond wanted to extend the territory of the Outremer, so he permitted his knight to build a castle out here. The fellow thought he would grow rich on the silk trade between Baghdad and Damascus. Unfortunately for him, his sense of geography was not as good as his skills as an architect," he added with a wheezing laugh. "He built it fifty miles off the Silk Road!" He paused to laugh again, and I smiled politely. There didn't seem much that was funny in undertaking such a mammoth project and getting it wrong.

"Raymond of Toulouse was enraged, of course, but before he could punish his man, the count died. His successor did not trouble himself, and so the Provençal knight lived here, out of the way and alone with only a few servants to attend him. When he died, the castle was abandoned, although pilgrims and travellers have used it when they have wandered astray. Gradually, all has fallen to ruin except a few small rooms." He drew close to the base of the tower then applied the brake. "I have some supplies and I think we can be comfortable here for the night. Then we will make our plans, shall we not?"

Gabriel had slept heavily the entire trip with the result that he was so hideously stiff he almost couldn't move at all. Herr Doktor helped him from Mother Mary, gingerly lifting one of Gabriel's arms to put about his shoulders. Gabriel didn't swear for once, but he went white to the lips and for one horrible moment I thought he would faint.

Instead, he ground his teeth together and walked under his own power into the wrecked castle. Schickfuss led us through a half-roofed corridor and into a tiny suite of rooms that were in better shape than I'd expected.

Herr Doktor settled Gabriel and turned to me. "I will go and hide Mother Mary. There is a bit of rubble behind the place, and I think I can just manage to squeeze her in there. I will come back with food and water and another bottle of schnapps," he added with a guarded look at Gabriel.

"I'll make sure he doesn't drink it all," I assured him. When he left, I took a good look around. There were traces of animal habitation, but they were old and whatever had lived here last had been long gone before we arrived. Gabriel had eased himself onto a window embrasure and was sitting with his forearms braced against the stone surround. His colour wasn't any too good, and I didn't like the look of his hands. They were shaking and he gripped the stone until the knuckles were bloodless just to keep himself upright.

"Well, it isn't exactly the Ritz, but it's a damn sight better than some of the places we've spent the night," I said, thinking of a particularly nasty little hotel in Northumberland.

He didn't reply. It was clearly taking all of his effort just to stay conscious, and I waited, my nerves strained to breaking, for Herr Doktor to return. It seemed an age before he emerged from the little corridor, and when he came I saw why. His arms were full to heaping with supplies—bags of food, goatskins tight with water and even some bedding. He arranged the latter to make a comfortable pallet for Gabriel. I'd expected

Gabriel to protest, but he simply landed on it facedown and was out for the count.

"You need to eat something," I told him. He didn't reply, and Herr Doktor gave me a kindly smile.

"Let him sleep now. It is the most restorative thing in the world, a good sleep. You and I will eat and drink, and later, when he rouses, we will feed him, as well."

He beckoned me to what had once been the hearthstone of the little room. There he set a candle to light against the darkening shadows and began to arrange the food. He unpacked the usual native flatbreads and dates as well as some tinned things and even an orange, wrinkled and soft from its day in the boot of the car, but at least it was something fresh. He gallantly insisted I eat the whole thing, and I borrowed his imperial knife to cut it into segments, sectioning out bits for him in spite of his protests.

We ate like compatriots, the little German and I, sharing the food he had brought, along with a modest supply of his schnapps. "I will save some, for I think Herr Starke likes it even more than I," he promised with a gleam in his eye.

"You never answered me when I asked if Daoud told you who he was."

He gave me a twinkling smile. "Is it because I am old that you underestimate me or because I am German?"

I considered. "Both," I replied. He broke into his peculiar wheezy laugh.

"I like a woman who is no stranger to honesty. It is a man's virtue." I opened my mouth to protest, but he waved me away. "It is not their shame that women do not have their share of honesty, my dear. It is our fault for making a world that demands they dissemble. But you are not like most women. You do not tremble and swoon when you see the man you love is so grievously injured."

I licked a drop of juice from the orange off my lips carefully. "Because I don't love Gabriel."

He wagged his chin at me. "I thought we established you were honest. Ah, very well. I am not here to force confidences. You are married to him, though, *nein*?"

There didn't seem much point in prevaricating considering how much he already seemed to know. "Yes. But the last time I saw him was in 1915. I was preparing to divorce him. Since that time I thought he was dead."

"Until very recently."

"Quite recently," I conceded. "Now perhaps you'll be good enough to tell me how you come to know so much about us."

He shrugged. "Because I am of little consequence."

"But, Herr Doktor—"

"No, child, do not protest. I speak the truth, and it is a truth you will know if you are ever my age

253

and your country is a conquered one." His old eyes were nostalgic. "The world is not as I once knew it. My upbringing, well, you would consider it medieval, I suspect," he said, his gleam beginning to reemerge. "I was brought up in the forests outside Breslau. My father had a hunting lodge there and always we were on horseback, testing our mettle. I was sent to school to learn to be a soldier, like any good Prussian lordling."

"Lordling? Your family is aristocratic?"

The full twinkle was in evidence as he smiled at me. "I no longer use my full title, my dear, but I was born Freiherr Wolfram von Schickfuss."

Something stirred in my memory—the pilots in the convalescent home talking about the Red Baron. His title was Freiherr, as well. "Freiherr? That's baron, isn't it?"

"It is. And as I say, the world then was a different place. I was taught to shoot and to ride and I came home fit for life as a country squire. But the stars sometimes rearrange our plans," he said, his voice low and dreamy. "I was out hunting my first autumn back at home. My horse stumbled and threw me into an icy stream. I managed to make my way up the bank, but I fell very ill and my lungs were damaged. My father decided to send me to the warmth of the Near East to recover. I had time, nothing but time on my hands, and nothing to do but sit and grow stronger. So I read. I read about excavations in Egypt and the Holy Land, and I paid calls to the sites where archaeologists were unearthing treasures. I learned much and I offered myself to the archaeologists. I did anything they needed just to be on hand to learn more. I picked through mountains of excavated dirt in the sieves. I tinkered with engines and made them run again. I drew maps and ran errands. Whatever I could to make myself valuable. And in time I learned so much, I myself *became* valuable. A dig hired me and I was sent to the Badiyat ash-Sham, this wondrous wasteland. And it was there I met her."

"Her?"

He smiled. "Of course, my dear. Every tale should have a love story within it. And mine does, a very little one. Her name was Anna, but I think you know her better by another name?"

"I know her?" I stared at him in mystification, then I dropped the date I had been about to eat. *"Gethsemane?"*

He nodded, his expression wistful. "It was one summer only, but it was the most glorious summer of my life. The feelings for her, I have never forgotten. And so, when she comes to me and says, 'Wolfram, you must help me. I think something is afoot,' what can I do but help her?"

I rocked back on my heels. It did not seem possible, but there was something so simple, so grave in his manner, I knew he was telling the truth. But this portly little German and the tall and tweedy Englishwoman! The mind reeled.

' "She was not always as she is now," he said, revealing again his trick of reading my mind. I looked away and reached for another date. "She was beautiful then, like a Rhine maiden. She was a Lorelei, with long golden hair and eyes the same bright blue as the sky over Silesia. She was everything I admired in a woman. And I was not as I am now, either," he said with a rueful glance at his rounded belly. "I was young and fit and my muscles were hard with vigorous work. I was a match for her then." He paused then drew out his handkerchief and wiped at his eyes. The Germans had a reputation for coldness but in my experience there were few people more sentimental. I looked away again until he had finished. He picked up the thread of his tale.

"We had that summer together in our youth but nothing more. I was no scoundrel, you understand. I offered her honourable marriage. Not wealth, for we were not a rich family, but comfort and ease and the title of Freifrau as my wife. But these gifts I laid at her feet, she did not want. She wanted only her work. This she loved, more than she loved me. And I left the Badiyat ash-Sham with a heart so broken I could never love another."

I caught my breath. "You never loved another?"

He laughed. "Of course I did. I am a man. I married three times and I loved them all. They were good women, my wives. But never do I forget my first love, my English Anna. And always I say to myself, 'Wolfram, someday you will see her again.' But the years pass and the wives come and go and I do not see her. And then the war. It was a terrible thing, that war. I am ashamed of it. Not of my people," he corrected swiftly, "but of the emperor and his kind. It was a stupid war and wars should never be about stupid things. It was years of blood and mud and pain and when it was over, I said to myself, 'Now, Wolfram. *Now,* you must find her.' And so I made inquiries and I discovered she was digging once more in the Badiyat ash-Sham. And I make my way to her."

"That is the most romantic thing I have ever heard," I sighed.

"It is not romantic," he said severely. "Romantic would be if she still looked like a Rhine maiden. She is fat and old and so am I. But I look at her, and for a moment I pretend I am twenty again, and I love her still. And so I am here, doing her bidding. For the sake of a boy I once was and the girl she used to be."

"I still think it's sweet." I paused. "What trouble did she think was afoot at the dig?"

He shrugged. "She does not tell me everything. But she notices the Hungarians, they keep their eyes close upon Herr Starke—Rowan, as he called himself. The Hungarians," he said again, and he spat into the corner. "They are scoundrels. The English and the German, we share a common ancestry. We understand one another. The Hungarians are a race apart, liars and thieves."

His face was an alarming shade of red, and I cleared my throat gently. He recovered himself and took a deep breath. "As I say, the Hungarians kept close eyes upon Herr Starke. And then Daoud comes to me and says he has heard of a great treasure, that he is not a fool but a clever man who has the means of bringing me a wondrous find if I can give him money enough for it. It does not take a genius to realise this is the thing the Thurzós intend to steal from Herr Starke. I discuss it with my Anna and she tells me she has looked into Mr. Rowan's things and discovered cuttings, all of them about the beautiful Frau Starke and her aeroplane trip. One of these has a picture of Frau Starke and her former husband, and Anna is clever. She has always thought to herself that Herr Rowan resembled someone she once met, but now she knows for certain. The photograph is clearer than her dim memory of a boy who once dug in the Badiyat ash-Sham as a student. She understands now that he has been passing himself off as someone he is not. But what can she prove against him? Nothing, for she knows nothing. So she follows him to Damascus and who does she find there?"

"Me," I said meekly.

"You! How suspicious does this look now. But to what purpose does Herr Starke pretend to be someone else? And to what purpose has his wife come to Damascus? My Anna is clever. She follows Herr Starke as he follows you. She believes you are not in league with your husband, but she cannot know for sure unless she brings you face-to-face."

"The dinner in Damascus," I murmured.

He nodded. "She watches closely when you are faced with him. She said you were very cool, very composed, and yet your face is the colour of new milk when you see him. You might have suspected he was alive, but not until this moment do you know for certain. Anna arranges then to bring you here, to the Badiyat ash-Sham, to determine what the purpose of your plots might be. But before she can do so, you disappear with Herr Starke, and then poof! So go the Thurzós and Daoud, as well. My Anna insists that I must go and discover what is happening. She has reason to be suspicious of Herr Starke, and yet always she remembers the boy she knew. She liked this boy, trusted him, and she was very hurt that Herr Starke did not trust her enough to confide," he added, wagging his chin at me.

"That was bad form," I agreed. "I am sorry Miss Green was alarmed."

"I do not like to see my Anna vexed," he said pointedly. "But I must be careful because I do not know if Herr Starke is a villain, you understand? So I am cautious. I make myself seen so that you may come to me if you need help. But you do not come, and what am I to think but that you are in league with the criminal Daoud? It is only when I find him that I understand he is not happy with Herr Starke and means to harm him. Then I think to myself I can help and I make myself friendly to him to work to get you free." He finished his tale, preening a little at his own cleverness.

"And very kind of you it was. But now," I said, brushing crumbs from my fingers, "I think we need a plan."

"No, Frau Starke. What we need is rest. You are a strong girl, and a brave one, but one can go only so far on one's courage. It is time to sleep now. I will go out to the car and keep watch to make sure you will rest in safety."

"But you must be tired, too," I protested. "You were awake all night and drove all day with us."

He shook his head. "I am old, my dear. I sleep like a cat, a little here, a little there. It is all the same to me."

I rose and helped him up as he groaned a little, his body creaking and popping. "I sound like an old wooden house settling," he joked.

He straightened and I put a hand to his arm. "I am glad you are here with us. You are a good friend."

He smiled and lifted my hand to his lips in a courtly gesture. "It is difficult to know who is a friend here," he said as he moved slowly towards the corridor. He turned back, taking one long look from Gabriel to me. "One will always need friends in the Badiyat ash-Sham."

TWELVE

He left me the rest of the food and water and the candle, stuck in a puddle of its own grease and burning slowly down. I blew it out and waited a moment for my eyes to grow accustomed to the dim scattering of starlight beaming through the narrow embrasure. When I could make out the shape of the pallet on the floor, I crept onto the edge of it, careful to keep away from Gabriel. He slept on, heavily, and I tumbled into sleep almost as soon as I lay my exhausted body next to his. Sometime later, deep in the darkest hours of the night, I woke as I felt strong fingers covering mine. He was shivering and muttering in his sleep, and when I touched his skin, it was scorching hot. I found the candle and lit it, half-afraid of what I would see when I looked at him. He was still on his belly, but his head was turned to the side, his face in profile. His cheek and eye were sunken and hollow-looking, and his brow was puckered. Somehow he had thrown off the blanket I draped over him, but I found it again and pulled it over both of us. I slipped close to him, careful not to touch him where he'd been wounded.

"I'm here, now hush and go back to sleep," I told him, hoping it would settle him down. But he stayed restless, his hands plucking under his body at the pocket of his ruined shirt. I sighed and reached into the pocket, tugging out the little tin box. "I know I promised to bury you with this, but you're not dying yet, if that's what you think." I pushed the box into his hands and he calmed instantly. The muscles of his face relaxed, and although he still shivered and shuddered with fever, he stopped mumbling.

After a few minutes he slipped deeper into sleep and his hands relaxed. I eased the box out of his fingers, but he was too far gone to protest. I opened it slowly, mystified as to what he could possibly carry in there that would be so important to him.

There was a wad of banknotes—a few very large bills and several smaller ones, tied with a bit of grimy twine—and a few newspaper cuttings, worn smooth from too much handling. They were cuttings about me, stories of my journey with the *Jolly Roger* and Aunt Dove, some with photographs, and one featuring a particularly warm embrace between Wally and me. I folded them back and put them aside. His signet ring was there, the gold ring he had always worn on his smallest finger. I could just make out the inscription under the shield, the same as on the knight's tomb at the dig site. *Nec Aspera Terrant.* There were cigarettes in the tin and a match or two, and there was a tiny rabbit's foot, the same one he had carried since boyhood on all his adventures. Half the fur was missing now, and it looked rather gruesome, but he would have sooner died than part with it.

And as I went to replace the contents, I realised something was sticking out of the roll of banknotes, something that had been tied inside them, perhaps for safekeeping. I untied the twine and opened the roll. It was a photograph, one I had forgot ever existed. It had been taken the day of our wedding and was the only image of the two of us together. We had just emerged from the registrar's office in Scotland, hand in hand, and Gabriel had spotted the tourist with his little camera snapping the picturesque street. He had darted over and pressed an enormous banknote in the man's hand along with his card. When he ran back, he was laughing his bright, merry laugh as he scooped me up into his arms as if to carry me over a threshold. The shutter clicked just as I had shrieked, and the image was a little blurry. But it was unmistakably us—and just as I had remembered us. I was impossibly young and so stupidly trusting, and Gabriel was the most beautiful boy I had ever seen. By the time the photograph had arrived in the post, Gabriel and I were packing for China. I had lost track of it soon after, and if I had thought of it, I would have assumed that it had

263

been lost, like so much drifting flotsam and jetsam left behind from the wreckage of our marriage. It was like stumbling onto a ghost, a dream I had long ago given up for dead.

The edges of it were soft with wear, and it was creased in a few places and even scorched a little on one side. It was battered and bashed and looked as if it had been to hell and back, just like the man who carried it. In the photograph I was staring up at him with adoring eyes, and when I looked at the expression on his face, I felt my heart turn over. I hadn't imagined it, not everything. He really had looked at me that way. Even if only for a moment.

I tied it back into the wad of banknotes and shoved everything back into the box. I thrust the box into his hands again and blew out the candle.

"This doesn't change anything," I said into the darkness. "Not a bloody thing."

By the time morning came, his fever had broken, leaving him looking disreputable as a buccaneer, and with a raging thirst. I gave him what was in the goatskin and a handful of dates and nuts.

"I see a tin of bully beef," he said accusingly. "Where's mine?"

"I ate it," I told him. "You slept through dinner."

He swore and got to his feet slowly. He moved like an old man, but when he stood, he didn't sway.

"That shirt is going to have to be burned when you find another," I said.

"At least I can move without wanting to scream or heave my stomach out," he said, his tone deceptively light. The skin around his eyes had tightened, and I knew that just moving at all was still excruciating for him.

"I'll go and wake Herr Doktor. He knows who you are, by the way. It's a long story, but for now all you need know is that he's on our side. He spent the night in Mother Mary to keep watch over us. Wasn't that sweet?"

Gabriel slanted me an odd look. "You and I have entirely different notions of sweetness, my dear."

I didn't bother to reply. I made my way through the narrow corridor and into the pink of the dawn. I paused a moment on the threshold to stretch and take in one long breath of clean desert air. If it weren't for being chased and shot at and nearly perishing of thirst and listening to Gabriel get thrashed within an inch of his life, I might have quite liked the place. There was an austere beauty to it, like an elderly woman whose youthful beauty still lingers in the bones of her face.

I took another deep breath and felt the promise in the air. It was going to be a very good day, I decided. We had an ally and we had transportation. The worst of our journey was behind us, and we had come out the other side, although Gabriel might well bear a few souvenirs on his back for a long while to come.

I stepped out of the doorway and turned to where we had left the car. I stood a long moment, making sense of what I saw, or rather, what I didn't. Then I swung around on my heel and went back to Gabriel.

"I'm afraid Herr Doktor is gone."

He flicked me a sour glance. "And I suppose he's taken the vehicle?"

I nodded.

What followed was a string of profanity so elaborate and original I couldn't even be offended. I folded my arms over my chest and waited for the storm to pass.

"Full marks for a towering display of rage," I told him. "Now what do we do?"

"I still can't believe the little bastard left us."

I shrugged. "I'm sure he had a good reason, but without the extra stores of food and water, we can't stay here. Do you know where we are?"

He rolled his eyes. "I wasn't precisely paying attention on the journey, Evie. You might have noticed but I had a spot of bother with our friend Daoud and I was a trifle preoccupied by the after-effects of that."

"There's no need to be nasty. And I know exactly the extent of your injuries since I'm the one who cleaned you up."

He paused. "Thank you for that. I don't suppose it was very nice."

"It was thoroughly disgusting, if you must know. There was a very good reason I nursed at a convalescent hospital instead of the front lines, you know. I don't much care for gore."

"I remember," he said, a sudden smile touching his lips. "You made me stitch my own leg after I collided with that rickshaw in Shanghai."

"Served you right for coming back to the hotel in the middle of the night and drunk as a lord. Besides, your skill with a needle always was better than mine."

"I got more practise. I think there wasn't a porter in China I didn't sew up at some point."

He was still smiling, but I was in no mood to reminisce. "Back to the problem at hand, Gabriel. The good doctor is out there wandering the desert for God only knows what reason and we're on very low rations. What do you suggest we do?"

"What do you suggest?" he countered.

I stared at him. "You're actually asking my opinion."

He shrugged, wincing as the gesture tugged at his ravaged skin. "I have been reliably informed that I am a very poor criminal mastermind. So, 'unrip your plan, Captain,'" he quoted cheerfully.

I thought a moment. "We should wait a little while, perhaps until sundown. If he hasn't come by then, we should leave and try to find water and friendly Bedouin. We crossed a wide track yesterday. I think it might have been a road. It couldn't be more than a mile or two back."

He gave a short nod. "Good enough."

I blinked. "That's it? You're agreeing? No fighting? No swearing?"

"Child, I am exhausted. I am thirsty. I have a back that has only just begun to heal from the sort of thrashing I wouldn't give a donkey. If you don't mind, I'll take a pass on scrapping with you. Let's save it for a day when I am feeling more myself, shall we?" He eased himself back down onto his pallet and lay on his belly. I stared at him uncertainly, but he turned his head, his expression taunting. "Don't worry. I'll feel much more like abusing you when I wake up. If there's something vicious you'd like to call me, I'm sure it will keep."

He turned his head and went back to sleep, leaving me with four or five choice things I'd like to call him. How he could sleep when we were stranded in the far reaches of the Badiyat ash-Sham was beyond me. And the fact that he showed no worry at all for what had become of Herr Doktor was a little disloyal, I thought. The old fellow had gone to great lengths to rescue us, and I hated to think of him on the loose out there, possibly at the mercy of Daoud, whom I suspected would not have taken his defection at all well.

I busied myself by organising our small store of

supplies and then passed the next several hours by working out a game of pitching stones into the tin of bully beef. It was useless playing against myself, but at least it passed the time. I had grown superstitious with it. When I put a stone directly into the empty tin I told myself everything was going to be just fine. But when I missed . . .

After I'd missed three stones in a row, I gathered the supplies and woke Gabriel. It took him a little longer to come to this time, and when he stood, he didn't seem terribly steady on his feet.

"I'm afraid you're starting a fever again," I told him.

"Have you a thermometer, nursie? I can drop my trousers and you can take my temperature if you like. I'm not shy," he said, moving the hand I had put out to touch his brow to someplace far less appropriate.

I snatched my hand back and led the way out of the castle without speaking. When we were outside he glanced up at the crumbling keep. "You know, it's a bloody miracle the thing didn't crash down on us in our sleep. It's a decrepit menace."

"It was perfectly good shelter," I reminded him. "And if you're going to criticise every little thing anyone does for you—" I carried on in that vein for the next two miles with Gabriel occasionally rolling his eyes or whistling a bit of one of his pan-pipe melodies to tune me out. By the time we'd exhausted ourselves quarrelling, we had come to the wide track. Gabriel leaned as far as he could comfortably and scrutinised the ground.

"The old fellow's been through here today. The tyre marks are quite fresh. He took the track southwest towards Damascus," he told me.

"He must be going for help," I said, determined not to think too badly of the little man for abandoning us. Gabriel bent a little further, wincing as he stared at the older marks on the track.

"What is it? What do you see?"

"It isn't what I see," he said slowly. "It's what I hear." He had his head cocked and he was listening intently. A long moment passed before he murmured a single word. "Camels."

He straightened and turned the other way, towards the northeast leg of the track. I saw nothing, but I put my hand up and stared into the distance until my eyes watered. Suddenly, a great cloud of dust and sand appeared and before it, a group of camels. They were coming fast in the peculiar loping run they had that covered ground swiftly as a horse. As they neared, I heard the jingle of bells from their elaborate harnesses, and I could see the men were draped in robes of black-and-white with distinctive scarlet cords upon their headdresses.

Next to me, Gabriel's posture had stiffened and he stepped forward, putting himself ahead of me on the road, but at the sight of them, he turned back.

"Evie," he said casually, "whatever happens, mind you don't flinch."

"Flinch? Why would I—" But then I saw. The Bedouin were not stopping. They rode straight for us, lances at shoulder height and pointed straight ahead. The warriors made an astonishing racket as they charged, racing their camels as if they would run directly over the top of us and never stop.

It took every last bit of control to steel my screaming nerves as one of them bore down on me. It was enormous, far larger than I realised camels could be, and it was a peculiar shade of creamy white, with a long neck and a lip that seemed to curl back in scorn. Just as I could see the pupil of its eye, wide and malevolent, the warrior mounted on the camel flung his spear to the ground at my feet, the length of the shaft wobbling as it struck home. Long streamers fluttered in the breeze, and he stood in his stirrups, shouting his war cries to his friends. The rest of them did the same, flinging their lances at my feet until an entire forest of them quivered in front of me. Not one had been thrown at Gabriel, and I turned to him for an explanation.

The lead rider, who had flung the first lance, dismounted his camel with a flourish. He was an extraordinarily handsome fellow, almost Gabriel's height of six feet, with a beautifully cut hawklike profile and arresting dark eyes. A pair of Persian greyhounds, sleek and handsome as their master, trotted at his heels, and perched atop his shoulder was a falcon that stirred its wings in the wind. He walked directly to Gabriel, his arms wide.

In spite of his injuries, Gabriel returned his embrace. "Thank Allah you're here, Hamid," he said.

His friend kissed him once on each cheek in the Bedouin custom and said something in Arabic. The only word I recognised was *akh*. Brother. The salukis, trained to a trice, had stood, quivering at their master's heel until he snapped his fingers. They sprang forward to Gabriel, rolling about in ecstasy as he gave them each a quick pat.

Gabriel and the Bedouin leader exchanged quick remarks, their expressions grim, but it was obvious they were very glad to see one another. Gabriel turned to me, almost as an afterthought.

"Sheikh Hamid ibn Hussein, this is Evangeline Starke. My wife. Evie, say hello to Hamid."

Stupefied, I inclined my head, but the fellow bowed deeply and made a gesture of welcome or blessing. "You are the wife of my brother, Djibril. You are welcome as my little sister." He turned and shouted a series of instructions to his men.

I flicked a glance at Gabriel. "Djibril?"

"It's the Arabic form of Gabriel," he told me. He grinned. "Relax, pet. Hamid is a sort of prince of his tribe. We're in good hands now."

"Then what was all that palaver with the lances?" I demanded.

"It's called a *ghazou*," he explained. "It's a test of courage. He wanted to see what you were made of. Now he knows. Don't scowl so, my dear. He's responsible for the safety of his entire tribe. He has to be cautious. Besides, I think he was amusing himself a little."

"He's rather dashing," I said faintly.

Gabriel gave me a cool glance. "And lucky for you he only has three wives. Play your cards right and you could be number four."

"Not unless I have him kill you first," I returned sweetly. "We are still married."

If Sheikh Hamid noticed anything amiss in our exchange, he had the good manners not to show it. He and Gabriel had a swift discussion of our situation—at least I thought that was what they said since the conversation was entirely in Arabic—and before I knew it, one of the men was walking towards us leading a camel. He gave it to Hamid, who led his own white camel to us. Hamid tapped it lightly with a crop and it gave a great gusty sigh as it knelt down.

"My friends, I offer you my own mount, Zahar." He crooned a moment to the camel then handed the reins to Gabriel and went to his new mount, a shaggier gold camel that stood looking bored as Hamid vaulted lightly into the saddle. Gabriel mounted gingerly but with an astonishing amount of expertise. He gestured impatiently to me.

"Hurry up, then."

I stood my ground. "Must I?"

Gabriel leaned over as far as he could without falling from the saddle, his face inches from mine. When he spoke, his words were low enough for my ears only and clipped off with barely smothered rage.

"Get. On. The. Goddamned. Camel."

"Why can't I ride with the sheikh or one of the others?"

"Because a Bedouin man doesn't touch a woman he isn't related to if he can help it," he explained swiftly.

"Daoud did."

"Daoud was kidnapping us, you imbecile. Now stop making an ass of yourself and get on the camel or, so help me God—"

I moved forward. "You needn't blaspheme, Gabriel. Heavens, you look mad enough to burst a vein. Now, how do I do this?"

"Put your boot on the ledge of the saddle and swing your leg forward over its head in one quick motion. There, just like that. Now grip the saddle with your knees and lean back," he instructed. I did, acutely aware of Gabriel just behind me, his chest firm against my back.

He made a clucking sound to the camel and it surged forward as it lifted itself onto its front knees. "Now lean forward,"Gabriel said, shoving me against the saddle horn. We rocked back and forth again as the animal straightened its back legs and then the front.

"Oh, my," I breathed.

Sheikh Hamid grinned. "You will like my Zahar. It is our word for flower and it suits her. Like all desert flowers, she is hardy and beautiful."

She didn't seem particularly beautiful—a camel is a distinctly unlovely creature to begin with—but I could see from the other animals that this one had a particularly fine head and a dainty way about her. She could move like the wind, and when Gabriel touched her lightly with the crop, she was off, nosing her way home. Gabriel kept her at a steady trot, and for such an ungainly animal she managed an even, almost silky ride with that gait. To my astonishment, I found myself relaxing, even humming a little tune under my breath as the miles rolled away.

"Do you mind?" Gabriel asked, his voice arctic. He pointedly brushed my hair out of his face and pushed me forward.

"What's the trouble?"

"Your hair is in my eyes and that tune is particularly annoying."

"It's 'Salut d'Amour,'" I said, my eyes fixed firmly on the track ahead of us.

"I recognised it," he returned. "It's still an appalling piece of treacle."

"You liked it well enough at our wedding," I reminded him.

275

"I had very poor taste in those days."

I laughed and he poked pointedly at my back. "You've gone dead weight again, and if you will forgive the observation, you seem to have put on a few pounds since the last time I saw you."

I jerked forward in the saddle. "I most certainly have *not*. If anything I weigh less now. A pilot has to be extremely conscious of such things. And of all the obnoxious and inappropriately personal remarks—" I carried on in that vein for the rest of the journey, but Gabriel didn't bother to reply. He simply directed the camel with a faintly supercilious smile on his face, and I realised he wasn't even listening. I finally huffed out a sigh and settled down, clutching at the saddle horn since I would have sooner walked the entire Badiyat ash-Sham on foot than touched Gabriel at that point.

But almost as soon as I'd stopped talking, the track veered off the straight course we'd been following and led us to a narrow gap between two steep walls of rock. The salukis ran ahead, tails held aloft like banners, and with a quick whistle, Sheikh Hamid set the falcon to flight. It disappeared ahead of us between the rock walls. The path was so tight we had to ride single file, and the flat rocky ground of the desert proper gave way to scrubby hills, and as we twisted and turned, the vast blankness of the desert fell away quickly. A stony outcropping stretched overhead where two of the hills clung together, and just beyond these, the path widened into a small fertile valley. The hillsides were green—nothing like England in the spring, but they had a lushness all their own after the barren wasteland we had just passed through. The ground was carpeted with low green bushes starred with little white flowers. At the lowest edge of the valley stood a circle of trees and what passed for a small meadow in these parts. Ranged around this pretty pasture were a series of low black goats'-hair tents, the tents of the Bedouin. Surrounding them were herds of horses and camels, and beyond these restless groups of sheep and goats dotted the hillsides as they cropped for the small shoots of spring grasses. Between the tents, cooking fires were tended by veiled women while children scampered about underfoot, stopping as soon as they saw us to carry the news that visitors were coming.

Gabriel tugged the reins to halt Zahar and Sheikh Hamid rode up next to us. "This is our spring pasturage. My people welcome you to this place." He turned to Gabriel, affection warming his dark eyes. "Welcome home, my brother."

I started to turn in the saddle, but Gabriel abruptly made a sharp clicking noise at Zahar and we were rocked back and forth as she settled onto her belly like a great ship coming to berth. "Get off the same way you got on," he told me.

I did, jumping free of the camel as Gabriel

swung himself slowly off. He patted its neck and murmured something in Arabic while she made grunting noises and fluttered her eyelashes.

"You appear to have made a conquest," I told Gabriel.

The returning men were greeted rapturously by their children and their veiled women as we stood by and watched. Sheikh Hamid gave me a wide grin. "We have been gone a few weeks. They will want news and goods," he explained. A slender figure in a long black robe had come near to him. She waited patiently, and although her face was veiled, I could see a pair of bright eyes shining over the edge.

"My wife, Sheikha Aysha," he told me. "She will take you to your tent so you may wash and when you have finished, you will join us for a good meal." He turned and gave instructions in rapid Arabic and she nodded. He leaned close to her and said something else and she gave a light laugh as he smiled down at her.

"Newlyweds," Gabriel told me sourly.

"Should I explain to her now or later about female emancipation?" I asked him with my sweetest smile.

His face was thunderous. "These are my friends and you will not disrespect them by attempting to change them in any way, is that clear?"

His eyes were ice-cold and I stepped sharply away. "You know perfectly well I would never do anything as rude as that. Hell's bells, you're in a rotten mood."

"You would be, too, if someone had sliced open your back and the best nursing around was yours," he said, his tone aggrieved.

I felt a rush of sympathy then in spite of myself. "I'm sorry, Gabriel. It was a beastly thing to have happen, and I'm sure it hurts like the very devil."

He opened his mouth, most likely to bark at me again, but he closed it suddenly and shook his head. "Forget it. Bedouins are excellent healers. I'm in good hands with them. Hamid has an old fellow, name of Faiz. He will fix me right up. Go on then. Aysha's waiting."

I turned to find those patient dark eyes resting on me, and she beckoned to me with a slender hand. I noticed her wrists were heavily laden with gold bracelets, and as she walked she jingled as much as the camels had.

She drew me into one of the dark woolen tents, where a gaggle of women waited, all chattering. As we entered, they fell silent and stared over the edges of their veils. They scrutinised me intently, pointing to my trousers and my undraped face, and for a moment, the mood wasn't entirely friendly. I gave them as respectful an inclination of the head as I could manage, and said slowly, "*Asalaam aleikum.*"

No doubt I mangled the pronunciation, but the attempt was appreciated and instantly the mood changed. Smiles broke out with more chattering, and they threw back their veils. Sheikha Aysha turned to me, holding her veil in her fingertips. She was older than I expected, almost of an age with her husband, but beautiful and dignified. She had plump lips and those magnificent eyes, and I wasn't at all surprised she had ended up married to the sheikh. Beauty must be as much of a commodity among the Bedouin as anywhere else.

She reached out her hand to me and I took it in mine. Before I could shake it, she leaned forward and touched her nose to mine three times. I blinked at her in astonishment, but from her smile I could tell it was a gesture of warmth. Several of the other women repeated the gesture, and soon a line formed of women waiting to touch noses with me. I touched them all, murmuring the same greeting over and over. *"Asalaam aleikum."*

When I'd finished, they pulled me to the center of a circle of women and started tugging at my clothes, exclaiming over each garment as they pulled it free. Under other circumstances I might have been at least halfway embarrassed, but their hands were gentle and kind and to my horror, I felt tears prickling the back of my eyes. My throat tightened, and as I clamped my lips shut, Sheikha Aysha leaned close into my face.

She shook her head and said something in low tones to the other women. Then she put out her hand and petted my filthy hair, crooning. The others did the same, one patting my hand, another putting a tender hand to my shoulder and I started to weep. I felt a perfect fool sobbing on them, but there was something so very kind about their manner, and before I knew what was happening, I was bawling my eyes out. I don't know if it was the gentle eyes or the nurturing hands or the fact that not one of them spoke English, but I told them everything, from the first time I met Gabriel to our whirlwind courtship to the disastrous trip to China that ended with me asking for a divorce I wasn't even sure I wanted. I told them about my flying escapades and Aunt Dove and Arthur Wellesley— I think the flapping may have confused them a bit since I used a wing gesture for both the *Jolly Roger* and Arthur Wellesley. For all I knew, they might have thought I was flying a parrot across the seven seas. But I kept talking. I told them about coming to Damascus and about shooting Gabriel and about him being lashed by Daoud. The only thing I left out was the Cross. There was no point in telling anyone about that, whether they understood me or not.

While I talked and cried, they kept up their gentle ministrations. They brought water in a deep copper can, a tremendous luxury in the desert, then washed me thoroughly and scrubbed every speck of filth from my skin. They washed my hair and rinsed it in rosewater, drying it with bits of silk until the curls were polished to a high sheen.

They wrapped me in a fine black robe lavishly embroidered in blue silk. It felt heavenly after days in my trousers and boots, and they even gave me a pair of the soft little leather slippers they wore. They carried my own clothes away and mimed washing, so I let them go with barely a protest. By that time I was finished with my story and was hiccupping a little. They bathed my eyes and gave me a hot drink of tea infused with cardamom and sweetened with honey to soothe my throat. They lined my eyes with kohl, miming the sun overhead, and I understood after a fashion that the purpose of the black stuff was to protect the eyes from the burning rays. Then they washed my hands a final time in rosewater so that when they stepped back and admired their handiwork, I was a clean, dry, perfumed and infinitely calmer woman than I had been an hour before.

Sheikha Aysha nodded to the other women, who were smiling. She thanked them with a phrase I recognised from my guidebook and they left us, pulling their veils firmly into place as they went. She turned to me and gave me a look of gentle approbation. "I think you are happy now, yes?"

I stood staring at her for a long moment before I remembered to close my mouth. "You speak English."

Her smile was gentle. "I needed no English to understand tears, *sitt*. I think you are better now."

"How do you come to know English out here of all places?"

She pointed in the direction of the men's tent. "My husband is pleased to teach me the languages he knows."

"Languages? Does he speak more than Arabic and English?"

She counted on her fingers. "And French, Persian and some Turkish, although this is not a language we like." She tipped her head and peered at me closely. "There is a saying here, *sitt*—a woman without her husband is the bird without a wing."

I covered her hand with my own. "This particular bird has her own wings. But thank you."

"You are most welcome."

She replaced her veil then and led me out of the tent and to another. This was the finest I had seen, clearly the domain of the sheikh. The ground had been spread with the most glorious Turkish carpets I had ever seen, light and silken underfoot, while the rough woolen walls of the tent were hung with the same. Pierced lamps hung from the tent poles, gently illuminating the dimness, and scattered about were dozens of cushions plump with feathers and dripping with fringe.

The tent was full of men, and I noticed Sheikha Aysha did not enter. She went as far as the flap and gestured for me to go inside. I recognised some of the men with Sheikh Hamid as those who had brought us to the village, but the others were strangers, watchful ones with the same bright eyes and assessing glances as their womenfolk. Another stranger sat next to the sheikh, his legs as carefully tucked as his sheikh's, the skirts of his robes folded formally under him as his glossy dark head bent over a map stretched between them.

Sheikh Hamid looked up and nudged his friend, who looked up sharply.

"Gabriel?"

It seems astonishing, but for a moment, I did not know him. He looked a far sight better than when I had seen him last. He, too, had been scrubbed within an inch of his life, and I realised it was the first time in five years I'd seen him without either desert grime or his wretched disguise diminishing his features. The lines I'd noticed in the photograph were there, but the grey had been washed out of his hair, leaving it dark as a seal's pelt, and his jaw had been shaved clean and smooth, revealing the cleft in his chin I had almost forgot. But the eyes were the same, as bright a blue as any forget-me-not in England, I thought numbly.

He gave me a warm smile for an instant, his dimples in evidence. Then, abruptly, his expression grew shuttered. He cleared his throat and rose casually.

"Evie. It's not customary for Bedouin women to eat with European men, but they welcome you to eat with the gentlemen of their tribe. Sit between

Hamid and me. It will make things less awkward for the others."

I nodded to the sheikh and scurried to take my place next to him, careful to keep my legs covered with my robe and my feet out of sight. "Any other tips?" I asked Gabriel, sotto voce.

"Yes, remember to eat with your right hand only and don't talk."

"Is that last bit also a Bedouin preference?"

"No, it's a Starke preference," he said with a glimmer of a smile.

"Have I missed anything important?"

"Only a ceremony of welcome. I was given coffee and there were certain exchanges of courtesies."

"I'm sorry I missed it," I said ruefully.

"What have you been doing?" he asked, peering at my telltale pink nose.

"Nothing. Nothing *whatsoever.*"

As soon as we were seated, the sheikh gave a signal and food began to appear. The map was whisked away and in its place were set great platters of food similar to what we had eaten with Daoud but of much finer quality. The platters were passed in a strict anticlockwise pattern, beginning with the seats of honour. There were piles of couscous soaked with the juices of roasted meats, and the meat itself shredded over the top in delicious titbits. There were dried fruits plumped in honey, and even a dish of eggplant, sliced and fried crisply. A mellow goat's cheese was offered, drizzled in more of the thyme-scented honey, and to follow, sweet pomegranate syrup in tiny glasses.

We ate until we could hold no more, and when the eating was finished and our hands were washed in rosewater, the men brought out their pipes and began to smoke and tell stories. I understood a little of what was said, but not enough to follow with any real interest although it was clear several of the men were born raconteurs. The salukis had slipped in with the food and arranged themselves between Sheikh Hamid and Gabriel, turning adoring heads from one to the other. Gabriel kept his hand resting absently on one shining head, and I noticed his signet ring, gleaming on his finger for the first time since I had seen him. He looked almost relaxed, and I realised he truly was among friends.

At one point, the sheikh looked at me and said a few words in solemn Arabic, then switched to English. "I have told them there is a great poem that carries the same name as the wife of Djibril." He cleared his throat and struck a sort of pose. "'This is the forest primeval. The murmuring pines and the hemlocks, bearded with moss, and in garments green, indistinct in the twilight, stand like Druids of eld, with voices sad and prophetic, stand like harpers hoar, with beards that rest on their bosoms. Loud from its rocky caverns, the deep-voiced neighboring ocean speaks.'"

I clapped in delight. "You know Longfellow!"

He shrugged. "It was on the syllabus at school."

I turned to find Gabriel grinning. "Hamid and I nearly came to blows over Longfellow when we were at Eton together."

The sheikh puffed out his chest. "A gifted poet with a turn of phrase to rival any of the great Arab poets," he maintained. "These American poets understand great spaces just as Arab poets do."

Gabriel snorted. "Longfellow's good for nothing but tawdry sentimentality. Now if you want to talk about real emotion, you need to get right back to the metaphysical poets—"

He went on to quote a few of his favourite passages, ending with a choice bit of Katherine Philips. " 'For thou art all that I can prize, my joy, my life, my rest.' Now I think we can all agree that, as a description of the ideal of love, that is pretty damned comprehensive. In fact—"

Sheikh Hamid curled his lip. "In fact, she wrote that to a woman, so the argument that the meta-physicals were more equipped to describe romantic love is entirely moot unless you accept the notion that Katherine Philips practised romantic love with another woman. This was a poem written to a friend of the heart and it says nothing of the love a man bears his woman. No, for love between a man and a woman, you must turn instead to the Romantics. What could be more heartfelt than 'The Bride of Abydos'? 'Be thou the rainbow in the storms of life. The evening beam that smiles the clouds away, and tints tomorrow with prophetic ray.' "

Gabriel gave him a disgusted look. "Do you hear yourself? You're quoting Byron, man. Is there anything so predictable as Byron? I suppose you'll say next that Shelley was a paragon."

Sheikh Hamid said stoutly that he would indeed say Shelley was a paragon and that led to an hour-long quarrel about the merits of the metaphysicals versus the Romantics. I half listened while the rest of the Bedouin sat, smoking politely while Hamid and Gabriel went at it hammer and tongs.

Just about the time Gabriel brought Suckling into it, I mimed a snore, and Hamid recalled himself. "Forgive us," he said with a smile. "It is a long time since we have quarrelled so happily."

He turned to one of his men and asked him for a tale, which sparked a sort of storytelling contest. Each of the men talked in turn, moving the group from laughter to tears. Gabriel translated quietly for me so I was able to follow most of what was said, and after the last man had told his story, they turned to me expectantly.

I blinked at Gabriel. "Why are they looking at me?"

"Because it is your turn," he said, smiling through gritted teeth. "It is an honour that they wish a woman to speak. Do not insult them."

I recognised the steel in his tone and I rose

slowly to my feet. I looked to Hamid, and he nodded encouragingly.

"Speak, *sitt*. I will translate for you," he encouraged.

I thought of the magical tales of *jinns* and beautiful princesses and desert raids they had shared, and I realised I had precious little of my own to offer. I flew an aeroplane, but without the *Jolly Roger* to back me up, I doubted they would believe it.

And then I had it. It was the thought of the *Jolly Roger* that did it, and I looked at Gabriel and grinned.

" 'All children, except one, grow up,' " I began. I couldn't remember all of it word for word, but I remembered enough. I told them the entire story of Peter Pan, from his sly entry into the Darling household to having his shadow sewn back into place by Wendy. I told them about the flight to Neverland that was navigated by stars, and I told them about mermaids and Lost Boys and a pirate named Hook. I recounted the epic battle on the *Jolly Roger* and how Wendy, tired of it all, asked Peter to make the necessary arrangements.

And then, as soon as it had come, the story seemed to slip away. I could not remember Peter's reply and I stood, silent before the expectant men.

" 'If you wish it,' he replied as coolly as if she'd asked him to pass the nuts,' " Gabriel quoted softly. " 'For would keep no girl in the Neverland against her will.' "

He looked directly at me then, his eyes piercing in the soft lantern light of the tent.

I swallowed hard. "I don't think I remember the rest."

Gabriel's eyes held mine. "Yes, you do. Peter takes Wendy home. And he tells her to leave a window open for him. Because he always comes back in the end."

It was wrong, of course. Peter said nothing of the sort, at least I couldn't remember it if he did. But it was a hell of a line, and I could not speak. I gave the sheikh an apologetic little smile and he translated the last bits.

I sat, and the men murmured and nodded, some smiling at me, others looking frankly puzzled. Only Gabriel's look was unequivocal. There was nothing but pain on his face, naked and raw, and I looked sharply away as the sheikh rose.

It was his turn, and for my benefit, he translated into English as he spoke.

"This is the story of the great love of Antar and Abla," he began. The story was long and beautifully detailed, chronicling the passionate affair between the warrior Antar and his beautiful Abla. It told of the challenges faced by the chivalrous fellow to woo his bride, and how patiently she waited for him to claim her. Hamid was a little too enthusiastic on the subject of armour—the details of that took far longer than any other part of the story—but by the time Antar was united with his beloved in marriage and then killed in battle, I was sniffling into my handkerchief.

When it was done, they took their leave with much bowing and kissing of cheeks although each of them was careful to give me a wide berth. The sun had long since set by the time they left the tent, and when Gabriel and I were alone with Hamid, the sheikh summoned one of his servants to bring coffee, thick black stuff with more cardamom. As we drank, Hamid lapsed into Arabic to speak with Gabriel and his expression grew grim.

"What is it?" I asked.

Gabriel put down his cup. "The Bedouin have had word from Damascus. While we've been out here running up and down the Badiyat ash-Sham, things have been happening."

"What sort of things?"

"The country has declared itself an independent kingdom and Faisal is king. Furthermore, he has made it clear he will rule without European interference."

I thought of the clever man with the long face and beautiful eyes who had featured so prominently in newsreels with Colonel Lawrence just after the war. Faisal had been reared in Constantinople but when war broke out, he had seized upon British promises of a pan-Arab state if Germany and its

Turkish ally were defeated. With the help of Colonel Lawrence, his men had won substantial victories during the war, and he had depended upon the word of the English when it was time to deliver on their promises. He had been deeply humiliated when they had been broken as easily as they had been given, and Lawrence had been so aghast he had retired to England to lick his wounds in private. I was quite glad to see Faisal had not given up the fight so easily.

"It's about bloody time," I murmured.

Sheikh Hamid smiled. "You approve of an Arab leading his own country, *sitt*?"

"I think British promises ought to be honoured," I returned firmly. "It's an absolute disgrace that this wasn't done as soon as the Arabs pushed the Turks out of Damascus." It had been a point of great pride to them that they had liberated their ancient city from Turkish control, and the fact that they hadn't been left to govern it was something of a black eye for the folks who had promised them autonomy.

"Have you any wish to take part in the government?" I asked.

He laughed. "No, dear *sitt*. The Bedouin has little use for government. What would we do with statesmen out here? We have tribal justice and it suits us well. Leave the cities to the men in suits and their books of rules."

"How does it work exactly, this tribal justice?"

He considered his words. "It works in the way that a family works. A family does not rely upon the law to keep its members in order. It relies upon the honour of the family itself, the understanding that one is always part of something larger than oneself. A man does not survive alone in the desert for long. So it is with the Bedouin. A man survives only as part of a community. If he has troubles with his cousin, his brother will stand at his side and defend him. If he has troubles with his brother, his father will come to decide who is right and both sons will abide by his decision. The role of the father in a family is the same as that of a sheikh among his people. He is the father of them all."

"How do the women fit into it?" I asked. Gabriel narrowed his eyes at me.

"Evie—"

Sheikh Hamid smiled indulgently. "It is not an offence to ask a question, Djibril." He turned back to me. "Our women do not have the same obvious freedoms that the Englishwoman has. For this you look at her and you feel pity. Because you do not live her life, you do not see her compensations."

"Compensations?"

"A Bedouin woman is never alone. She does not toil without help. She does not weep without the support of her sisters. There is always a pair of hands to aid her and always a shoulder upon which to cast her burdens."

I thought of the scene in Sheikha Aysha's tent when I had let my own tears flow. It had felt glorious to give myself up to the care of the Bedouin women and their gentle kindnesses. Of course, having another woman to help milk the goats or dry one's tears was small payment for having to wear a face veil and having all decisions taken out of one's hands, but I understood his point a little better.

I smiled. "We shall not agree upon this, but I thank you for explaining. And we English have not come so far down that road as we ought. We women still aren't even allowed the vote, at least not all of us."

He lifted his brows. "Then you might prefer to be a Bedouin woman. They do not sit on our councils or speak their opinions publicly before men, but there is not a man in our tribe who does not know precisely what his wife thinks on any subject. Much persuasion may be done when heads are close upon a pillow," he added with a meaningful smile.

I thought on what he said, and realised Gabriel had spoken the truth: there were no easy answers in this part of the world. They were resentments and blood feuds a thousand years in the making, and everything the Westerners had done—from the Crusades to the recent peace conferences—had only complicated matters. I smiled at Hamid. "Yes, well, I suppose if you've been doing something successfully for three thousand years there isn't much reason to change, is there?"

"You're both rather missing the significance," Gabriel said irritably. "If I might draw you back to the matter at hand—that is, Faisal's declaration of kingship. The French aren't very well going to take this lying down, you know." He turned to me. "Things are only going to get worse now that Faisal has declared independence. There will be a price to pay for this and it's going to be a bloody one."

I suppressed a sigh. "Do you suppose just once you could consider something without counting your own risk of bodily injury?"

Sheikh Hamid turned to me, his expression clearly one of astonishment. As we had just discussed, no Arab woman would have spoken to her husband in front of others with such disrespect, I was sure, but I was fed up to the back teeth with Gabriel's skulking around the desert and hampering our entire adventure with his endless carping about danger.

"But, *sitt* . . ." Hamid began.

Gabriel folded his arms lazily over his chest. "Don't bother, Hamid. Really," he said with a sharp glance at his friend.

Hamid shrugged.

"I apologise," I told him. "It's discourteous of us to share our marital woes with you."

"Yes," he said gravely, "Djibril tells me that you

will divorce. It is a complicated thing for the English with your courts. It's easier our way," he remarked to Gabriel. "You just tell a woman she is no longer your wife and it is done. She goes back to her people."

"I ought to have been born a Bedouin," Gabriel replied, his tone thoughtful.

"My brother speaks truly."

I cleared my throat. "I thought you were the one who wanted to get back to the matter at hand. When can we leave? Not that your hospitality hasn't been absolutely grand," I hastened to assure Hamid, "but I am rather anxious to get back to Damascus."

The sheikh shrugged. "When it is safe to go."

"When will that be?" I persisted.

Hamid looked at Gabriel, who merely threw up his hands.

"*Sitt*," Hamid said with great patience, "it is not the job of a man to change the stars or the wind. These things belong to Allah. We will go when we may go. Until it is safe, you will remain here as my guests."

I stared from one to the other. "You must be joking," I said, spreading my arms to encompass the furthest reaches of the desert as I thought about the empty miles stretching between us and the Cross. "Can't you let us have a few men and some horses or camels to ride?"

Hamid spread his hands. "It pains me to refuse

you, *sitt.* But not even for my brother can I do such a thing. I will not open my men to attack. The French are angry now, and any Bedouin they see they are likely to fire upon. This is not our fight."

"How can you say that?" I demanded. "King Faisal is fighting for a united Arab state here."

Hamid shrugged again with the cool indifference of a desert dweller whose perspective is shaped by the vast land at his feet. "Governments come and governments go. Yes, I hope that King Faisal succeeds. But I have sacrified many of my men already in this cause. If the fight comes to us, we will take up arms for a united Arab state. Again," he said pointedly, a sharp reminder that they had fought for a free state and had it snatched back by European hands. "But we will not go to the fight. It must come to us. There is a band of deserters, men from the French Foreign Legion who have made their way here. They are brigands, I believe, and desperate men without honour. But if I attack them without cause, I will give the French in Damascus the excuse to post troops here. It is better to wait and give them no reason to disturb the peace of my people. They will go away, and then, when these men have moved on and it is safe, I will lead you out and you will have the best of everything I can offer you—horses and camels and men. This is a fair offer, is it not?"

I looked to Gabriel, who was watching me

closely. There was something coldly assessing in his eyes, and I knew he was waiting for me to blunder in and offend his friend. "Very well," I said calmly. "I understand and accept your generous hospitality. I have heard there is no more generous friend in all the world than a Bedouin."

"It is true," Hamid said, giving me a wide smile. "You will see. Now, I think it is time for you to go to your tent. You will want rest."

He rose and stepped back to make sure I did not touch him as I passed. Gabriel was behind me, and when I hesitated at the flap, he pointed. "That one," he said, gesturing towards a smaller tent a little distance away. When I got there, I stopped, startled to find Gabriel right behind me. I huffed a little at him.

"Don't fuss, Gabriel. I don't require a body-guard. You yourself said the Bedouin were the most hospitable folk on earth. I'm hardly likely to get into trouble on my own."

"What you do is not my concern," he said blandly. "But you're blocking the way."

"To my tent."

"To *my* tent," he corrected with a lazy smile.

I folded my arms. "Absolutely not."

He stepped close, his voice pitched low. The lazy smile was still in evidence but there was no mistaking the tone. "You are my wife. In this culture that means one thing—you are my property and my property stays with me."

"Your property? I don't see anything that marks me as yours," I retorted.

He lifted his hand, and with agonising slowness, stretched a fingertip to the neck of my robe. He slid it down, lightly skimming the skin between my breasts, then stroked upwards.

"Don't you?" he asked softly. Dangling from his fingertip was the chain with my wedding ring. He dropped it abruptly and gave me a cold smile. "Don't screech, woman. You sound like a particularly unattractive species of Patagonian monkey. And yes, you heard me correctly. You sleep here with me."

I crossed my arms and planted my feet firmly. "I refuse. Categorically and emphatically."

He shrugged one broad shoulder, clearly bored with the conversation. "I don't see what bother it makes. You've spent the last few nights with me."

"As abductees," I pointed out. "I had no choice."

"And you have no choice here. There is no place for you. The other women will be with their families."

"Then I can sleep outside."

"You cannot. They would be scandalised, and I'll not have you offending my friends by implying there is something wrong with their customs."

"But—"

Something in his face stopped me. He would take any amount of abuse at my hands, but not if it were directed at his friends, and I understood why. To insist upon different sleeping arrangements would seem critical of their ways, and even though I was raging at Hamid's reluctance to take us back into the desert, their hospitality had been profound. Lifesaving, in fact.

"Fine," I said stiffly. I turned on my heel and went into the tent. It was furnished simply with more of the silken Turkish rugs on the ground and a pierced lantern to give light. A carved chest stood in the corner, and the top of it had been laid as a sort of dressing table for Gabriel with razor and toothbrush and bowl for washing. There was a decanter of something that looked suspiciously like whisky and a *nargileh*, as well. Thickly padded silk blankets had been left for us on a sort of pallet, and I took one and rolled myself into it as far away from Gabriel as I could. I heard him groaning a bit and turned back to find him struggling with his boots.

"For heaven's sake," I muttered. I got up and went to him, cupping my hands behind his heel. I yanked off the first boot then the second.

"Bless you," he murmured, easing himself onto his side and closing his eyes.

I hesitated. "How is your back? Do you need more salve?"

He shook his head without opening his eyes. "No. Hamid's fellow larded it with something and it feels miles better. Stung like hellfire, but since then the pain has been almost nothing."

He opened his eyes suddenly, a spark of something brilliant and mocking in that forget-me-not shade.

"Don't come over all wifely now, Evie. It doesn't suit you."

I repeated one of the bad words he used so liberally and went back to my pallet to roll up in my blanket. Within minutes I heard him breathing the slow deep breaths of the heavy sleeper, but I lay for a long time, staring into the darkness of the woolen tent and thinking.

THIRTEEN

The next few days crawled past with the slow, measured effort of life in the desert. Each day Sheikh Hamid and his men rode out a little way to assess conditions in the desert and hunt, and each evening someone of their acquaintance— a neighbouring tribesman or scout—would come into camp and add his observations. I was sometimes included in these conversations, but as they were conducted in Arabic, I took my cues from Hamid's patient expression.

"Not yet," he would say after each of these men left.

So the days passed in acute boredom. I followed the women about, helping to fetch water from the well or bake bread, but I hadn't the knack for either.

I spilled more water than I carried back, and I managed to burn the bread. I irritated the other women by breaking the rhythm of the coffee-grinding song, and when I attempted to spin wool, I ended up with a snarled mess that Sheikha Aysha untangled with patient fingers. It was she who finally set me to gathering camel dung for the fire, supposing even I couldn't bungle that. Of course, she hadn't reckoned on my spooking Hamid's prize *naga*, or camel mother, just as she was about to give birth. He politely discouraged me from going near the camels after that, and I spent hours just sitting in front of the tent, staring out at the desert.

Each night we ate with Sheikh Hamid and afterwards, Gabriel and I retired to our tent to pass yet another night in excruciatingly polite silence. Those long quiet nights were almost the only time we spent together. During the day I was left with the women while he slept, claiming he needed the rest to heal, or sat in on timely discussions of the political situation. As a result, he was enjoying a rather relaxing holiday and hearing the latest from Damascus, while I played endless games of charades with the women in futile attempts to make myself understood. They taught me several new words, a few of which I tried out one evening on Gabriel after we'd retired to our tent.

He stared at me in openmouthed shock. "Yes, I know that word. And you are *never* to repeat it again, particularly in mixed company." He busied

302

himself lighting the *nargileh*, drawing in a deep breath of the sweetly scented smoke then exhaling it ever so slowly through barely parted lips. There was something hypnotic about the process, and I looked away quickly, plucking at a loose silken thread on a pillow.

"This isn't mixed company," I pointed out sullenly. "It's only you." He settled himself against the cushions, one hand tucked lazily behind his head as the other worked the pipe.

"Still, I am a man," he countered, his expression a little wounded. "And no man wants to think that women discuss such things. We'd never have the courage to face one again. My God, is that really what they talk about?"

"All the time. You'd think they'd be more interested in their children or what's going in the cookpot or the fact that King Faisal has declared their independence. But no—nothing but sex, sex, sex."

He shook his head slowly. "I knew the men were inclined to be frank with one another about such things, but the women . . ."

His voice trailed off and I gave him a keen look. "What do the men say?"

His expression turned stern. "None of your business." He took another deep pull from the *nargileh*, his big body relaxing as he blew out the smoke.

It was deeply fragrant stuff, and the scent of it

filled my head, clouding my thinking a little. I felt slightly euphoric and not a little relaxed. I flapped a hand at him with an insouciant gesture. "Gracious, Gabriel, I don't remember you being particularly prudish. In fact, I can think of one or two things you demonstrated on our honeymoon that still make me blush." He choked a little on the smoke but recovered himself nicely, puffing furiously for a moment as I talked. "Besides, it can't be any worse than what the pilots talked about when they thought I wasn't listening. The words I learned from them would curl your hair."

"Don't tell me," he instructed, taking a long, deep breath of smoke that he blew directly over me like a slow caress. "I'd rather keep my pretty illusions if it's all the same to you."

I shrugged. "Have it your way. But I hope something happens soon. The waiting is playing havoc with my nerves. All I do is sit in the tent and struggle with verbs and nod while I understand one word in a hundred."

"And apparently only the obscene ones," he commented. He switched from long, lazy draws on the pipe to quick little bursts complete with elegant little smoke rings as he exhaled.

I pulled a face. "Show-off."

"Oh, come now," he said, mischief lighting his eyes. "You could make yourself useful. Why not learn to bake bread like a good wife? Or weave me a nice blanket?"

I rolled my eyes. "Yes, because women ask no more of life than to make the perfect pie or starch a proper collar."

He puffed another smoke ring. The atmosphere was getting thick with the fragrant smoke, and my head began to swim a little. "You could always borrow a child and see if you come over all maternal."

I shuddered. "The children are all right, I suppose. They're terribly sweet and even their English is better than my Arabic, but I didn't realise how often they needed a good nose-wiping. I haven't any clean handkerchiefs left," I said darkly.

He held up a commanding hand, looking for all the world like a pasha ordering his harem about. "Not another word. You forget I was gently reared. I shock easily."

"They're quite well, you know," I said softly.

He roused himself. "Who?"

"Your family. I know you're thinking of them. That's the same expression you always had when you talked about them. Do you ever miss them?"

He shook his head. "No. Too many years trying to please the old man and coming up desperately short. It was rather freeing to let them all think I was dead and not have the bother anymore. Now I only worry about disappointing myself." He paused still smoking thoughtfully. "Were they awful to you? After I 'died,' I mean?"

"Yes, frightful, actually. They opposed the annuity you'd arranged for me and questioned every detail about the funeral itself. We even quarrelled about the music."

"Really? Who won?"

"I did," I told him with noticeable satisfaction. "I insisted upon Palestrina with a lovely bit of Purcell to finish."

A slow smile curved his mouth. "Good girl." Wordlessly, he handed me the mouthpiece of the pipe and I took a puff. I coughed a little—this mixture was stronger than the one Daoud had favoured. But the second puff was smoother, and by the fourth, I felt nothing but silken smoke slipping down my throat. I handed it back as my head buzzed.

"You needn't look quite so pleased," I told him. "I gave way about the monument. There's a bloody great pile of stone with your name on it in a churchyard in Norfolk."

"But no cherubs," he pleaded. "Please tell me you didn't let them have cherubs."

"Enormous fat ones with wreaths of stone roses and a particularly gruesome dove that looks as if it might have a wasting disease. It really is the most revoltingly sentimental thing I've ever seen." I paused. "But I had an inscription of my own carved into the back."

There was a moment where he said nothing, as if weighing whether he dared ask. But he put aside the pipe and held my gaze levelly with his own.

"What does it say? Not some bloody Psalm, I hope." He attempted a light tone, but there was an edge of something sharper there as he must have steeled himself.

"It says, 'We hope our sons will die like English gentlemen.'" Nine words, but each one a laceration to a boy who'd grown up waiting for the Lost Boys to walk the plank and make good ends.

He mouthed a word and looked away. When he looked back, he had mastered himself. "Well done," he said, the edge still in his voice. "I thought you might try to break my heart a little."

"Only a little," I said, venturing a small smile. "It's funny. When I was sailing home from China, I always thought if I ever saw you again, I'd want to torture you, to pay you back pain for pain what you inflicted on me."

"And now?" he asked.

I shrugged. "I've lost the habit of hating you. At first, I couldn't because you were dead and it's so difficult to hate the dead. So I tucked it away and promised myself I'd take it out for a good airing later. I thought after a proper amount of time had passed, I could indulge myself and hate you lavishly. But there was war work, and then I discovered flying—the only thing I was really good at."

"Oh, I don't know," he said mildly as he picked

up the pipe again. "I think you could probably do just about anything you set your mind to."

It took me a moment to realise he had just paid me a compliment, but the camaraderie between us was so new, I didn't dare to draw attention to it. After another few breaths of pipe smoke I was floating a little, wrapped in a velvety warmth that seemed to come from within my own blood.

"Flying is the only thing I'm good at," I repeated. "Well, that and posing for those wretched photographs. I loathe dealing with sponsors. Nothing but grabby hands and silly slogans—as if it makes the slightest bit of difference which brand of tea biscuits I buy. But somehow people think it's important, and I can only afford to fly if I have sponsors, so it all gets muddled up somehow. But it's that sort of blurry dishonesty I loathe. I tell people I use things and so they go and buy them, but I hate myself for it. And I hate them for believing it."

"So what would you do if you chucked it all?"

I shrugged. "I haven't the faintest. This trip will be over soon. We've only the Caspian left. That will finish us, provided the *Jolly Roger* makes it that long. And then it's back to England to find something new."

He had smoked more than I had and his voice sounded drowsy. "Is the *Jolly Roger* so elderly?"

I smiled. "She's on her last legs, poor lamb. She flew like a bomb in the war, and I've asked so much of her. But she's held up beautifully thanks to Wally. If I can coax one last big flight out of her, she'll have earned a happy retirement."

"And what becomes of you after that?"

"I haven't thought of it. I haven't thought beyond this trip. It helps keep the nerves at bay, you know. If I think too hard about a particular bill or what I'll have to do next, I can't sleep for the worry. So, I put it all aside in a neat little box and tell myself I'll take it out when the time comes and worry over it then."

"Does that work?"

"Of course not. I fret myself to ribbons, anyway. But it keeps me from running mad all the time." I paused. "But I think I'd like to do something different, something nice and clean, where I won't have to pose for photographs or tell lies about soap flakes. And I want the same for you. Whatever trouble you've been in, it's never too late for you to go straight, Gabriel. It's never too late to be what you might have been."

His face was thoughtful as he pulled on the pipe but he said nothing.

He rose, and I noticed for the first time that he had done so without wincing. The constant sitting on the ground was playing hell with my knees, but Gabriel was sinuous as a cat.

"Your back must be healing up," I told him. "You're not making those awful old man noises anymore when you move."

He rolled his shoulders experimentally. "Healing, yes, but it itches like the devil. The healer fellow, Faiz, gave me more salve, but I haven't bothered to put it on."

"Why are men always so perfectly stupid when it comes to taking care of themselves?" I demanded of no one in particular. "Take off your robe and turn around."

"Yes, Nanny," he said with a smile that managed to be meek and mocking at the same time. He handed over the tin of salve and stripped off his robe. He had dressed like a Bedouin since our arrival, wearing the long loose robe they favoured. I don't know what their men wore underneath, but he had on a slim pair of trousers, and I wasn't sure if I was relieved or disappointed. He dropped his robe to the ground and turned to show me his back. The lash marks were still there, the slashes freshly pink against the olive flesh. But they had closed up and were healing nicely. He would scar, but not deeply.

I scooped up a bit of salve and began to work it gently into the marks. He sucked in his breath sharply, the sleek muscles jumping under the skin of his back.

"Did I hurt you?"

"No," he said in a strangled voice. "Just get it over with."

I sighed. "I know you're upset that I insisted on going after the Cross. And I know you blame me for everything that's happened. And you're quite right. I was thoughtless and I didn't consider the consequences properly. But I want you to know I am sorry you were hurt. It was never my intention."

"I know that. Careful, pet," he said with a wince. "That one's deep."

I softened my touch and went on. "And I want you to know I understand. I've had a lot of time to think out here, nothing but time," I added wryly, thinking of my long hours staring at the camels. "And I've realised what I ought to have seen before. Marriage frightened you. We rushed off into it, and I don't know if you were already up to nefarious deeds or if that came later, but it all happened so fast—the elopement and then the expedition to China. I think it only came home to roost then that you had to be responsible for me. And I suppose it scared you terribly. But I don't blame you anymore. It isn't your fault."

A stillness came over him, stiffening his muscles.

"It's not my fault that I'm a coward?"

"No. Some men just don't handle responsibility well. They break under the pressure of it. They simply can't bear having to take care of another person. And it makes perfect sense in your case considering your willingness to turn to crime. Clearly your character is just lacking somehow. It's actually quite understandable when you think about it like that."

He said nothing and I finished rubbing the salve into his back. "There, is that better?"

"Quite," he said, biting off the syllable as if it tasted bitter in his mouth.

"Now, Gabriel, you're not sore, are you? Because of what I said? I'm trying to show you I understand what you were going through. And I'm not angry at you anymore because it doesn't make sense to be angry at someone for something they can't help. It's like being angry with a person because they're left-handed or tone deaf. It's simply who you are."

He turned, his eyes glittering oddly in the lamplight. "Thank you for that. Now, if you're finished eviscerating my character, put out the lamp. I'd like to go to sleep."

"Oh, don't take it like that," I said, pleading only a little. "I didn't mean to upset you. I was trying to make friends again."

He stood up and went to where the lamp hung and took it down. "I said, put out the lamp." Then with great care he hurled it outside the tent. I heard it strike a rock, shattering into pieces and leaving us in blackness. Without another word he threw himself down onto his pallet and lay there, simmering with rage.

I rose and went to the flap of the tent, pushing it back. High above us the moon hung like a baroque pearl, just beginning to wane, its edges blurred by the fronds of the palm trees. The moonlight softened the scene below, lending the sleeping tents a sort of glamour. "It looks like a picture from a fairy tale," I said, almost to myself. "Something out of *Arabian Nights*."

Gabriel got up and gripped my shoulders, his fingers insistent. "Goddamn it, Evie, when will you grow up? Not everything is a fairy tale, you know. Sometimes life is just what it is, brutal and hard and dangerous. And it's real, Evie. It's real, and so am I," he repeated, digging his fingers in harder.

And before I knew what he intended, he bent his head to mine. I didn't fight him. I didn't want to. He was the one who broke the kiss, pulling my hands out of his hair and pushing me away. The kiss hadn't been gentle, but the gesture was when he shoved me back, rocking me on my heels. He pushed his hands through his hair and I could see they were shaking.

"I'll apologise for that in the morning," he said, his voice rough.

"Don't bother," I told him lightly. "After all, we are still married. Still, if it's all the same to you, I think I'll sleep on my side of the tent tonight."

I crawled into my pallet, wrapping my arms hard around my body to stop the trembling. He stepped through the flap and into the desert air, blocking the soft moonlight with his silhouette. I could smell the scent of his cigarettes, acrid and sharp after the soft seduction of the *nargileh*, and he must have smoked several, one after the other, waiting for me to fall asleep. I heard him move towards the tent, and I closed my eyes tightly. I didn't fool him; I was sure of it. But it was the excuse we both needed not to look at each other. "As long as I live, I will never understand men," I murmured to myself.

The next day, a messenger arrived and spent some time closeted with the men before Sheikh Hamid and Gabriel emerged from the tent, grim-faced and resolute.

"What is it?" I asked.

Hamid busied himself giving orders while Gabriel brought me up to speed. "There has been an attack. One of Hamid's scouts found an injured traveller in the desert and he's sent a pair of warriors back with the scout to fetch him. Hamid wants to question him about what he's seen."

Just then, a faint commotion stirred at the edge of the village. The warriors had returned, each of them carrying someone pillion. The first dismounted and I caught a glimpse of the slender youth mounted behind him.

"Rashid!" I hurried forward, wholly delighted to see him and just as mystified.

He sprang from the camel to make a graceful gesture of welcome. "Greetings, *sitt*."

"Rashid, what on earth are you doing out here?"

"I told you I would return to my tribe," he told me with a broad grin. "Sheikh Hamid is my uncle by marriage."

"Uncle by marriage?" At that moment Sheikha Aysha stepped forward and greeted Rashid warmly, offering him water. He drank deeply and as he did, Aysha nodded towards me.

"My nephew, *sitt*, the son of my sister."

He finished drinking, wiping his mouth across his sleeve. "You like the desert, *sitt*?"

"It's magnificent," I told him truthfully. "Were you the scout who found the injured traveller?"

He puffed his slim chest out. "Yes, *sitt*. I am the best scout in the eastern desert. I have information for my uncle, and I bring him this pitiful man," he said with a nod to the second camel.

A group of Bedu had come forward to lift the unconscious man from the camel, but even before they turned him over, I knew him.

"Herr Doktor!" I cried.

He did not hear me. He was still senseless, a dead weight in the arms of his rescuers, but they coped manfully, lifting him with all the gentleness they could muster. His pink complexion was blotched red and white from too much exposure to the sun, and his clothes were filthy, but none of that mattered compared to the horror I felt when they shifted and his arm fell free . . . the sleeve drenched in blood.

● ● ●

They put up a small tent for him and I stayed outside while Faiz, the healer, attended him. Faiz was as unlikely a healer as any I could imagine. He was enormous—tall and with a belly so round he looked like Sheikh Hamid's favourite *naga*. His hands were the size of two of mine together, but with the delicate touch of a child. His face was adorned with blue tattoos that might have given him a menacing air were it not for the broad smile that always wreathed his face.

I went to the little German and held his hand.

"He won't know you're there," Gabriel said flatly. "He's quite unconscious."

"I don't care," I snapped. "He ought to have someone here who cares whether he lives or dies."

Gabriel shrugged. Faiz turned to Gabriel, asking a series of questions in Arabic.

Gabriel answered him quietly, then reached into his robes and took out his medical kit. Faiz peered into it thoughtfully before pointing to something in the kit and giving Gabriel instructions. He spoke calmly and Gabriel asked a question or two before they seemed to settle something between them. To my astonishment, Faiz stepped aside and folded his arms over his belly, smiling benignly.

"What's he doing?" I demanded of Gabriel. "Surely he won't just let the old fellow die."

Just then, the German's eyes fluttered open. He

looked around, his eyes rolling a moment until they focused on my face.

"Hello, Herr Doktor."

"Frau Starke," he said faintly. "I am glad to see you."

But his smile did not reach his eyes, and he moved his injured arm fitfully.

"I'm sorry you were hurt," I told him.

Herr Doktor gave me a sad smile. "I do not blame you. It was not gallant to leave my friends in such a place."

"Then why did you?" Gabriel demanded.

I flapped a hand at him. "Hush. There's no call to be rude when the poor man is wounded." I turned back to Schickfuss. "Who did this to you?"

He nodded his head, his white hair standing on end. "Daoud. Not such a nice fellow, I think," he said with a gallant attempt at a joke. "He shot me." He made a vague gesture towards his wounded arm, and I peeled back the filthy remnants of his shirt to find a neat hole on one side and a mess of blood and splintered bone and torn muscle on the other.

"Heavens, it's a good thing he's got rotten aim," I said with an attempt at lightness. "If that bullet had hit you anywhere important you might be in real trouble instead of just a spot of inconvenience."

He gave me another of his sad smiles. "This is a consolation? I think it is better not to be shot at all,

Frau Starke." He attempted to laugh at his little joke, but he was ghastly pale and the wound did look unpleasant. From the pile of soiled rags on the ground it was clear he'd bled rather a lot, and when he put his hand in mine, it shook.

Gabriel moved forward, his medical kit in his hands. He opened it and inside was a tidy array of miniature surgical tools.

Swiftly, he prepared a hypodermic syringe. It was a lethal-looking thing, and I had no idea what it was filled with. Neither did Herr Doktor, but when he turned his rheumy old eyes on Gabriel, he merely smiled.

Gabriel paused. "Shall I go on or don't you trust me?"

The old man managed a laugh. "It is rather late for that, *mein herr.* Do what you must. God will take care of the rest."

"God doesn't bloody care," Gabriel said softly, but he went ahead, sliding the needle into the shoulder and slowly depressing the plunger as Herr Doktor let out a soft exhalation. Then, with perfect nonchalance, Gabriel took out a bottle of antiseptic and swabbed out the wound, then fished a scalpel from his kit. He did not even hesitate before plunging it into the wound, and within a moment, it emerged with a bullet perched neatly on the tip. He flicked it to the corner of the tent then proceeded to stitch up the old fellow, while Faiz watched in approval.

There was something ghoulish about Gabriel's unnatural calm, and I was still put out that Faiz hadn't lifted a finger to help. Gabriel gave Herr Doktor enough morphine to knock out an elephant, and proceeded to wash his hands while chatting calmly with Faiz. I made certain Schickfuss was resting comfortably before I turned on my heel and left. I went into the tent and helped myself to a healthy swallow of Gabriel's whisky. I washed my face and hands and combed my hair before I ventured out again.

Sheikh Hamid was just outside the tent, chatting with Rashid. He dismissed him as I emerged, and the boy trotted off, smiling at me over his shoulder.

"He likes you," Hamid told me with a grin. "But you must believe he would never bring dishonour to the wife of Djibril. He knows better."

"And I know better than to bat my lashes at a fifteen-year-old boy," I retorted.

Hamid laughed. "He is twenty, little sister."

"You're joking."

"And he has two wives already. And three children with another on the way."

I shook my head to clear it. "It all seems so different out here," I murmured.

I don't know if he caught the words or the wistful tone, but his eyes were warm with sympathy.

"I understand, little sister. I felt the same when I

went to England. All of it seemed impossible to me, so many people in so small a space! How does a man breathe?" he asked, not expecting an answer. "But it is good enough for Englishmen, I suppose."

I faced him, careful not to touch him. "I wanted to thank you for your hospitality, Hamid. You and your family have been very kind to take us in."

The smile deepened. "This is the Bedouin way, to care for the traveller. But even if it were not, what else could I do for my brother Djibril and his honoured wife?"

I tipped my head. "I'm curious, Sheikh, why do you call him your brother?"

"He is my milk brother. My mother nursed him when he was born in Damascus. We are connected, as truly as if our blood were linked."

I was still standing openmouthed when he walked away.

The sun was just setting when I went to the little tent where they had put Herr Doktor. Outside, Gabriel was dumping the load of bloody bandages into the fire. His hair was tumbled and his jaw was darkened by the shadow of his beard, but his eyes were brilliant and he was whistling a bit of Palestrina. He was happy, I realised with a start, and this handsome, enigmatic man, cool in a crisis and in command of any situation, *this* was the man I had married. I wondered if perhaps, even for a moment, I could break through the wall he had put up against me.

He looked up from the fire. "Doesn't do to leave bloody things lying around," he told me. "Attracts jackals."

I moved to stand next to him, but he edged away, sitting with his robes folded carefully beneath him. "Why wouldn't Faiz help him?"

Gabriel seemed to choose his words carefully. "The war has been finished less than a year, Evie. And Faiz and Schickfuss were on different sides. If Faiz had tended him and Herr Doktor died, there would have been repercussions, grim ones. Europeans in these lands love nothing better than having a good excuse to ride roughshod over the natives and the French are itching for any justification to take over."

"He helped you," I pointed out.

"Not the same thing at all. England was allied to these men in the war."

"And you're a friend to them still. Hamid told me the story of how he came to call you 'brother.' You've been keeping a few secrets," I told him. "You made fun of me, but it *is* like something out of *Arabian Nights*, the pale, starving baby suckled by the desert princess."

He rolled his eyes. "For your information, I was fat as a tick. My mother simply wanted a wet nurse because she was too vain to spoil her figure with nursing. I warned you about fairy tales," he said, frowning. "Leave it alone, Evie. You won't find what you're looking for so just stop searching."

I went to sit next to him, careful to keep a little distance. "What are you really doing out here, Gabriel?"

He shrugged and said nothing, stirring the burning rags into the fire with the toe of his boot.

"I don't know why you won't tell me, but I think you're here for a purpose—something more than just petty crime. Won't you tell me what it is?"

He turned, his eyes bright in the firelight. "Don't you ever get tired of asking questions?"

"No, I am tired of not getting answers."

"Perhaps your questions just aren't very interesting," he said in the same blandly bored tone I had come to hate.

"Then I'll try a different tack. Did you send Rashid to Damascus to look after me?" I held my breath, wondering for an impossible moment if he might have given way to some softer emotion where I was concerned.

He leaned close, his eyes wide, his lips slightly parted. His voice was a soft, deliberate caress.

"Actually, I sent him to spy on you. I followed you a few times myself, but I couldn't always be there. Rashid was my eyes and ears."

He sat back with a malicious smile.

"And just when I was beginning to think you might not be a complete bastard," I said sweetly.

He laughed, a genuine laugh this time, and something in him uncoiled. He eased back and I edged closer to him, watching the flames for a long time. It was peaceful, companionable even.

"Unnerving, isn't it?" he asked.

"What?"

"How easy it is. Like the old days."

"It's nothing like the old days. To begin with, back then I didn't know how to fly a plane and you weren't dead."

He laughed again, but the joke was on me. It was like the old days, much more than I liked to remember. There had only been a handful of weeks before he had changed and the beautiful idyll was over, but every night before that had ended just like this—with the pair of us staring into a fire, dreaming.

"I've almost got the knack of it now," I said finally. "I can almost remember you without hating myself for being such a fool."

He shook his head. "You were never that, Evie. You were young and in love and that's a recipe for blindness. You saw what you wanted to."

"I saw a man who had so much potential, so much strength. All you needed was a little polishing to be really great."

His lips curved in a mocking smile. "And look at me now."

"Yes, not so much polished as ground down to nothing. You should have had a hero's death and lived on as nothing but a sweet memory instead of this," I said, flicking a glance from his tousled hair to his scuffed boots. "I suppose when I go back to Damascus I'll have a good wet weep over you."

"Don't bother," he said, his tone amused. "I assure you I'm not worth it."

"Oh, now you're being flip again, but I mean it. It's absolutely heart-wrenching to think of you like this, probably broke and rotting away out here. I'm beginning to think it's only the grossest sort of fluke you even found that Cross," I said, warming to my theme. "You won't have a legacy at all, Gabriel, except as a footnote, an explorer who died before he did anything of real note."

"What a lovely picture you paint," he said sounding marginally less amused.

"Well, it's true. You didn't summit Masherbrum, after all. You *almost* did. You didn't find the source of the Nile. You *almost* did. You didn't find Machu Picchu. You *almost* did. It's the story of your life, and no one ever remembers the folks who almost did things."

"Not true," he returned brightly. "Plenty of folks remember Napoleon. He almost won Waterloo."

"That isn't the same and you know it. He conquered Europe first. You never conquered anything."

"Not even you," he said, his gaze fixed on the fire. "I have a fine catalogue of failures, my dear, and you have kept perfect account of them. But the greatest failure of my life is you."

He levered himself up off the ground and walked quietly away. I wrapped my arms around my knees and stared into the fire until my heart stopped jumping. He had always had that effect on me. My pulse always raced when he was near. It was more than a little unsettling that after five years apart, he could still do it with a flick of his eye.

FOURTEEN

I went later to look in on Herr Doktor and found him awake, his eyes dreamily unfocused, but his faculties sharp.

"How are you feeling?"

"I have been better," he said with a small smile. "There were wars, you know. Many of them, and I was a good Uhlan."

"Uhlans? Those are Prussian cavalry fellows, aren't they?"

"Were." The word was simple but carried all the weight of the world with it.

I settled myself next to him and poured out a tin cup of water. I held his head and he took a few sips. "I am sorry," I told him.

"For what? That the water tastes of camel? Pah. It is what happens in the desert, child."

"No. For the war. I mean, you started it, of course. One doesn't like to be indelicate, but it was down to Germany getting all ruffled up. But I am sorry it happened. So many lives lost and for what? Germany's crushed now, monarchies toppled like toy bricks, entire cities destroyed and millions of men who either never came home or will never be the same. It's something we all ought to be sorry for, don't you think?"

His eyes were shrewd. "You are a rare woman, Frau Starke. Few victors ever think of how the weight of their victory burdens the conquered."

"It's always been that way, hasn't it? Here we are in the middle of a desert war in the same desert people have been fighting over for thousands of years. It's madness."

"Then why do you not go home?" he asked simply.

I started to answer, but he shook his head. "No, *gnädige Frau*. Do not give me the easy answer. Give me the real one."

I sighed. "I don't know. Well, I do know, but I wish I didn't. The truth is, I feel quite sorry for Gabriel."

His silvery white brows rose in little tufts. "A man seldom welcomes pity from the woman he loves."

"Loved," I corrected. "It's terribly complicated, but the short version is that I blame myself. Make no mistake," I warned, "I blame Gabriel plenty, too, but I have to take at least half the responsibility for the way he's turned out."

"And why is this?"

"Because I let him leave me when I ought to have fought for him. I think it may have been his one chance at real happiness and I took it from him. He turned to a . . . well, let's just say a life of bad choices, I suspect."

"How could you have anticipated such a thing?" he asked gently.

I shrugged. "I don't know. I was a child myself, really. But Gabriel was always so full of energy, so much larger than life. He seemed driven at times to do the things that were most impossible." I shook myself briskly. "Now, why don't you tell me exactly how much Miss Green is paying you to retrieve the Cross from us."

The smile faltered and in its place a sheepish flush brightened his cheeks. He spluttered and fumed a few minutes until I held up a hand. "That's quite enough. You're going to tug those stitches out if you aren't very careful. You might as well tell me, you know. I've already figured it out, anyway."

"You have not," he said, his jaw set mulishly. "This is a trick on an old man to make him tell things he ought not to—things you do *not* know."

"Feathers. I think Miss Green knows exactly what the treasure is, and I think she sent you to get it. I've had time to think out here, and I don't believe she is concerned for Gabriel at all. I think she wants the Cross. She's desperate for a great find, the sort that will establish her reputation once and for all." His expression was stubborn, but I went on, supplying the broad strokes. "I think Daoud told her about the Cross, but she wasn't able to offer him as much money as the Hungarians, and since Daoud is a mercenary soul, he chose to throw in his lot with them. Realising she'd been betrayed, Miss Green turned to her old flame to do the dirty work for her and sent you out after the Cross. Which," I finished, "isn't very nice at all. She's rather more spry than you are. She ought to have come after the Cross herself like any modern and independent woman would. Her thinking is painfully Victorian."

Herr Doktor didn't just splutter then. He positively *howled* his outrage. He was fussing at me in German so I understood about one word in fifty, but when he trotted out the word *blamage*, I held up my hand again.

"That's quite enough. Really, you will burst those stitches and I don't know that I would trust Gabriel's hands to be quite steady a second time. The fellows have been entertaining themselves for some time now and I suspect Gabriel is halfway to being tight." I rose and dusted off my hands. "I'm leaving the water for you. Make sure you drink plenty. It wouldn't do to get dehydrated out here. It would be a pity to leave you behind."

He was still shouting when I left him.

No sooner had I emerged from the tent than Gabriel strode up carrying a length of flatbread heaped with dried fruit, a few nuts and something that looked like an old shoe.

"What is this?" I poked at it a little.

"A sort of dried meat."

"It looks like leather," I told him.

"Tastes like it, too, but it will stop you being too hungry. What's Herr Doktor fussed about?"

I shrugged and nibbled a piece of the dried meat to avoid telling him. There seemed little point in going into the details of Herr Doktor's thwarted romance with Gethsemane Green. The poor man had little enough dignity left as it was. There was no need to make him a laughingstock.

"He isn't our friend," Gabriel said sharply.

I jerked. "I do wish you wouldn't do that. It's rude to read another person's thoughts."

"Hardly clairvoyance when what you're thinking is writ large all over your face," he returned with a bland smile. "You've just rowed with him about leaving us and discovered for yourself what I told you all along—that he is not to be trusted."

"You trusted him well enough when he turned up in the middle of nowhere with a car," I pointed out.

"No, I used him to get us the resources we needed."

I rolled my eyes heavenward. "If you were so successful, we would have been left with the car."

"Be glad we weren't," he said, his expression grim. "Apparently that's what caught the eye of Daoud and his dangerous friends."

"How do you know?"

He nodded his head towards the low fire where Sheikh Hamid and his men were gathered. "Rashid did a bit of sniffing around and met up with a cousin of his who told him that a band of Bedouin from the south had followed a car along the track from Palmyra."

"Daoud," I murmured.

"That means the good doctor was telling the truth. Daoud is still hanging about. And we have to assume he's coming for us."

In the morning, in the grey still hours before the sun has risen but after the black cloak of night had slipped off the edge of the world, Gabriel shoved me awake. "Drink this," he ordered, pushing a cup of steaming liquid into my hands.

I sniffed. "What is this?"

"White coffee. Hot water flavoured with almonds and sweetened. Makes a nice change from their wretched habit of putting cardamom in the tea. Drink up and come with me. We've got a council of war on."

He was exaggerating only slightly. The men had gathered around the fire, stoking it just enough to boil their drinks and talking with serious expressions.

"What's the trouble?" I asked Gabriel.

"Rashid met with his cousin again this morning. The cousin's village is a little distance away, a few hours by camel. He said they've been disturbed for the last day by two aeroplanes flying overhead."

I shrugged. "Surely that can't be so odd. This desert was crawling with planes during the war. The villagers must be used to it."

He gave me a patient look. "The planes that flew over during the war were just as likely to drop bombs. These people are a trifle touchy about anything that flies and they're quite happy to shoot at anything that does. These two were flying a little high for that. Their rifles didn't have the range to touch them. But the curious thing is that they were flying search patterns."

"Search patterns?"

"They're looking for something out here," he said, his jaw set.

"The Cross," I breathed. "What if that's how Countess Thurzó has arranged to get the Cross out of the desert? It's brilliant. She wouldn't have to go to Damascus at all! She could head right to Turkey or Baghdad with the money already in her pocket."

Gabriel shook his head. "Baghdad is under British control, remember? We've been through this. She would have better odds with the French, I think."

"Except for one thing," I reminded him. "French control is teetering. With Faisal declaring independence and the government slipping into Arab hands, the last place Countess Thurzó would want to be is Damascus. She'd want to go quietly, and what better way than by flying over the border into Mesopotamia or Turkey?"

Gabriel rubbed his chin thoughtfully. "Not exactly a subtle entrance, but you could be right. It is possible that the arrangements were already made and they're hanging about because the countess is lost in the desert."

"Of course! If the planes are still flying, then the countess hasn't made contact yet," I told him, reasoning it out as I spoke. "That means she still has the Cross. We'll get it yet," I promised him.

He sighed and put a hand to my shoulder. "Evie, it might be time to let it go. Hamid and his men can see us safely to the Damascus road—hell, they'll take us all the way to the city if we want. Or they'll escort us to Baghdad, which sounds a damn sight safer at this point."

I shrugged off his hand, stepping closer until we were toe-to-toe. "Have you forgot that my Aunt Dove is in Damascus? What sort of cad are you that you would leave a defenceless old woman in a city that could fall any day?"

He groaned. "God, I did forget. Still, we could have Hamid send men to Damascus with a message to put her on the first train to Baghdad, or

Palestine even. They'd get her out faster than we could."

I waved an airy hand. "Don't be stupid. Damascus isn't going to fall. They have a king in Faisal but if there's one thing I know about the fellow, he's *nice.* He isn't going to throw the French out completely, and he isn't going to let anything happen to foreigners."

He fisted his hands at his sides as if clenching them were the only thing preventing him from fitting them around my neck. "You just called me a cad for even thinking of leaving your aunt there and now that's precisely what you're suggesting."

"I would back Aunt Dove against a revolution any day. She's been through fourteen, you know. I just wanted to remind you that there are factors to consider besides what is most convenient for you."

"Convenient?" His nostrils flared like a bull's. "Do you think any of this has been bloody convenient for me?"

I shrugged. "Oh, don't be such a bear. I know you got whipped and you're still a little upset that I shot you, don't deny it. But I have priorities, too, Gabriel. And not just Aunt Dove. Wally should be in Damascus with the *Jolly Roger* by now, and I have to consider them, as well."

"Of course you do," he said.

"How ever do you get your upper lip to curl like that? It's the most wonderful sneer. Do you practise in the mirror?"

"For God's sake, Evie, if you make one more joke—"

"Really, Gabriel," I said seriously. "All this time I've been annoyed with you for making a joke of everything, but now I see it's marvelously effective—almost as effective as your sneer. Now, you must teach me how to do it. I'd like to be able to raise one eyebrow, as well. I bet you can do that, too."

"I remember this mood," he said dangerously. "It's no use talking to you when you're like this."

"Like what? Oh, I know you think it's foolish, but I can't shake the feeling that everything's going to be all right in the end."

"You *always* think everything is going to be all right in the end."

I blinked at him. "Well, isn't it?"

His mouth went slack. "Is it? Evie, I've been officially dead for five years. Our marriage ended on a steamer in Shanghai. I haven't been with another woman since. Do you know what that does to a man's insides? I have been in this bloody desert killing myself to make one single discovery that I can leave as a legacy to show that I actually did something with my life, and when I finally do discover it, I manage to put you in danger, get whipped, chased and shot at as well as kil—" He choked himself off abruptly but I scarcely noticed.

"You haven't been with another woman? Not since me?"

"You sound incredulous," he said with a nasty, clipped quality to his voice. "May I presume you've not been quite so assiduous in maintaining your own marital fidelity?"

"Well, since I thought I was a widow, there wasn't any marital fidelity to maintain, was there?" I gave him a cheerful smile that concealed much. "You really ought to rectify that situation. You're quite right. It isn't healthy for a man's insides. Perhaps you can find a nice girl in Damascus. I hear they have quite good prostitutes there."

His mouth went from slack to hanging fully open. He closed it with a snap that must have rattled his teeth.

"Now," I said briskly, "what is Hamid's plan?"

"Hamid insists upon going to the aid of Aysha and Rashid's people. Hamid feels it would be a disgrace not to support them. His rifles are longer range. He thinks he can shoot at least one of the planes down and perhaps both, *inshallah*."

"Does Hamid know that the planes are most likely not after the Bedu at all?"

He hesitated. "Hamid is a trifle intractable on the subject of aeroplanes. I tried to explain that they were most likely just searching the desert for oil surveys or something equally innocuous, but he thinks they're French reconnaissance after Bedouin rebels. I couldn't reassure him completely without explaining about the Cross, so I went along with it."

Just then the sheikh beckoned to us.

"I hear some planes have been spotted to the east," I said. At this half a dozen men broke out in fervent Arabic, and I caught one word repeated several times. *Saqr.*

"What does that mean—*saqr*?" I asked Gabriel. "I've heard the word before."

He shrugged. "It's a bird of prey, a hawk or falcon, I think. Their flowery Bedouin way of referring to an aeroplane," he said smoothly.

I turned again to the men, but the swiftness of their colloquial Arabic flowed right past me. They argued back and forth, and several times Hamid shot Gabriel a meaningful look only to find Gabriel was studying his shoes or cleaning his fingernails.

Eventually, they seemed to come to some understanding and the men dispersed, clearly excited.

It was only when I saw Rashid trotting away that I remembered where I had heard the word *saqr.* "It's not just an aeroplane," I said to Gabriel. "It's a sort of folk hero among the Bedu, the Falcon of the Desert, they call him."

He lifted a lazy brow. "I'm surprised you've heard of him. He's just a bit of local folklore."

"But he isn't just folklore," I said slowly. I was trying to remember everything Rashid had told me. "He's real. He led the Bedouin during the war, united them against the Turks."

"Did he?"

"Of course he did. Why on earth would they still talk about him if he didn't exist?"

His look was pitying. "My dear child, do you have any notion of what the Turks were up to out here? They were committing atrocities that would have made Attila the Hun blush. They raided all through this part of the Badiyat ash-Sham, doing whatever they bloody well liked, and killing as many as they possibly could as nastily as they could."

"I'm sure it was horrible," I began, but he waved me to silence.

"Horrible? What a dainty, drawing-room sort of word to describe what they did. In one village, they dug a pit and hurled every last soul—man, woman and child—into it before pouring burning pitch over the lot of them. The lucky ones died quickly," he said, his jaw tight. "They raped women and nailed their corpses to the walls with bayonets. They pulled entrails out of men and staked them out for the jackals to feed on while their victims still lived. They lanced children," he said, his eyes glittering. "*Children.* And nothing could stop them, not even your famous Colonel Lawrence."

"Lawrence did try," I pointed out.

He laughed, a hollow, mirthless sound. "In the first place, Lawrence spent most of his time far south of here—in the Hejaz, bolstering Faisal's shaky popularity with any tribe that wasn't Hashemite. And in the second, Lawrence was captured by the Turks and do you know what he got for his pains? He was beaten and raped by them. I'll wager that didn't end up in one of your little newsreels."

I gaped at him. "How on earth do you know that?"

He hesitated only a fraction of a second. Anyone else might have missed it. But I did not. "Word gets around in the desert."

And suddenly, with a flash of something I can only think of as inspiration, I knew one of the secrets Gabriel had been hiding.

"During the war, when you were dodging your responsibilities and poking around the desert for treasure, you must have heard of the Saqr."

"I heard of him," he said reluctantly. "But his identity was a closely guarded secret. The Bedouin learned from Lawrence's mistakes. His showmanship got a bounty put on his head and distracted from the matters at hand. The Bedouin were much quieter about the Saqr—to speak of him would have been dangerous for him and lethal for them."

"But you must have run across him," I persisted.

He said nothing, and I thought furiously for a moment, the truth dawning so suddenly I nearly fell over. "My God. It's Hamid. He's the Saqr, isn't he? The desert prince who leads his people wielding the sickle blade of a crescent moon and riding a milk white horse? It is Hamid," I said in quiet triumph.

Gabriel fixed me with a hard stare. "I trust you will keep this information to yourself," he said, his voice clipped and cold. "I don't think I need to tell you what might happen if that fact fell into the wrong hands."

"You mean Herr Doktor," I said furiously. "You are absolutely wrong about him, you know. He is a darling old man, and I happen to trust him."

Gabriel's expression was bored. "Well, I don't. Be a good girl and keep Hamid's secret, will you?" He thrust his hands into his pockets, whistling a bit of Purcell as he went.

Herr Doktor had spiked a fever and Faiz kept a watchful eye upon him while the rest of us set off to visit the village that had complained of the aeroplanes flying overhead. It was a glorious morning, with a pink wash of sunlight over the landscape, and a quick breeze picking up the streamers tied to the lances. Each man carried not only the traditional weapons of sword and lance, but there was a rifle tucked into each saddle, as well. The camels were hung with richly tasselled saddle cloths and I realised for the first time that each camel bell sounded a unique note, blending together in a strange melody as we travelled. The horses were fitted with embroidered headstalls held by a single rein, but they were so well-trained and light of foot they hardly seemed to touch the ground. Hamid's mount was a beautiful creature called Hadibah. I noticed with interest that she was the colour of a pale grey pearl.

Gabriel had sunk into a sort of sulk—no doubt because I had forced his hand about admitting Sheikh Hamid was the Saqr—and I ignored him, as much as I could in light of the fact that we were sharing a camel. I chatted with Hamid, who pointed out the desert landmarks that would have gone completely unremarked by the casual observer.

The sheikh looked at me in surprise when I said as much. "But of course, the desert has landmarks. How do you think we navigate?"

He explained about the system of wells and faint tracks that linked them, the ancient ways through the desert and the fluid and elegant system of navigation that enabled them to thrive in such a place. It was deeply fascinating, but behind me, Gabriel sat rigidly and said nothing.

We were still some distance away when Hamid slowed, his hooded eyes watchful. He held up a hand for silence and after a moment a high, tiny sound emerged from the stillness.

Gabriel cocked his head a moment then barked a word in Arabic, and suddenly Hamid gave a signal and the entire company charged forward. The camels covered the ground as swiftly as horses, their odd, rocking gait eating up the distance to the village. As we approached, we could hear the shouts from these Bedouin, some calling hurried greetings to Hamid and his men, the others crying out warnings as two tiny dots dropped down from the sky.

They were no bigger than insects at first, but they came nearer, growing larger as the noise of their engines filled the air. The village horses began to stamp at their pegs and the men raised rifles, shouting curses and threats at the incoming planes.

It was folly; their weapons were ancient things, far too unreliable to hit a plane at any distance, and these two were still just out of reach for even a decent infantry rifle. One of them was sitting smoothly, the wings holding steady, but as they closed the distance and dropped a little lower, I saw that one was bucking hard, fighting the pilot every inch of the way.

Next to me, Sheikh Hamid raised his Enfield and sighted the struggling plane. He paused, his finger poised on the trigger. Ammunition for an English rifle was too expensive to waste, I realised. He would wait until the shot was clean. I held my breath, wondering if this was what it had been like for all those boys I had nursed at the convalescent hospital—this impossible moment when every nerve stretched like elastic, taut and vibrating and very nearly broken.

My palms ached, and I realised I had dug my nails straight into them.

"You might not want to watch," Gabriel suggested, his voice mild.

"I can handle anything you can," I muttered. But before the last word was out of my mouth, I was standing on the edge of the camel saddle, high on my mount, straining my eyes into the morning sun.

The planes had dropped lower still, and the one in back was barely holding itself together, shaking and bucking until it seemed it must fall to pieces. Hamid tracked it with the sight, and just as he began to squeeze the trigger, I launched myself out of the saddle, shoving his rifle into the air so the shot went high. I landed on his horse's neck and she began to plunge and shriek, tossing us both onto the hard ground. I landed on Hamid and it took a moment for Gabriel to jump from our camel and disentangle us.

"Evie, what the hell was that? Not only did you ruin his shot, you fell on top of him! Do you have any idea how much you have insulted him?"

I looked up to find the rest of the men staring at me in horror, and Hamid, his face purple with outrage, waiting for an explanation.

I dusted myself off. "*Aasif*, Sheikh Hamid. I am so sorry, I do hope that's the right word. I really do beg your pardon most awfully, but you see I couldn't let you shoot that plane," I told him. I turned to see both aeroplanes dropping to the road, landing neatly and rolling to a stop as the villagers began to surge towards them.

Hamid's jaw was tight with anger. "And why could I not shoot that aeroplane, *sitt*?"

"Well, because it's mine."

FIFTEEN

I made a rushed explanation as we hurried along with the villagers and by the time we reached the planes, Hamid was able to persuade the local folk who were preparing to drag the pilots out and hang them that they were friendly visitors and not French spies at all.

He finished by turning to me and asking me to vouch for them. "Of course, I vouch for them. The lady is my aunt," I said, pushing through the throng of people to reach her. I threw my arms around her. "Darling, what on earth are you doing here?" I hugged her as tightly as I could. "Don't mistake me, I'm desperately glad to see you, but don't hug me again. I smell of camel. But what are you doing here?"

Aunt Dove pulled off her leather flying helmet and fluffed her white curls then reached into her pocket for a folded newspaper clipping.

"Have a look for yourself," she told me.

"What's this?" I asked. I opened it to find my own face staring back at me under the headline

Celebrated Aviatrix Missing in Desert. I sucked in a breath as I skimmed the article. *Famed aviatrix Evangeline Merryweather Starke has been reported missing from an archaeological site in the desert outside of Damascus,* it began. It went on to say that I had vanished along with the expedition's co-leader, a man of whom remarkably few facts were known, although the piece ended with lurid speculation as to why we had disappeared.

"Oh, dear. However did they get that story?"

"I'm afraid it's my fault," said a smooth voice. The crowd parted and John Halliday walked towards me, tugging off his own helmet. He looked a good deal less clean and tidy than he had in Damascus, but there was something decidedly attractive about him in his pilot's rig.

He put out his hand to take mine. "Evie, do forgive the dramatic entrance, but we've been combing the desert looking for you. I don't mind telling you, we've been rather frantic." He looked at the assembled crowd and immediately his eye fell upon Hamid, and with the homing instincts of a true diplomat, he realised at once that Hamid was the sheikh. Halliday made a low bow and a few silken sentences of his fluent Arabic did the trick. Within moments the headman of the village had vacated a tent for us and Hamid acted as host. A shrieking Arthur Wellesley was retrieved from the *Jolly Roger* with the ghastly cage Rashid had bought for him. Aunt Dove talked soothingly to him as the Bedouin bustled around.

"Oh, my poor little darling. Would you like something to eat?" She crumbled a biscuit from her pocket, but he merely hopped up and down, scolding. She shook her head and turned to me.

"He has been in a wretched mood ever since we left Damascus. I am beginning to think he doesn't much care for aeroplanes," she said thoughtfully. She slipped a flask from her small travel bag and gave him a sizeable drink. He perked up then, telling the kaiser to bugger off a few times, much to Hamid's amusement.

"That is a clever bird," he remarked.

"He's a nuisance and ought to be drowned in a bathtub," I muttered. Arthur shrieked again, and Aunt Dove gave me a repressive look.

"He understands you, you know." She soothed him down again and by the time he was settled with some nuts and a few bits of dried fruit and several more sips of brandy, we were given the fullest hospitality the village could offer. Water was brought for washing and then food—a simple meal of stewed vegetables and flatbreads and nuts, but I was too happy to eat. I hadn't realised how much of a strain the past several days had been until I saw familiar, friendly faces. Of course, Gabriel's face had been familiar, but it certainly hadn't been friendly, and it had grown even more sour since the planes had landed. I would have thought he'd have been pleased to know the villagers weren't being surveilled by hostile French, and was nearly on the point of telling him so when Aunt Dove peered through the dim light of the tent, staring intently at him for the first time.

"Bless my soul, it's Gabriel Starke!" she cried. "So you've been here all the time, have you? Well, that is interesting."

John Halliday's head snapped up. "This is a turn-up for the books. I say, weren't you given up for dead after the *Lusitania*, Mr. Starke?"

Gabriel was quietly consuming his food. "Yes, and being dead suited me, so I think we'll dispense with the questions if it's all the same to you."

"Gabriel!" I nudged him as hard as I could in the ribs, hoping I'd hit something vital. "Don't be rude. I do apologise, Mr. Halliday. My husband always did have a filthy temper and death hasn't improved it."

"Oh!" Aunt Dove exclaimed. "He is still your husband, isn't he? Now, I see it—you were masquerading as that interesting archaeologist Rowan in Damascus, the one we had dinner with, the fellow with appalling table manners. I can't believe I didn't recognise it then, but it's all in the eyes, I think. No one could mistake those beautiful blue eyes—so wasted on a man! Well, come and give me a kiss and later on you can explain how you managed to survive a shipwreck,

346

to say nothing of why you've been pretending to be someone you aren't."

Gabriel went and kissed her papery cheek with a loud smack. She slapped him lightly. "There's a good boy. I'm sure you had your reasons. The Gabriel Starke I knew wouldn't do something so frightfully stupid without a good reason."

He stared at her a long moment with something like gratitude before turning away.

I held out the newspaper to him. "Read all about us. Apparently I've been abducted and you are possibly a sex criminal."

"Jesus Christ," he muttered, snatching it out of my fingers. I turned back to Aunt Dove.

"How did you come to be flying the *Jolly Roger*, Auntie?" I asked. "And where's Wally?"

She gave me a sorrowful smile. "I'm afraid he had to leave, dear girl. Trouble at home." She turned to the others to include them. "Wally's father is Viscount Walters, you know. Wally is heir to the title. A very pretty estate in Hampshire, I'm sure you've heard of it—Mistledown? Doesn't that sound ethereal? Such a charming name for a house, although the Walters men have always run to eccentricity. Anyway, the old fellow had a bad turn and poor Wally was wanted at home, no doubt for some hearty deathbed recriminations. It was all quite sudden and the dear boy was wretched about the whole thing, but I packed him onto the first train out of Damascus and told him not to worry, that I would manage the *Jolly Roger.*"

"I still can't believe you flew her—and all the way from Damascus!"

"You needn't look so shocked. It may be the furthest I've flown, but I did a splendid job, if I say it myself," she said, her tone a trifle miffed.

"Lady Lavinia was quite capable at the controls," Mr. Halliday affirmed. "I'm afraid this was all my idea. You see, Lady Lavinia grew quite concerned when she hadn't heard from you, Mrs. Starke. I offered to borrow a friend's Nieuport to fly out to the dig site and have a look around— see if I could turn up a bit of information and perhaps bring you back with a bit of luck."

"Naturally, I refused," Aunt Dove added smoothly. "My niece is my responsibility. I told him I was perfectly capable of flying the *Jolly Roger* myself, but he insisted on coming along."

"I thought it might be useful to have a member of the diplomatic corps since the situation out here can be tenuous at the best of times," he said, his voice carefully neutral.

Hamid gave a booming laugh. "You are tactful, Mr. Halliday."

"Thank you, Sheikh."

They bowed to each other and Gabriel gave a gusty sigh. "Fine, we're all getting along like a house afire. Time to get things sorted. Dove, my heart, I'll pull the ballast sack out of the *Jolly Roger*, and Evie can fly you back to Damascus.

I'm sure Mr. Halliday would be only too happy to act as escort," he added with a bland smile in the gentleman's direction. "In the meantime, Hamid and his fellows and I can secure some sort of transport for Herr Doktor Schickfuss and get him medical attention."

"Herr Doktor Schickfuss? Do you mean Herr Doktor Wolfram von Schickfuss?" Halliday inquired. His light sandy brows were arched in curiosity. "Isn't he one of the fellows attached to your . . . that is to say, Mr. Rowan's dig?" He flushed just a little, but he was not a diplomat for nothing. He covered the awkwardness easily.

"Yes," Gabriel replied shortly. "He's had an accident." He paused, flicking a quick glance at me, and I realised he intended to minimise the danger in order to reassure Aunt Dove that it has all been perfectly safe. "I'm afraid the old fellow's been shot. Just a flesh wound, but it's turning septic and the sooner he gets to a proper hospital the better."

"Shot!" Aunt Dove turned to me. "Darling, what *have* you been doing out here?"

"Well, I didn't shoot him," I protested in some irritation. "I only shot Gabriel."

Mr. Halliday blinked and stared from Gabriel to me. "You shot your husband?"

Gabriel bared his teeth in a wolfish grin. "Square in the chest. Luckily I had something in my pocket to deflect the bullet."

Sheikh Hamid was watching me with new

349

respect, his expression one of amused interest. "You are a new Zenobia, little sister."

"I only shot him because he wanted me to," I confessed modestly.

"Still, it is only a warrior of cool head and temperament who can shoot when he must and keep his aim true. More so for a woman. Their emotions run hot as the noonday sun."

"How poetic you are, Sheikh?" Aunt Dove asked, fluttering her lashes a little.

I frowned. "That really is the rankest untruth, Hamid, if you'll forgive me. In my experience, men are far more emotional, particularly under life-and-death conditions. I remember one incident at flight school when two of the fellows came to blows over—"

"Evie," Aunt Dove said, gently recalling me to the matter at hand.

"Oh, of course." I smiled at Hamid. "Just as well. It was about to get nasty. One of the fellows shoved the other right into a spinning propeller."

Mr. Halliday swallowed thickly, his complexion a little green. "I say, I do have a few questions. How did this Doktor Schickfuss come to be shot, anyway? Were you potting birds out here?"

I could feel Gabriel's eyes boring into me, willing me to be quiet and I ignored him.

"No. Gabriel discovered something of value, a relic of sorts, and it was stolen. Herr Doktor Schickfuss happened upon the folks who stole it from us and we thought he was in league with them."

"And so you shot him?" Halliday's voice was incredulous.

I gave an impatient sigh. "No, *they* shot him. Mr. Halliday, do try to keep up. Now, of course, you see why Gabriel's suggestion is ludicrous. We can't possibly just let them get away with it. We have to go after them and get it back."

"We?" Aunt Dove perked up considerably.

"Not we," Gabriel contradicted.

"Your jaw is going to lock like that if you grind it any harder," I told him. I turned back to the rest of the group. "Now, at first we thought the planes were French authorities reconnoitering the area to look for renegades and deserters, but now we know it was just you, and it was very sweet of you to come looking, and I'm delighted you did. But we're not ready to give up yet, so you can either stay and join in the fun or head back to Damascus and I'll meet you there." I paused and furrowed my brow. "Unless Baghdad would be better? We have heard some strange things about the goings-on in the city. Is it still peaceful?"

"For the moment." Halliday's tone was dry. "But I won't lie, Evie. We're sitting on a tinderbox here. I, for one, will feel much safer when you and Lady Lavinia are safely out of the country. Baghdad is—"

"Out of the question," Gabriel interrupted. "This

351

thing has got quite out of hand, and if you would get Evie back to Damascus, Halliday, I would be personally grateful."

I turned to him, my mouth agape. "I am not baggage to be carted around at your pleasure, Gabriel Starke. I am my own woman and I think you abdicated any authority over what I do the day you put me on a steamer out of Shanghai, to say nothing of the fact that you faked your own death—a fact I would be *delighted* to present to the authorities at the nearest embassy because I am terribly certain it's not legal." I turned to Halliday. "You're a representative of His Majesty's government. Can't you arrest him?"

Halliday looked awkwardly from my inquiring face to Gabriel's insouciant one. "I'm afraid, that is to say, really, it isn't my place—"

"That is diplomatic-speak for 'no,'" Gabriel stormed. "I'm not afraid of anything official you care to threaten me with, so just drop it, Evie. Can't you see I simply want to forget the whole bloody thing?"

"Of course you do," I returned coldly. "Because it's difficult. Because it's hard. Because that's your way, to run at the first sign of trouble. Well, it isn't *my* way, thank you very much. I'm going to see this thing through."

Gabriel went white to his lips and rose without a word. He left the tent and an uncomfortable silence fell.

"Always so awkward when married people quarrel," Aunt Dove murmured.

"We're not married, not really," I told her. "I was halfway to divorcing him when he died, remember?"

"Yes, dear, but he didn't die, did he? You are still married to him. And married people always seem to get into the silliest quarrels."

"I do not quarrel with my wives," Hamid said blandly.

"Because your culture gives you complete authority over them," I reminded him.

"No, because I find my wives are usually right and it is more harmonious to simply agree with them." He stroked his beard thoughtfully. "Now, what was this about a theft?"

I should have known it was a mistake to mention the theft in company. Halliday seized on it as soon as Sheikh Hamid had spoken.

"Here, now. What's all this about a relic? If Mr. Starke really has found something of value in the desert, surely it belongs to the sponsors of the archaeological expedition. And the French government—" He broke off, darting a quick glance at Hamid. "Well, perhaps not the French anymore. I suppose it will fall to Faisal and his people."

"King Faisal," Hamid corrected coldly.

"My apologies, Sheikh," Halliday said, inclining his head. "My government has not officially recognised the kingship of Prince Faisal, you understand."

"And if the British government does not recognise it, it cannot be so?" Hamid's voice was pleasant, but his eyes glittered dangerously, and I was reminded of precisely how ferocious the Bedouin could be.

"Recognition by His Majesty's government would go a very long way towards legitimising the rule of King Faisal," Halliday pointed out practically. "Surely you see that, Sheikh."

"What I see is once again it becomes the business of the European to direct the destiny of the Arab," he replied.

"As much as it pains me to say it, Sheikh," Halliday said, his voice calmly reasonable, "it would indeed help Prince . . . that is, King Faisal's cause to have British support. If this relic is so very significant, perhaps joint ownership would reflect well upon both nations. If nothing else, it would cut out the French, something I think both of our peoples can agree is not a terrible thing?"

Hamid looked mollified for the moment, and I tipped my head thoughtfully towards Halliday. "Considering the upheaval in the government, I'm a little surprised they sent you out to find me. After all, one aviatrix is hardly as noteworthy a story as the toppling of the French government."

"It hasn't toppled yet," he reminded me. "This

trouble with Pr—King Faisal may be a tempest in a teacup."

"You think an Arab king declaring his country independent is so trifling a thing?" Hamid asked, his hand settling with lazy purpose on his dagger.

But Halliday wasn't a diplomat for nothing. He smiled at Hamid. "I would love nothing better than to see Faisal succeed in tossing the French out on their ear," he said with disarming bluntness. "But the French are better armed and firmly entrenched. It will take a miracle, *inshallah*."

Hamid inclined his head and his hand dropped from his dagger. Halliday turned back to me.

"But your disappearance was bigger news than you think. It was picked up by wire services and has spread around the world. Everyone is waiting to see if you're all right or if you've been carried off by—"

"By an archaeological sex maniac," I finished.

He rose and dusted off his trousers. "If you will excuse me, Sheikh, I would like to make the necessary repairs to Mrs. Starke's plane."

I jumped up. "What's the matter with the *Jolly Roger*?"

He gave me a reassuring smile. "Nothing very serious. Just a bit of tightening up, and a leak I need to patch." I hesitated and the smile deepened. "You needn't worry, you know. I'm perfectly qualified, and I promise not to touch a wire on her frame without permission."

I felt a warm flush in my cheeks. "I'm being beastly and you're only trying to help. Yes, of course, do what you must. And thank you."

Sheikh Hamid rose, as well, his good humour apparently restored. "You may need the services of some of the village men and the blacksmith. I will help you with this."

Halliday brightened. "I say, that's awfully nice of you. Perhaps you can tell me a bit more about these hostile fellows we're up against."

They left together and I made to follow, but Aunt Dove's voice was sharp.

"Sit down."

"Yes, ma'am," I said. I folded my legs under me and took a seat on the carpet, arranging my features into a wide-eyed expression of patient obedience.

"Meekness doesn't suit you," she said, her lips thin. "Now, suppose you tell me, Evangeline Merryweather Starke, *precisely* what you are doing gallivanting around the desert with your not-quite-dead, not-quite-ex husband?"

I took a deep breath and launched into a detailed explanation. I left nothing out, at least nothing of importance, and she had only asked a few probing questions. Her expression was thoughtful, and when I finished, she nodded. "I suspected something like this."

I blinked. "How on earth could you have possibly suspected something like this? Have you added clairvoyance to your talents?"

"Don't be pert," she said, arching an imperious brow. "When I saw that photograph of him, I knew exactly why we were going to Damascus. I just wish you had confided in me sooner."

I gaped at her. "When did you see the photograph?"

She gave a long, slow-lidded blink. "The day it arrived, child. I went through the post before you did and there was one blank envelope. Since it didn't have either of our names on it, I opened it and found nothing but that photograph."

"There was no envelope when I saw it," I pointed out.

She flapped a hand. "Of course not. I threw it out. It was *filthy*. Besides, it had no distinguishing marks of any kind, not even a postmark."

"Then how did it even get to us in the first place?"

"The ambassador's people in Rome had kindly delivered any post that was sent to their office. This was among those things. I made inquiries at the ambassador's office, but the witless fellow I talked to merely said that the outer envelope had been so soiled and badly torn he thought it best to throw it away and simply pass along the interior envelope. He said the postmark had come from Damascus, but there were no other markings on it. So that made for a tidy little dead end. No more information to be had beyond what was on the photograph itself."

"But why didn't you tell me you knew about the photograph?" I felt a little aggrieved that she had kept it from me all this time. I thought of the long days of travel, the sight-seeing in Damascus, and through it all there hadn't been the slightest hint from her that she'd known.

"Why didn't you tell me that was why we were going to Damascus?" Her gaze was sharp, but her tone had softened.

"I suppose," I said slowly, "I didn't want you to worry. Wally thought the whole thing was the wildest sort of goose chase at first, but then we decided I had no choice but to go and see the thing through."

"And do you always do what Wally tells you?" There was a touch of asperity, and Arthur fluttered irritably in his cage.

"I'm not marrying him, am I?" I regretted the sharpness the moment the words were out of my mouth. "I am sorry, Auntie. It's all gotten out of hand. And Gabriel—"

"Isn't living up to your expectations?" she guessed.

"My expectations where Gabriel is concerned are quite low."

"But not your hopes."

I looked up quickly, but her face had gone sweetly sad. "I know, child. I know what these last five years have cost you. I know you blamed yourself for pushing him away, and I know you fretted yourself to distraction about whether you made a terrible mistake in Shanghai."

"And it turns out, I didn't. I thought he was something he wasn't, and that illusion is what I married. The real man is so capricious he makes my head spin. He's exactly the man I was afraid he was. He's feckless and unreliable and he's got himself mixed up in all sorts of nasty business out here. My mistake wasn't misjudging him. It was marrying him in the first place."

She gave me a thoughtful look. "When this is all finished and you're quietly and thoroughly divorced, you might give some thought to choosing a nice beau from all those suitors you have flocking around. Someone besides Wally."

I shuddered. "That's the last thing I want to think about. I won't marry again," I swore. "One time down that particular road is plenty for any girl."

"And too much for some," she reminded me. "I've done quite nicely for myself without bothering to hitch my wagon to anyone else's star. But you aren't me, Evie. You like having someone around. That's why you took up with Wally after you lost Gabriel. He was a sort of husband for you, albeit the kind who wouldn't pester you in the bedroom."

I narrowed my eyes at her. "Have you been reading those psychoanalysis books again?"

She shrugged. "Well, it's perfectly obvious, dear.

In a woman with a slight Electra complex whose father issues were never entirely resolved—"

I held up a hand. "Let's leave Electra out of this. Now, I want to see what damage you've inflicted on the *Jolly Roger* and whether Mr. Halliday really can fix her up."

The *Jolly Roger*'s repairs proved minor—a leaking fuel line and some loose guy wires—and while Halliday was finishing up, Gabriel reappeared. He'd been gone the better part of the afternoon with no word he was even leaving. I had no notion of where he'd gone when he stamped off in a sulk, but apparently he'd decided to check in with Herr Doktor. He returned in a nasty mood.

"How is Herr Doktor? Is he feverish?"

"Missing," he said, his mouth set in a grim line.

"But that can't be! He was far too ill—" I broke off at the frankly sceptical look in Gabriel's eye as he waited for me to figure it out.

"You think he left to go after the Cross. I won't believe it. How is that even possible?"

"He took the drugs in my medical kit and one of the camels. They didn't stop him because they assumed Hamid had given his permission."

"Not that nice old man," I said stoutly. "We were helping him!"

"I wish I knew what he had up his sleeve," Gabriel said slowly. "If he's loose, he could be planning on throwing in with the countess. In fact, they might have been in league the whole time. She could have sent him to keep an eye on Daoud and follow us to the rest of the Cross."

I thought it over then shook my head. "I don't believe it." I told him briefly about Herr Doktor's love for Gethsemane, and Gabriel's eyes narrowed.

"It might have been useful to have this information sooner," he said with a touch of asperity.

I shrugged. "It didn't seem relevant at the time. Besides, you have plenty of secrets of your own," I retorted. "But now you understand why he wouldn't throw in with the countess. He loves Gethsemane."

"He *told* you he loves Gethsemane," he corrected. "You haven't seen them together, have you? He could have made up that story just to play on your sympathies. In fact, he could have been in league with the countess the whole time. With her brother dead, she'll be on her own out in the desert, and that means she's desperate. I wouldn't put it past her to find a way to use Herr Doktor to help her get out of the country."

"How on earth would he be of use to her?"

He shook his head slowly. "Devil if I know. But he is Prussian nobility. She might suppose he has wealthy relatives somewhere who could pay a ransom or pull some strings to get her out. Or, if she's really up against it, she knows he wanted the bloody Cross, too. She could seize the chance to sell it outright to him now and be done with the damned thing. Believe me, she's a far more clever woman than people give her credit for."

"But how do you know what she might do? You can't read her mind, and it isn't as if you were all that close . . ." I trailed off. "Oh, *Gabriel*."

He had the grace to look uncomfortable.

"You said you hadn't been with another woman for five years," I said accusingly.

"That may have been a technicality," he acknowledged.

"A technicality? But Countess Thurzó is beautiful! And Rowan is so . . . so . . ."

"Thanks for that. It wasn't *that* extensive of a disguise."

I shuddered. "But you had those gruesome false teeth."

He grinned. "That was the most amusing part. You see, I figured quite early on that Countess Thurzó wasn't above doing whatever it took to get information for herself and that ratty brother of hers. I thought I'd see exactly how far she was prepared to go. It was quite instructive."

"I'll just bet."

The grin deepened to a real smile, his blue eyes shining with amusement. "If I didn't know better, I'd say you were jealous."

"Jealous! Heavens, Gabriel, you do have a high opinion of yourself. I assure you, if we compared our activities of the last five years, you would have *much* more cause to be jealous than I would."

"Is that right?" He moved a fraction closer to me, but before he could say a word, Halliday approached.

"I've got very good news, Evie. I'm all finished with the *Jolly Roger.* Went back to tighten the prop and she's right as rain now. I say, am I interrupting?"

"Nothing I'm interested in continuing," I said sweetly.

Gabriel's eyes narrowed as he looked at Halliday, but his tone was cool. "Didn't think you diplomat chaps liked to get your hands dirty," he said with a nod to Halliday's grease-streaked palms.

Halliday flushed a little and fished a hand-kerchief out of his pocket to scrub at his hands.

"Don't mind Gabriel," I told him. "He's been in a very bad mood for five years."

Sheikh Hamid joined us then, his expression grave. "Trouble is on the horizon, my brother," he said in a low voice to Gabriel. He rattled off a quick explanation in Arabic and strode off, leaving Gabriel to explain.

"It's the deserters, the fellows who were French Foreign Legion. They've apparently set up camp in an old Turkish outpost, and this morning they attacked a village of Mezrab Bedouin. The entire place was put to the sword. There were no survivors."

I turned away, sickened, but there was more horror to come.

"There is fear this village will be next."

"Gabriel, these people are shepherds, for heaven's sake!"

He glanced around, pitching his voice low. "The deserters found a European woman wandering the desert, half-dead from dehydration and claiming she'd been robbed by her Bedouin guides."

"Countess Thurzó!" I breathed.

"Based on the description of the lady, there's no question. After we escaped his clutches, Daoud must have decided to take what he knew he could get his hands on. The countess was no doubt expecting him to return with results of his 'interrogation,'" he said, his mouth tightening on the word. "Instead, he must have robbed her then and turned her out into the desert to make her own way out. Or she's still got the Cross and has concocted the whole story just to get deserters to help her get out of the desert. Personally, I like the notion that she might actually have been robbed and left for dead."

"Considering her willingness to see *us* dead, you'll pardon me for not shedding violent tears at the notion," I retorted. "So, the deserters are outraged that a European lady has been treated so shabbily by the natives and they're out for blood, is that it?"

"More or less."

"And it doesn't matter to them at all that the Bedouin who left her for dead are not the same as the villagers they plan to attack?"

"Evie, to most Europeans a Bedu is a Bedu. They don't bother to split hairs about it."

His words were matter-of-fact, but his expression was thoughtful.

"Hamid and his men are going to fight, aren't they?"

"Hamid doesn't want to give the deserters time to recover from this morning's attack. They suffered some losses when they destroyed the Mezrab village, and Hamid wants to strike while they're still recovering."

I took a deep breath. "Then we have to help him."

"You have no idea what you're asking."

"I do," I told him firmly. "I worked in a convalescent hospital, you're forgetting. Oh, I tried to stay away from the worst of it, but I saw plenty. It was vile, and I can't even imagine inflicting that sort of horror on defenceless women and children. If there is anything at all we can do to help, we must."

Sheikh Hamid returned in time to hear my last remark, followed by Halliday, who had obviously been brought up to speed. "It may be too late for that," Hamid began.

I cut in sharply. "We can't leave this village unprotected," I said, digging in my heels. "We've come here and brought trouble among them. It's our responsibility to protect them if they are in danger."

Hamid gave me a broad smile. "Lady, these are *my* Bedu. They could fight demons and leave nothing to send back to hell. But," he added, turning to Gabriel, "this is a winter camp. There are elderly people here, and women and children. These are not just warriors. If the deserters have sufficient men—"

"Then we must act," Halliday said quickly. "We ought to assess the threat properly and if it is indeed a threat, we must direct attention away from this place."

"And how do you propose we do that?" Gabriel asked in a slow drawl.

"I can take up my plane and fly over to see what sort of numbers they have. A sort of reconnaissance mission," he said. He spoke calmly but there was a barely contained excitement simmering just under the surface. I wondered how often a junior diplomat got to engage in acts of derring-do. No doubt he thought himself a great champion of the noble Bedouin. The fact that his attitude might be construed as patronising seemed not to occur to him.

"I think it's a smashing idea," I said. "But I'm coming with you."

Halliday smiled regretfully. "Nothing I'd like more, but I've only got the one seat."

"I meant in the *Jolly Roger*. You said she's fine

now, and I haven't taken her up since Venice. I miss the old crate."

Halliday hesitated. "Evie, I hardly think, that is to say . . ." He turned to Gabriel. "Mr. Starke, as her husband, surely you possess the authority to deal with Mrs. Starke. It's really most unsuitable for a lady to even consider such a thing."

Gabriel shrugged. "Evie will do as she pleases."

I blinked at him. I had half expected him to bully me out of flying just to spite me.

"Thank you, Gabriel."

Halliday was spluttering. "But surely, Mr. Starke, you understand the danger." He lowered his voice. "The remnants of that Turkish outpost may have some anti-aircraft artillery we don't yet know about."

Gabriel turned to me with a bland smile. "Isn't that what all those aces used to call a 'beautiful death'?"

I put my fists on my hips. "You're both being completely outrageous. Well, not so much you, Mr. Halliday. You're just being a man, and an Englishman at that. You've spent too much time with traditional, old-fashioned girls. You need a modern girl to bring you up to speed. But that is quite enough out of you, Gabriel. You were right before—I shall do exactly as I please and it doesn't concern you in the least."

With that, I turned on my heel and strode to my plane. I didn't have my flying leathers with me, but fortunately Aunt Dove and I were of a size and I slipped into hers. "Shall I come with you, dear?" she asked.

But she was lounging on a pile of woolen cushions and wearing a loose Bedouin robe, drawing peacefully on a *nargileh* while Arthur twittered happily in the background.

"Not a bit of it. You look perfectly relaxed, and you ought to rest. That flight from Damascus must have been frightful."

She shrugged, but I noticed she moved her shoulders a little stiffly. She puffed on her pipe as I changed and nibbled a few dried dates. "You know, I begin to see what Jane Digby was thinking in coming to live like this. It's quite restful in its own way. If they could only mix a good whisky and water, I'd be tempted to stay."

"Not an option for us," I told her, dropping a quick kiss to her cheek. "The Bedouin seem to think the whole desert is going to be afire soon with resistance to the French since Faisal has declared independence."

She puffed again. "That's something I should like to see. It's about bloody time some of these fellows took their own country back. We've had our claws in these places long enough."

I left before she had a chance to work herself up into an anti-Empire rant and ran smack into John Halliday. He was pulling on his flying helmet and he gave me a regretful smile.

"I don't suppose there's any point in asking you to reconsider?"

I grinned. "None. In fact, I'll race you."

I pounded towards my plane and he ran for his. Hamid and his kin, having been given a short tutorial on how to start a propeller, were standing at the ready. I stepped onto the wing and swung myself into the cockpit. I was just settling my goggles into place when I felt the *Jolly Roger* give a shudder. I whipped my head around to find Gabriel standing in the rear cockpit, tossing a hundred-pound ballast bag over the side as if it weighed no more than a feather.

"What the devil are you doing in my plane?" I demanded. "Get out at once."

"Not a chance," he said, settling himself in. He buckled his safety belt and gave me a dry smile.

I looked to Halliday, who gave me a shrug and a thumbs-up. I turned back to Gabriel.

"Have you ever flown before?"

"Are you afraid I'm going to fall out?"

"I'm not that lucky. Now listen up, you can't make sudden movements back there. Anything too quick could upset the *Jolly Roger*. She only weighs thirteen hundred pounds and if you start bouncing around, we'll be upside down before you can blink. So sit down and be quiet and let me do what I do."

He gave me a meek thumbs-up and I turned back to the front. Halliday's plane was already fired up, and I waved him on to take off first. He hesitated then rolled out to shouts and ululations from the villagers.

I followed, lifting off smoothly just after Halliday. He had done a bang-up job on fixing her. The *Jolly Roger* was rising as sweetly as she ever had, and for a moment I gave myself up to the sheer joy of flying. I took her nose up, not too sharply because she had been known to stall if she didn't like the incline, but Halliday had already climbed quite high. He led us over a few ridges of rocky hills to the east, and a long, flat sandy plain dotted with brown bushes lightly ruffled in pale green. Spring in the desert.

We passed over another ridge of hills, and just as we topped the rise, bullets screamed out from the ground, strafing past us. One hit the back of Halliday's machine, and he immediately put her in a climb, just steep enough to get himself out of danger but not so sharp to stall. I followed suit and came up next to him as we levelled off.

He was mouthing something excitedly, but I pantomimed that we had indeed found the deserters.

They were firing furiously at us, but the bullets fell far short, and we banked sharply back towards the village, circling a few times in wide arcs. Gabriel hung over the edge, peering down at the outpost, noting the details, and when he gave me a thumbs-up, I motioned to Halliday that we should start back.

We landed without incident, and as soon as we killed the engines, Halliday jumped from his machine to give me a hand down.

"I say, that was jolly exciting," he said, his eyes alight.

I grinned. "How's your crate?"

He gave his plane a rueful look. "Sheared the aileron cable," he told me. "It's a bloody mercy I made it back at all."

He looked abashed at his language, but I grinned. "Never mind. I promise I heard worse every day in flight school. Can you fix her?"

He shrugged. "If I can find a bit of cable, it's simple enough. Without it, I'm grounded. Still, it's been a devilish good plane, although nothing as pretty as yours," he added with an admiring glance at the *Jolly Roger.* She was rather beautiful, I thought, her slender black wings shimmering in the desert sun.

Gabriel gave us both a long, level look then strode off to find Hamid.

"Is there something amiss with Mr. Starke?" Halliday asked, his brow furrowing slightly.

I looked to where Gabriel was having an intense conversation with Hamid. It seemed that Hamid was pressing him and Gabriel was refusing something. Their expressions were grimly similar.

I shrugged. "Heavens, I don't know. Just because you're married to a man doesn't mean you understand him."

He flushed faintly. "I say, Evie, it's all rather complicated with Mr. Starke in the picture— That is to say—" He looked distinctly uncomfortable and I put my hand up.

"Never mind, John. My marital entanglements seem to be taxing your diplomatic skills to the utmost. Now, let's go and find Aunt Dove and see what mischief she's got up to while we've been gone."

SIXTEEN

We found Aunt Dove and ate a quick meal, but it soon became apparent that the coming clash with the French deserters had heightened the atmosphere to a fever pitch. Nerves were taut and excitement thrummed in the air. Gabriel found me as I emerged from Aunt Dove's tent.

"Where is Aunt Dove?"

I nodded towards the tent. "Inside. Reading to Arthur."

He blinked. "She's reading to the parrot?"

"Yes, the *Q'uran*. She said it's only fair since he heard Mass in Rome."

He snorted, and held up his hand as I started to explain. "I don't want to know. But I'm glad she's out of the way. Hamid and his men have just about finished their preparations. They mean to attack at dusk and take the deserters by surprise."

My heart thudded uncomfortably as I glanced at the sky and its lowering sun. "An hour, then?"

"Give or take. Evie—" he began.

"Oh, don't. I can't bear scenes, you know that. Besides, you're not going without me. I want to help."

"Out of the question," he said flatly. "In fact, if you give me trouble about this, I will tie you up and dump you in a tent until I'm back. There's not a Bedouin in this place who would cut you free, either. Remember, you're my property as far as they're concerned," he warned.

I stepped up to stand toe-to-toe with him. "Don't feed me that rot, Gabriel. I'm certainly not your property, and I have a suspicion that the women would be most inclined to see my point when I explain that I might well be able to save a son or two."

He narrowed his eyes. "How do you intend to do that?"

"By doing precisely what I did earlier today— flying over the outpost. Those deserters can't resist shooting at an aeroplane, even if it's out of range. Every rifle aimed at the *Jolly Roger* is one less aimed at a Bedouin."

He fell silent a moment, and I didn't press the point. I simply let him think it over, and to my astonishment, he gave a grudging nod.

"I suppose you're right."

"Gabriel! Do you mean it?"

"I must be mad, but yes." He gave a heavy sigh as I hurtled myself at him, throwing my arms about his neck.

"Oh, you won't be sorry! Heavens, I don't know why I'm thanking you because I was going to do it, anyway, but it will make it so much easier not having to sneak around—" I broke off, uncomfortably aware that my arms were still looped about his neck, his face inches from mine, his lips so very close.

I stepped down from my tiptoes, pulling my arms away and shoving my hands in my pockets.

"Good thinking, pet," he said, his eyes mocking. "Unless you'd like to indulge in a bit of marital congress before sending me off to face possible death at the hands of the enemy?"

"Of course not. And don't be vulgar," I said automatically. But even as I refused, I realised I did not entirely mean it.

He gave me a quick nod and a smile and strode off then, disappearing into a tent. One of Sheikh Hamid's men gave a signal, a cry of summoning, and within moments all of the warriors of the tribe had assembled. They carried ancient rifles and some of their bandoliers were only half-filled with bullets, but they were a magnificent sight, standing at the edge of the camp, their saddled horses nearby, draped in tasselled finery and tossing their heads as they stamped their feet impatiently. They were as ready to go as the men were, but there was some sort of ceremony that had to be observed first. Several of the men came forward in turn to speak briefly, and as they spoke I kept a watchful eye on the sun. If it sunk too far, I'd be flying blind on the way back, and I slipped away from the edge of the crowd to find Aunt Dove seated in front of her tent, Arthur's cage hanging from a tent pole beside her. She was watching with rapt interest, and I almost regretted telling her I was going. The last thing I wanted was to worry her.

I should have known better. "Of course you are," she said roundly when I had finished explaining. "I would expect nothing less. What can I do?"

I sketched out my request and she nodded. "Of course. I'll get Halliday to help. He's been having such a moan over that wretched plane of his. I'm sure he'd love nothing better than to be in the thick of things, but I'll smooth it over. I shall explain to him how it will ease the minds of the ladies left behind to have such a strong fellow to defend them should worse come to worse. Men lap that sort of thing up."

"Mind you don't trowel it on too thickly or you might find yourself betrothed by morning."

She made an airy gesture and the waning light caught the sparkle of the paste rubies on her fingers. "All in a day's work, child. Besides, I suspect he has other fish to fry," she added with a knowing glance.

I widened my eyes. "I haven't the faintest idea of what you are talking about."

"Of course you don't. But it's a pity he doesn't realise it's a futile effort. You'll never look at another man so long as you have eyes only for Gabriel Starke."

"Eyes only for Gabriel?" I spluttered. "Of all the ridiculous— Really, darling, are you starting on senility? Tell me now so I can take over your affairs."

She waggled her fingers at me. "Oh, 'methinks the lady doth protest too much.'"

I said a bad word and turned to go. She put out her hand and caught mine, turning me back to her. Her expression had turned serious. "No, darling. You can be as angry as you like, but you can't leave without a kiss. I should have thought you'd have learned that by now. After all, you never know when you just won't see someone again, do you?"

She kissed me soundly on both cheeks and put a hand to my face. "Now, go and fly your beautiful *Jolly Roger* and give them hell, is that the expression?"

"It will do," I told her, blinking back a tear.

I went back to the crowd, which was still seething with excitement. I heard a single word repeated over and again, an invitation. Saqr. I caught their fervour as they waited outside his tent for Sheikh Hamid. They raised their voices higher still, chanting his name—"Saqr!"—and at the fever pitch of it, when the people had grown hoarse, Rashid came to find me.

His eyes were bright. "*Sitt*, the Saqr wishes to see you."

He gestured for me to follow him to Sheikh Hamid's tent and I did, uncertain of what to expect.

I entered the tent to see the Saqr standing before me. Garbed in the robes of a Bedouin prince, he was warrior and king, a creature striding straight from myth. He wore blinding white from head to foot. Only the black of his boots and the bright polish of the bandoliers spanning the breadth of his chest broke the purity. A narrow gold cord bound the white headdress to his brow, and under it, the bluest eyes I had ever seen held mine with a calm and level forget-me-not gaze.

"Surprised?"

I gaped at Gabriel. "But I don't understand. You said Sheikh Hamid—"

"You said Hamid. I didn't correct you."

I shook my head to clear it. "I don't understand," I repeated. "How are you the Saqr?"

"It's a long story, pet, and one I don't have time for now. The short of it is that what your Colonel Lawrence was doing in front of movie cameras in the south, I was doing up here in secret. I built a legend for them to use to rally their own people, but it's over now."

"How is it over when you look like . . . like that?" I demanded, still unsettled at seeing him looking so shatteringly heroic.

His expression was resigned. "It has to be." He buckled on a wide belt with a glittering gold sword. "Ready, pet?"

The crowd was chanting the name of the Saqr, and I wondered fleetingly if he had summoned me for moral support. I followed him out of the tent, and as he emerged, the cheers were deafening. The crowd parted, calling blessings upon him as he moved through them.

He strode to his horse, a mount they had put aside for him—an unblemished animal of solemn white, whiter even than the beautiful Hadibah. It was caparisoned in white and gold and as he held the headstall, he drew out the sword, a magnificent thing with a long curved blade, the golden hilt gleaming in the setting sun. He held it high overhead and waved it three times, each time pointing it directly to the east. And every time, the people chanted, louder and louder, and then Gabriel turned and led the horse to where Sheikh Hamid stood.

Gabriel bowed his head until the people were silent. A breeze had sprung up, rustling veils and robes as it passed over the land, the only sound amid the throng. When they were still, Gabriel lifted his head.

"Sheikh Hamid, brother and friend, it is no

longer—and never was—my place to lead you. For too long my people have meddled with yours." He turned to the crowd and lifted his voice. "I am no longer the Saqr. But I will follow he who is. I will fight for him and for you—but as your friend, Djibril, if you will have me." He bowed his head again and lifted the sword to Hamid.

For a long moment, no sound, no movement came from the crowd. But then a voice, a single voice—was it Rashid's?—called Hamid's name. He looked from the sword to the crowd, and they erupted in cheers, chanting his name and calling him Saqr. Slowly, he reached out and took the sword from Gabriel. He waved it three times overhead, and the cheers multiplied.

He turned back to Gabriel. "You will always have a place among us, my brother."

A thousand questions tumbled in my head, but it was not the time for answers. For now, the mantle of power had been shifted, and Gabriel, who had looked hunted a moment before, now relaxed as he passed the rein for his milk-white mount to Hamid. The others hurried to their waiting mounts as the women lifted their voices in farewell.

Sheikh Hamid signalled for his own lovely Hadibah to be brought forward and Gabriel swung himself into the saddle, touching Hadibah's flanks lightly, springing her to join the warriors just behind the Saqr.

"My God!" I hadn't heard Halliday approach,

but he was staring openmouthed, as I was at the spectacle of the warriors preparing to ride out.

I said nothing as the men moved out. There was nothing to say. I could not think of it now, how utterly, unspeakably wrong I had been. I burned with shame at the thought of the things I had said to him, the way I had mocked his pride, his courage, and all the while—no, I could not think of it or I would go mad. I put it aside as Ryder had taught me, forcing myself to think only of the job ahead.

The men moved out, the women trailing after a little distance. But the men spurred their mounts, their swords waving high, and within moments they were out of sight of the little valley, only a cloud of dust hanging in the pink light of dusk to show they had been there at all.

I hurried towards the *Jolly Roger*, Halliday trotting along in my wake. I clapped on my leather helmet as Halliday hefted the ballast bag into the second cockpit. He hesitated and I turned to him. "Do you want to come along?"

His smile was wry. "Is that all I'm fit for? Ballast?"

"I didn't mean it like that."

"I know. Don't trouble yourself, really. I do think it's best I stay here. The women are quite undefended if those rotten deserters carry the day. I'd hate to think—well. Best not to, then." He paused. "Did you have any idea?"

I paused, my fingers tightening painfully. "About Gabriel? No. I'm afraid I've been very stupid indeed."

He gave me a wry smile and touched my hand. "Haven't we all?" He stepped back and saluted smartly. "Godspeed, Evangeline Starke!"

I found them in less than ten minutes, a tightly bunched group of men riding fast and hard to the east. I flew high enough not to choke them with dust and waggled my wings as I passed over. I looked back to see them raising their rifles in salute, and Sheikh Hamid at the front, pointing them in the direction of the outpost.

I eased back on the stick, pointing her nose upwards as I approached the outpost. The noise of her engine carried far on the desert air, and I heard the crack of gunfire as I came into sight. They were waiting for us, and I pulled a barrel roll just to give them a show. I trotted out every trick Ryder ever taught me, every bit of showmanship and razzle-dazzle I could muster. The deserters poured out of the outpost, each of them trying for the chance to take down the *Jolly Roger.* I kept her far out of range, but the sight of her taunted them, and they were staring up and to the east when the Bedouin rode into their outpost out of the westering sun.

I watched them scramble for weapons, but there was no time. One or two tried to rally, but faced with the discipline of the Bedouin, the rest turned and fled. Determined to see justice done, the Bedouin pursued the deserters while a few remained behind to finish off the handful who stayed to fight. The harshness of it was more than I could have imagined, even circling high overhead, and as soon as the shooting stopped, I brought the *Jolly Roger* down and sat for a long moment, my hands still wrapped tightly about the stick.

After a long while, the shouts and shots faded and I could smell smoke from one of the out-buildings as it burned up. The Bedouin were making their way back, calling jubilantly to one another as they picked their way through the litter of destruction.

Still wielding the sword of the Saqr, now sticky with blood, Sheikh Hamid appeared at my shoulder, his face set in an expression of deep satisfaction.

"You're pleased, then?" I asked him.

He nodded. "Justice has been satisfied. Those who survived run like frightened hares into the desert where most will die for lack of water." He smiled grimly. "You will observe they did not take provisions and they are fleeing to the south when the roads to the north lead to cities. In their panic, they have chosen poorly."

"I don't imagine you gave them much time to think it all out," I replied.

The smile deepened, and his manner was so calm we might have been discussing a Sunday cricket match on the village green. "Little sister, a woman will never truly understand the burden a man carries."

"Burden?"

"The burden of responsibility for the lives and the happiness of all his people. We did not seek this bloodshed. They brought this upon themselves by their attack upon our allies, the Mezrab. And we have made our point—that so long as there are Bedouin in the Badiyat ash-Sham, we will never surrender. The men who survive this will wander into the desert, and as I said, most will die. But some will live. They will see their cities again and they will tell this story. They will talk of the day when the Bedouin rained fire upon them and sought vengeance. And these deserters will know they have made enemies of us and that we stand with our king and the legend of the Saqr lives on."

His eyes gleamed in the dim light. Darkness was fast falling, and here and there his men were lighting torches and paraffin lamps. They had moved into the outpost itself and were searching for any survivors who might have taken cover inside. There were storerooms for supplies, various offices and a sort of dormitory for the men with a few small private rooms for the officers. In addition, there was a large open space that functioned as a mess hall. Yellowing notices in

Turkish were still pinned to the walls, and the leaves of the calendar had been torn off until October 1918. It was here I found Gabriel, his white robes filthy but unbloodied. Sheikh Hamid's men had broken open a barricaded door and brought out a woman. She moved slowly, as if underwater, and her clothes and face were caked with grime. They brought her to where Gabriel stood. He flicked his eyes to the door and they left us, but he did not look at me. I moved to the sideboard, where a pitcher of water stood. I poured her a glass and looked around for a napkin of some sort. There was nothing of the sort, so I took out my handkerchief and gave it to her with the water.

"Would you like to wash a little, Countess?"

She looked at me with tired eyes. "Yes, thank you. They fed me, but there was little in the way of polite conveniences in this god-forsaken place." She gave a little wry smile.

She drank neatly and tidily from the glass then dipped a corner of the handkerchief in the rest of the water to wipe her brow and wrists. "That is better. One can face anything now." She gave Gabriel a level look. "I had a good reason for wandering the desert, as I suspect you know."

Delivered in another tone, the words might have been an accusation. But from the countess, they were stated calmly.

"Countess, you should sit down."

Her smile was pitying. "I am Magyar and I will stand for the truth, thank you."

"Very well," Gabriel returned. "You need look no more. You will not find him."

"Was he at least buried?" she asked, as evenly as if they had been discussing the weather.

"Under a fall of rock. On a ridge not far from the well where we found the Cross."

She nodded slowly. "Thank you for that. I should hate to think the animals—" She faltered a little then, but recovered herself quickly, folding her shaking hands together firmly. "You must not think I blame you. I warned him, so many times did I warn him. I told him this was a dangerous game to play. But he was insistent, and the fault is mine."

Gabriel remained silent, letting her talk.

"What András was, he was because of me. He was younger, half a dozen years, although I do not think it showed," she said. In another woman it might have been an invitation to flattery, but in the countess it was a simple recognition of fact. They looked so close in age they might have been twins. "Our mother died when András was born. Our father married again and our stepmother had many children. They were very happy together, but always András and I were different, the only children of our mother. And so we clung to one another, and I looked after him. I taught him his letters and his sums. I schooled him in languages and showed him how to button his shoes. I became his mother in a sense. I could not bear to see him hurt, you understand. I could not bear to say no to him, to disappoint him."

She took a deep breath and carried on. "As we grew older, our interests grew apart, but always we found a way to mingle them so we would always have the pleasure of one another's company. When he studied archaeology, I learned to apply my skills as an artist to assist him. In this way we carried on together, happy. And then the war came. When the empire fell, we lost everything—home, money. We had only each other and our titles. We were determined to build a new life for ourselves, or rather, I was determined to build a life for us. You see, that was András' fatal weakness. He could not take initiative. That was left to me, always. If it were not for me during the war, he would have starved. I arranged he should be kept from the army on the grounds of a medical condition. I scrounged for food and I secured our posts here. I thought in time he would meet a lovely girl and marry her. I could keep house for him, care for their children."

"That doesn't sound like much of a life for you," I blurted out. She turned as if seeing me for the first time.

"It was as much of a life as I wanted," she told me. "So many young men of our class were killed during the war or ruined after the fall of the empire. I gave up on the idea of a life of my own," she added with the first touch of bitterness I had seen in her. "But I think it would have been enough if András could have been happy. If only he could have contented himself with a nice girl and a family of his own, with work as an archaeologist. But he brooded after the war. Always he thought of what we had lost—the little castle in the woods, the hunting lodge, the city house. He wanted it all back. He believed it was owed to him," she explained. "It became an obsession with him, and when Daoud approached him with the story of treasure, I overheard them talking. I realised that this is the dream that had been driving him all along. He hoped to find something beyond belief, a treasure so profound it would make up to him all that he had lost."

She paused and patted her face again with the damp handkerchief. "I saw at once that I should have to become involved. András tried to hide it from me." She chuckled. "He was such a child, he wanted to surprise me when he discovered it, to present it to me as a king of ancient times would present a treasure to his queen."

Gabriel flicked a quick glance my way and I lifted a brow. The countess might believe it, but I had my doubts. Perhaps András Thurzó had seen an opportunity to finally rid himself of the domineering older sister who had controlled his life since infancy.

She was still speaking, her voice clear and calm. "We talked for a long time, and we decided we would wait for Mr. Rowan," she said with a nod towards Gabriel, "to return for his treasure. We were too afraid that Daoud would not be able to find the treasure again on his own, and it seemed much simpler just to take it once you had retrieved it. Daoud promised the help of his friends for a little money, and the arrangements were made. We argued several times over the amount of money, and at one point Daoud even said he had made the whole thing up and there was no treasure."

"That must be when he decided to try his luck with Gethsemane," I murmured to Gabriel.

The countess heard me. "Yes, this is so. He went to her, as well, but we did not discover this until much later. We did not realise the Cross was missing the most essential component, the heart of the relic," she added with an accusatory look at Gabriel. "But perhaps we were foolish thieves. You must blame our inexperience. We ought to have looked at the Cross immediately, but I was so nervous. I wanted only to get away. I do not know what came over András," she said, burying her face in her hands. She looked up a moment later, her eyes damp. "It was as if a stranger had taken the place of the brother I loved. When we left you after you were—" Her voice broke then and she could not say the word. "When we left, we quarrelled bitterly. I thought we would simply tie the pair of you up and leave you, but when I told András this, he laughed at me and said I had no spirit for this sort of thing. And when he discovered the heart had been taken from the Cross, he was so angry. I have never seen him in such a temper. When he left, I was in a state. I hardly knew myself. I understood, you see, that he would return to kill Madame Starke."

She balled her little fists at her sides. "It was wrong, monstrously so. And I told him this, but he would not hear me. He was a man possessed. When he did not come back, I did not understand. I thought an accident perhaps. I could not imagine that Madame Starke could harm him. But when I saw you," she said to Gabriel, "alive and unharmed, I understood. He would not have expected you."

"No, he did not expect me," Gabriel said quietly.

"I do not wish to know anything more except this—was it quick? I do not say you were unjust. But I think of that beautiful little boy whose curls I once stroked, and I think I will die if you tell me he suffered."

"He never saw me," Gabriel told her. "It was over in an instant."

"How?" She barely mouthed the word.

To his credit, Gabriel gave her the truth. "I broke his neck."

She considered the words a moment and then nodded. "I do not care if you have given me a lie.

It is a lie I can live with." She gave a deep sigh and all the life seemed to go out of her. "Now, will you be so kind as to tell me what will become of me? The French promised to escort me to Damascus, but there was not time."

"There's little point in going to Damascus," Gabriel told her. "King Faisal has declared his country independent and the government is in the hands of its people."

He went to the door and called out a few words of Arabic to a pair of Sheikh Hamid's men. One of them asked a question, and Gabriel responded before turning to the countess.

"These men have agreed to see you safely to the Turkish border. What becomes of you then is your own affair."

She stared at him, her eyes almost but not entirely blank. "I do not understand."

"I'm letting you go," he said coolly. "I suspect everything you've just told me about your upbringing is absolute rot. It's a lovely story, designed to win you the greatest amount of sympathy, and I daresay on some, it might work a treat. For my part, I've always considered you the cleverer of the two, and possibly deadlier. But you at least understood the stupidity of killing me, and you tried to talk him out of having me shot. It wasn't your fault he didn't listen. A life for a life, Countess. You spared mine. I'm sparing yours."

She opened her mouth to speak, but he cut her off.

"Don't thank me yet. The ride will be hard. You've hundreds of miles to cover and these fellows will be eager to get home again, so they won't be any too gentle with the pace. But if you can keep up, you have a chance."

She moved slowly to the door. "I do not know what I will do with myself," she said, her voice hollow.

"At least you will have a chance to find out," I told her. She did not look at Gabriel as she left. Perhaps it was too much for her to acknowledge the man who had killed her beloved brother. Or perhaps it was too difficult to find the words to thank the man who has just spared one's life. In any event, she passed out of the door and out of our lives.

I looked at Gabriel. "You told me he fell. Why did you lie?"

The arch manner and mocking expression were gone, perhaps forever. There was nothing in his eyes except a fathomless pain. "Because every death is a burden, Evie. I didn't want you to have to carry this one."

He turned on his heel and I followed him. There were few other rooms at the outpost and it took only a little time to search them. In the former commander's office, cabinets had been broken open, but in the desk, a single drawer was still firmly locked.

Gabriel drew a small pair of picklocks and made

quick work of it. He reached into the drawer and pulled out a familiar goatskin bundle.

I gasped. "She *was* lying. Daoud never robbed her."

"And she wasn't about to tell us the French deserters took it off her. I'm guessing the Turkish commander left his key to the desk behind and they locked it up for safekeeping. They wouldn't have had time to retrieve it before haring off into the desert. No doubt the countess hoped to elude Hamid's men and come back for it," he mused. He slipped the bag onto his shoulder and gave a sharp nod. "Time to go, pet."

I walked out into the clear purple night. The stars were just beginning to appear, and here and there the remaining Bedouin were working by lamp-light to pack up the last of what they wanted to bring with them. The dead lay as they had fallen, and I looked around me, shaking my head.

He led me to the *Jolly Roger.* "Can you fly her in the dark? The moon is almost up."

I nodded. "I've made arrangements. But, Gabriel, there was something—" Before I could finish the sentence, a figure loomed out from the shadows, a sword raised high as it swung the blade slashing down at Gabriel. I shrieked just loudly enough to warn him and he dodged as the sword went wide.

Gabriel dropped to his knees, flinging the Cross aside as he went. He rolled to the side, and in the rising moonlight, I saw Daoud's face, twisted with rage as he bore down on him a second time.

Gabriel lifted his arm to deflect the next blow, and only his elaborate robes saved him. The blade tangled in a woolen sleeve, and Gabriel twisted free, landing two hideous thuds to Daoud's midsection in quick succession. Daoud groaned and fell to his knees, but he did not drop the sword, and I understood then that this would be a fight to the death.

They fought for what seemed like hours, although I realised later it could only have been a matter of minutes. First Gabriel landed a series of blows that would have crippled a smaller man than Daoud. But Daoud was wiry and strong and he was fueled by the desire for revenge. He came at Gabriel again and again, slashing Gabriel's robes to ribbons. Both of them were heaving, their faces pouring with sweat and blood when I saw Gabriel lose his footing and slip to his knee.

Daoud pressed his advantage then. I would have leaped on him, but I knew one false move, one distraction, could cost Gabriel his life. I did not even think he remembered I was there until I heard his voice, thick with pain and fury, call out a single word to me. *"Contact."*

My hands were busy before I even had a clear thought of what he wanted. Somehow my body understood, and within seconds I started her up. Gabriel had gathered up the shreds of his sleeves and was using the thick pads of wool to shield his arms as he rose, pushing himself at Daoud. With the last reserves of his strength, he came at him, swinging hard, moving him closer and closer until finally, with one last final thrust, he pushed him backwards into the propeller blades.

Daoud never saw what happened although it is a sight I will remember for the rest of my life. It was over in an instant. One moment he was there, his sword raised high, flashing in the moonlight as he prepared to bring it down in one final blow on Gabriel's head. The next he was gone, his remains scattered on the sand.

Gabriel lay on his back, breathing hard. After a long moment, he staggered to his feet and pulled me up. There were still clots of desert earth in my hands as I walked, and I forced my fingers to open, leaving the dirt and sand behind. He retrieved the Cross and shoved me towards the plane. "It hasn't hit you yet. Get out of here before the adrenalin wears off and you start to shake." He pushed me up onto the wing and into the cockpit. He put my leather helmet onto my head and tightened the buckle. "Evie, can you hear me?"

"Yes, I think so."

"Good. Now forget what you just saw. Don't think about it. Can you do that?"

"I don't know," I told him honestly. For the first time, my pilot's training seemed to have deserted me and all I could do was stare at my hands.

Seeing a few deserters killed from the air had been nothing compared to the bloody awfulness of watching pieces of Daoud strewn across the sand.

He hesitated. "Christ," he muttered. Then he reached into the cockpit and hauled me out bodily, dropping me neatly into the rear cockpit. He buckled my safety belt and took my goggles, strapping them onto his own head.

"What are you doing?"

"I'm flying the goddamn plane," he yelled. He strapped himself in and before I could object, we were airborne, leaving all the carnage behind us. He had never told me he could fly, but if that night had taught me anything, it was never to under-estimate Gabriel Starke again. I sat in the rear cockpit, letting the cold wind rush past me as he flew us back to the village. He pointed us in the right direction, pulling us high to avoid the hills he could not see. By the time we were past them, a living line of light beckoned us down to the desert below. It was the women of the village, organised by Aunt Dove to stand with torches to guide the *Jolly Roger* home.

He brought her down with a bump that would have sent me flying out of the cockpit if he hadn't buckled me in, but we were down. Within moments he'd unstrapped me and set me on my feet. I fell to my knees, washing my hands in the sand as the Bedouin did before prayers. Without a word, Gabriel scooped me up and carried me to the tent.

Aunt Dove peered over his shoulder. "What's happened to her? Is she all right?"

"Perfectly fine," he answered. "Just a bit of shock. She needs warming up and some whisky. Take care of her, will you?"

He dumped me down like a sack of meal and left. He must have told the women their men were coming home safely, for the cheering began. They carried on outside while Aunt Dove tended to me. She helped me wash and change into a soft robe of green silk. She poured me a stiff drink and tucked me in then, telling me to rest, but when she left, lowering the flap of the tent behind her, I could not close my eyes. I saw Daoud, or the bloodied bits of what was left of him, lying on the dark desert floor.

"You're thinking about it too much," said the voice from the tent flap. I opened my eyes to see Gabriel, washed and changed, his hair still damp and his robes fresh and clean. His bruises were spectacular, but the blood had been washed from his face and hands, and he was carrying a tray of food and a familiar goatskin bundle.

"Are the others back?"

"Just now. They'll probably be up the better part of the night making merry and they're planning a feast for tomorrow. Ought to be quite the party," he added, coming near. He brought the tray of food down next to me. "I wasn't certain if you were hungry."

"Are you?" I asked, sitting up.

"Ravenous," he admitted.

"So am I. I'm a little ashamed," I confessed. "That's why I came over so funny, you know. It wasn't because of what you did to him. It was because I wanted you to. I knew what you intended as soon as you yelled 'Contact.' I understood what was going to happen and I didn't even hesitate. I never thought I had it in me," I said soberly. "And if I suspected, I would have thought there would be some regret or some guilt with it. But there isn't. I've been lying here, waiting for it to come, expecting the shame or horror to set in. But I haven't felt a damn thing except plain, quiet satisfaction. Can you explain that?"

He gave me a knowing look and poured out a whisky for each of us, raising his in a toast.

"It means you're one of us, pet. You're a Lost Boy, too."

We ate then, the usual Bedouin fare, cold meat and fruits and flatbread with nuts and some little pastry with honey. We said little until we had washed our fingers in the bowl of rosewater and poured out more whisky.

"This is very good whisky," I told him at one point.

"A little single malt courage for the ordeal to come."

"What ordeal?"

His expression was grave. "The one where I answer all the questions you've had. The one where I make a clean breast of it and confess all. The one where I try to begin to apologise for everything I've put you through."

I took another sip. Oh, it was lovely stuff, burning right through all my resentments and doubts and leaving nothing but clean and pure instinct behind it.

"No," I said slowly.

"No?" His dark brows arched skyward.

"No. I mean, yes, I want you to tell me all about it. But not now. After."

"After what?" he asked, his brows still raised.

I rose onto my knees and leaned forward, putting my arms about his neck. He opened his mouth, but if he meant to speak, I had other plans.

I had never undressed him before. I had never taken him before. But that night I did as I pleased with him. He was very still at first, holding himself in check as if he did not dare to move. Did he wonder if I was a mirage? Did he wonder if speaking or touching me would somehow break the spell? I did not ask him. But when I pulled his clothes away and covered his body with my own, his perfect control suddenly snapped. He gave a great shudder and rolled me roughly onto my back, moving within me and twisting his hands in my hair until I cried out his name into his own mouth.

Afterwards, we lay together, damp and still in the warmth of the tent and the silence between us was like a perfect living thing, holy and complete. It was enough to be together. The questions and the imperfect answers could wait, and wait they did until we had slept and roused again. It was leisurely then, as if we had all the time in the world and no one to care. Old pleasures were resurrected and new ones discovered. We made no promises and expected none. It was flesh and bone, striving together and stoking new fires. He murmured poetry, snatches of Marvell and Donne and even some Traherne, as he traced his lips over each part of me as he spoke. " 'These little limbs, these eyes and hands which here I find, these rosy cheeks wherewith my life begins, where have ye been?' "

When it was finished, we picked over the remains of the food, nibbling bits of fruit and bread as we lounged on leather cushions.

"You have spoilt me for another life, Evie," he said lightly. "I think I shall take up the job of pasha in an eastern *harim*. All this lying about suits me."

"You'll need at least three more wives. I can't be responsible for keeping you occupied all the time," I returned.

He gave me a serious look. "I know you want answers. Ask."

"Anything?"

"Anything and everything. I owe you at least that much."

I sat up and put the pieces together as best I could. "All the time I thought you were dead, you were here, in the Badiyat ash-Sham. Have I got that much right?"

He shrugged. "For the most part, yes. There were the odd trips abroad, but I've spent the better part of five years right here."

"And during the war, you were acting the part of the Saqr, this mythic sort of hero who organised the Bedouin into active resistance against the Turks?"

He winced a little. "I wouldn't put it like that. The Saqr is no myth. He's a very real fellow, you know—just a bit of theatre, something for the Bedouin to rally around."

"As Colonel Lawrence was doing in the south?"

"Only with rather fewer movie cameras about," he said with a smile. "I warned you not to romanticise it too much, Evie. I was simply an agent provocateur, albeit one with a rather dashing wardrobe. My job was to keep them focused on the task at hand, which was keeping the Turks too occupied to help the Germans. And, in time, to help chuck them out altogether so the Arabs could have their own lands back."

His mouth tightened a little on the last sentence, and I began to understand where the trouble lay.

"Who did you work for? The same Arab Bureau in Cairo that directed Colonel Lawrence?"

He shook his head slowly. "No. My orders came directly from London."

"London? But there are field offices in Cairo and Baghdad—" I broke off. "You weren't part of a regular mission, were you?"

He sighed and helped himself to a date. "My orders came from a place in London known only to a handful of rather important people."

"What place is that?"

"It has no official name, and even if it did, no one who knew of it would dare say it aloud. Those of us who work there refer to it as the Vespiary."

"The wasp nest?"

His smile was tortured. "An apt description. It's a hive of activity with no one in this part knowing much about that part. Only a very few people know all that happens there."

"Prime Minister being one of them?"

A brief smile flickered over his mouth. "He might know my name."

"And this Vespiary oversaw your activities here?"

"And other places," he said carefully.

I stared at him, openmouthed. "China. You were working in China, weren't you? The whole of that trip you were so odd, always dodging off at strange times to meet with people I didn't know. The peculiar messages, the disappearances. You were working even then."

"That was when I realised what a bloody great mistake I'd made," he said brutally.

"In marrying me?"

"In marrying anyone. I was a fool to think I could combine the work with a wife. They warned us when we signed on it was a wretched idea, but I wasn't really thinking of that when I met you," he finished, his smile rueful. "I danced with you once and all thoughts of little grey men in little grey buildings went right out of my head. I swear to you, it didn't even occur to me what I'd done until we were already back in London after the elopement and I was supposed to report."

"I suppose they weren't pleased," I managed to say.

"With the possibility of war looming, they thought it best to send me out on a sort of fact-finding mission. I was ostensibly going to China to do some climbing in the Tian Shan, but really I was there to assess the likelihood of the Chinese coming in on our side if the Germans pushed us into a war. I thought I could prove to the power-that-be that I could still do my job perfectly well with a wife in tow. Instead, I mucked it up with rare talent."

I held him even closer, horrified at all he had endured without my ever knowing. "And I picked a fight with you about the fact that you wouldn't enlist with Kitchener," I remembered. "I said terrible things to you, awful things. I called you a coward."

"Yes, I remember," he said dryly. "Of course, I

knew I wasn't, but it did sting a little that you should think so. I wanted to tell you so badly."

"I don't imagine your superiors would have approved of that."

"No, in fact, it was the one thing they insisted I must never do. They pointed out, quite rightly, that I had endangered you terribly by marrying you at all. And I had compounded the risk by bringing you along on the mission. I thought I'd been so bloody clever, that no one would ever think a spy would haul his wife around the world on a mission, but apparently it did occur to the Germans in Shanghai. As it was, I barely got you out of there with your skin intact. An informant told me the Germans there were getting suspicious and were forming a plan to take both of us. I couldn't let that happen."

"What would they have done to us?"

"I was junior enough in the Vespiary they wouldn't get much information out of me, but they'd have a bloody good time asking. And I had no idea what they might do to you. It was a chance I couldn't take. My superior at the Vespiary ordered me to put you on the first steamer out of Shanghai and get myself out the best I could."

"Tell me how you managed the *Lusitania*. Surely your superior didn't sink a passenger liner just to fake your death."

He managed a smile. "No. Even Tarquin wouldn't go quite that far."

"Tarquin? Tarquin March? *He* is your superior?"

"Was," he corrected. "I severed ties with the Vespiary at the end of the war."

I shook my head. "But Tarquin March! He's a friend of yours—and the dullest man I know. How on earth did the pair of you end up working for this place?"

The smiled turned nostalgic. "Poor old Tarquin. I don't think he'd appreciate being described in those terms. Actually, it's an image he's worked hard to cultivate. He might just thank you."

"I can't make sense of this," I told him.

"You can if you realise that Tarquin is merely carrying on the family business. The Vespiary was actually begun by his uncle by marriage nearly thirty years ago. It was right when Germany started building up their navy and Lord Salisbury felt it was his responsibility as prime minister to keep a closer eye upon things. He was worried about espionage at home and abroad, and he permitted one of his aides to create the Vespiary with the help of a private enquiry agent. The pair of them built the place into a small but select and highly specialised group. They had a habit of recruiting from within their own families and friends, but always with the tightest secrecy. I had no idea Tarquin was involved until he recruited me."

"When was that?"

"The autumn of 1914 I had just completed field

training when we met at Delilah's New Year's Eve party."

"Field training? What sorts of things did they teach you? How to break a man's neck with your bare hands?" I asked softly.

A lesser man would have flinched. "Yes. Or a fountain pen or a shoehorn or a bit of sealing wax." He picked up the thread of his story. "The Vespiary were recruiting a fresh batch of operatives just then with the start of the war, most of us only right out of university. I was chosen because I fit precisely the profile of the person Tarquin needed. You see, it was he who devised the idea of bringing in an English agent provocateur and using him to rally the various Bedouin tribes together. He knew the Arab Bureau meant to do something similar in the south, but he felt the Turkish border was the place to focus attentions. He drafted a list of qualifications he would require and gave them to his recruitment agent—Quentin Harkness."

I goggled at him. "Quentin Harkness? The same Quentin Harkness who married Delilah Drummond after her first husband died?"

"I hear she's married to a Russian prince now." I blinked as he grinned at my surprise. "I do still get all the major periodicals out here, pet. I have to stay informed."

"I'm sure you do." I was still dazed by all he told me, but I knew instinctively it was merely the tip of a particularly mammoth iceberg.

"So, Tarquin had a list of requirements—for someone to play the Saqr, is that right?"

"Precisely. He sent the list to Quentin, who told him about me immediately. Within a week I'd been vetted and offered a position in the Vespiary. I couldn't believe it when they explained what I would eventually be doing. It was like a dream, everything I had ever wanted—adventure, danger, intrigue. I accepted on the spot and they put me into training the same day. I finished with flying colours and was preparing for my briefings on the eastern situation when Delilah threw her party."

"And you met me."

"And I met you. And my whole world turned upside down. I couldn't believe my bad luck, really. I had everything I could ever dream of wanting, but I had to choose between them. I chose you."

"But not for long," I reminded him. There was no judgment in my voice, only acknowledgment.

"Not for long," he agreed. "I thought, you see, that the Vespiary would come around. Occasionally they did. We weren't supposed to marry or have attachments, but they would make exceptions for agents who were indispensable. It was my own bad luck to be less important than I thought," he said with a grim smile. "They fired me as soon as I got back to London. But I begged Tarquin to give me a chance, anything. I told him I'd ride a desk in the city and write reports for the whole of the

406

war, whatever he wanted. He sent me to China. Told me to assess the German chances there, and said if I did a good enough job he would consider letting me come to Damascus, after all."

He paused and ran a hand through his hair. "I think you can guess what happened next. I botched it—so badly I nearly got us both killed. And I knew then I could never do that to you again. I had vowed to protect you. How could I expose you to that kind of danger out of my own stupidity and arrogance? There was only one way out."

He stopped again and it was a long moment before either of us were able to continue. The sacrifice he had made for me was almost greater than I could comprehend. I said as much, but he shook his head angrily.

"I thought it was a sacrifice, but what if it was just another stupid mistake, Evie? What if I had trusted you and told you the truth of who and what I was that night in Shanghai? What if . . ."

"*What if?* The two most torturous words in the English language, Gabriel. You were twenty-one. And trying desperately to be a man. You made the only choice you thought you could at the time, and there is no point in trying to rewrite history. What's done is done, and we both have to live with it."

He swallowed hard. "I did live with it. Every day out here, I thought about what I did to you."

"I'm surprised Tarquin let you come after what you did in China," I said evenly.

He pulled a face. "So was I. But he knew how shattered I was by it. And I had proven to him I was willing to do anything to serve, and I had shown my resourcefulness by getting myself off the *Lusitania* and letting the name Gabriel Starke go down with the ship."

"So you were on board."

"I was. I made my way to the shore and stole some clothes, then walked until I came to a proper town where I could wire Tarquin. Gabriel Starke's name was on the list of lost souls by the next morning, and I was in London, being commended for my quick thinking. Tarquin gave me my own group of agents, nine of us, and shipped us off to Damascus to take care of one another."

"That sounds cosy."

"It wasn't. We fought like cats and dogs, but we were a family of sorts," he said, nostalgia lighting his eyes. "We were all young and wild and so convinced we were going to change the world starting right here. We were so different, but we had that in common, that love of danger and that thirst to prove ourselves. Tarquin had his doubts, I think, about setting us loose on our own. I suspect he believed there might be safety in numbers. But we didn't care. We called ourselves the Lost Boys and we came to Damascus. Tarquin knew I'd already been here as myself a few years before, but I was given a new cover identity—Rowan's— and a disguise to make me look older than my years. I was told to make contact with Hamid again and when he agreed, to introduce the character of the Saqr. I spent most of the war with them, but from time to time I went to Damascus to rendezvous with one or other of the Lost Boys and exchange information. It was during one of those meetings that one of the Boys shared a collection of mediaeval manuscripts he'd found when he was in the desert. Some of us were good with languages, one was a cartographer, one was a history scholar—among us we realised we were sitting on a treasure trove. When pieced together the documents gave the whereabouts of two extremely valuable finds. One was the Cross. We talked it over and couldn't agree on what was to be done with them. Our compromise was to cache the manuscripts in a safe place and come to a decision when the war ended. I went back to Hamid and his people and continued to act as the Saqr through the course of the war. When it was done, I expected they would get their own country, as London had promised them. As *I* had promised them," he added bitterly.

"And when they didn't?"

"I resigned," he told her with grim satisfaction. "I've never been more ashamed of anything in the whole of my life, Evie. At least what I did to you, I was able to justify that by telling myself it was for your own good. But what had I done to the Bedouin? I had urged them to fight, led them to fight. And for what? A handful of broken promises made by chaps in London who've never set foot in the Badiyat ash-Sham. I was disgusted with the lot of it. I couldn't face myself, what I'd done in my arrogance, believing it was for the best. And that's when I realised it's been our greatest failing all along—treating them all, Baghdadi, Damascene, Cairene, Bedouin, every soul from the Bosphorus to the Nile, as if they were children. It's despicable. We had no right ever to interfere in the first place, and I was furious at myself and at everyone else—London, the Vespiary, even you."

"Me?" I was startled out of the spell his words had cast.

"Yes, you. I thought back to how it was in Shanghai, how it really was, and I saw that at the first sign of trouble, you were ready to bolt. As soon as things were too real, too hard, you were ready to leave me. I know I picked a hell of a fight with you that last night, but you didn't fight back, you didn't fight for us. And I started to wonder if I'd imagined it all."

"Imagined what?" I asked, my mouth dry.

"The way you'd looked at me, the way you'd loved me. I began to wonder if I was crazy. I must have taken out that photo of us on our wedding day a thousand times, just staring at it for hours to see if it was really there—the way I thought you'd felt, the girl I thought you'd been."

I thought of us, leading parallel lives, never

touching, but wondering the same things, feeling the same pain. It was almost more than I could bear.

"And was I?"

"God help me, I couldn't tell. I wondered if everything I'd ever done in the whole of my life had been just a series of extravagant failures. And I thought, if I could just do one thing right, make it up to you—"

"The Cross," I whispered.

"The Cross. After the war, the Lost Boys were scattered. Some were dead, some were back in England. So I went for the manuscripts alone, but when I got there, I realised someone had beaten me to the punch. All the information about the greater treasure had been taken."

"There's something bigger than the Cross?"

He nodded. "I presume you've heard of Lady Hester Stanhope?"

I rolled my eyes. "She's only Aunt Dove's idol. I must have heard the story a hundred times—how she left England a century ago to travel through the East and settled in Syria to live out her days in lavish eccentricity."

"Quite," he said. "She also collected manuscripts and antiquities, and she started the first proper archaeological excavation in this land when she dug at Ascalon. She had purchased a particular manuscript, a medieval chronicle that detailed the whereabouts of a hoard of Templar gold stashed at

Ascalon since the days of the Crusades. The Turks were resentful of her digging, and to show them she didn't mean to profit from the excavation, she destroyed the only good thing she turned up—a statue of a goddess. It placated the Turks, and she was left in peace. But she found something else, as well—the Templar gold. She never had the resources to remove it, but she added her notes to the medieval manuscript and bundled it with the one describing the whereabouts of the Cross. Somehow the manuscripts passed out of her possession and eventually came to where we found them. I wasn't sure exactly what I would do with the Cross when I found it, but when I realised one of the other Lost Boys had been there first and had broken trust with the rest of us . . ." His face darkened, and he seemed to be struggling with strong emotion.

"In any event, I decided then it was every man for himself. I decided to take the Cross and give it to you."

"For atonement."

"For atonement," he echoed. "And I promised Hamid I would stay close should he have need of me."

"Why me?" I demanded. "Why give it to me instead of Hamid? You care for him and for his people. You could make a very good argument for it being rightfully theirs. And you owe him atonement, too, yet you wanted me to have it. Why?"

"What do you think would happen to the Bedouin if I gave them a priceless relic that every Christian European nation could make a claim to?"

"It would be taken," I said softly. "By force."

"Exactly. Besides, there was another reason it had to be you."

He stared at the floor a moment then raised his eyes, those brilliant blue eyes, piercing me with raw, ungilded truth.

"Because I wanted to see you one last time."

The vulnerability on his face was too much. I looked away until he mastered the emotion.

"So sorry to interrupt," said a voice from the tent flap. Halliday was standing on the threshold, a small revolver pointed at both of us. "But I'm afraid I simply can't wait any longer."

Gabriel moved to shield me, but Halliday cocked the revolver. "I think not, old man. Stay right where you are. You, too, Mrs. Starke, and no sudden movements, if you please."

I crossed my arms slowly over my breasts. "I presume you will allow me to cover up at least?"

"And take the chance you've a weapon hidden under your pillow? No. I promise to be a gentleman and not look if it consoles you." He turned to Gabriel. "You know what I want."

Gabriel rose with as much dignity as a naked man could manage. He held up his robe and Halliday shook his head.

"Take it out. I want to see it, and I don't think I ought to put the gun down, do you?"

Gabriel gave him a bored look and proceeded to retrieve the goatskin bundle.

Halliday smiled. "Open it, if you please. I'll keep my gun trained on your wife just to make quite certain you continue to cooperate."

Gabriel started to pluck at the knots, but I was in no mood to humour anybody.

"How do you even know about the Cross?" I demanded. "No one in Damascus knows."

Halliday smiled, never taking his eyes from Gabriel's deft fingers. "Dear lady, this is the East. There are no secrets here, and Miss Green is rather more talkative than most. I owe you a great deal of thanks, Mrs. Starke, for introducing us. As it happens, she was in need of some semi-official assistance."

He gestured towards Gabriel. "It seems she was suspicious of you, Mr. Starke. She was worried you were about to make a great find and intended to cut her out. But Miss Green is an ambitious woman. She planned to nip in and take it before you could remove it to Damascus. She thought a man with my diplomatic contacts would be just the person to help her get the find out of the country for herself." He paused and flicked a glance to me, holding me in place with his gaze. "Now, I am an amenable fellow, but it did occur to me, I would far rather have the treasure than let

414

her keep it. And if I liberate it before she gets it, she can't very well make a formal complaint, can she? Her hands would be tied and I would have the dosh. Rather a tidy plan, I thought."

"Very neat," I said, but sarcasm was lost upon him. He merely gave me a beatific smile and continued to hold his gun on us. "You yourself provided me with the final bit of the puzzle, my dear, when you admitted to the sheikh that Mr. Starke had unearthed a relic. I did a bit of judicious listening after that, and put the pieces together. It occurred to me that the last known person to have the Cross was the Countess Thurzó, a lady you saw last night and a person who would not have had the opportunity to dispose of the relic. It seemed obvious to me that Gabriel Starke is not a man to let such an opportunity pass him by. He would have retrieved it at the first opportunity."

I looked to where Gabriel had just got through the goatskin and was busy with the velvet wrapping.

"I suppose this is where we ought to tell you that you will never get away with it," I said pleasantly. "In most cases of sensational fiction it's an over-statement, but in this particular scenario, we do have rather a number of well-armed Bedouin allies," I pointed out. "Do you have a plan?"

"I most certainly do. Hurry up, Mr. Starke. I'm in no mood to be trifled with." He turned back to me. "That's the trouble with having such a pleasant face. People always think I'm not entirely serious when I am. In fact, just to prove my point," he said, his voice chillingly conversational, "I think I will shoot one of you in ten seconds if that Cross isn't open. Ten. Nine. Eight."

I whipped my head to where Gabriel's fingers were still working methodically. "Gabriel?"

"Five. Four. Three."

"Gabriel!"

"One," Gabriel said, tossing the relic down on the ground in front of Halliday. It landed at his feet, and in the shimmering lamplight of the tent it glowed as if from an inner light. Halliday's face creased into a smile. Gabriel stood, feet planted wide apart, arms folded over the breadth of his chest, still as blessedly, gorgeously naked as the day he was born.

"Gabriel, perhaps Mr. Halliday will let you put some clothes on now," I murmured.

"Why? I have nothing to be ashamed of. But I can see why it might make him feel inadequate," he added with a cold smile at Halliday.

Halliday gave a low chuckle. "You cannot force my hand, old man. I don't give a damn about you, not anymore. I don't need you at all. In fact, you're just a complication at this point."

He reached down, his eyes still fixed on us as his fingers closed around the Cross. He rose, clasping the Cross to his breast.

416

"Now, I will bid you both adieu." With that, he gave a single polite nod of the head, aimed the gun directly at Gabriel and pulled the trigger.

The gun was small and the sound barely made a pop. I whirled to see the pool of blood welling on Gabriel's shoulder. He clapped a hand to it as he fell to his knees, cursing as Halliday fled.

I was at his side in an instant, shoving a bit of cloth into his shoulder to stop the bleeding.

"Put some clothes on," he said through gritted teeth. "Both of us. I'd rather not chase that bastard in my bare skin."

I threw a robe over my head and grabbed another for Gabriel, the plain white *abba* he'd worn the night before. First I ripped a length off the bottom to tie the cloth to his shoulder. It was a wretched bandage, but it would have to do. He kept barking orders at me, and I obeyed, blindly, even to wrenching his shoulder as I pulled the robe over his head. He swore through gritted teeth, but when he saw my face, he mastered himself.

"It's fine, Evie. He shot me through and through. It just hurts like a son of a bitch, and I've lost a little blood. Now get that damned pistol of yours and come *on*," he ordered, shoving me through the tent flap. Some members of the camp were peering into the darkness from their tent flaps, but most were still yawning and scratching themselves. Dawn was just beginning to silver the eastern sky, and I had lost sight of Halliday, but Gabriel knew exactly where to find him.

I heard the engine before I saw him. He had started up his plane, and he glanced back and saw us emerging from the tents just as he pulled back on the stick. It bounced and shuddered, but it lifted into the cold morning air, carrying him upwards.

Gabriel swore again and shoved me towards the *Jolly Roger.* I jumped into the cockpit while he started the propeller. He dodged into the rear cockpit, hoisting himself with his good arm.

"Thank God for stupidity," he shouted, and I nodded. If Halliday had been smarter, he would have done something to put the *Jolly Roger* out of commission so we couldn't follow him. But she purred instantly to life, ready for anything.

I had nothing with me—no flying leathers or helmet or chart, but I made the best of things. I gave her all the power I could, pulling back smoothly on the stick to get her airborne. Halliday had a lead, but his Nieuport was older than my Strutter, and her engine was smaller. I gave the *Jolly Roger* everything I could, pushing her as fast as her engine would go. I glanced back once at Gabriel and he gave me a single determined nod. His features were set and his eyes were fixed on the small dot ahead of us in the morning sky.

But the dot was getting bigger. The *Jolly Roger* was closing at lightning speed, and I felt the rush of the cold morning wind freezing my fingers to the stick. Within minutes we drew even with Halliday and his Nieuport. He turned his head at the sight of us, clearly astonished. He reached into his cockpit and pulled out a revolver. A smarter man would have aimed it at me since putting the pilot out of commission meant taking out the whole plane, but he pointed it straight at Gabriel.

Without thinking, I stamped hard on the rudder paddle as I pulled on the stick and she slipped into the prettiest dive I'd ever made. The *Jolly Roger* protested, screaming a little as we fell—or that might have been Gabriel. The dive must have taken him by surprise, but the idea was to surprise Halliday more. It took him several seconds to figure out what I was up to, but by the time he followed me down, I had banked sharply to the west, pulling her out of the dive and climbing again as we returned back over the ridge of dusty hills.

Suddenly, I realised what I was doing. It was morning, which meant I was flying into the sun, a cardinal mistake under the circumstances. I looped around again just as Halliday put a few rounds into my tail section.

Gabriel was shouting something unintelligible, but he seemed to be complaining about how close Halliday had gotten to him, and when I glanced back he put a finger into the hole in his sleeve. The bullet had passed right through, but I didn't blame him for being sore. I'd made an error the likes of which Ryder would have tanned me for, and I couldn't afford to make another.

I climbed again, this time even sharper, looping around until the sun was at my back. I climbed higher still, pushing the *Jolly Roger* until her engine screamed and her frame creaked. Halliday was in front of me, twisting and turning. He'd lost me in the sun, and I closed, coaxing from Baby every last bit of power she had to give.

It wasn't enough. Halliday turned the Nieuport quicker and came up on me. I dodged him, and when I glanced back, I saw Gabriel had taken my pistol and managed a few shots on Halliday—nothing that stuck but just enough heat to persuade him to dive.

I turned back and pushed the *Jolly Roger* again, higher and to the east, lifting up into the rising sun. When I turned her again, Halliday was circling below me like a great black bird of prey riding slowly and waiting. He didn't have to pursue me, I realised. He could just stay down there. He knew I'd have to come down sooner or later. The *Jolly Roger*'s fuel tank was smaller than his machine's, for starters. He could just swoop in those long, lazy circles and wait, biding his time until I fell into his clutches.

Unless . . . I put my back to the sun and turned the *Jolly Roger*'s nose downward. I darted a quick look behind me, and to my astonishment, Gabriel seemed to know exactly what I was doing. He gave me a sharp nod and I pushed her nose further down, as far as I dared. It was a delicate balance, because if I pushed her too far, the wings could shear off. But I held her just above that point, and as I held her, she felt like a part of me. The wind whipping on her canvas wings was my breath, the pulse of her engine was my pulse. And then I cut the engine.

There was silence as we fell. Nothing but silence and the long fall, the earth rising up to meet us as we answered gravity. Halliday never heard us, and he didn't see us until it was too late. He managed to get one shot—a lucky one that hit the *Jolly Roger*'s tail—but before he could get off a second, Gabriel had put a bullet into him and Halliday fell hard against his stick. His Nieuport surged downward in a long, pretty spiral. One of his feet must have got wedged against the rudder pedals, holding it in that circle as it drifted down, down, down.

I'd switched the *Jolly Roger*'s engine on again as soon as he'd started to fall, and she wasn't too happy about it, but she revived herself. I pulled the stick to steady her.

Nothing. I tried again, but when she didn't respond, I realised she was dry. Halliday had done exactly as he intended. He'd kept me airborne long enough for the *Jolly Roger* to burn up all her fuel. We were going to crash. I glanced over the side to where Halliday had gone down. The plume of oily black smoke reached skyward. His plane had crashed hard into the rocky slope below, and the rocks had torn his fuel tank the minute he'd hit.

I turned to Gabriel and pointed down. We were going to have to fly low and slow and try to set her down and hope to God that whatever was directly in front of us wasn't going to kill us.

I started to ease her down, but just as I did, I realised we were too close to the next line of hills. There was no way to lift her. All I could do was cut a sharp turn and hope for the best. I banked her until my palms were wet on the stick and my thighs ached from standing on the pedals. Her wheels almost skimmed the dusty top of the nearest hill, but I kept her just this side of airborne. And over the top of the rise, a hidden outcropping of solid rock loomed just in front of us, too high and too close to miss.

We crashed into the outcropping. The *Jolly Roger*'s beautiful nose, with its gallant rotary engine, was completely crushed, but that same engine ate the brunt of the impact. I was thrown against the control panel, but my belt held. Gabriel didn't have that luxury. He was thrown from the tail, and I jumped out of the plane to find him.

He was lying a few dozen feet away. He had landed hard, and when I ran to him screaming his name, nothing answered me but stillness and silence.

"Gabriel Starke, you answer me," I ordered him as I grabbed his shoulders and shook him violently. "You are not dead, do you hear me? I won't allow it. Now you say something, say something this very minute."

I shook him harder and suddenly he gave a hideous noise like a death rattle. He wheezed hard for several minutes, and I realised he'd had the wind knocked out of him. He rolled onto all fours and coughed hard, getting his breath back, then settled back on his haunches and patted his empty pocket regretfully.

"Damn me, I've left my flask back at the camp. I could use a drink right now."

He tested his shoulder, but the wound was clean and the blood had clotted. Gabriel rolled his eyes. "He can't even make a good job of shooting a man. Amateur."

I looked back to the crumpled wreckage of my beloved plane and saw the engine beginning to smoulder gently. "The *Jolly Roger*!" I cried.

Something wet was blurring my vision, but whether it was tears or blood, I couldn't say. I wiped my eyes on my sleeve and turned to Gabriel. He held me a moment, then pulled back.

"I've got to go see about him," he said, nodding once to the tall plume of oily black smoke a little distance away.

"Why?"

His eyes never left my face. It would have been

easier to lie, but he told me the truth, unvarnished and unlovely.

"Because I have to take care of this."

"No, you don't," I said.

He did not argue with me, and we leaned on each other as we walked. We climbed over tumbled rocks and scrubby bushes, and over it all, the rose-pink light of the most glorious morning sun shimmered like a benediction. It seemed obscene that it should be such a morning when a man lay dead in the desert, but I had already learned that this was the truth of the desert; that life and death and beauty and pain existed together. That one was heightened by the other, that pleasure was sharper for being fleeting and that joy was keener for being snatched.

Halliday had gone down in a pillar of fire that reached to heaven like a minor prophet translated to the presence of God. The fire was still burning when we reached the plane. The frame was still intact, but parts of it had fallen to flaming rags. We picked our way through the small fires to the wreckage. I steeled myself for the worst, but when we reached the cockpit, it was empty. There was no sign of Halliday or the Cross.

"He's not here! How on earth—"

And then I saw the trailing silk of the parachute, discarded like a spent cocoon, and streaked with blood. Gabriel picked it up, turning the silk over in his hands.

"I must have winged him," he said ruefully.

"And we never saw him bail because we were too busy crashing ourselves," I said. We stood and I looked at the footsteps leading into the desert, towards Baghdad hundreds of miles away.

"I have to go after him," he said simply.

"I know you do." I could have argued with him, but I finally understood it would have been wrong. This was something Gabriel had to do. The man he was, the man I had loved with all of my heart, the man I had always known I married, finished what he started.

My throat ached but I wouldn't let him see my cry. Not then. Instead, I lifted my chin. "What? No poetry?"

He grinned. "A bit of Marvell, I think. 'I would love you ten years before the flood.'"

Then he lowered his head. When he pulled back, we were both shaking, but I carried the taste of his mouth on my lips and the feel of his body in my arms.

He smiled again, and it was that beautiful smile I would take with me. "Time to go," he said. "What did Peter say to Wendy? ' "Now then, no fuss, no blubbering. Goodbye." ' "

I nodded, wiping my eyes on my sleeve. "I've only just realised— I thought you were Peter Pan. You've been the Scarlet Pimpernel all along."

"No, love. Once a Lost Boy, always a Lost Boy."

I turned and began to walk, but he called my

name. I looked over my shoulder to where he was silhouetted, a tall black shadow against the rising sun. " 'Just always be waiting for me, and then some night you will hear me crowing.' " And with that he threw his head back and crowed like a rooster.

I was still laughing and wiping my eyes as I turned and walked into the west, back to the camp and out of his life while he walked east, towards the man who wanted to kill him. It was the hardest thing I had ever done, but it was the most perfect moment we had ever shared. I did not look back again.

I walked back to the village, a long and dusty trek, and after explaining Halliday's villainy, I fell onto my pallet and slept straight through until night-fall. Aunt Dove was there when I awoke, and I told her the whole story from start to finish, and she listened, asking nothing as I talked myself hoarse. I owned every mistake, every doubt, every failure I had made. And when I was finished, she nodded briskly.

"I'm not at all surprised," she said seriously. "I never liked him. You'll remember I said so on several occasions."

I didn't bother to argue. I stared out of the tent at the setting sun. The eastern horizon was already dark and I would not look there. It was dangerous to hope too much for what might never come.

"So, what do we do now?" she asked, bright-eyed as Arthur hopped on her shoulder and pecked at her jewellery.

I thought of the long days in the desert, of how easy it would be to stay another day, a week, a month or more. Waiting, endlessly waiting, until the whole of my life was lost in it.

"We go back to Damascus," I told her. "And then to England. It's time to go home."

SEVENTEEN

Leaving the Bedouin was not quite as easy as I had expected. First, they wanted to hold a feast, and it took an entire day to cook the sheep.

"A whole sheep?" I asked Sheikh Hamid.

"A whole sheep," he assured me. "We will cele-brate our victory and honour our guests."

And so I bowed my head gravely and we sat a day waiting for the feast. It was carried in on great platters, heaps of mutton dripping in grease on top of masses of fruit-studded couscous. There were a dozen other dishes, none of which I recog-nised, and Aunt Dove and I were placed at the right hand of Hamid as honoured guests. They danced and told stories, and eventually, when we had eaten far more than we could ever have imagined, Aunt Dove fell to snoring gently and I turned to Hamid.

"The Saqr. I had no idea what Gabriel did out here."

He smiled. "Every cause needs a myth to believe in. During the war, the story of the Saqr inspired our men, gave them hope during dark hours when the Turks raided. It was a black time for us. Whole villages were burned or driven to caves to starve. Livestock were killed, tents put to the torch and more men than I care to count were thrown down wells to drown. The Turk wrote his resentments with the blood of the Bedouin, and even now, the sight of a Turk can anger a desert-dweller like nothing else. They had a talent for cruelty."

"Did Gabriel, in his role as the Saqr, drive them out?"

"No, little sister. The Bedouin is warrior enough to defend his own. But the Bedouin are scattered across the desert like so many grains of sand. Over the generations, our ways have changed. The Bedu of the north does not love his brother from the south. The Bedu of the east does not love his brother from the west. Howeitat, Ruwallah, Mezrab—and a hundred more. We are brothers, and yet we forget to understand one another. We share blood, but blood feuds, as well, and it is these quarrels that keep us divided. We needed something to unite us, to remind us that we are one and the same. Your Colonel Lawrence did so in the south. But here, we had the Saqr, the falcon who flies with us." His eastern cadences and poetic language slipped for a moment and he grinned. "Besides which, Djibril is a bloody brilliant fighter."

I returned the smile. "You have an acute grasp of the power of an image in popular imagination."

He shrugged. "Not unlike your picture in front of an aeroplane holding a packet of washing powder. Does not the common Englishwoman see such a thing and think to herself, 'I, too, can be like this daring and beautiful woman if only I wash my things in Daisy Biological Washing Powder'? Of course she does. And the Bedu looked to him and believed they could be like him, like they once were, princes of the desert, sons of the wind."

"They might have looked to you for that example," I pointed out. "You have all the same qualities as Gabriel."

He shrugged. "But I am known to them. There is a mystique about the foreigner, don't you think? You like us because we are different from you. We live in tents and tend our sheep, and we live as our people have since the days of the Prophet, peace be upon him. Our language, our laws, our customs, all are different and strange to you. And yet yours are just as curious to us. We are amused and puzzled and intrigued by you, and if one of your kind finds our cause just, perhaps it persuades us even more that we must prevail."

"So you found Gabriel to be useful, a propaganda tool," I said slowly.

429

He smiled again. "I would not have phrased it thus, but yes. It suited my purposes to have him here. And it suited him, as well. You must know he served our cause out of a belief in its rightness. And we have loved him for that, as he loves us. It grieved him deeply when the promises he made in the name of his English colleagues were not honoured."

"I am starting to understand," I told him. "I think he must have felt he failed you."

"He did. But the dishonour was not his. He put his trust in men who were not worthy of it, but that was his only crime."

I lifted a cup. "A toast, then. To your new king, Faisal. Long may he reign."

Sheikh Hamid bowed his head. "Your sentiments are kindly, but I do not think he will last."

I blinked. "What do you mean? Surely he will rally the rest of the country behind him. Look how easily a handful of your men routed the deserters from the outpost."

He regarded me thoughtfully. "Tell me, little sister, when you were in Damascus, could you tell the difference between a fruit seller from the land around Hebron and a merchant from Aleppo? Can you look at a man's robe and know he is from Palestine or hear a man speak and know he is Egyptian?"

"No," I admitted.

"Precisely. To the English, one Arab is like another. We are interchangeable to them. But as we say, people are like the hand—all fingers are different. We are no more alike than a Welsh coal miner is to a Kentish farmer or a London barrister. Always the English, the French—they look at us and see nothing but men in robes with camels. But King Faisal is a Hashemite from Arabia. It will take much for a Syrian to accept him. He has cooperated too much with the French in the past, given in too easily to the whims of the English. We want a strong king, and I fear he will not be the one to lead us. It is like expecting a Cornishman to rule over a Highlander. It will not happen easily. But perhaps I am wrong. Only time will tell, little sister. Only time will tell."

In Damascus, we packed up our things as quickly as we could, and in two days we had made our preparations to leave the city. The trains were thronged with fleeing Europeans, but with Aunt Dove's connections we managed to make our way to Beirut, where we found a small cabin on a tiny steamer bound for Greece. From there we booked passage on a much more comfortable ship to Southampton. The voyage would last the better part of a month, but neither of us was in any hurry to get home. The events of the past weeks had been exhausting and exhilarating, and although we did not speak of it, I think we both wanted some time to think matters through before we had to face the press.

The afternoon before we left, when our suite was in a riot of tissue paper and farewell fruit baskets from Aunt Dove's admirers, I received a note. It had been handwritten, hastily, and it had been carried by messenger. There was just a single line, but it was enough.

I found a hat and clapped it on, calling out to Aunt Dove as I went.

"I'm going out for a bit, darling. I'll be back by dinner."

Aunt Dove was busy fussing over Arthur. "As you like, my dear. You might think about finding a bookstrap when you're out, if you don't mind. I seem to have acquired too many books to tuck in my bag, and I do hate to leave them behind now that we've got the luxury of travelling with as much baggage as we like."

I pulled a rueful face. "That's the one blessing to not flying home, I suppose," I told her.

She gave me a fond smile. "Never mind, darling. We'll find you a spiffing new plane when we get back to England. You'll see."

I waved goodbye and left her. There was no point in mentioning that I couldn't buy a new plane as I simply didn't have the money. There had been a pile of telegrams waiting for us at the hotel, and most of them had been from sponsors outraged that the *Jolly Roger* had been wrecked in the desert. No successful tour, no proud newspaper mentions or short films for them. A few had even threatened to ask for their money back, but a quick trunk call to our solicitor in London had assured me they couldn't go quite so far. But they could, and did, remove their support entirely and immediately. Only the last of our meagre funds and the generosity of a few friends had settled the hotel bill and paid our passage back home. What we were to do there, I could not imagine, but I refused to think of it until I absolutely had to. The afternoon was brilliant, soft spring sunshine gilding the ancient stone to warm honey, and somewhere, tantalising, just out of reach, the scent of jasmine rose above the odours of donkey and charcoal and leather.

It was astonishing to see how much Damascus had changed in the few short weeks I had been gone. The streets were teeming with men, most of them in groups and talking, the Arab-speakers loudly and with passionate gestures, while the Europeans looked tense and preoccupied. Mindful of Sheikh Hamid's questions, I looked at the people in the streets, searching out the differences. And for the first time, I began to see. I saw them not as exotic window-dressing of a land I had come to love, but as individuals. I saw the students of the Q'uran walking quickly with their heads together, discussing their studies. I saw the pearly toothed smile of a tiny girl eating her first rose toffee, and I saw the same laughter in the eyes of her grandmother above the veil that concealed her face. I saw the *halal* butcher sharpening his knife as he prepared to teach his son his trade, and I saw a stout matron quarrelling with a vegetable seller over his courgettes. They might have been characters from any English village—the schoolboy, the tradesman, the housewife—but they were unique to this time and this place, and I wanted desperately to know their stories. To know them and to tell them.

But there was another story to learn first. I walked quickly, stopping only once at a florist's shop for an armful of blooms, and in a few minutes I was at the European hospital, knocking at the door to a private room.

"Come in," came the sharp reply.

I entered, closing the door softly behind me.

"I am glad you have come," said the plump little figure in the bed.

"And I'm glad you're all right. You are going to be all right, aren't you, Herr Doktor?"

He smiled and patted my hand. His other arm was in a sling against his chest, but his colour was good and he seemed cheerful. "I am Uhlan, child. It would take more than a desert to kill me."

In a chair next to the bed, Gethsemane Green was looking closely at me.

"It's all right, you know. I'm not going to smother him in his sleep," I told her a touch acidly.

She flushed a little. "I do not blame you for

434

being cross with us— Oh!" She broke off suddenly.

"That is a dreadful pun," I told her. I took the other chair in the room, handing the flowers off to Miss Green. "You might want to put those in some water. I should think the nurse could oblige you."

She withdrew discreetly, leaving Herr Doktor and I alone while she took the warmly fragrant jasmine.

"I don't think I will ever be able to smell that scent again and not think of Damascus," I told him.

He spread his hands. "It is a city of miracles, child."

"It is indeed. I'm rather going to miss it, I think."

"You are leaving soon?"

"Tonight. There's a train to Beirut and a steamer bound for Greece. My aunt and I will be on it."

His eyes gleamed brightly. "Just the two of you?"

"And her parrot, but I'm afraid that's all. If you're thinking of intercepting us to get your hands on the Cross, you'll be courting disappointment. We haven't got it. I can't prove that, of course, but you must simply take my word for it."

He puffed up a little, his complexion turning bright red. "Och! Did I suggest such a thing? No, I want nothing to do with your Cross," he said, his vehemence ringing in every word. "I want only to be left in peace with my lady."

435

"Is she your lady, then?"

"I am," she said coolly. She had come in quietly, carrying a heavy vase full of starry white blossoms. "I don't know if Wolfram has told you yet, but I am his wife. We married this morning."

I gaped at them, managing to stammer my congratulations.

She fussed with the flowers a moment then put them on the windowsill. She went to him, taking his hand almost defiantly as she looked at me. "You needn't sound so surprised, Mrs. Starke. Wolfram and I have been very fond of each other for many years. And when I thought I had lost him over this absurd business with the Cross, well . . ." She stopped and cleared her throat, patting her British reticence firmly into place. "I was being a fool. There's no other word for it. Wolfram helped me to see that, and I am very honoured to be his wife."

She gave him a fond look and he patted her hand adoringly.

"Well, you seem beautifully suited. I wish you both every happiness," I told her sincerely. I rose and shook hands with both of them. "I doubt our paths will cross again. But I am glad to know you are both well."

"We did not ask you to call just to wish us well," she said hurriedly. She glanced at him and he gave her a nod of encouragement. "We wanted, that is, I wanted, to apologise most awfully. It was my fault for bringing you into the Badiyat ash-Sham. Because of me, you were put into terrible danger. There is no possible way to make amends, but I do hope you will forgive me."

She looked stiff and uncomfortable, and I knew the little speech had cost her something.

"You were responsible? So you did seek me out, then, that day by Saladin's tomb. It wasn't a chance meeting."

"No. You see, I know Wolfram has explained, but I must own my part in all of this. As he told you, I had suspicions of Mr. Rowan—that is, Mr. Starke. But I could not understand what his plan might be. I am not proud of it, but he is not here to receive my apology, so I will tell you that I searched his things. I knew there was a connection between you, and I thought if I threw you together, it might perhaps shake something loose, make something happen." Her expression turned rueful. "I suppose I was right about that. But rather more happened than I anticipated. And I certainly never suspected that Daoud could be capable—"

She broke off, her complexion mottled with anger.

"Yes, well, I suppose the least said about that, the better," I told her.

"Nevertheless. My own actions were inexcusable. I behaved in a low, common manner, and completely unbefitting a professional. I hope you will convey my apologies to your husband. If I knew his whereabouts I would speak to him directly," she added, her breath coming very quickly. She was truly distraught, and as much as I deplored what she had done, I hadn't the heart to torture her.

"Never mind, Miss Green—I apologise, baroness now. I forgive you."

She swallowed hard, her high colour ebbing. Herr Doktor stroked her hand gently.

I managed a light tone. "So, do you mean to stay here in Damascus?"

"No," he said firmly. "When I am fit to travel in a few days we will go to Egypt. We will honeymoon on the Nile, on a cruise. It will be very romantic."

The newly minted baroness blushed then, a proper bridal blush, and I found myself smiling.

"Then I will wish you both bon voyage," I told them. We shook hands again and I left them. Miss Green, now the Baroness Schickfuss, had taken one of the jasmine flowers from the vase and broken it off just below the bloom. She tucked the little stem tenderly into his sling as I closed the door.

The voyage home was as uneventful as we had hoped. Arthur, as it turned out, had a particular fondness for sea air, and he spent most of his time in his painfully gaudy cage, talking up a blue streak to anyone who would listen. The reporters were thronging the dock when we landed, but we fought our way through and straight down to the little cottage in Kent. It was damp and gloomy, and before the week was out, Aunt Dove caught a terrific cold. I had one, as well, and we spent the next fortnight with streaming noses and mustard plasters. But when the first roses bloomed and I was well on the mend, Aunt Dove was still in bed. Her cold turned to pneumonia, and as the weeks passed, her condition grew worse. We had a hospital nurse down from London at horrifying expense, but all the care in the world could not help her, and as the weeks slipped away, so did her vigour. She began to wander in her mind, confusing me sometimes with my mother, and she kept to her memories, living out her girlhood again.

On the last evening of her life, she lay in her bed, her face to the window, and asked me not to draw the curtains. Her expression was lucid and her voice was calm.

"I want to see the light as I go, child," she said.

I threw open the window, letting in the soft purple light of May Day evening. The scent of wild hyacinth was heavy in the air and she sighed in contentment.

"Oh, that is lovely."

I went to sit beside her on the bed and she took my hand.

"You mustn't fret, you know. I'm very tired. I

have been for years now. But I wanted one last good adventure. Like the old days. And that's what it was. Just like the old days. I'm only sorry not to give you a better story. It's not very exciting to die in one's bed, child. I ought to have fallen off a camel or got myself poisoned by a pit viper or drowned in a waterfall. So lowering to die in bed like an old woman," she murmured, her voice trailing off.

I held her hand for hours, stroking the papery white skin with the map of blue veins along the back.

"It's a perfect map of the Thames and its tributaries, so long as you don't look too closely," she told me, opening her eyes. "Ought to have been a lesson to me, that wherever I went, I took home with me."

I smiled through my tears, and opened my mouth to say something, but before I could speak, she gave a soft little sigh and her hand relaxed in mine. I did not weep. We had seen the end coming for weeks, and all that we need say to one another had been said.

I covered her face and went to the window, breathing in the soft violet air and wondering for the thousandth time where Gabriel Starke was and what he was doing.

The weeks passed with no word from him. Aunt Dove had demanded cremation, but a committee of the London Geographical Society insisted upon holding a small memorial service for her. I was deeply touched at how many members attended, and they presented me with a small plaque in recognition of her accomplishments. I thanked them and went directly from the service to the solicitor's office in Bloomsbury, where her will was formally read. I daydreamed a little as he doggedly made his way through all the proper papers, but in spite of all the legal gibberish, it was clear that I was the only beneficiary to her estate— even if she only had Arthur and her paste jewels and her travel papers to leave behind. I told the solicitor I meant to donate her papers to the Society and assured him I would take good care of Arthur. I also informed him I would be leaving the cottage at the end of June when the lease was up and that I intended to stay with friends until I decided what to do with myself.

"I have been invited to stay at Mistledown with Lord Walters," I informed him. "You can reach me there if there's anything of importance to discuss, although it all seems quite straightforward."

"Very good, Mrs. Starke," he said, rising. "I will inform the landlord of the cottage that you do not mean to renew the lease, and I will contact the Society about arrangements for the collection of Lady Lavinia's papers. Her estate—and by extension, you—should in no way bear the cost of packing them up and transporting them to London.

I will also notify you as soon as I have a buyer for the Orinoco Green."

"But I don't mean to sell Arthur," I repeated. "He's a terrible nuisance, of course, but I wouldn't feel right about it."

He blinked behind his thick spectacles. "I don't think you understand, Mrs. Starke. Arthur Wellesley is a common green parrot. I am speaking of the Orinoco Green, Lady Lavinia's emerald."

"What emerald?"

He blinked again. "Surely you noticed her emerald, Mrs. Starke. She wore it on a daily basis. In fact, I am given to understand it never left her person."

I groped back to my chair. "Do you mean that lump of green glass she used to pin in her turban?"

His face relaxed into a smile. "I'm afraid the Orinoco Green is not glass. It is, in fact, a rather significant emerald from Colombia. Lady Lavinia acquired it on her travels in South America." He cleared his throat gently. "I believe it was the gift of an admirer."

"But it can't be real—it's massive!"

"Yes, and quite valuable," he said rather sternly. "And that is why I counseled her many times to leave it in a bank vault or on our premises for safekeeping. However, your aunt was—well, she was a very headstrong lady, I think I may say without giving offence. She insisted upon wearing it, but she was not entirely unaware of the danger she courted by wearing such a spectacular jewel. That is why she had it placed in such an obviously cheap setting and wore other similar pieces with it. The thing looked like a bit of glass instead of the significant gemstone that it is."

I perked up my ears. "You said valuable."

The smile was back. "It is. Not as much as these things used to be, you understand. With the White Russians selling off all of their imperial jewels, there's a glut in the market just now and you won't get as much as you might have before the war. But I think I can assure you of a tidy little bit of capital that will generate a modest income. You could keep a flat in London, if you liked, although nothing extravagant," he said, his tone firm. "Just a pair of rooms with a kitchen and a cook-housekeeper. There should be enough left for a little travel and some modest entertaining. Nothing more," he warned.

I was practically floating as I left his office. I ought to have been furious with Aunt Dove, but my fingers flew as I threw my things into a bag and caught the train for Mistledown. My euphoria lasted until I stepped off the train and into Wally's arms when I promptly burst into tears. I sobbed on him all the way to the house and up to my room, where the maid poured me a stiff drink and stuck me in a hot bath. I went to bed early and didn't get up for two days by which time I was feeling miles better, like something newborn: fragile and fresh and beginning anew, and the last time I dried my tears, I burned the handkerchief and put on my brightest scarlet lipstick. I was finished looking behind me.

Wally and I spent weeks rambling about the countryside and gardens and talking about all that had happened. He pointed out his projects to me with a proprietary air, and I smiled.

"You've done it, Wally. You've gone and become the lord of the manor, just like your father wanted."

"I have not," he said indignantly. "I'm still the same fellow I ever was."

"Yes, but in tweed plus fours and talking about drains and the tenant farms," I teased. I looped my arm through his. "I think it's grand. You're bringing new life to this place, and I'm rather proud of you."

He preened a little. "I'm rather proud of myself, I suppose. I always thought the people around here would always see me as the boy I was. But once I got down here, when Father was too sick to give orders, I just sort of rose to it. There was no more 'Master Vyvyan' from the staff. And when we came back from the funeral and the first one addressed me as 'milord,' I turned and looked behind me to see if Father had risen from the grave. I don't mind telling you it spooked me. But I liked it. I felt like a 'm'lord', like I was happy to be responsible for the place." He shook his head.

"Odd, isn't it? I only wish Father had known. It might have eased his mind to know I would take to it so well."

"I think he did know. I think that's why he wanted you down here. He knew Mistledown would get hold of you and never let you go."

He raised his brows. "Legacies, eh? And what of yours? Aren't you furious with Dove for not telling you that bloody piece of glass was really an emerald that might have saved the family fortunes?"

I shook my head. "I ought to be. But I can't seem to muster the rage. She was terribly wrong to have lied about not having anything of value, of course, but I quite see why she did it."

"Do you?"

"Not knowing about the emerald forced me out of my safe little cocoon."

"Cocoon?" He howled with laughter. "My darling girl, you were already learning to barnstorm. I would hardly call courting death on a daily basis a cocoon."

"Well, perhaps not *cocoon*. But it was a safe spot, just taking lessons and not doing anything in particular. She told me once she was worried I would just bump along in life and not have any more grand adventures since my marriage had turned out so disastrously. She was afraid I had soured on living a large life. I think keeping the emerald up her sleeve was her way of making certain I took risks. And we did have a grand adventure, didn't we?"

He smiled. "We certainly did. And what will you do now?"

I spread my arms open wide. "Whatever I like. Another adventure, of course, large or small, I don't care. Maybe learning shorthand. I could take a job and see if it suits me. Or I could rent a cottage in the Shetlands and learn to keep goats. Or is it sheep in the Shetlands? I can never remember."

His tone was decidedly casual. "Well, if you've a hankering for country life, you might as well stay here."

"Don't be stupid. I can't stay here except as—" I broke off. "No, Wally. You're a dear, but I can't."

"Don't fancy life as the lady of the manor, then?"

"Oh, I could, particularly this manor."

"Just not my lady," he added lightly.

I shook my head slowly. "No, not yours. I love you dreadfully. You know that. But it isn't enough, pet. Not for either of us."

"Besides," he said, tucking my hand in his arm, "you're still married and I don't fancy visiting my wife in gaol when she's taken up for bigamy." He paused. "Have you heard from him?"

"Not so much as a postcard," I said.

"You're being awfully brave about it."

"Do you think so? Then I'm a better liar than I thought."

"What's the latest news from Damascus?"

"It isn't good. The French are insisting on a mandate and it looks as if they'll win. Poor Sheikh Hamid," I said, thinking of the courteous gentleman with his strong profile and love of poetry.

"I rather wondered if you'd go back there," he said. "You know, to have a nose around and look for him."

I gave him a careful smile. "No, Wally. Gabriel will know how to find me if he wishes. But I'm finished with his adventures. It's time to find mine."

I stayed with Wally for the whole of July and by the end of it, I was restless. I had followed developments in Damascus, snatching up the newspaper as soon as it was delivered each morning—a fact that enraged the butler since it was his job to iron it before the ink could sully his master's hands. But I didn't mind if my fingers got grubby. I tore through the pages, searching for something, anything. The news was never good. In the middle of July, King Faisal surrendered, and on July 25, the day after the devastating Battle of Maysalun, his government fell officially and the French regained control. The brief dream of a free Arab kingdom was over. At first I expected word from him. I gave a start each time the telephone bell went or the butler brought the post. But it was never him. I did not believe he was dead. Had I ever? I thought back to the years after the *Lusitania* when I had been told he was lost forever. Had I ever truly believed it? I wonder. Even now, I think there must have been some part of me, something buried in blood and bone that understood he could not die and I would not know it. Something of him would always survive in me. I was part of him and he of me, and I believed so long as I lived, something of him would endure, as well.

So I did not weep again—not when I packed up, not when I took Arthur Wellesley and boarded a ship out of Portsmouth; not when we put to sea and the salt air blew in my face, carrying me far from England and into the waters of the Red Sea. I did not even weep when I went onto the deck late one afternoon when the long golden light stretched over the deck and shimmered the sea to brilliance. I wore a dress made of the green silk Rashid had chosen for me in Damascus, the colour he promised would bring out the green in my eyes and make me irresistible to men. In one hand I carried Arthur in his ridiculous Damascene cage. In the other I carried a wooden box from Bali, carved with flowers. I set Arthur carefully on the deck and looked around, but no one was about. The dressing bell for dinner had just sounded and everyone was busy with their ruffled silks and pearls. There was no one to disturb us.

I stood a long moment, watching the golden shimmer of the sea. I thought of Aunt Dove, with her brilliance and her own magnificent sparkle, and it seemed like as good a time as any. I opened the box and threw her ashes to the wind, watching the feathery grey cloud scatter over the sea. Most settled on the surface of the water, hesitating, then drifting gently into the depths. But some were caught on the wind, skimming gently out to sea, far from the Arabian coast, mingling with the perfumes and spices of fabled lands.

"I think she would like that, Arthur," I said. He flapped a little, but his expression was solemn.

"I think talking to birds is a sign of incipient mental breakdown," drawled a bored, high-pitched male voice.

I turned to see another passenger approaching. He wore an eyepatch and walked with a stick and his hair was entirely white although his skin was remarkably firm for a man so old. He carried a battered attaché case in his free hand.

"And what if the bird is a better conversationalist than the other passengers?" I retorted.

"Then you ought not to be travelling alone, dear lady. I think you need to be under someone's care."

From under the bushy white eyebrows, the eye that stared at me was a brilliant forget-me-not blue.

"I think I can take care of myself," I replied.

"I've no doubt of that," he answered softly, dropping the affected voice.

I swallowed hard against the tight knot of joy in my throat. "Have you really lost an eye or is that part of the disguise?"

He glanced around, then flipped up the eyepatch, winking.

"The limp is real, though. Bullet to the thigh at Maysalun," he said with a rueful grimace.

"You're getting too old for that sort of thing," I told him. "I read about the battle in the newspapers. I'm sorry."

He smiled thinly. "No more than I am. They had a chance, you know."

"I know. How is Hamid? And Rashid? And Aysha, and oh, all of them!"

"They're well. They send their regards. Hamid is philosophical about the whole mess. He says change is slow in the desert, but it will come in time."

"Have you finished there?" I asked. "Really finished?"

"I have," he said, his expression resigned. "The French got their way this time, and the powers-that-be will go back to the conference tables and draw the maps again and make new kings. But they shouldn't. And I've lost the taste for meddling in other men's wars." His tone was light, but there was a dark edge of bitterness to his words. He would regret much of what had happened there for the rest of his life, I had little doubt.

"So since I last saw you, you've been in a war and got yourself shot. Perhaps you're the one who needs a keeper."

"Yes, I think I do. Tell me, where are we bound?"

"Don't you know?"

"I haven't the faintest. I caught up with you just as you were boarding at Portsmouth and barely made it onto the ship myself."

"And it's taken you a fortnight to find me? It isn't that large a ship, you know."

His expression was grave. "I thought you might like a little time to yourself."

"You mean you had second thoughts."

"Well, it did occur to me I might not be welcomed with entirely open arms."

I tipped my head. "I ought to pitch you overboard. You promised me the True Cross and all I got was a wrecked plane and a decrepit parrot for my troubles."

"And the heart of the Cross," he said blandly.

I blinked. "What the devil do you mean? Gabriel—"

He held up a finger. "Colonel Clutterbuck, please. That's my current alias."

"Clutterbuck? I will call you no such thing. It's absurd."

He huffed a sigh. "Is that any way to talk to a veteran of the Crimean War?"

"Gabriel, all the veterans of the Crimean War died decades ago. Now, what do you mean I have the heart of the Cross?"

He grinned. "I told you I took it from the Cross when I first discovered the thing. It shows a decided lack of curiosity on your part that you never asked where I stashed it."

He paused, waiting, and I stamped my foot. "Don't play games, you maddening man. Where is it?"

He rolled his eyes. "Oh, very well, but you're a disappointment to me, you really are. I would have thought you'd have discovered it ages ago."

He put down the attaché case and bent over Arthur's cage, unscrewing the gaudy finial. The thing was in three parts, and he deftly freed the top and bottom bits leaving a centre-piece with a cavity of sorts. He gestured for me to hold out my hands and as I did so, he upended the middle bit. For one agonising moment, nothing happened. Then, with an audible sigh, the thing slid free and into my hands, a single enormous piece of crystal. Embedded within was a piece of wood the size of a man's hand. It was jagged at the edges, and deep within the grain of the wood was a dark stain. Blood? Rust from a nail that had been forged in a blacksmith's fire in Jerusalem?

I could scarcely hold it steady, my nerves were rattling so badly. Here in my hands was the single most valuable thing I had ever seen, would ever see. And Gabriel had risked his life to give it to me.

"It's yours," he said. His voice was quiet, almost reverent. "I will write a letter as to its provenance and I will detail everything that happened. There will be doubters, of course, but I think you should be able to convince quite a few people as to its authenticity. And when you have, it will be easy enough to find a buyer. My word isn't worth much," he added with a wry smile, "but you could get corroboration from Gethsemane and Herr Doktor Schickfuss if you needed."

I did not take my eyes off the heart of the Cross. "I can't use your testimony. You are a ghost, remember?"

He shrugged. "I will come clean and tell the whole story. It will be a nightmare, of course, particularly once my parents get hold of me. And there will most likely be a bit of detention involved, but no matter."

"*Detention* is a nice word for prison," I reminded him, watching the setting sun brighten the gold setting of the crystal.

"Only until we get it all sorted," he assured me. "The government won't want me spilling my guts about what we got up to during the war. I'm sure we can come to some sort of arrangement."

I finally looked at him. "After you killed John Halliday? I hardly think so."

He shook his head. "I didn't kill him, pet. He got

damned lucky. He was picked up by a caravan less than a mile from where he landed while I had to walk all the bloody way out of the Badiyat ash-Sham. I tracked him down in Baghdad. He was hiding out in some filthy hovel in a room he rented under an assumed name."

"You didn't kill him?"

His solemn gaze never left mine. "No, I didn't. Now, I'm not saying I left him without a few bumps and bruises. After all, I owed him a little," he added, widening his eyes innocently. "But I didn't kill him. I decided that would have been unsporting. Besides, I may no longer work for the Vespiary, but I didn't want them dragged into any of this. They've enough troubles without arranging favours for me. It was simpler just to take what I went for and leave him alive."

My heart began to drum in my chest, a slow, heavy rhythm. "Gabriel, did you find—"

He lifted a brow. "Did I find? Oh, you mean this?" He reached into his attaché case and drew out a familiar goatskin bundle—a little the worse for wear after all of its travels. Gabriel had the instincts of a showman. He unwrapped it slowly, drawing out the anticipation as I peered over his shoulder.

At last, he folded back the final layer of the wrappings and lifted the Cross. I saw a flash of gold and jewels, but before I could look at it properly, he took a moment to restore the heart to its home, fitting the crystal into the open setting at the centre of the Cross. Carefully, he handed it to me.

I looked down at the relic in my hands. It was a piece of history, the wood that been part of the most famous execution in all of the world, stained with what might well be the blood of Christ. This relic had passed through the hands of kings and bishops; it had been carried in triumph before armies and witnessed the passing of ages. It was the single holiest artefact in all of Christendom, and it was mine.

And without hesitating, I took a deep breath and raised my arm to fling it overboard. The last flash of the setting sun sparked off the crystal and the gold and it seemed to catch fire as it arced, destined for the cool green waters below.

At the last possible second, Gabriel vaulted to the rail, catching it in his fingertips. He turned and stared at me in astonishment.

"You were going to throw it away," he said, his expression one of shocked bewilderment. "I've never seen anything so daft in my entire life. What the devil were you thinking?"

I stood on my tiptoes and kissed his open mouth until he pulled back.

"I don't understand," he began. I looped my arms around his neck.

"I don't want your relics. I want you."

"But—"

I put a finger to his lips, silencing him. "Gabriel, you wanted me to have the Cross as atonement for what you did to me. It's just a way to buy me back. But I forgive you. Without the Cross, without the money or the fame it would bring. And I wanted you to know that. I wanted you to know that when I am with you for the rest of our lives, it is because I choose to be."

He pushed my finger gently aside. "What shall we do with it?"

I thought a moment then grinned. "I think we ought to pack it up and send it to Tarquin March to deal with. He's the one who got you into this business. He owes me a favour."

He bent his head to kiss me, and when he finished, I was as dizzy as if I'd just pulled a barrel roll. "I know you said you were chaste during those five years, but I have to wonder," I murmured, fitting my head to the hollow of his shoulder. "I don't remember your technique ever being quite so, so—"

"Quite," he said dryly. "Perhaps I'm simply inspired. I've never had a woman give up a priceless treasure for me before."

"This is where I ought to tell you that the priceless treasure is *you*. I shan't, of course. It's far too sentimental and I don't want you to get a big head." We stood there some time, watching the purple light of the evening change to a deep violet as the first stars began to appear.

Gabriel's voice rumbled in his chest. "By the way, where exactly are we going? I booked through and the ticket said Australia."

"That's just where we change ships," I informed him. "Our final destination is the Cook Islands. Nothing but white sand beaches and deep blue sea and lovely people who don't care who Evangeline and Gabriel Starke are at all. I rented us a cottage right on the beach for the rest of the year. We'll have nothing to do but swim and sun ourselves and plan the book I mean to write."

"You're writing a book? On what?"

"Ethnography," I told him, relishing his groan of despair. "You might not think stories and people are important but I do. I've brought a trunkful of books to begin my studies and whatever I don't already know, you can help me with."

"You were awfully sure I'd find you."

I turned my face to the east and the first star that shimmered on the horizon. He held my hand, and it was the hand of the man I had married, lost and found again in the Badiyat ash-Sham, the fabled land of camels and caravans that lies just beyond the walls of the city of jasmine.

To live with him would be a very great adventure indeed.

ACKNOWLEDGMENTS

The word that comes to mind when I write acknowledgments is always *"generosity."* The people I am fortunate enough to know and name here are among the most generous and gracious I have ever had the pleasure to meet. I am humbled to know them.

Tremendous thanks:

To the entire Harlequin MIRA team—art, sales, PR, marketing, editorial, digital and all their supporting staff. I am, as ever, entirely grateful for all that they do. Particular thanks to Margaret Marbury, Michael Rehder and Leonore Waldrip for making all of this hard work so much fun.

To Tara Parsons for shepherding this project with as much care and enthusiasm as if it had been hers from the start. This is only the beginning. . . .

To Pam Hopkins, agent and friend, for taking me under her wing and providing endlessly patient support and laughs.

To the brilliant and generous Susanna Kearsley for providing research links, and the ever-lovely Jayne Hoogenberk for patiently explaining how to find them.

To Ava Miles for research support.

To my family—my parents, my beloved, my child. They are my past, my present and my future.

And to a kindly spirit halfway across the world—a person whose name I do not know but who generously shared her language with me. *Shukran*, and I hope that peace comes soon to you and yours.

QUESTIONS FOR DISCUSSION

1. Evangeline Starke is a dynamic young woman with all of the energy and spirit of the 1920s. How does she embody those qualities?

2. How do Gabriel's experiences as the Saqr change his views on British involvement in Syrian affairs?

3. Gabriel and the Lost Boys of the Vespiary did dangerous work during the war. What challenges might they face in adapting to life after the fighting stops?

4. Damascus is a city at the crossroads of history. How does the political climate of Damascus in 1920 influence the characters?

5. Honour and duty play a strong role in the book. How do the characters view their own responsibilities? How far will they go to satisfy honour?

6. Evie and Gabriel are reunited after life-changing events. How have the years in between affected the dynamic of their relationship?

7. How does the Badiyat ash-Sham, the great Syrian desert, function as a character in the story? What does their time in the desert reveal about Gabriel and Evie?

8. What is Evie and Gabriel's potential for a happy ending?

Center Point Large Print
600 Brooks Road / PO Box 1
Thorndike ME 04986-0001 USA

(207) 568-3717

US & Canada:
1 800 929-9108
www.centerpointlargeprint.com